A ~~Poem~~ ~~for~~ This
love

VIOLET BLOOM

Copyright © 2022
All rights reserved. No part of this publication may be reproduced, distributed, or transmitted in any form or by any means, including photocopying, recording, or other electronic or mechanical methods, without the prior written permission of the publisher, except in the case of brief quotations for reviews and certain other noncommercial uses permitted by copyright law.
ISBN:9798427861243
Any similarities between real people or real places are used fictitiously. Names, characters and places are products of the author's imagination.

Cover illustrated by ljm.art
Edited by Sandreanic Davis
Formatting by Brady Moller

www.violetbloom.me

For my mom,
who is no longer here for me to ask to
please skip over the sex scenes,
my gratitude for being your daughter is
eternal.

CONTENT WARNING:

This book contains subject matter that may not be suitable for all readers, including domestic violence, drug use, insinuations of sexual assault, gun violence, and graphic descriptions of sex.

PROLOGUE

THE FIRST DAY

Haley

Have you ever been told that you should hate someone? You didn't know why, but for as long as you can remember, you were told to hate them?

I never questioned it—not until I was eighteen and had already spent my entire life hating him.

I could still remember my first day of pre-kindergarten, clear as day—I'd just turned five. That was the problem with having a summer birthday. Snake, my dad's best friend's son, was three months younger, and my parents wanted us in the same class, so they started me in pre-kindergarten as one of the oldest students. I was always the oldest in the class, except for Will, he was three days older than I was.

When I got on the school bus, I sat with Snake and Sassy, the three of us crowded in the large seat. We weren't nervous, because the three of us spent every day of our lives together. Sassy's house was at the other end of the trailer park, and Snake's was right next to mine. Snake and I were royalty in the trailer park. My dad was the leader of the Southside Gang, something I'd known for my whole life. Snake's dad, Bull, was his number two.

We'd driven through the poor side of town, with the trailer park, the run-down houses and the overgrown parks, but as soon as we crossed the railroad tracks, it was like we'd literally driven into a separate town. The houses were big and modern. The parks were luxurious, with soft tiles, and frequently updated to prevent the rich kids from getting hurt. At the time, I didn't think anything about the differences; I hadn't realized that things were kept that way expressly.

I was sitting between Sassy and Snake and there hadn't been room for anybody else, but I noticed Will as soon as he'd gotten on the bus. He was loud—even as a kid, he'd drawn attention to himself immediately.

When we'd gotten to school, Sassy and I were separated from Snake. He'd been placed in the other pre-kindergarten class. Will was in ours. I hadn't known his name then, but I learned it soon. When our teacher, Ms. Stillwater, called our names, we exchanged a small smile before walking up to the class together.

"Hi," he'd said loudly to me. "I'm Will."

"I'm Haley," I'd told him. Even then, his smile had been bright, and I'd thought he was cute. At the time, I hadn't known those thoughts would be forced to change.

"Haley and Will have summer birthdays. Will's is August 18th and Haley's is August 21st," our teacher told the class. "So I'm giving them their birthday cards and special birthday treats today. The rest of you will get yours on your birthday."

The rest of the class protested, also wanting their special treat, which consisted of bite-size pieces of candy we got to choose. Will cheered loudly, running around and showing it off to everyone. When I was five, I thought it was cute, and even as we grew older, I still was somehow attracted to his obnoxiousness. But through the years, I'd learned to push those feelings away because I *had* to hate him.

It was a family requirement.

But I didn't know that on my first day of pre-kindergarten. Ms. Stillwater, who we'd gotten to call Ms. S, sat us together, right in the front row, and when it was lunchtime, he'd saved me a seat next to him. "My mom packed me carrots, but I don't like them." His nose scrunched up, and he'd offered them to me.

"I'll trade them for my tomatoes," I bargained with him. Will's lunch was homemade, but I'd bought lunch. My mom didn't work, but she'd never made me lunch or breakfast either.

"Deal."

Will and I shared lunch that first day, switching whatever we didn't like for the other. And when it was time for dessert, we split his cookie in half and shared one spoon for my chocolate pudding.

"Did your Mom make this?" I asked when I'd taken a bite of the delicious cookie.

"She always bakes cookies," he said.

"It's yummy. My mom never bakes," I told him. "She always buys them from the store, but they're never this good."

"She says it's 'cuz she bakes 'em with love." *Love?* I knew the word even though nobody ever said it to me. "Maybe you can bake them with us sometime," he offered. "She always lets me lick the batter off the egg beater. But we can't tell Dad that. Dad says it's bad for me, but it's the best part."

"Moms and dads are weird." He laughed while bobbing his big head up and down in agreement.

Sassy sat on the other side of me, but she'd spent all of lunch talking to Snake. That was before Snake and Sassy realized we were supposed to hate Will too.

When we went back to class, we had to line up two by two and hold hands with our partner. Before Sassy could claim me as her partner, Will grabbed my hand. Friends held hands all the time; I held hands with Sassy and Snake all the time, but I liked holding Will's hand the best.

Ms. S constantly had to tell Will and me to stop talking during class. By the time class was over that first day, I'd felt like Will was my best friend, just like Sassy and Snake.

On the bus ride home, I sat next to Will, just the two of us in the seat. Sassy and Snake sat in the seat across the aisle from us. Sassy always said Snake had cooties, but even then, she'd smiled at him all the time. As the years would go on, she'd smile at him less and less and I would end up embarrassed at how long it took me to realize why.

Will got dropped off first. "See you tomorrow, Haley," he said while he'd waved goodbye to me.

"I'll save you a seat," I told him, a broad smile on my little face.

I smiled happily all the way home, knowing I'd made my first friend who I hadn't known my entire life and didn't live in the trailer park with me.

My mom was waiting for us when we'd gotten off the bus the first day, only because if no one was there, they wouldn't let us off. "How was school?" She asked. She hadn't hugged me. Neither of my parents had ever been very affectionate, even when I was younger. And that hadn't changed with the years. My younger sister, Chloe, was on her hip, she'd been almost two then.

"I made a friend!" I shouted excitedly.

"You have friends," she said, somewhat annoyed. Even as a child, I knew she didn't even like me, let alone love me. It was evident in the way she spoke to me.

"I made a *new* friend," I told her seriously. "His name is Will."

"Will what?" She snapped angrily. I'd been confused about why making a friend made her so mad.

"Will Roberts." I remembered because Ms. S called him Mr. Roberts quite a few times when correcting him, which didn't make him change his behavior.

"You cannot be friends with him!" The tone of her voice and the volume of her shout terrified me. It wouldn't be until I was much older when she didn't scare me anymore, even when she used that tone of voice on me.

"Why?" I hadn't meant for the question to annoy her more, but it was a serious one. Why couldn't I be friends with a nice boy?

"He's Sheriff Robert's son," she said. "His daddy is the reason your daddy spent the weekend in jail."

That was the last time my dad spent any time in jail, but certainly not the last arrest. When I was older, I'd finally figure out why.

"Oh."

She huffed heavily before turning and walking away from the three of us. I followed, my little legs chasing after her. I wanted her to be happy with me. Things were always better when she was happy with me.

"It's okay," Sassy said. "We're still your friends." She'd rubbed her hand along my back soothingly while I felt sad for the loss of a friend.

"We'll be best friends forever," Snake affirmed.

The next day, even though I'd promised to save Will a seat on the bus, I sat squished in with Sassy and Snake again. When Will had gotten on the bus with the rest of the kids from the rich side of town, he smiled brightly at me. "Hi, Haley. Wanna sit with me?"

I hadn't even given him an answer.

I'd been so young that I didn't really understand Mom's reasoning, but all I knew was that I didn't want to make her mad. So, I ignored him.

As the years went on, we ignored each other less and less and started tormenting each other. He was the town's golden boy, the sheriff's son, destined to be the next sheriff. The teachers kissed his ass because they wanted to stay on the sheriff's good side. At best, he was mediocre at sports and at school, but he was praised and worshiped like he was a god.

Was I judging him too harshly based on the way I had to hate him? Maybe.

But the feeling was mutual, mutual hatred that had both of us sent to the principal's office more than once throughout elementary, middle, and high school. In high school, it was a lot. He'd make snarky comments about my dad being the leader of the Southside

Gang, which encompassed basically the entire Southside. I'd make comments about him being a goody-goody whose future was only set because of who his daddy was.

But every year, I remember his birthday. Three days before mine made it hard to forget. And he didn't know it—nobody knew—especially not my parents and certainly not my friends, but every year on his birthday, I sent him a birthday card. When we were younger, from first to the sixth grade, I'd brought a homemade card with me to the first day of school and slipped it into his backpack or his cubby and eventually his locker. When I'd gotten old enough to afford to buy one, I stopped making them. I never signed my name, and I had no idea if he knew who they were from, but I always felt lonely on my birthday since it was in the summer. I thought it might make him feel nice to have a card on his special day.

Senior year of high school, though, something changed. We stopped playing enemies. I hadn't realized for the last thirteen years we'd still been playing pretend. But the boy I liked so much that very first day of school was still buried in there somewhere, underneath the cocky exterior I pretended to hate.

I'd always thought people who claimed there was a thin line between love and hate were spouting cliche bullshit. I stopped thinking that when I realized even if it was a cliche, it was true. Even so, I was more shocked than anyone when he fell for me. It didn't make any sense. Not after thirteen years of built up hatred.

It wasn't supposed to be love.

It was supposed to be a one-time thing, something to never be repeated. It was supposed to be a momentary lapse in judgement, which led to a stupid decision. That same stupid decision wasn't supposed to happen again and again and again. A decision I wasn't supposed to want to happen again. One he wasn't supposed to want and encourage. We weren't supposed to tell anyone. It would ruin us.

I had plans, secret plans. And nothing would stand in the way of them, not even a tall, blonde-haired, blue-eyed man-boy who I hated. But there was no such thing as a kept secret, only if you were the only one who knew said secret.

Would sex lead to love? Would hate change to love?

But still, the answer to the biggest question would change both our lives and possibly be the end of one of them: would I be the love of his life, or would I be the cause of his worst heartbreak? Or, worse yet, would our love get us killed?

CHAPTER 1

THE LAST FIRST DAY

Haley

Rolling over in my bed, I looked at the clock, seeing it was only five thirty in the morning. I still had forty-five minutes before my alarm would go off and wake me for the first day of my senior year of high school. The last first day of high school ever. If my parents were smart, they would have started me early and I would have graduated last year, turned eighteen last week and been off to college.

Although, they could never know I was planning on going to college. It wasn't in their plans for me. A wedding to Snake straight after graduation—who I didn't even like as more than a friend, let alone love—was their plan. Chloe's soft snoring filled the room. Our trailer was only two bedrooms and we'd been sharing a room since she was born three years after me. She was starting her freshman year of high school today. She was nervous, but she didn't need to be. She had friends her age. Sassy, my best friend, had a brother in her year.

Instead of laying awake in my bed for the next forty-five minutes, I took advantage of the alone time and privacy I had. I hardly ever got that. It was difficult when you shared a two bedroom, one bathroom trailer with your parents and younger sister. The kitchen was small and so was the living room, and even if it wasn't small, it was usually full of my dad's associates. By associates, I meant members of the Southside Gang he ran.

I fucking hated it.

Thankfully, Chloe was a sound sleeper. Leaning over the bed, I reached under the mattress and pulled out the stack of college flyers and went through them. I only had a limited amount of money to send my applications in. Who the hell knew just *applying* for college could cost so much money? I'd have to narrow my list of six to three. The one thing all the colleges had in common—they were thousands of miles from my house. I hated it here, hated my parents, hated Carver High School, and I hated Lake City, California. Most people dreamed of coming to California. All in all, it wasn't a bad place to live; it was gorgeous plus the weather was nice, and the town was nestled between the mountains and the ocean perfectly. The problem was the fucking politics of the town, that and my dad was a criminal. Not just a criminal, he was the biggest, at least according to Sheriff Roberts. Because of that, I needed to get the fuck out. I didn't want this to be my life. I wanted more than a marriage to Snake, more than wondering if he'd be arrested, and more than that, I wanted freedom. I couldn't have freedom here, and I certainly couldn't have love—if I ever decided that was what I wanted. Snake would be the only one to ever attempt to date me. Sure, I'd fucked around with a bunch of people, but nobody wanted to really *be* with me, scared of what my dad would do if he found out.

Sitting up, I sat cross-legged on my bed and looked down at the flyers in front of me. With my grades, I had a pretty good chance of getting a scholarship. All the schools were on the east coast—Virginia, North Carolina, Pennsylvania, or New York. Dartmouth was in New Hampshire and was my reach school. I definitely had a shot, but I'd read that they didn't do merit scholarships, only financial ones. I'd be applying for one. Despite my situation, it didn't seem worth it to take out a bunch of student loans. Grabbing my phone, I pulled up a few tabs and searched for scholarships that I could apply for that weren't dependent on what school I went to.

Three schools, I thought to myself. Chloe stirred, rolling over in her bed. She and Sassy were the only ones I felt bad for. Chloe was my sister by blood, and Sassy may not be blood, but she was as good as my sister. I'd been lying to both of them since I was twelve when I finally figured out the only thing I wanted in life was to get the fuck out of this town. But I couldn't tell them. I'd break both their hearts by sneaking away in the middle of the night, taking my beat-up car and everything I had and slipping over the town's border. I'd be halfway to Utah before anybody even realized I was gone. And by the time they did, I could have been anywhere—halfway down the California coast to Mexico, halfway up the coast towards Washington.

Anywhere.

Definitely Dartmouth, I thought to myself. East Carolina University wasn't somewhere I actually wanted to go, but with my grades, I was basically a guaranteed entry. I needed one of those because I couldn't risk not getting in anywhere and having the plans I'd worked so hard for these last eight years just vanish. Where else did I really want to go? Virginia seemed like a nice place to live. It seemed similar to California, having both mountains and ocean. Grabbing my phone again, I googled Richmond, Charlottesville, and Blacksburg.

After reading about the size, population, nature and location of the cities, I decided the University of Richmond was my best bet. Richmond was a decent sized city with a small-town feel. Cary Street looked so cute, and the Museum of Fine Arts looked like a great place to study, plus it was only two hours from the beach, two hours from the mountains, and close to Washington, D.C.

I planned on applying for early admission to all of them and making sure I only received electronic correspondence. The last thing I needed would be an acceptance or rejection letter coming through the regular mail.

Suddenly, the phone in my hand blasted my alarm, catching me completely off guard. I jumped, sending the papers for college scattering everywhere. Quickly, I picked them up and shoved them back under my mattress, hoping it would take Chloe a few minutes to wake up fully. Turning the alarm off, I glanced over at my sister who was still dead asleep.

"Chloe," I said, climbing out of bed and walking the short distance to her. "Chloe," I said again, louder this time.

"Yeah?" She asked groggily, turning her body away from me.

"We've got school today, you need to wake up."

"Mmkay," she mumbled. Grabbing my towel off the back of the door, I walked to the bathroom and showered quickly. Long showers were not allowed in this house; my mom would lose her shit if she didn't have any hot water left, and she was always the last to shower. Dad took showers at night, but Chloe and I both needed them before school.

Quickly, I washed my body, scrubbing from head to toe while avoiding getting my hair wet. Once I was done, I turned the water to cold, rinsing with cold water. It was shit, but it was better than dealing with my mother's potential wrath. Shivering, I turned the water off and stepped out, wrapping the towel tightly around myself and walked back across the hall to my shared bedroom.

"Chloe!" I shouted at her this time. "Get your ass up. If you want a ride to school, we need to leave at 7:15. You've got less than an hour!"

"Okay, okay," she grumbled before finally climbing out of bed. When she was gone, I dropped my towel and searched through our closet for something to wear. Our school had a uniform policy, either khaki pants, plaid skirt, or khaki skirt and a white, blue, or cream-colored blouse. The boys had to wear ties, girls could, but it wasn't mandatory. Usually, I wore one loosely around my neck because I liked the way it looked. It was still warm out, so I opted for a short plaid skirt and a white button down. I pulled on short socks and a pair of old worn converse. I desperately needed new shoes, but there wasn't any money for them. I worked part time during the summer at the movie theater a few towns over, not wanting to work in Lake City. But every penny I made needed to be saved for my escape. My parents didn't have any money. Running a gang wasn't exactly a lucrative business, at least not the way my dad did it.

I was standing in front of the full-length mirror situated in the corner next to my bed, combing my light brown hair. I'd curled it a few days ago and today would definitely be the last day I could pull off the ringlets, but that was fine. I'd wear it up tomorrow and then wash it the next day. I applied some mascara and grabbed my bag I'd packed the night before, tossed my phone into it and headed to the kitchen. Chloe was coming out of the bathroom as I was passing.

"Can you make me something for breakfast?" She asked.

"Sure," I told her. I had a hard time telling her no.

My parents were still asleep, so I quietly tiptoed past their room into the kitchen. Grabbing four pieces of bread, I put them in the toaster. Quickly, I cracked four eggs in a bowl, whipped them and sprinkled some cheese in it before tossing it in the microwave for ninety seconds. It was so much easier than trying to scramble eggs in a frying pan on a busy morning before school. While that was cooking and the bread was toasting, I cut up some tomatoes. I liked to add avocado too, but those weren't always in the food budget. When the bread popped up, I slathered all four slices in mayonnaise, layered tomato on it before sprinkling on some black pepper and salt. Next, I divided the cooked eggs onto the bread, smashed the pieces together and cut them. I set each one on a paper plate and grabbed two apples.

"Buck texted me," Chloe said when she emerged from our room. Buck was Sassy's little brother. "Sassy said he had to ride the bus since she did when she was a freshman and he wants me to ride with him."

"That's fine," I told her.

"Thanks for breakfast," she said.

"No problem, but tomorrow you've got first shower and breakfast duty."

"Good thing you like Pop-Tarts," she countered. Rolling my eyes at her, I grabbed my breakfast sandwich, the coffee I'd made, and my apple and left the trailer, careful to not let the door slam shut behind me. Sassy was already waiting by my car. Snake would take his motorcycle to school for as long as he could, and then he'd take his own car.

"Not riding with Snake?" I asked her.

"Not on that death trap. He drives like a maniac."

I snorted. He was nearly eighteen and thought he was fucking invincible. Teenage boys were so fucking dumb.

"You should ride with him," I told her as I unlocked my car. "He drives safer when you're with him."

Some sort of emotion I couldn't place flashed crossed her face, but I ignored it. If she wanted to talk about it, she would.

"You know," she said. "If you'd let me burn the school to the ground at the end of last year, we wouldn't have to go."

"I'm pretty sure it doesn't work like that," I told her. She just shrugged.

Her comment about burning down the school came up at least weekly, sometimes twice a week. I was surprised she and Snake hadn't actually done it yet. It would be a miracle if they got through this year without getting expelled. Somehow, Snake always convinced Sassy to do the dumbest shit that wouldn't just expel her, but also land her in jail. He had protection from jail because of who his dad was, but Sassy didn't. Her dad died eight years ago, and her mom wanted nothing to do with the gang, leaving her unprotected. I'd protect Sassy with my life, and Snake would too, but that courtesy wasn't extended by my father or his.

Honestly, it could very well have been my dad who killed her dad. We didn't talk about it, but I knew we both thought about it.

The circumstances surrounding his death were... suspicious. He'd been working on a car in the shop when it fell on him, crushing and killing him. The investigation concluded it wasn't an operator error for the lift machine, and it hadn't malfunctioned. Foul play couldn't be ruled out, but it also couldn't be proven, and years later, it was still an open investigation.

I could never figure out what the motivation was. Hound, Sassy's dad's gang name, wasn't a ranking member. If it were betrayal, everyone would have known, and my dad would have proudly, and with honor announced he was the one to do it, but since he hadn't done that, the motivation must have been something different.

"One more year and we're out of this shithole school," she said. Sassy wanted to open her own full-service salon with hair, nails, massages, facials, and waxing services. She wouldn't be leaving, so she assumed I wouldn't be leaving either. She only thought the school was a shithole while my feelings extended to the whole of Lake City.

I turned the radio on and ate my sandwich, not in the mood to talk while we drove. When we pulled into the back parking lot, it was already full. Everyone had a leather jacket on and half of them had a fire red and blue eagle on it, which was the symbol for the Southside Gang. Snake was leaning against his bike, his flavor of the week on his arm.

Despite the fact that he and I were expected to be together and make lots of future gang member babies, it didn't bother me in the slightest that he fucked anything that moved and gave him the slightest bit of attention. I didn't want him, never had, not like that anyway.

"Ready?" I asked Sassy.

"Let's get this over with."

Every single one of the kids we walked up to lived on the same side of town we did. I'd seen them all summer long so there was no need to exchange fake how was your summer conversation. I sent up a small thank you for that because I hated small talk.

"What's up, Haley?" Snake asked, tightening his arm around Bridgette, a petite blonde who was a year behind us.

"Same old fucking same," I said with a shrug. Sassy handed me a cigarette and lighter. Taking it, I lit it and inhaled, trying not to go too deep. I hated cigarettes, the taste, the smell, but I had to look the part. I also only smoked around my friends. Sassy smoked too, keeping her eyes on Snake. I finally fucking figured it out halfway through junior year. My best friend was in love with Snake. I didn't get it, I didn't understand the attraction. He was probably the reason she was still a virgin, never taking anyone up on the countless offers to bed her.

What I did understand was why she didn't talk to me about it. She knew I didn't want him like that, but she also knew what our fathers were expecting of us—like it was some medieval times bullshit. I didn't understand why Snake couldn't just take over the gang and pick whoever he wanted to have his little Snake babies. It wasn't my fault that my dad never had a son and didn't have someone to take over.

It was all fucking bullshit.

Thank god I had no intention of ever letting it happen.

After I finished my cigarette, I flicked it to the ground and stomped on it, pissing myself off in the process. I wanted to pick it up and put it in the trash can, but even just that small action would open up a can of worms I didn't need opened.

Sassy and I left everyone else standing there and headed for the school's back doors. As soon as we were walking down the hall, Will fucking Roberts walked right towards us. His blonde hair was shaggier than it had ever been, looking like he hadn't cut it all summer.

He looks cute.

I pushed the errant thought from my mind.

"Winters," he spat my last name. I didn't even understand why he felt the need to address me.

"Wade?" I said, tilting my head to the side. I wouldn't give him the pleasure of calling him by the name I'd known since I was five. He rolled his eyes at me. He was walking slightly in front of all his friends, and they all looked the exact same, but I guess that was to be expected given we all had to wear uniforms. They all had the same shaggy style of hair in varying shades or brown and blonde, same dull eyes which looked like they held no knowledge for school or the real world that existed beyond the four walls of Carver High School.

They probably didn't even know that it was called Carver high school for the man who founded the town and that it wasn't named Lake City High for that reason.

He and his friends tried to block mine and Sassy's path. I stood there, examining my nails, refusing to look up into his crystal blue eyes and pretended I was bored.

"How many times did your daddy get arrested this summer?" He asked.

I glanced at Sassy and shrugged my shoulders. "Just once," I said, tilting my head again. "But it cost your daddy two black eyes." Of course, Dad didn't fucking go quietly or peacefully. Will's dad wasn't stupid, he must realize whenever my dad got arrested he was released less than an hour later.

"Bitch," he spat at me. He took a menacing step closer, his body towering over mine even though I was taller than average for a girl. I looked up at him, giving him my best '*fuck you*' face because he sure as fuck didn't intimidate me. The only good thing my dad ever did for me was teach me how to defend myself.

"A bitch is a female dog," I said, continuing to make my voice sound bored. "Or something a man with a small dick calls a woman to make himself feel powerful."

I watched Will's face turn red in anger and heard Sassy chuckle next to me. Glancing down at the front of his pants, I shrugged. "Tiiinnnnyyyyyy," I said, making my voice high and squeaky. Before he could say anything else, I brushed by him, making my shoulder bump into him, ignoring the tingles that spread out where my body came into contact with him.

It was just a physical reaction, a stupid one that meant nothing.

Sassy and I walked to our lockers. Carver high school was so small that freshman year, we got to pick our lockers and those had remained our lockers for the past four years.

"He's a tool, just like his dad," Sassy said when we were standing next to our lockers. I just snorted out a response. "What do you have first block, again?" She asked.

"I have a free period," I replied.

"Why did you come in so early?" She didn't give me time to answer before saying. "I've got statistics."

"I probably won't see you until lunch," I told her, not answering her question.

"I'll save you a seat."

With that, she was off to first period, which also doubled as homeroom, where our attendance for the day was taken. Each teacher took it, however, this attendance counted us as tardy for the day or not. Since I had a free period, I walked to the office to sign in. Technically, since I was a senior, I didn't have to come in early, but I'd been planning on taking Chloe and I liked having time to myself in the library.

My day passed relatively easily. I had creative writing first thing in the morning after my free period, followed by AP chemistry, then AP statistics. After that, I had lunch. Sassy saved me a seat like she said she would. I waited until the line was almost completely gone before going to buy a sandwich and a bag of chips. Will was sitting at his usual table in the front of the cafeteria, surrounded by his friends. He had his arm wrapped around Mackenzie. They must have gotten back together over the summer because last I heard, he'd broken up with her right before the end of junior year because he was spending the summer at his grandparents's beach house.

Not that it mattered.

I was dipping my chips in ketchup–yes, I said what I said–and listening to Snake and Sassy talk about school, how stupid their classes were. If Snake wasn't careful, he might not even graduate. But that probably wouldn't bother him and it would in no way affect his job prospects. His job was set.

When I'd finished my lunch, we still had about ten minutes left. "I'm gonna go to the bathroom," I said.

Sassy didn't even look up at me, too busy staring at Snake, but waved me off.

While I was walking to the bathroom on the first floor, I rounded the corner tightly and walked straight into a chest.

"Sorry," I said before looking up and realizing who I'd bumped into. But the way my body tingled, I should have known anyway.

"Winters," he said gruffly. His tone was always just a little bit softer when he wasn't around his friends.

"Watch where you're going," I said in annoyance. It probably actually was my fault, but I was definitely going to give him the blame.

"Me?" He asked in annoyance.

"Yes," I snapped. "You're supposed to walk on the right side of the hall, just like you drive that shiny truck of yours on the right side of the road."

"You paying attention to what I drive, Winters?" He asked with a hint of a smirk.

"Fuck you," I said, brushing past him again.

Before I could get far, he grabbed my wrist and hauled me back. There was nobody in the hall and no way we could be seen from the cafeteria, not with the way the wall and door were structured.

"Careful, Winters," he husked in my ear. "One of these days, I may just take you up on that offer."

Heat flooded my core, but I didn't let him see the reaction. Pulling my hand away, I turned around and pushed him roughly back into the door.

"You fucking wish, Roberts," I said before turning on my heel and walking to the bathroom. Once I got there, I let out a shaky breath, my hands braced on the sink. Looking up at my reflection, I saw my cheeks were flushed. I hated him. He was the biggest fucking douche in the school, probably the state and the country too. But my body continued to react to him, momentarily forgetting that I was repulsed by his mere existence.

After my breathing finally returned to normal, I slipped inside a stall. Once I was done, I washed my hands before splashing cold water onto my face. As I walked back into the cafeteria, I felt someone's eyes on me. I didn't need to look to know they were Will's.

The rest of the afternoon passed quickly. I had AP English, AP Spanish and finally AP Calculus. I thought I'd gotten lucky and not had a single class with Will, but god didn't look down on me with that much favor because as soon as Ms. Smalls, the calculus teacher, walked into the classroom, Will walked in right after her and took a seat in the middle of the classroom. That was his typical seat, making sure he was the center of attention.

Great.

I'd have to spend the last hour of my school day looking at the back of his head and listening to his ridiculous voice and obnoxious ways.

I paid little attention while Ms. Smalls passed out the syllabus and went over what we would learn during the semester. It was the same as every class I'd had that day.

Finally, at two thirty, the bell rang and we were free.

"You're in an AP class?" Will snorted when he finally noticed me.

"Yup," I said, attempting to give him as little attention as possible.

Part of me wanted to tell him I was actually in five, plus creative writing was a class you could only take if you were in AP English, so really it was like six, but he didn't need to know that. There was no reason to tell him.

"I'll tutor you if you need to," he said.

"And make sure I fail? No thanks."

Before he could say anything else, Mackenzie was coming up to him and wrapping her arms around his middle. His eyes held mine while he leaned down and kissed her.

Gag me.

I flipped him the bird before turning and heading towards my locker so I could take Sassy and myself home.

I fucking hated him.

And nothing would ever change that.

CHAPTER 2

THE CONCERN

Haley

"**H**arder!" I demanded of Bobby. I was on my hands and knees in front of him, and his hands dug into my hips harshly while he took me from behind in his bed. Somehow, Bobby's parents were never home.

"Fuck, Haley," he groaned. "I'm gonna come."

"If you come before me…" I threatened menacingly.

"Fuck. Then get there," he panted. Reaching between us, he stroked my clit like I'd taught him to.

"Yes!" I cried. I was finally close. "Yes! Yes!"

"Fuck," he grunted. I felt him slam into me, hold still and release himself inside the condom just as I came too. I always used condoms with the guys I messed around with. *And* I was on birth control. No way was I going to let a pregnancy derail my college plans and dreams of getting the hell out of Lake City.

Bobby and I worked together at the movie theater. I worked way less hours during the school year, but I still worked once a week to have gas money and money for whatever other activities I deemed worthy of spending from my sparse college fund.

Pulling out of me, he rolled to the side of me. My body collapsed onto the bed. It was almost two in the morning. We'd worked the evening shift together before he invited me back to his place. I was never one to turn down one of his invitations. He was pretty decent in bed and didn't know who my father was, knew jack shit about Lake City and therefore had no reason to be terrified of him.

"Tell me again why you don't have a boyfriend," he panted. I watched him discard the condom before walking to the attached bathroom. Bobby's bedroom and attached bathroom were almost the same size as the trailer I lived in with my entire family.

"Because I don't want one," I snorted. "Boys are only good for one thing."

"Glad to be of service." He winked as he spoke and came back to the bedroom, tossing a wet washcloth in my direction. On his way back to the bed, he stopped at the beverage fridge in his room and grabbed two bottles of water. "Here."

"Thanks," I said, taking a generous sip after I'd cleaned myself and tossed the used washcloth into the hamper in the corner of the room. "And why don't you have a girlfriend?" I asked.

"The only girl I want is in love with my best friend." That was the thing about mine and Bobby's friendship—friends with benefits status—we weren't jealous and we were also the only two people that the other knew from our respective towns. Having unfiltered honesty with someone was refreshing. I got that from Sassy. Unfortunately, I couldn't give her the same.

"Yikes," I said.

"It gets worse," he said. I furrowed my brows, waiting for him to continue. "She's got this kink." My eyes rose and widened. How did he know about her kinks? "She likes to be shared. And Adam shares her with me."

"He doesn't know you're in love with her?"

"Fuck no," he snorted. He'd put boxers back on, but I was still lying there naked. I didn't care about it; he'd seen everything there was to see on more than one occasion. "He can never know. They're literal soulmates. She loves being shared with more than just me." Damn, I'd like to meet this girl too. "And I wouldn't be able to share her. She thinks the sun rises and sets on Adam's ass and is beyond in love with him, even if she wants dick from more than just him."

"And he doesn't mind?"

"He loves it, gives him some sort of possessive high from knowing that other guys are only participating because he allows it."

"They do sound kind of perfect for each other," I said.

"They are. But it sucks at the moment. I'm applying to different colleges than they are. Which means I'll find someone there."

"And in the meantime, you're still gonna screw her whenever he decides to let you."

"Obviously," he said while rolling his eyes. "Unless you finally decide you want to be my girlfriend."

"You gonna share me too?" I deadpanned.

"You wanna be shared? I can have two guys here in ten minutes," he quipped, reaching for his phone.

"Not a chance, bud." I was not ever going to let myself be shared, it was not on my list of kinks. Men who liked to share women were dominant in bed, and I was anything but submissive. Bobby could attest to that. "I gotta go." He laughed at me. He wasn't really being serious about me being his girlfriend anyway, especially after he just told me he was in love with someone else, but I felt bad for him. Bobby was a good guy, and good guys were hard to find.

"When do you work again?" He asked as I was opening the door to his bedroom.

"Next week."

"I'll see you," he said with a wink.

"Bye," I said through my laughter.

It was freezing when I walked out of his house. September was that magical month where it was still boiling hot during the day, but the nights were down right ice cold.

The drive home took about thirty minutes since Bobby lived one town further away than the movie theater was.

When I got home, it was about two in the morning. It was good I didn't have a curfew. The lights were still on and there was a row of motorcycles parked in front. Why the members of my dad's crew felt the need to ride their motorcycles when they all lived within a thousand feet of us was something I would never understand.

Taking a deep breath, I prepared myself for what I was about to walk in on. It was the same for as long as I could remember, and this time wasn't any different. When I walked in, my dad was sitting on the big reclining chair that was his throne. Mom was on his lap, where she always was when he was trying to put on a show for his men. She was bent forward, one of her nostrils plugged while the other had a rolled up bill in it. My timing was perfect as I walked in just in time to watch her snort the cocaine off the table. Using her thumb, she wiped under her nose before leaning back against my dad, the effects already hitting her. Snake was there too. He had become a more and more permanent addition to the living room meetings. Along with Snake, there was Snake's dad, Bull, and Trent, Marcus, and of course, Judge Richardson.

"Join us," my dad said. It sounded like a polite invitation to everyone else in the room, but to my ears, it was a threat. If I didn't, there would be hell to pay. Dad wouldn't be the perpetrator of the violent beating I'd get, he'd force Mom to do it. I'd once read something about the cycle of abuse, and I didn't buy into it fully, but in this instance, it was true. Dad beat my mom. My mom beat me. Thankfully, the cycle ended there and nobody had ever been abusive towards Chloe.

Snake caught my eye and patted his legs in invitation. We'd gotten good at pretending that there was something between us when the watchful eye of my father was around. He didn't want me either. Setting my bag down on the kitchen counter, I walked towards him and sat on his lap as my father nodded his head in approval.

Despite not having romantic feelings for Snake, I felt safe in my best friend's arms. He laid his arms closely around my waist, pulling me close. It looked like an act of possession to the others in the room, but it was an act of protection towards his best friend. The few times we'd talked about what would be expected of us after graduation, he'd agreed it would be weird for us to sleep together since we'd been best friends our entire lives, but he was also adamant that he would have no trouble falling in love with me. I'd rolled my eyes, especially when that turned to how *it would be impossible not to fall in love with me based on nothing more than my body*.

If that was the case, Sassy stood a fighting chance because that girl was genetically gifted. She looked like a damn Instagram model without even having to try for it. Me? I was average size, not skinny, but certainly not plus sized, just perfectly average. I had fat around my stomach, and my boobs were too small for my body, plus my ass could be a little bigger for my liking, but I was happy with the way I looked. I'd decided a long time ago that I wouldn't let society dictate how I felt about myself. I had enough self-confidence that, even if someday I ended up gaining a hundred pounds and became too big for society's standards, I would settle for no less than a man who thought the exact same way I did.

"Relax," Snake whispered low enough for only me to hear. "And Jesus, you smell like sex," he said even lower. I turned and gave him a sheepish look.

"Shit, you probably do too," I said, taking a deep breath of him. "Yup." We both laughed, and instead of getting reprimanded, my dad thought we were having a cute couple's moment and let it slide. He didn't know that we were commenting on how the other smelled distinctly of sex… with another person.

"As I was saying," Judge Richardson continued, clearing his throat awkwardly. "Currently, there are no warrants of arrest out for anyone in the club." The last time he'd slipped and called it a gang, Dad nearly beat him to death. It *was* a gang. But whatever.

"Thank you."

Mom was leaning forward and doing yet another line of coke. The rest of the guys were passing a joint back and forth, but it wasn't offered to Snake or me. I zoned out, not caring to listen to my dad and Judge Richardson go back and forth about whatever illegal activities the club was involved in. It couldn't be anything all that interesting since everyone in this room was broke. That or they either snorted or shot the money they made, like my mother was currently doing.

When Judge Richardson finished speaking, my dad just waved him off without a care, rudely dismissing him from the conversation. The power dynamic between them was strange. Judge Richardson probably didn't throw him in jail for fear of his own life or his dirty secrets being exposed.

My father would surely kill him if he needed to.

"You can go too," he said, dismissing both Snake and I.

"Come outside with me." Chloe was asleep in our room so we couldn't go in there. I nodded, heading outside into the chilly night air. Snake lit a cigarette and offered me one, but I shook him off, too tired to partake. "Who were you with?"

"Some guy from the movie theater. You?"

"Bridgette." I rolled my eyes.

"Do you actually like this one?" I asked.

"Fuck no. There's only one girl for me." Snake said the words like a joke, implying it was me, but one time last year I'd actually gotten him to admit that there was someone he wanted to be with, but because he and I had to be together, he didn't even want to let himself get a taste of her. He was also adamant that I didn't know her and that it didn't matter, which is why I could never convince him to tell me. I should tell him my plans that way he could be with whoever he wanted without having to worry about me. But that would require me telling him about my plans to leave, and nobody could know. "You need to be more careful."

"I didn't know there was a meeting tonight," I told him.

"Still. Be more careful."

"I will," I assured him.

The door to the trailer opened and the rest of the men came stumbling out, including Snake's dad. "Later, sweetie," he said seductively, leaning in and kissing my cheek.

"Bye," I offered him my best seductive smile.

We'd gotten good at this game. How our parents didn't know that Snake was a man whore, sleeping with anything that moved, was beyond me.

I watched the bikes roll away, waking up everyone in the trailer park before heading back inside.

"You dumb, stupid, fucking whore," Dad seethed. He wasn't shouting the words, which made them somehow even more terrifying. "I told you that you could do one line, not fucking three. You used up everything for the week. What the fuck am I supposed to do now? How the fuck am I supposed to keep supporting your habit? Go spread your fucking legs again, but this time get paid to let some fuck inside your tight little cunt and then you can buy your own shit." I watched my father pull my mom's head back roughly, using her hair, before he slammed her face forward into the coffee table she'd been snorting her lines off of. "Fucking slut," he spat the word at her before tossing her now limp body to the side and stepping over her.

He glared at me, taunting me, daring me to say something. But I didn't. I never did. My father and mother were the only people who scared me, so, like every good kid from an abusive home, I kept my mouth shut and went to my bedroom. Tomorrow I'd be on the end of a violent beating from my mother; I always was after she had to suffer one from my father. But it was fine. As long as I was here to take them, she wouldn't turn on Chloe.

I had to protect Chloe.

But how was I going to do that when I was all the way on the other coast?

I couldn't stay. Not even for her.

I couldn't.

"Get up! Get up! Get your lazy ass out of bed right fucking now!" I woke to the loving sound of my mother's voice screaming at me to get up. "You didn't clean the living room before bed last night. Get up and do it right fucking now!"

It didn't matter that it was barely eight o'clock in the morning and because of her and Dad I hadn't gotten to bed until after three.

"I'm up, I'm up." I said groggily. What I wanted to say, and what I would have said to anyone else was *fuck off and do it yourself.* But, if I played the dutiful daughter, I may be able to prevent the beating I was expecting. Those hopes and dreams vanished as soon as I was out of bed when my 'mother' kicked me in the back of the leg, behind my knee, making me fall to my hands and knees, hitting my head on the door on the way down. She then proceeded to kick me once, harshly in the stomach, before stepping over me. The wind was knocked out of me and I was struggling for breath on my bedroom floor.

"Haley?" I heard Chloe's voice. Turning, I found her squatting next to me.

"Go back to bed, Squirt," I said, calling her by her nickname. "I'm fine. Get another hour of sleep. I'll make pancakes when you're up."

"Haley," she said my name again, this time only sadder.

"I'm fine. And then, this afternoon, I'll take you to lunch at the diner and we can get ice cream after." Chloe was the only time I put my stingy budget and savings plan aside.

"I can help you clean."

"I'm fine. Go back to bed." Begrudgingly, she nodded and trotted back to her bed. My breath had finally returned, so I stood. Quickly, I made my bed before heading out into the living room. There wasn't a trace of either of my parents, thank God. Dad would show up sometime this afternoon, presumably from whoever his side piece of the month was and he'd have flowers and chocolates for

Mom and a big apology and encouragement to make her not piss him off so much that he *had* to beat her.

There were remnants of drugs all over the coffee table. Using a paper towel, I swept them into a glass before rinsing it and washing it. The best thing about a trailer? It took me less than an hour to clean all the surfaces and the bathroom.

The place was spotless. It had to be otherwise I'd get another beating from Mom. I was sure I'd get another one anyway today for some reason or another, but it wouldn't be for my lack of cleaning abilities.

Once I was done, I started making pancakes for breakfast. The pre-made stuff was too expensive, basic ingredients were cheaper, so they were from scratch. Not being able to afford the pre-made stuff wasn't necessarily a bad thing. I was a good cook because of it, and making things from scratch always tasted better. There was bacon too, surprisingly, must have been on sale. I grabbed it and fried it all, but Chloe and I would only each get one slice. I didn't know if it was for something else and if we finished all of it, I'd be in for a beating.

I may even get one for the two pieces I took, but the way Chloe's face lit up when she came out and had a stack of pancakes and one single piece of bacon on her plate made it worth it. "Thanks, Hilly." You'd think Hilly would be short for Hilary, but when Chloe was little for some reason, the 'a's' gave her a hard time and Haley always came out sounding like Hilly. It stuck, and she was absolutely the only person allowed to call me that nickname.

We were both finished when there was a knock on our door. It opened before I could say anything, which meant it was Sassy. "Hey," she smiled happily.

"Go," Chloe said. "You cooked." I looked at her nervously. "Don't worry," she whispered. "I'll make sure it stays spotless."

"Thanks, Squirt." I kissed her head, something she'd hated since turning thirteen and becoming a teenager, but she was my little sister, so I did it anyway. "I'll be back to take you to lunch."

"How was last night?" Sassy asked when we stepped out of the trailer.

"I hooked up with Bobby again," I told her.

"Was it good?"

"It's good because I taught him exactly what I like," I laughed. "You might still be holding onto your V-card, but trust me, babes, you'll have to teach them all."

"Even if they've had tons of sex?" Sassy was so sexually naïve and I couldn't figure out how. She was best friends with Snake and me, and we were anything but.

"Yes. Because women all like different things and men can't figure that out, so we have to teach them."

Bobby was easy to train. It helped that the equipment he was working with was adequate.

"Whatever, enough sex talk."

"Yeah, why don't we talk about crushes instead?"

"What?" She asked, looking at me confused. "I don't have a crush on anyone," she lied horribly. "Do you have a crush on anyone?"

"Please. We both know I don't do the whole feelings bullshit."

"How do you have sex without developing feelings?"

I shrugged my shoulders. "I just do." She nodded, biting her lip. "I figured it out, you know."

"Figured what out?" She asked, her beautifully drawn eyebrows furrowing as she looked at me.

"Who you're crushing on."

"There's nothing to figure out," she said. We'd been walking around the outskirts of the trailer park like we always did. And right on cue, Snake pulled up. I heard the way Sassy's breath hitched as she looked at him. I might not like him like that, but that didn't mean I wasn't aware that he was damn fine to look at. He had tan skin, piercing green eyes that were nearly emerald colored, and his jet black hair was always slicked back. He could be described as every girl's dream bad boy. Sure, I liked to look, but there was no romantic attraction, just pure acknowledgement of a beautiful human.

"Then why are you drooling?" I asked her.

"I don't want to talk about this," she mumbled.

"Okay," I told her. "We don't have to, but know that we can, if and when you want to."

She looked at me and nodded, the thanks clear in her eyes. If she didn't want to talk about it, that was fine. I'd gotten the admission I needed, and now my determination to prevent Snake and me ending up together was only more solidified.

"Do you want to go to lunch with me and Chloe?"

"No thanks. I've got to start working on my history presentation."

"Okay. I'll see you tomorrow morning."

Sassy knew that my mom hit me sometimes. But she didn't know the extent of it and she didn't need to. She'd only ever found out accidentally when my mom backhanded my face, leaving a mark from one of her rings. She'd smartened up since then. Although when she'd hit me this morning, my face had come down against the door, but it didn't hurt and probably wouldn't bruise.

"ARE YOU FINISHED?" I ASKED CHLOE. THANKFULLY, THE DINER FOOD was cheap. I could feed both of us a three course meal for less than fifteen dollars. But we'd only gotten one course and were going to get ice cream across the street.

"I'm so full," she said, pushing away the few remaining fries and remnants of the burger that were left on her plate. She'd ordered a double bacon cheeseburger that was bigger than her head.

"Guess that means you don't want any ice cream, then."

"Well, you see," she said, sitting up seriously. "My food stomach is full. But my dessert stomach, the little stomach above my stomach, that one is demanding ice cream."

I laughed at her. She was too good and too pure for this world, especially the world she was born into with our father as a gang leader. I flagged down Suzie, the waitress who had to be in her late seventies. She was a Lake City fixture. Everyone in town knew her. "Here," I said, handing her a twenty which was plenty for food and tip.

"Thanks, girls. Have a great day."

Chloe and I walked across the street to the ice cream place. She ordered a scoop of chocolate chip cookie dough and dark chocolate in a waffle cone. I had to tease her mildly for being so basic. I ordered salted caramel and butter pecan for myself, asking for chocolate dip and chocolate sprinkles. It gave me the best of all the worlds—salted caramel, sweet and salty pecans and chocolate to cover it all with. Did I feel superior about my ice cream order? Yes.

We were walking out of the shop and back towards my car when I spotted Will walking down the street towards us. He would never give me the satisfaction of just ignoring me. "Take the keys and get into the car," I told Chloe. He wasn't a threat, but I didn't want her interacting with him. His taunting about our parents would affect her more than me.

"Haley," he said, using my first name. He was always so much nicer when it was just the two of us.

"Roberts," I said, using his last name like I knew he hated. "No bimbo today?" I asked.

"I don't date bimbos," he said.

"Oh. You broke up with Mackenzie then?" I asked, fake concern lacing my voice. He inhaled sharply. "Oh, you're meeting her here. Poor girl doesn't even know she's a bimbo then?" Was it low to be talking negatively about another woman? Should I be more feminist than that? Absolutely, but Will made my blood boil and talking about his precious girlfriend would be a sure-fire way to get under his skin.

And I enjoyed getting under his skin.

"Watch-" he cut himself off as he took a step closer to me. "What happened to your eye?" He asked suddenly.

Shit, it must be bruising.

"I fell," I said. He looked concerned, more than he should and more than I wanted him to.

"What happened, Haley?"

"I fell. Drop it Will. We're not even friends."

"Do you need me to talk to my dad?" He asked. He was acting like he was genuinely concerned.

"No!" I snapped at him. "Leave it alone, Will. I'm fine. We're not friends. Let it go." I brushed past him. But again, just like in school last week, he caught my wrist.

"Are you sure you're okay?"

"Will. I'm. Fine." I bit out each word through gritted teeth. "Go find your girlfriend."

Pulling my wrist away from him, I headed back down towards my car. I could feel his eyes staring at me, which was absolutely not the reason I swayed my hips a little more than usual.

That and the ridiculous tingles my body and stomach got whenever he touched me.

No.

It had absolutely nothing to do with that.

CHAPTER 3

THE FINAL WARNING

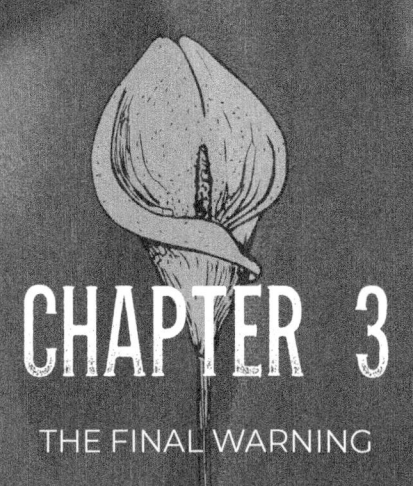

Will

The Monday after I'd ran into Haley outside the ice cream shop, I couldn't stop myself from looking at her, unable to not notice how much makeup she wore when she usually hardly wore any. Had Snake given her that bruise?

They were together, supposed to be anyway, but she let him cheat on her all the time. Maybe she'd finally had enough.

And why the hell did I care so much? She was right, we weren't friends. We'd been friends one day in pre-kindergarten and since then, we'd been enemies.

After that first day, over twelve years ago, I'd been so excited to run home and tell my mom all about my new friend. I remembered that day like it was yesterday. I could even still tell you what Haley had been wearing—a pink dress with yellow hearts. Her hair was combed back out of her face, but all throughout the day she'd played with it, messing it up to where she kept having to push it out of her face.

Once I'd gotten off the bus, I'd run into the house, telling Mama all about the friend I'd made. Lifting me up, Mama placed me on the counter, my little feet kicking excitedly as I spoke too quickly. She'd listened to me tell her all about Haley while she handed me a brownie and some milk.

"I'm happy you made a friend, sweetie," she'd said once I was finished.

The next day, when Haley wouldn't even speak to me, I'd had no idea what I'd done wrong. And I wouldn't figure it out until I told my mom about it.

"What did you say her name was?" My mom had asked.

"Haley Winters," I said.

"Winters?" I'd been eating a piece of homemade banana bread. Mama baked nearly every day, letting Dad take whatever was left down to the sheriff's office to feed his deputies. "Oh sweetie," she said sadly. "I don't think her parents want her to be friends with you."

"Why not?" I asked, my little voice full of confusion.

"Her dad is the dangerous man from the other side of town. The man your daddy has to arrest all the time."

That was the narrative my entire life. Her dad was a gang leader, my dad was a good guy, the local sheriff. He'd been re-elected so many times I couldn't even keep count.

I hated Haley now. The feeling was mutual. Our destiny had been predetermined. We had to hate each other. We were born into and bound to those feelings thanks to who our parents were. It wasn't something we ever had a choice in.

But if she truly hated me, why did she send me birthday cards every year? It took me a long time to figure out they were from her. I hadn't figured it out until my seventeenth birthday. A few days after my party, we started junior year of high school. When I'd seen her handwriting on one of the assignments she'd turned in, I knew it was her. It had always been her sending them to me and slipping them into my cubby or locker.

But why?

She hated me.

And I hated her.

Yet somehow, I was still worried about her when I saw that bruise forming on her face yesterday.

I blamed the damn birthday cards.

She didn't seem like she was in a lot of pain, going through the day like she usually did. The fact that I knew that meant I was paying too much attention to her.

"What's up with you?" Jordy asked when I sat down at our lunch table. "You're weird today."

"I'm good," I said, waving off his concern.

"Hey dreamboat," Mackenzie said, sliding up next to me before Jordy could continue his interrogation. I hated that nickname. I asked her repeatedly not to call me that, but I'd given up. She never listened.

"Hey," I said, bored, but I kissed her cheek anyway.

For some unholy reason, Mackenzie and I were the school's power couple. Apparently, everyone in our class thought we were going to end up getting married and be the next power couple or some shit. I would take over my dad's role as sheriff after getting a degree in criminal justice while she went to college and then law school and eventually took her father's judgeship. It was like everything in our lives was meant to be predetermined.

I didn't want to be married to Mackenzie. She gave me a headache and was incredibly whiny, especially when something didn't go her way. Yesterday at the ice cream shop, they were out of chocolate chip cookie dough and she'd basically thrown a tantrum. She was almost eighteen-years-old and couldn't handle the stress of an ice cream parlor not having what she wanted. She was spoiled, entitled, and mostly just annoying, but we'd been dating on and off since freshman year and I just couldn't seem to escape her completely.

"Are you coming over after practice tonight?" She asked.

"Probably," I said noncommittally. If I said yes and then bailed, there would be hell to pay. I faced forward, not even looking at her the entire time we ate our lunch. My back was to the table Haley always sat at with Snake and Sassy. As discreetly as possible, I turned to watch their interaction. They all bantered playfully, like they were normal teenagers and not about to take over the Southside Gang after graduation. Haley's head was back while she laughed. When she stopped, she rolled her eyes at Sassy, but I wasn't interested in watching her interact with Sassy; I wanted to watch her interact with Snake, to look for signs that he may have been the one hitting her. It wasn't because I liked her or some shit. It was because I wanted to be the sheriff and I wanted to protect *all* women from being abused. Men too if they were victims of intimate partner violence, but that was a different story.

It was hard to watch, to be discreet with my back turned. "I'll be right back," I announced, getting up from the table. Mackenzie's hand, that had been resting on my leg, fell off of me and she pouted while I walked away. At some point, I was really going to have to cut the cord and end it with her for good.

When I walked out of the cafeteria, I hid myself behind the door. It was the perfect spot to watch if you wanted to. Fuck, why did that sound so creepy? I was just making sure she was okay. I watched Snake lift his hands and move them around wildly, flinging them. Haley didn't even flinch. Later, she reached across the table and cuffed the back of his head while she scolded him for something he'd said.

Yeah, it wasn't Snake, but then who was it because someone had hit her.

Haley was like wildfire, unpredictable, strong willed and not easily tamed.

Hot.

I could hate her while still appreciating how gorgeous she was.

But who would she allow to hit her without fighting back?

Shaking my head, I walked away. It wasn't my business. *Haley* wasn't my business. One day, I was going to have to arrest her and her boyfriend. Until that day, whatever she did wasn't my problem.

Walking back to the table, I sat in the seat next to Mackenzie again. She offered me her best cheerleader smile, and I returned it reluctantly.

By the time last period rolled around, the one class I had with Haley, I'd finally been able to push her from my mind. Obviously, that changed once we had to share a space. Ms. Smalls was a great teacher, and she loved me even more than the other teachers. With a bit of luck, I'd be able to get her on a talking point that had nothing to do with math and I wouldn't have to learn a damn thing.

Taking AP calculus was the worst decision of senior year. Hands down.

As I was walking into class, I got bumped in the chest and pushed back out the door. "The hell," I grumbled, rubbing my chest where someone's bony head bumped into me.

"Watch where you're going," Haley seethed.

"For fuck's sake, Winters. If I didn't know any better, I'd think you *enjoyed* running into my chest. Can't get enough of a man with real muscles? Snake not doing it for you anymore?" I taunted her. "I know I'm stronger than he is."

"And way more of an asshole," she said. "And for the last time, he's not my boyfriend." The words may have been true, but that didn't mean that everyone in school didn't know their dads wanted them to get married.

"Well, if you want a real man before you have to tie yourself down to him the rest of your life, let me know," I offered with a wink.

Her head tilted to the side, her eyes flicking downward towards the zipper of my jeans. Her eyes had been there last week too—before she called me small. She had no idea.

"A real man?" She scoffed. "I'll pass. I had one of those this weekend." She smiled at me like I was dumb. "Couple times. And what would poor Mackenzie think if she found out you went slumming with slutty Haley Winters?"

Why did speaking to her turn on the douchebag part of my brain?

She drove me crazy.

"You wouldn't know a real man if he was standing in front of you," I said, taking a step closer. For the first time, I noticed that her breathing changed when I stepped into her personal space. Looking down at her, I watched her eyes, pupils dilated.

Was she affected by me?

"And I'm sure you think there's a real one standing in front of me right now?" Before I could answer, the bell rang and she pushed past me, presumably on her way to the bathroom.

I watched her go, noticing how short the stupid uniform skirt she was wearing was, and I couldn't stop myself from imagining what she was wearing underneath it.

Yeah, she definitely activated the douchebag part of my brain.

For the rest of class, she was all I could think about, consuming my thoughts. It was a damn good thing I was successful in getting Ms. Smalls to talk about her weekend instead of actually teaching anything.

The entire time I was sitting in class, the only thing I could think of was Haley. Why did I react to her the way I did? I had Mackenzie and if I didn't have her, I could have literally any other girl in the school. Sure, it may have been cocky, but I was a big fish in a small pond.

It was purely a physical attraction. It happened all the time, the good girl falling for the bad boy. This was the opposite. The good boy, with the good grades and the good family, was stupidly attracted to the bad girl. She smoked, she drank, but who didn't as a teenager? She didn't pay attention in class, didn't participate in extracurricular activities.

Yeah. This was just a stupider version of whatever that was.

And it was just passing lust. She was the most attractive girl in the school. Beautiful. And that damn nose ring and tattoo that peeked out from her side whenever she lifted her arms up, did things to me too. Her eyes were a light brown, looking almost honey colored in the right light. Her hair was brown with multicolored highlights to it, but they were all natural. The random streaks of dark blonde and auburn gave her a one of a kind look.

Why did I know all this about her?

I was just a good boy lusting after a bad girl. Someone I *hated*, something that could never and would never happen. She was someone I would never be with. Could never want to be with. The problem was my raging hormones made me forget whenever I saw her in her school uniform. But I had self-control. Nothing would ever happen.

Neither of us wanted anything to happen.

"Ms. Smalls." I heard Haley call out about halfway through class.

"Yes, Miss Winters?"

"You do realize that Will distracted you so you wouldn't teach us anything, right?"

"Fucking seriously?" I turned to growl at her. "Based on who your dad is, I'd never beg you for a snitch."

"I have a headache. Both of you get out. Go to Principal Potter's office," she said. "And for the love of God, one of you switch out of this class. The semester has only started and I can't deal with the drama."

"Yeah, Will," she said, voice taunting. "Maybe you should just drop the class before it gets too late and has to go on your record. We all know how hard getting into the community college down the street is."

"At least one of us is going to college."

I'd still been looking at Ms. Smalls when I said the words, and a look of confusion crossed her face. Why was she confused? Everyone knew I was going to community college.

"Go. Now."

This was the first time this year Haley and I had been sent to the principal's office. Last year, our longest streak *without* being sent was six weeks.

We ignored each other while we walked down the empty halls.

"Again?" The secretary asked when we walked in.

"It was his fault." Haley smiled widely at her as she spoke, her head tilted to the side as she tried to appear innocent.

"I'm sure," she said noncommittally. "Sit down." She hit the button on her phone that would buzz Principal Potter. The words were always the same. "Miss Winters and Mr. Roberts are here." She put the phone back on the hook and looked at us over her glasses. She had a serious look about her and the gray roots of her hair were starting to show. "You can go in."

Haley stood first and waltzed into the room.

"Last year," Principal Potter began before even letting us sit across from him. "Last year, you set a record of being sent to my office sixty times. That's once every three days of school on average. And the reality is, it felt like so much more. Who can forget the two-week period where you were sent every day?"

Haley and I went to protest at the same time, to give the other the blame.

"No," he said, holding his finger up and shaking his head. "We are not doing this again this year. I've been very lenient with both of you, all things considered." The unspoken truth of his words was that I was the golden boy, and he couldn't give me detention. The other side of that coin was that he was afraid of Haley's dad and wouldn't give her detention either. "This is your final warning. Next time you land in my office, you're both getting detention. Do I make myself clear?"

"Yes," we said at the same time.

"Go," he said, waving his hands at us.

"Better behave," I told her.

"Take your own advice, Roberts," she retorted before disappearing the opposite way down the hallway.

Rolling off of Mackenzie, I caught my breath and rolled the condom into a tissue. "That was great," she smiled before attaching herself to me like a leach.

Don't break up with her post sex.

I was fighting an internal battle. I definitely could not break up with her post sex, but I did not want to keep doing this. *Avoid her for the week and then do it next week. No more sex.* "Yeah," I agreed. It was sex; it was fine. But I wouldn't classify it as great. There was no excitement, no rush. Mackenzie let me do pretty much whatever I wanted to her, and although I used to like it, it just didn't do anything for me anymore.

I was turning into such a cliche. I hadn't been with her for the chase because if that was the case, I would have dumped her sophomore year after the first time we'd fucked. I just wasn't into her anymore, and if I wasn't into her, it was hard to be into the sex.

"I should go," I said, rolling away from her. "I promised my mom I'd be home for dinner."

"Okay," she said. "I'll see you at school tomorrow."

"Bye."

I walked out of the gigantic empty house. Judge Richardson worked long hours and his wife was a typical trophy wife—always engaged in some charity event or another in an effort to improve the town. Shockingly enough, her charity efforts only ever benefited the rich side of town and not the poor side where charity would actually be beneficial and could potentially change someone's life.

When I pulled into my own driveway, my dad's sheriff's truck was just pulling into the driveway too.

"Son," he said.

"Hey Dad, how was work?" He shook his head. "What's going on?"

"Something's brewing, but I don't know what."

"What do you mean?" I asked.

"I don't know. The Southside has seen an increase in activity lately. Whatever they're planning, it's big."

"It can't be that big a deal. I know they're trouble, but if they were into something serious, wouldn't they all be rich? Everyone is still so poor."

I guess I could understand the benefit of being in a gang or involved in illegal activity if it was profitable, but it wasn't, not the way they did it anyway.

"I don't know because Judge Richardson won't give me a warrant to raid their warehouse."

"Why?"

"I don't know because we have probable cause."

Something was definitely going on.

"Do you think it's drugs or guns or something else?" I asked.

"I know they're dealing drugs, but they're small fish when it comes to that. Last time I tried to involve the DEA they said they wouldn't intervene. It don't know, could be anything, but something just doesn't feel right."

"That's enough shop talk," my mom said once we'd slowly made our way into the kitchen. "I made your favorite."

"Mine or his?" My dad asked her before kissing her.

"Who's my favorite man?" She asked in response.

"Dammit, you know I don't like fajitas," he said.

"Good thing you're my favorite man then," she smirked at him. My parents were young. I was born when my mom was just nineteen. Her parents forced them to get married, but it didn't seem like either one of them regretted it. That was the reason I was an only child. They didn't want to have another kid and the financial burden when they were still struggling, and by the time they were financially stable enough to have a second, I was like six and they didn't want to go through the newborn phase again. Having parents who'd had me as a teenager made me obsessive with condoms. That would not be happening to me.

"You guys are gross."

"Someday, you'll be in love and you'll get it," my mom told me.

Mackenzie told me she loved me regularly, but I'd never said it back.

Was it worse for me to stay with her when I didn't love her and probably never would? She stuck around anyway. And I wasn't lying to her by telling her I loved her when I didn't.

"How was school?" Mom asked when we were sitting at the table.

"School was fine," I said. "Ms. Smalls sent me to Potter's office again."

"Were you fighting with the Winters girl again?" My dad asked.

"Fighting is a strong word."

"Let her be. She got dealt a rough hand. You don't need to be making it worse for her," my dad defended her. "It's not her fault who her parents are."

"But," I began.

"No buts, leave the girl alone."

Did he know something I didn't?

We ate spaghetti and meatballs with homemade garlic bread, my dad's favorite, in relative silence after that. Mom served us chocolate cake with peanut butter frosting, also my dad's favorite, for dessert.

After dinner, I was dismissed and spent the rest of the night in my room.

I couldn't forget what my dad had said. Leave Haley alone, she's had a hard enough time as it was. Something was brewing.

But what?

And why, even after he'd told me to leave her alone, why couldn't I get her out of my head?

CHAPTER 4

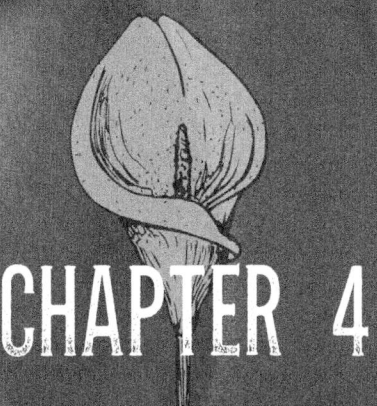

THE ARREST

Haley

For the last week, Will and I managed to stay out of trouble, kept our snarky comments away from Ms. Smalls and out of her classroom, and avoided being sent back to Principal Potter's office. That didn't mean that we didn't see each other around or exchange snarky words. It just meant we were both smarter about how we went about degrading the other.

Despite all that, things were… peculiar.

I caught him staring at me regularly, at lunch mostly, but I only knew that because I was looking at him too.

Ever since he'd shown so much concern over my bruised eye, it seemed like I was thinking of him less negatively, silently wondering how different things would have been if we'd been able to stay friends after that first day of pre-kindergarten.

It was a ridiculous notion. We weren't friends, couldn't be friends. Ever.

Will broke up with Mackenzie on Wednesday, right in the middle of the cafeteria. She'd come strolling in, calling him dreamboat—what a ridiculous nickname—and he just dumped her. Had I laughed when she'd screeched at him with her banshee-like voice echoing through the cafeteria?

Maybe.

He clearly could have picked a better time to do it.

"William!" She shouted at him. "You cannot be serious."

I never heard anybody else call him William.

"Look," he began. He'd been trying to keep his cool, but was losing it, especially since she was making a scene. Maybe he'd done it in the middle of the school day in hopes it would keep her calm. I'd snorted at the thought, since it obviously backfired. "You care about me way more than I care about you. That's not fair to you."

"But I love you," she said dramatically, dragging out the word love.

"Yes, I know. And it's not fair to you, because I don't love you," he countered, speaking slowly, as if she was a child.

Burying her face in her hands, she cried into them loudly before running out of the cafeteria, the cheerleading squad hot on her heels.

I hadn't laughed.

Okay, I'd tried not to laugh.

Later that same day, in AP calculus, Will winked at me. I'd spent most of that period staring at the back of his beautiful blonde head.

Not beautiful.

Average. Nothing but an average fuckboy head.

That day, when we'd walked out of class, Ms. Smalls spoke. "I don't know what's changed, but I appreciate you not disrupting my class."

Will flashed her his signature grin while I'd just rolled my eyes.

"Nothing has changed," I muttered before leaving class.

But something *had* changed, even if I couldn't figure out what.

"What are we doing today?" Chloe asked me, pulling me out of the memory of what happened at school during the last week.

"What do you want to do?" I asked her.

"Can we go to the diner again?"

"No," I said, shaking my head. I hated saying no to her, but I needed to save money. I couldn't make our diner adventure a weekly thing. Twenty bucks a week would add up too quickly, plus I wasn't working at the movie theater again until next week.

"I'll pay," she offered.

"You'll pay?" I asked her. "With what money?"

"I've been babysitting all summer."

I felt like a terrible sister because I had been so busy with my own life, working my own job, and hanging out with my friends, I hadn't even realized she had a job.

"Who can afford to pay a babysitter around here?"

"Um," she began, nervously. "I was working on the other side of town." My eyebrows rose, giving my face a shocked expression. "My science teacher from last year. She really likes me. She works during the summer to supplement her income. She needed someone to take care of her three-year-old little boy while she worked. So she asked me if I wanted to."

"Wow, Chloe, I'm so proud of you. That's amazing."

"So, wanna go to the diner?" She asked again, this time with a grin on her face.

"You buying me ice cream afterwards?" I asked.

"Duh," she laughed.

"All right, Squirt, no more free loading for you, now that I know you're rolling in dough." She rolled her eyes dramatically, a new habit since she'd started high school.

Swiping my keys off the counter, I double checked that the trailer was clean before we left. Both Friday and Saturday nights, I cleaned it spotless in an attempt to avoid another beating. So far, I've been successful.

Mom also hadn't been home a lot. She and Dad were barely speaking, just another part of their cycle of abuse. She'd get angry after he hit her, but instead of leaving, she'd go out and find guys to hook up with before coming home. He'd beat her again, which would lead to her beating me, and then we'd get to pretend to be a normal family for a month or so before the cycle started all over again.

It was exhausting.

I'd thought multiple times about forgoing college until Chloe was eighteen and I could legally take her with me, but that would be another three years after I graduated. If I stayed that long, I feared I'd get sucked in.

Maybe I could get Will to watch out for her.

What a stupid thought.

Why would Will do anything for me? He seemed truly concerned someone was abusing me, but I doubt he could have guessed it was my mom.

But maybe if I told him and the sheriff knew, things could be different. I didn't care enough about myself to go through the trouble. It wasn't worth it when I already had an escape plan, but for Chloe, I'd do anything.

"So, since you're paying, do I get to order the most expensive thing on the menu?" I teased her as we slid into our usual booth.

"Be my guest," she grinned.

I wondered how much her teacher actually paid her to babysit.

"I wouldn't do that to you," I dismissed. I was going to get something different than I usually got though. "Oh, the sampler looks good though." It was a combination of all the diner favorites—a mini bacon cheeseburger, a chicken strip that rivaled Chili's, half of a club sandwich, a spicy chicken slider, along with curly fries, cheese fries, and onion rings.

"Oh, let's share that," she said. "And then we can get the dessert sampler too."

"And I still get ice cream after?"

"Duh." I chuckled at her expression and closed the menu.

"Let's do it."

I let Chloe take the lead ordering since it was her money we were spending.

"So, how are you liking school?" I asked her once we'd ordered.

"I like it a lot. My grades are actually really good." Hm. Smart like me. Where did we get that from? Was one of our parents actually smart and had been destined for more than the trailer park life they'd been given?

"That's great," I told her. "Just don't get distracted."

"What would distract me?" She asked.

Our home life, I wanted to say, but I didn't. "Boys. Or girls. You know, either is fine with me."

"Boys," she said seriously. "And I won't. All the boys in town are either headed nowhere because they're from the Southside or they want nothing to do with me because they think being rich makes them too good for me."

"You're too good for all of them," I told her seriously. It was also the truth, Chloe was absolutely too good and too pure for this world. "But what about Buck?" I asked.

"Not going to happen," she said. "He's my best friend. But I don't have any interest in him romantically at all. The thought of it actually makes me kind of nauseous. He's like a brother to me."

It was nice to hear her say that. "In any case," I continued. "You're going to be fifteen soon. And if at any point, there is a boy who catches your eye, I want you to be smart and safe." I knew my mom wouldn't have this conversation with her. But it needed to be done. Neither one of us needed to end up a teenage mother like ours had. "Let me know, and I'll drive you to the clinic. You can get birth control for free."

"Hilly!" She shouted at me. "Hilly," she said, this time in a whisper yell. "Quiet."

"Stop," I told her. "Don't be so dramatic. I'm sorry Mom didn't even talk to you about your period before you got it, but you need to know how your body works. How birth control works. And even if you're on birth control, you still need to be using condoms," I told her seriously.

"I'm not even having sex," she protested. "And I'm not planning on it. And I know how my body works."

"Health class doesn't even cover ten percent of what actually goes on with the female body."

"I know!" *Oh.* "I can find everything I want to know online, even on social media. I know how to use google if I want to know something. And I promise that if I ever have something that I can't get answered, I'll come to you. Now, can we *please* stop talking about this?"

"Okay," I told her. "But just remember, my offer stands. Sometimes birth control is a necessary evil."

"I'll remember."

"Good."

With that, our platter of food showed up. It was so much. Good thing the Winters girls could eat. "I love this place," Chloe sighed before digging in.

I was so full by the time we finished the first sample platter, but that did not stop us from ordering the dessert sampler, and it would also absolutely not stop us from walking to the ice cream shop when we were done.

"This one is my favorite," Chloe said as she dug into the apple crisp with bourbon vanilla ice cream on top of it.

"I like this one," I said, digging into the ultra fudge brownie that had double chocolate chip ice cream covering it. I was going to end up in a chocolate coma. I'd definitely need to forgo my usual chocolate drip on my ice cream but maybe get some rainbow sprinkles.

"And you call me basic," she snorted.

After finishing the rest of our lunch, Chloe paid the bill, leaving a generous tip while I downed the rest of my soda and climbed out of the booth.

"I'm so full," she whined. It was the same thing she always said whenever we were leaving the diner. "But don't worry, we're still getting ice cream."

I flung my arm around her shoulder and pulled her into me, kissing the top of her head.

We definitely needed to pick a different day to go to the diner and the ice cream shop, because just like last week, Will was walking down the street towards us. This time, he already had his ice cream in his hand. "Go ahead without me," I told Chloe. "I'll catch up."

She nodded reluctantly, but left anyway. She stood at the entrance for a moment, giving me one last look before finally opening it and disappearing inside. "Haley," Will said. His voice held less disdain than usual.

"Roberts," I said.

We stood there, staring at each other. Why didn't we just ignore each other? We clearly had nothing to say to the other. Why would we? We weren't *friends*.

"Your eye looks better." Of all the things I'd expected him to say, it hadn't been that.

"Thanks."

We stood there somewhat awkwardly while his ice cream melted. I watched as he licked around the ice cream, preventing the sweet creamy substance from dripping onto his fingers. Absolutely ridiculous, the image of said tongue doing that same motion to me filled my mind. I could see it all in front of me, his blond head between my thighs with his hands wrapped around them. Based on how he was licking his ice cream, it seemed like he might actually know what he was doing.

No wonder Mackenzie lost her shit when he'd broken up with her.

I wouldn't want to give that up either.

"My offer still stands," he said. "If you need help." His words pulled me out of my ridiculous fantasy, and when he looked at me, I was sure he knew exactly what I'd just been thinking.

"I don't," I said, cutting him off. "But thanks," I said so softly I was sure he could barely hear me.

With that, I brushed by him, more confused than ever.

Which one of our interactions was the facade? Was the way he treated me when we were alone the facade? Was the nice guy thing just an act? Or was the way he treated me when we were at school, when all of his friends were around the pretend version?

I wasn't sure which answer I wanted to be true.

The knock on the trailer pulled me away from where I was working on my homework. Walking to the door, I opened it to find Sassy standing there. It was getting late, nearing eight, and the sun was almost setting.

"Wanna go for a walk?"

"Sure, just a second."

"Squirt," I called for Chloe.

"Yeah?" She yelled back from the bedroom.

"I'm going for a walk. If Mom and Dad come home, go to Sassy's."

"Okay."

Slipping my shoes on, I met Sassy where I'd left her standing outside the trailer.

"What's up?" I asked her.

"Just had to get out of the house."

"Everything okay?"

"Yeah. I just," she began and stopped. "I know you know," she told me.

"Know what?"

"That I'm ridiculously and hopelessly in love with Snake."

"Ah, yeah, I do know that."

"How?" She asked.

"You're my best friend, I've known you all our lives. Of course, I know."

"He's known me just as long. How does he not know?"

"He's a boy," I said in a *duh* tone. It was the only explanation needed.

"But he's yours."

"I don't want him, not like that."

"It'll be hard for me to watch you guys together," she said gloomily.

"But I don't want him," I told her again, this time more forcefully. "Take a chance, he might want you too."

"Only to have us break up when your dads force you guys into whatever bullshit arranged marriage they've cocked up?"

"I know," I told her. She was visibly upset. "But I'm working on getting out of it."

"How?"

By running away.

"I'm not sure yet. But I've still got some time to figure it out."

"What am I supposed to do in the meantime? He's got girls all over him."

"He's got no idea you're into him. Be a little more obvious," I told her.

"How? You know I have zero experience with boys. I've never even kissed one because all I want is Snake."

"So kiss him," I told her. "Push him up against a locker or a tree or a car and just kiss him."

"That's sexual assault, Haley," she said seriously.

Yeah, she could potentially be right.

"So tell him to kiss you."

"What?"

We'd made it almost all the way around the trailer park, still on the edges of it before we'd weave our way through them and back to my trailer.

"Next time you're alone, put your hand on his leg and lean in. Whisper something to him, how sexy he is, how strong he is, whatever, just make it sexy and whispery—they love that shit. And then lean in."

"And if he doesn't take the bait."

"He will."

"Okay, that's fine," she said. "But what happens when I fall even harder for him and he just wants me for sex, like all the other girls he's with?"

"Oh." I hadn't thought about that. "I'm not the one you come to for feelings advice. I told you, I don't do the feelings bullshit."

"I guess I'll give it a try," she said.

I was worried she'd just end up hurt.

But before I could voice that fear, sirens were blaring everywhere. The red and blue lights were still flashing, lighting up the trailer park like it was the Fourth of July. Sassy and I hid in the tree line, not wanting to get caught in any potential crossfire. My only hope was that Chloe was inside our trailer, that she'd stay there.

"Douglas Winters," Sheriff Roberts's voice boomed through the megaphone. Nobody called my dad Douglas, everyone called him Viper. I guess it was fitting that Snake was set to take over for him. "We have a warrant for your arrest," he said. "Come out with your hands up."

"Why's your dad being arrested?" Sassy whispered at me.

"I have no idea," I shrugged. "Could be anything."

"Is he not going to come out?"

"He won't go quietly."

She made some type of noise of disbelief, but we both knew the truth. Dad never went quietly even though his arrests got further and further apart and the time he actually spent in the holding pen was less and less.

"Do not make us come inside where your wife and daughters are," Sheriff Roberts spoke again.

He had four of his deputies with him, one woman and three men. They looked bored.

In traditional white trash fashion, multiple people stepped outside. Some of the women were in their robes with their hair in curlers like it was still the sixties or some shit. The men stood with their arms folded, but itching to support their leader if it came to that.

Suddenly, the door to my trailer swung open and my dad appeared, standing menacingly in the doorway. All four of the deputies drew their guns, no longer appearing bored. "Stand down,"

Sheriff Roberts's voice commanded. Relaxing their posture, they still didn't put their guns away.

"Come on out, Doug," he said.

"It won't stick and you know it," my dad said. "Why not save everyone here the show and the trouble and just go home?"

"Just doing my job. Come on." Sheriff Roberts held his arm up, inviting my dad to join him. He had handcuffs in his other hand.

He couldn't really think my dad was going to go quietly, could he?

I watched as everything seemed to happen in slow motion. My dad skipped the steps of the trailer, instead jumping down onto the ground. When he rose to his full height, he stood evenly matched with Sheriff Roberts. "Douglas Winters, you're under arrest." Whatever the charges were, I didn't hear them because my dad did the stupidest thing he'd ever done. Well, not ever. It seemed like he always did it. His fist pulled back, and he landed a right hook right to Sheriff Roberts's left eye. Falling to his knees, he didn't have time to recover before my dad was tackling him, punching his face repeatedly.

Disgust filled me.

I couldn't even look at him.

How had that man fathered me?

I was nothing like him.

One of the male deputies and the female one jumped on my father's back, attempting to restrain him. When a few of my father's men took menacing steps forward, the other two deputies whirled around, pointing their guns at them. "Stand back!" Their wives wrapped their arms around them and pulled them back.

My dad was still struggling, but he had been subdued. The woman straddled his hips and sat on his lower back, keeping him down. Standing to his feet, Sheriff Roberts spit on the ground, barely missing my father.

There were calls of abuse and police brutality, and although, in general, I wasn't the biggest fan of any police force, in this case, I found their actions more than justified.

Sassy and I waited until my dad was put in the back of the car. Ridiculously, he was still struggling against them.

Bull and Snake stood in the middle of the circle that formed, trying to calm down the rest of the guys.

"I need to go check on Chloe," I told her.

"Okay. I'll see you in the morning."

Great. I thought to myself. This news would be all over the school tomorrow morning. I wouldn't be able to hide from it.

CHAPTER 5

THE MOMENTARY LAPSE IN JUDGMENT

Haley

The day after my dad's arrest, I pulled into the parking lot of school at the same time I always did, all alone this time because Sassy chose to ride with Snake. Maybe she was going to take my advice to heart and tell him how she felt. Parking my old beat-up car, I braced myself for another day of bullshit, and today was sure to be worse than usual. So much worse.

I'd never given too much thought to growing up on the literal wrong side of the tracks. It was what it fucking was. But things with Will had been so strange lately, and now after Dad got arrested—again—I didn't know what to do with myself. I wasn't accepted in any of the preppy circles, despite being valedictorian of the class. But nobody knew that. And sure, it wasn't set in stone yet, still having most of senior year to get through. Besides, they wouldn't until I gave my scathing commencement speech because that was how I wanted it. The number one in our class had been a mystery since seventh grade when I'd finally surpassed Mackenzie. Everyone assumed she was lying about only being in second place out of the hundred some kids in our graduating class.

They'd fucking know soon enough.

Lighting a cigarette, which was forbidden on campus, and something I still hated, I walked across the parking lot ready to face another day. Just the action of lighting the cigarette calmed my nerves. It was a habit I could break easily, one I planned on breaking as soon as I wasn't under the watchful eye of my father, as soon as I didn't have to keep up appearances anymore.

Sighing, I certified my own thoughts, trying to manifest myself out of this bullshit life, the life I didn't want, but the one that was being demanded of me. I didn't fucking want it: the guns or the violence or the drinking. I wanted a chance at a life I could choose for myself. And as soon as I heard from the colleges I applied to, I'd know if it would finally be happening now. Step one, get into college. Step two, figure out a way to pay for college.

But for now, I'd still play the part of the bad girl. I kept my shitty attitude in all my classes, despite my excellent grades. I talked back, I smoked, I cussed, and I slept around.

That part I did willingly. Sex was one of life's greatest gifts. Good sex anyway. But still, it helped my reputation.

"You're in for it today," Sassy said, walking up to me. She grabbed the cigarette out of my hand, taking a drag before handing it back to me.

"Don't I fucking know it. They're already whispering."

"Can we just burn this shithole to the ground?" She asked the same question she asked nearly every week. One of these days, I may just take her up on her offer, probably right before I snuck out of town in the middle of the night. Snake would be more than willing to help us.

"What are the charges against your dad this time?" She asked as we started walking towards the building. The warning bell was about to ring.

"Racketeering, money laundering, possession of controlled substances." My mom was able to find out after he'd gotten taken in, and I'd finally known what Sheriff Roberts had been about to say before my dad punched him.

"Are they going to stick?"

"They never do. That's what happens when you find out the only judge in town has a thing for the eighteen-year-old boys in the gay club a town over."

"Of course, he ran for the judgeship on a family values platform." I snorted at Sassy's words.

Last night, in her post arrest drunk and high stupor, my mom let that little detail slip. I'd always wondered how none of the charges against my father seemed to stick, and now I knew. The princess of the preppy kids had no idea her dad got some on the side from boys barely older than her. Her mama had no idea either, apparently, and my dad, ever the businessman, found that information and used it against him. It was the only reason he wasn't locked up for life.

So much fucking corruption.

That's what the preppy kids in the school didn't realize, and the thing I was finally starting to realize—their parents were just as fucked up as the bad kids' parents. Was Will's dad corrupt too? Were all the arrests just for show? To keep up appearances? The parents of the rich kids had enough money to buy their way out of problems and pretty family names that went a long way. Fucking small town bullshit politics.

"Can't believe you had the nerve to show up here," Will said. He thought being a big man on campus gave him free range to do whatever he wanted, to say whatever he wanted. Was this really the same kid who'd stood in front of me yesterday, eating his ice cream, making me imagine what his tongue would feel like against me? It didn't seem like the same one. Maybe he had a twin who the family only let out on Sundays and he was the one I was impossibly attracted to.

That would explain the act.

"Why wouldn't I?" I shot back at him.

"Because your daddy got arrested. *Again*." The group of guys behind him snickered stupidly.

"I don't know anything about that," I said, blinking my eyes at him.

"My dad arrested him last night."

"And that's somehow your accomplishment?" I asked. Two could play whatever game he was playing. And I could play it better.

His face turned red with anger. "It will be."

"Sure. When you become sheriff."

"Yup. And then I'll arrest your misfit boyfriend, Snake. And you."

"He's not my boyfriend."

"Yet," Snake said from behind me, wrapping his hands around my waist. He thought he was being helpful, defending me from Will, but all he did was antagonize him and make it worse.

"Back the fuck up. You're not helping," I seethed at him.

"Trouble in paradise?" Will laughed at his own joke.

I glared at him. Why was he so popular? He wasn't even *that* attractive. There was nothing unique about him, standard blonde hair and standard blue eyes. Nothing I hadn't seen on thousands of other guys.

Sure. But you weren't imagining a thousand other guys with their head between your thighs last night.

My inner monologue needed to shut her damn mouth.

But she wasn't wrong.

Before I could snark at him again, the bell rang. Flipping him the bird, I pushed by him and walked to the office to sign in before I'd take up my usual first period hiding spot in the library. Today really should have been the day that I didn't come in until second period when I was required to.

Thankfully, the rest of the day passed without much incident. Will stared at me during lunch, a weird new habit of his. What bothered me wasn't that he was doing it, but how much I noticed he was doing it, how much I *liked* he was doing it.

But all of that only lasted until AP calculus. Ms. Smalls had been right, one of us should have dropped the class. I knew as soon as he walked in that he was going to try and start something. I could read it all over his smug fucking face.

"Who'd you have to blow to get your daddy released?"

"What the fuck are you talking about?" I seethed.

"Just heard all charges were dropped."

That was faster than I'd been expecting.

"We all knew you were a whore, but I'm curious. Who'd you blow?"

"Back the fuck off," I snapped. We were standing close, his tall frame towering over me. But I wasn't afraid. He wouldn't be stupid enough to hit a girl, not with all these witnesses. Besides, even if he did, I was sure I could take him. Then I remembered Will's concern when he'd seen my bruised eye. He wouldn't hit a girl, not just because there were witnesses, but because Will wouldn't hit a girl. That was the end of the sentence, full stop. He wasn't the type.

He wasn't like my father.

"All that experience must have made you an expert, how else would you get him released in twelve hours?"

"I heard that Mr. Roberts," Ms. Smalls said. "To Principal Potter's office. Now!"

"I didn't do anything!" I defended myself.

"That may be true, but you're both being disruptive. Now go."

Fuck. We'd already gotten a final warning. Detention was coming.

Pissed off, I stormed out of class, hearing Will try to sweet talk Ms. Smalls into letting him stay. When I heard him behind me, I knew it hadn't worked.

"Have a seat, Ms. Winters." the secretary said. "You too, Mr. Roberts." She said the words with a heavy sigh. It was too early in the year for this. Will sat, leaving a seat between us free. The principal's door opened shortly after that and we were both called in.

"What happened?" He asked.

"Nothing," I smiled easily.

"A simple misunderstanding." Will said.

I could easily throw him under the bus. His actions had been harassment. Sexual in nature by calling me a whore.

But I wouldn't stoop to his level.

"Nobody wants to tell the truth?"

We were both silent.

"Detention for disrupting. This afternoon until five pm."

"That's not fair!" I said.

"Seriously." That was probably the first time he'd ever agreed with me. The only time he'd ever agreed with me.

"Disrupting class for whatever lover's quarrel you were having-"

"We are not lovers!" I snapped.

"She wishes," Will snorted.

"Not if you were the last person on this planet."

"Enough," the principal said harshly. His hands were rubbing his temples. Honestly, I'd have a headache too if I had to deal with snarky teenagers all day. "I told you what would happen if I found you two in my office again. Apparently, you didn't take me seriously. Well, the basement supply closet where the janitorial staff keep their supplies needs to be cleaned and reorganized. I'll be down at five to check on the status of things. I trust the two of you are responsible enough to be in charge of yourselves. No fighting."

"Not a problem. We won't even be speaking."

"Just go." Poor man was exhausted.

We stood at the same time. Will held the door open for me and mockingly bowed in my direction. I flipped him off and brushed past him.

I'd hated him since pre-kindergarten, and the feeling was mutual. There wasn't ever another option for us. Our parents hated each other in high school and our grandparents before that. It was like some Romeo and Juliet shit, except we were not star-crossed lovers destined to be together. We were destined to hate each other. And if I stayed in this shitty town and let my father determine my life and marry Snake, our kids would be destined to hate each other too. We were more like the Hatfield's and the McCoy's, and not Romeo and Juliet.

"I'll do this side. You do that one," I tossed over my shoulder while pointing to the other side of the room. The one far, far away from where I was.

"You're such a bitch," he said.

"And you're an asshole, douchebag, dumbass. Need I go on?" He growled at me. Literally growled. "I hate you so fucking much."

"Feeling's mutual, baby."

"Good," I seethed.

I walked away, but I could feel his eyes on me. I hated it. He shouldn't be staring, and I shouldn't be aware enough of him to feel his eyes on me. But just like the rest of this year, it was all I could feel and my body broke out in delicious tingles because of it.

My own body was betraying me for him.

Ignoring it, I went to my side of the storage room and started rearranging. Honestly, it didn't need cleaning that badly. Who actually knew what the principal was up to by trapping us down here, some ill-guided attempt to restore relations across town lines?

What a stupid concept.

Cats and dogs never got along.

A tiger never changes its stripes.

A leopard never changes its spots.

The Roberts and the Winters families would never get along. It wasn't meant to be. I hated him so fucking much, and he hated me the same. Just a few more months of high school and then I would be gone, never to hear from or see him again.

"Fuck!" I cursed. I'd been standing on my toes, trying to lift a bottle with distilled water in it from a high shelf, distracted by thoughts of Will, and it fell on my head, soaking me.

Without thinking, I pulled my blouse over my head.

"What-" I heard Will ask. "Oh shit." Turning, I saw him staring at me, the lace bra I was wearing unable to hide the way my nipples pebbled from the cold water and the look on his face. "I always knew there was a rockin' body hiding under that school uniform." I'd never heard him use that tone of voice on me. On Mackenzie? Sure, whenever they were together or he wanted to get back together. He moved closer to me, eyeing me like I was his next meal. I backed up, but whatever sexual tension he was putting out there, I wasn't opposed to it. It had been bubbling for weeks. Our Sunday meetings, the angry words within school, were all laced with sexual tension.

When I was pinned up against the door with nowhere left to flee, his hands went to the outside of my head, caging me in. His hips pushed against mine and I could feel him, hot and hard, behind his khaki uniform pants.

"I hate you," I said.

"I hate you too, dollface."

Dollface? What a stupid thing to call me. And before I could tell him exactly that, his lips were on mine. Grabbing the white button-up shirt he wore every day with his uniform, I pulled him closer, kissing him back urgently, aggressively moving my lips against his, before shoving him off.

"This doesn't change anything." He didn't say anything back, but pushed my hands away and pinned them above my head. Fuck. He could kiss. And I hated him more for that. His lips commanded mine, forcing me to submit, a fact I hated more than the fact that I was kissing him. I knew if I wanted to, I could get my hands out of the grip he had on them, but for the moment, I was content to submit to him. His tongue worked against my own, making me moan into the kiss. Fuck, I was getting lost in the kiss, no way out, no way to stop or pull back. And fuck, I did not want to stop because, *goddamn*, he could fucking kiss. I said that already, didn't I? But it was so goddamn true, I'd kissed countless people, but nobody ever made me feel the way Will Roberts was currently making me feel from just a kiss. Moisture flooded my panties. I tilted my head back, letting him kiss me harder, rougher, deeper. When he finally pulled away, I could barely breathe. For good measure, he sunk his teeth into my bottom lip, pulling on it as he separated our mouths. "On your knees, Winters," he whispered in my ear.

And that was where my submission ended.

Quickly, I snapped my wrists out of his grasp and dug my hands into his shirt again. "I don't know about the little bimbos you've been with, but I'm in charge."

"I don't know what kind of *little* boys you've been with, but I'm in charge."

With those words, he spun me around and pushed me roughly against the wall, my chest against the cold brick. His hands pulled my skirt up, bunching it around my waist. "This ass," he groaned. His hands groped me, making me moan. His body pushed into me, forcing me harder against the wall. I pushed back but he was too rough. He'd only let my ass lift, pushing into his groin and feeling just how hard and big he was for me.

So much for his good boy reputation.

His hand snuck between my legs, pushing my panties aside until he got to where he wanted, finding my dripping pussy. "Will," I moaned as he tortured me with slow circles. My hips bucked against him. "More!"

"Who's in control?" He whispered. I bit my lip, not justifying that with a response. Sliding his hand further down, he pushed two fingers into me. "Who's in control?"

Fuck.

His fingers were unmoving inside me, holding completely still and making me crazy while he waited for my answer.

"I hate you," I groaned. His fingers may have been inside me, but it was still true.

"I hate you too, but this pussy is too fucking wet," he groaned, pulling his fingers back. "And squeezing the hell out of my fingers like the greedy girl you are." He pulled his fingers back, his words smug as he spoke and slammed his fingers back inside me. "And I can't wait to sink my dick into you. Tell me who's in control, Haley."

"You are," I whispered, the words betraying everything in me.

"Good girl."

Fuck. This boy definitely didn't deserve his good boy reputation, not with the wicked things his fingers were doing to me, certainly not with the wicked words spilling from those sinful lips. My hips moved against him.

What the fuck was I thinking? Letting this fucking prick touch me. Will's hand beside my head came around my throat, holding it there without squeezing while he pulled my head to the side. His lips pushed against mine, in total control again while he fucked me with his fingers. He curled them inside me expertly. Fuck. How was he so good at this?

And then I came. A loud cry tore from my throat where one of his hands was holding me while the other made me come for him. "Fuck!" I yelled. I was sure I could be heard somewhere in the building, but I couldn't care less at the moment.

Will pulled his fingers from me and brought them to my mouth. "Suck," he ordered. Opening my mouth, I let him push two of his fingers in. I moaned around them and sucked them clean. "On your knees Haley." His lips moved against the shell of my ear, making me shiver, but I didn't comply. Not yet.

"Say please," I whispered. It was a warm up, but I'd be taking back the control. "You want me on my knees for you? Slutty Haley Winters? Beg for it."

He groaned in my ear. "Fuck. Haley, please get on your knees for me, dollface."

"Don't call me dollface," I snapped.

"Yes, ma'am." The last words were a joke. Spinning against him, I dropped to my knees. Looking up at him, I undid his khaki pants and slid them down.

He was bigger than I'd expected. Much bigger than Bobby and any other guy I'd been with before. But he didn't need to know that. He could never know that.

Taking him in my hand, I stroked him, teasing him. When he moaned, I licked around the head, still teasing him. "Haley," he grunted my name sexily, like I was the only thought in his head. "Suck my dick."

Begging.

I had Will Roberts begging for me to suck his cock. Spitting on his cock, I slid down on him, hallowing my cheeks and sucking. Going all the way down, I let him gag me, grabbing his naked ass cheeks and forcing more of him into my mouth. His knees buckled at the pleasure and I smiled triumphantly.

"Who's in control now, Will?" His hands went to my hair, holding me in an attempt to dominate me. I pulled him off immediately. "Touch my head again and I'll stop. Or restrain you with your own tie. Maybe both?" He gulped. "Who's in control?" I asked. His blue eyes were mesmerized as he looked down at me. I watched as he reluctantly said the words. He definitely wasn't used to a girl in charge of her sexual nature like I was.

"You are."

"Good boy."

Taking him back in my mouth, I continued to suck him sloppily, letting spit fall out of my mouth, stroking him and spreading my saliva everywhere. Using my tongue, I worked the underside of his shaft, along the prominent vein every time I pulled back. I kept my eyes trained up, glued to his while he stared down at me. His mouth was open, pleasure washing over his features.

"Damn," he groaned. "I'm gonna come."

"Not so fast," I said, pulling off of him. "Fuck me."

"Beg for it," he repeated my words.

"No," I said defiantly. "I'll leave you here to finish the job." My words weren't a threat, but a promise. "And I'll go find someone else to fuck my tight, wet pussy."

"I hate you," he reiterated, as if I could have forgotten. "This changes nothing."

"Nothing," I echoed him. Will pulled me to my feet, lifted me by the back of my legs and pinned me against the wall. My hands dug into his hair, tilting his head back as he slammed into me. "Yessssss!" I hissed.

Fuck. I couldn't tell him he was the best, how good it felt to have him stretch and pound himself into me. He could never know. "Fuck, you're already squeezing the life out of my dick."

"Shut up!"

He grunted in my ear before pulling back and slamming back in. I moaned, the sound nearly a strangled cry as he stretched me. He'd taken my words to heart and stopped talking. He moaned sexily in my ear, the sounds sending more pleasure through me. "Harder." I was begging, but I wanted him to think I was demanding.

Setting me on my feet, he spun me around, forcing me to my hands and knees. The concrete felt cold and hard against me. Hands on my hips, he slammed back into me. My back arched and my head fell back. I moved my hips, pushing them back with each one of his forward thrusts, forcing him deeper and harder inside me. I could feel my orgasm building, coming on like a freight train I couldn't and didn't want to stop. "Will," I moaned his name before biting my lip and reminding myself that his name should not come from my lips that way. Or any other way.

But it was too fucking late.

"You feel so fucking good." The sounds of his hips slapping against my ass, my sopping pussy filled the basement around us.

Pulling his hand away, he slapped my ass. "Yes!" I wanted him to spank me again, but before I could tell him that, his hand came to my throat, pulling me up so I was against his chest. He squeezed.

"You're so fucking wet. I'm soaked," he groaned. "Tell me again how much you hate me."

"So much, I hate you so fucking much." His hand squeezed on my throat, making my pussy clamp down on him.

It felt so fucking good, but he had too much control. Bucking my hips, I forced him off of me, using enough strength to make him fall to his back. Holding my skirt up, I straddled him, dropping roughly onto him and enveloping him in my pussy again.

His hands squeezed my hips, digging in. I might have bruises from where his hands were, but I didn't fucking care. My hands went to his throat, both of them. His head fell back, exposing his neck to me, and he moaned long and loud as I used his neck for leverage. His hips thrust upward, fucking into me while I rode him. "I'm gonna come!" I shouted.

"Fuck, me too dollface." I groaned at his use of the nickname but I was too close to care.

I could tell before I even came that it would be the hardest I'd ever come in my entire life. "Yes! Yes! Yes!" I screamed.

I gushed, squirting and soaking both of us, something I'd never done before. Will's hands dug into my skin and I squeezed his neck while he came, releasing inside me.

As soon as he was finished, I stood, putting as much space between us as I could. Ignoring him, I pulled my skirt back down and put my soaked shirt back on.

"If you tell anyone about this, I'll kill you."

With those words, I left, not caring that I'd get detention again tomorrow for skipping out early.

I made it to the top of the basement stairs before I realized the magnitude of what had just happened.

I'd fucked Will Roberts.

Not only had I fucked him, I'd done it in the school.

And I'd been too caught up in the moment to even think about a condom.

Fuck I hope he used them with Mackenzie.

I need to make an appointment at the clinic.

Fuck.

Fuck.

So stupid.

Fuck.

CHAPTER 6

THE BLAME

Haley

W hat. The. Fuck.

How could I have been so stupid? A few moments ago, I'd called it a momentary lapse in judgment, but I'd clearly lost my damn mind.

I hated him.

He hated me.

But fuck, had it been amazing.

His cum was pooling in my panties, combining with my own as I attempted to not look thoroughly fucked while I strolled through the empty halls to my locker. I had no idea how long we'd gone at it, or how long we'd been 'cleaning' the space before everything changed and everything I thought I knew went to shit.

No, no. Nothing went to shit because this hadn't happened. What just went down in the school basement had absolutely not been reality. It was forgotten, a long memory that I'd never ever think about again.

Because why would I?

Because he just rocked your damn world.

My inner monologue never knew when to be quiet.

Finally at my locker, I took a deep breath, opened it and looked in the mirror I had hanging there, quickly trying to brush my hair with my fingers, combing out the knots he'd put there when he'd fisted it in his hands.

Hands that knew exactly where and how to touch.

Shaking my head, physically trying to push the thoughts of Will Roberts from my mind, I grabbed all my books and stuffed them into my bag. Obviously I didn't need all of them, but I couldn't focus, and I had assignments due, assignments I had to do in order to maintain my number one spot in the class and guarantee myself a scholarship to school.

Shit.

I still needed to find a few to apply to that I could use to pay for Dartmouth if I actually got in there. Because if I got in, I had to go—it was one of the best schools in the country. Stanford was also one of the best schools in the country and much closer to home. If I went there, I could be closer to Chloe, but that would never work because it also meant being closer to my parents, and if they could reach me, they'd either kill me or drag me back kicking and screaming. Maybe both.

Leaving through the back door of the school, I all but ran to my car, scared somebody might see me and read what I'd done all over my face. Once I got to my car, I tossed my bag in the passenger seat before strapping myself in and burning rubber out of the parking lot. Will's truck was still parked in its usual spot. Was he still in the basement cleaning?

Fuck.

How could I forget a condom? Using a condom with guys was my only sex rule. And I'd let him finish inside me. So stupid. Guess I was about to find out how effective my birth control actually was.

No matter how hard I tried, I couldn't keep myself from thinking about Will as I drove home. His lips felt too good against mine, better than any of the other boys or girls I'd kissed. I never let people speak to me the way he did, take control, but I'd wanted him too, almost as bad as I'd wanted to take it from him. His fingers against me and in me, he'd known exactly how and where to touch me without having to be told.

And when he'd called me a 'good girl'. I had no words.

The one time Bobby tried that shit, I'd put a stop to it immediately. I was nobody's good girl.

Except Will's apparently.

Fuck.

When I pulled into the trailer park, I slammed my fist against the wheel before climbing out. Sassy was waiting for me.

"Hey," she called.

"Hey," I said, doing my best to act natural.

"The entire school heard about what happened."

"What?" I asked too quickly. I cleared my throat, attempting to compose myself. "What are you talking about?" I asked slower.

"Everyone knows Ms. Smalls sent you and Will to Principal Potter's office. What happened?"

"We got detention, no biggie," I shrugged.

"Why did Ms. Smalls send you?"

"Will asked me who I blew to get my dad released." As if I'd do anything to help my father get released, let alone something as degrading as blowing someone I didn't really want to.

"If only he knew it was his precious girlfriend's father doing the blowing that keeps getting your dad released."

"They're not together anymore," I said before I could stop myself. "I mean, you were there. You saw the hissy fit she threw when he dumped her in the middle of the cafeteria."

"They'll be back together before next week."

Why did I find myself hoping that wasn't true?

"Who knows?"

"Well, I'm gonna go. My mom needs me to cook dinner tonight. I just wanted to make sure you were okay."

"I'm fine," I told her. "Are you riding with me tomorrow or with Snake?"

"Snake," she said. I smiled at her. She'd tell me if something was happening between them, but right now, it looked like she may finally be taking my advice, letting him know she was into him.

"I'll see you at school then."

"Let's hope it's a less eventful day than today."

"I fucking hope so."

I watched Sassy walk away before climbing the few steps into the trailer. Chloe was sitting at the table doing her homework. "Hey Squirt," I called.

"Hey," she said, looking up from her homework. "Can you help me for a minute?"

"What are you asking her for help for?" My mom's bitchy voice asked as she came out of her bedroom with a cigarette in her hand. "Her grades are horrible."

That's how much attention she paid to me. She had no idea that I was top of my class, never went to a single parent teacher meeting and paid as little attention to me as she could get away with. How would she know?

"Sure. Let me try. Geometry wasn't that hard."

My mom scoffed, then took a long drag of her cigarette all before grabbing a beer out of the fridge and heading out of the trailer. She was probably going to Denise's, the neighbor across the way. They were sometimes friendly, depending on my mom's mood.

"Area of the circle," I said, looking down at my sister's homework. I'd gotten an A+ in geometry. "It's easy, just Pi times the radius squared."

"No, I get that," she said. "It's just a simple formula, but we weren't given a formula to find the radius once we had the area."

"Okay," I nodded. "Just plug in all the information you have into the equation."

"So the area is 75, which is equal to Pi times the radius, which I don't know, squared."

"Correct. How many decimals of Pi are you supposed to use?"

"Just two."

"Okay, write it out." I watched as she wrote 75 = 3.14 x radius squared.

"And how do you get rid of the value of Pi?"

"Divide by 3.14." I watched her break down the equation, 23.89 = radius squared. "And now I need the square root." She hit a few buttons on the calculator and came up with the answer. "Radius equals 4.89."

"Good, now do you know how to check your work?"

"No," she said, shaking her head.

"Write the formula again, but this time plug in the radius as your answer."

I watched as she wrote A = Pi(radius squared) and then broke down the equation.

"Seventy-five point one," she said when she was finished. "That's not seventy-five."

"No, but when breaking down things into tenths, the backwards isn't always perfect. Especially with Pi but it's still correct."

"Thanks."

"Think you can manage the rest on your own?" I asked.

"Yeah." I rubbed the top of her head and kissed it before heading to our bedroom to do my own homework. Chloe was smart, hopefully she wouldn't let our home life stop her from reaching her goals, whatever they may be.

When I pulled up my school email on my phone, I had an email from Ms. Smalls with the assignments Will and I missed when we'd been dismissed from class early, and just like that, he was back on my mind.

Was he thinking about me too?

Stop it!

It didn't matter if he was thinking about me too, and even if he was, he shouldn't be. Just like I shouldn't be thinking about him, it was a one-time thing. A very, very good one-time thing, but it was a mistake that could never be repeated.

We hated each other.

But then our interactions from the start of the school year played in my mind. There were definitely times when Will had been flirtatious, hell, I'd even been guilty of flirting with him. But flirting and sexual chemistry didn't mean we were a good match, that we should even be speaking to each other. Then there were a couple of times outside the ice cream shop when he'd seen my bruise, he'd been concerned, nearly sweet and caring.

He would have helped me… if I'd asked.

I could ask.

But I wouldn't. I didn't care what happened to me because I was eighteen and could get out if I wanted, but Chloe still had to turn fifteen. If she spent three years in the foster care system because she got removed from the house, it would break her. Sure, her life was shitty at best, but there was no guarantee that a foster home was any better, a lot of them were probably worse because the system was broken. Would they let me take custody of her? I was eighteen—technically an adult—but I'd have to prove that I could take care of the both of us, and I couldn't, not if I was going to college.

I'd get her out. Someday I would.

If this nicer side of Will was still around at the end of the school year, I'd ask him to look out for her while I was gone, to make sure she didn't take my place in my mom's violent outbursts. He'd do that for me.

Wouldn't he?

Yes.

Ah. There she was, my snarky inner bitch.

I ignored her and got to work on the math problems in front of me, wishing they were as easy as geometry.

I had no idea how long I'd been working, but Chloe finally came into the bedroom long after the sun had set. "What's for dinner?"

"Shit, what time is it?"

"Almost eight thirty," she answered.

"How do you feel about macaroni and cheese?"

"Can you add extra butter?"

"Is there another way?"

Setting my books aside, I climbed off my bed, stretched my legs that were crossed underneath me for too long and headed to the kitchen. "Do we have hamburgers or something to go with it?" She asked.

"Check the freezer."

While Chloe dug around in the freezer, I grabbed a box of macaroni and cheese and put a pot of water on the stove to boil. "I found these." She came back with a bag of frozen meatballs from the discount grocery store. I was sure there probably wasn't a lot of meat in them, and I didn't particularly care for them, but I would make them for Chloe. "We can just microwave them," she said.

"Grab a bowl."

Chloe moved her homework to the counter and kept working while I made us dinner.

"Here," I said when it was done, setting the plate in front of her. "Do you want ketchup?"

"Duh." Grabbing the ketchup, I doused my macaroni and cheese in it before handing it to her. She sat while she ate and I stood with my body leaning against the corner. "Thanks for cooking," she said.

"No problem."

I would need to teach her how to make a few basics—macaroni and cheese, pasta, even if it was just boiling water and heating a sauce, boiling eggs and potatoes. I wouldn't be around to cook for her next year and, clearly, my parents wouldn't cook for her.

"Hilly?" She called while I was distracted by looking down at the food in my bowl.

"Yeah?"

"You've had sex before, right?" I nearly choked on my macaroni and cheese.

"Yes." I coughed. And cleared my throat.

"What's it like?"

"I thought you had people on Instagram for this," I said. I could talk to her about the process, but she was too young to know the details of my sex life.

"For the basics and stuff, but like. Is it worth the hype?"

"With the right person, yes."

"So when you're in love?"

"No, that's bullshit. With the right person I mean a partner who focuses on your pleasure as much as their own. Someone who wants to make you orgasm more than they want to orgasm themselves." Someone like the way Will was with me only a few hours ago.

"And how do you know that person is like that before you start?" She asked.

"You don't always. Sometimes you think they will and they don't." Like Tim, the fuckwad I'd lost my virginity to. He'd almost made me never want to have sex again. "But you'll feel some type of pull, an attraction, and sometimes your partner will need a little guidance, instructions, you telling them what you like." She nodded before shoving a meatball into her mouth. "I thought you weren't ready for sex?"

"I'm not, but that doesn't mean I'm not curious about it."

"Whatever you do, don't get your ideas from porn, it's not realistic."

"Okay."

I let out a heavy sigh. Even with Sassy, I didn't really talk about my sex life, mostly because she was still a virgin and didn't ask about it. "I'm glad you felt you could ask me." That was the right thing to say. It was good that she was curious, asking questions. I'd rather she come to me instead of asking one of her friends that probably didn't know anything. She offered me a shy smile. Truthfully, I didn't love the idea of her having sex. She was still my baby sister, but I had been fifteen when I'd lost my virginity—only a few months older than she was. I'd be a hypocrite if I told her anything else.

"You cooked, I'll clean," she said when I was setting my bowl into the sink.

The roaring of a motorcycle engine and the yelling that could be heard when it cut off had me on edge. "No, get your stuff and go to our room."

"But Hilly."

"Now."

Chloe let the dishes drop and quickly gathered her stuff. She was barely safely inside our bedroom when the door to the trailer opened and my mom was roughly pushed inside by my dad. "Fucking bitch!" He yelled at her. His loud voice boomed inside the small, cramped space of our house. "You're so fucking stupid." I was trapped, so I played dumb, ignoring the yelling and continued to wash the dishes in the sink, but I could hear every vile word they hurled at each other. "How fucking hard is it to take the money I give you and put gas in the car?" He shouted at her. "This is the second time in three weeks I've had to come fucking get you because you ran out of gas!"

"Viper, please," she begged. I heard the sound of his hand connecting with her body, most likely a backhand across her cheek. He wasn't shy about leaving bruises on her. She was an expert on makeup and even if she wasn't, everyone in the trailer park knew he beat her, but nobody ever did anything about it.

"Stay on the ground you fucking cunt." She yelled in pain, and I heard another hit, most likely his foot into her stomach.

Has he always been like this? I couldn't remember a time when he wasn't.

"Next time, I'll fucking leave you stranded there. You can call one of your boyfriends to come get you. You can suck dick for the gas money for all I care."

I was finished washing our dishes, but I didn't dare turn around to look at the scene behind me. But I felt my dad behind me before his hand tugged my hair and my neck backward. "You got shit to say?"

"No, sir."

"Good." He released my hair harshly, pushing me forward as he did.

Ten seconds later, I heard the door to the trailer slam, followed quickly by the sound of his bike engine starting again. I let out a deep breath, glad it was over. His violent streak was escalating.

Something must be going on with the club.

But what?

"Enjoy that?" My mom snarled at me. She'd pushed herself off the ground and was coming towards me. I wouldn't have to wait until tomorrow until she took her anger at him out on me. It was coming right now. "You think you're so much better than us. Don't think I don't know what your plan is."

"What plan?" I managed to ask without stuttering and keeping my face straight.

"You and Snake taking over. Your father thinks it's a great idea, but Snake is weak, just like his daddy. The only person who ever should have run the Southside was-" Her eyes went wide as she looked at me. She'd almost just given something away, but I literally had no idea what. I'd stopped paying attention or caring about the gang a long time ago. "You'll never be good enough to take my place."

"Why? Because I'd never let a man get away with laying his fucking hands on me?" I never talked back because it made the beatings worse, but I was in for it no matter what tonight. I may as well say my piece before she started lashing me.

"Just wait," she muttered. "It'll all change after you get married and have a kid. Kids ruin everything."

Ah... there it was. Classic, blaming me for her problems. Before I could remind her that having kids was her fucking decision, she had the cutting board from the counter lifted into her hands and was swinging it at my abdomen. She landed two blows to my right side before I collapsed to the floor, gasping for breath. The lashes had knocked the wind right out of me. Tossing the cutting board to the ground next to me, she stomped her foot harshly into my back once before walking away, leaving me laying on the floor, gasping for breath, while I clenched my eyes, fighting the pain.

When I could finally breathe normally again, I pushed myself off the floor and made my way to my bedroom, but not before picking up the cutting board. I didn't need to take another beating because I didn't clean up her mess.

"Are you okay?" Chloe asked when I walked into our room.

"F-fine," I managed to get out, gritting my teeth as I spoke. "Come on, let's go to bed. We've got school again tomorrow, and it's getting late."

She nodded, turning on the lamp next to her bed while I turned off the big light in our room. I needed to shower, to wash the sex off of me, but I was in too much pain to do it. So, I stripped naked, tossed my clothes in the hamper, and pulled on a pair of loose cotton panties and an oversized t-shirt before climbing into my bed and hoping I fell asleep before the pain got too bad.

THE NEXT MORNING WHEN I WOKE UP, I GROANED AS I SAT UP. "I'll shower first," Chloe said. I nodded, happy to let her, needing a few more minutes to collect myself anyway. Grabbing my phone, I texted Sassy.

> Me: I'm gonna go in late today. I'll see you at lunch.
> Sassy: Okay. I'm riding with Snake anyway.

I let my phone fall back to the bed and rolled back over. Ten minutes later, Chloe came back into the bedroom, her towel wrapped around her.

"I'm going in late today," I told her. "I've got a study hall first period, so I don't need to be there until second period."

"How bad is the bruise?" She asked.

"I don't know, I haven't looked yet."

"Let me see."

Standing from the bed, taking more time than usual, I lifted my shirt and turned to the side.

"Hilly," my sister said. "It's horrible."

Turning, I looked at the mirror. "Fuck." Chloe was right—it was one of the worst bruises she'd ever given me. It was a nasty blue and purple, taking up almost half my stomach. "Good thing it's not bikini season anymore," I joked.

"Hilly," Chloe said again. When I looked at her, she looked scared and had tears in her eyes.

"I'm fine," I told her, pulling her in for a gentle hug. "I promise I'm fine." She sniffled against me. "I just need to take some Tylenol and take it easy for an hour before I have to go to school."

"You're sure?"

"Yes."

"Okay."

"Have a good day," I told her, walking out of our room. I went into the bathroom and turned the shower back on. Hopefully, my mom was hungover and would sleep until noon and not notice that I used up all the hot water like I was about to.

When I went to pee, I could smell myself. I smelled like Will, like the sex we'd had. I needed to rid myself of his scent and push what happened out of my mind. Stepping into the shower, I let the warm water rain down on my straining muscles. I couldn't be sure which muscles were sore from the way Will had fucked me and the ones that were sore from the beating.

Either way, I wanted to forget them.

Once I was done with my shower, I rubbed Arnica salve across my stomach, hoping to help with the bruising and swelling.

As quietly as possible, so as to not wake my mother, I got dressed for school, choosing a pair of high pants that were a little looser than the ones I usually wore and a blouse with a sweater over it. The blouse was white and almost see through; I didn't want the bruise to be visible.

I grabbed a pop-tart, too tired to make any other breakfast and did a sweep of the living room and kitchen, making sure things were neat and tidy before I left.

When I pulled up to school, I had about ten minutes before second period started. As I made my way into the side entrance,

I saw Will's truck pulling into the parking lot. Did he have a free first period too? Shit. That was not information I needed to know. I attempted to walk quicker, but the pain in my body prevented me from making my escape as quickly as I wanted.

"Haley," he said when he caught me.

"Will," I said.

"About-"

"No," I cut him off. "There's nothing to talk about because nothing happened."

He gulped, but nodded.

"Nothing," I said louder.

"Okay," he said, putting his hands up.

That didn't stop him from following me to the office so we could sign in. I could feel his eyes on me the entire time. Did he notice I was limping a little? Did he think it was from him? Was it from him?

"Morning," I said to Pattie, the school receptionist.

"Morning," she smiled back. I signed in without further word and made my way towards my second period class, ignoring the way my proximity to Will was making me feel.

Lightheaded. Dizzy. Aroused. Making a split second decision before I stepped into class, I grabbed my phone and texted Bobby.

> Me: Wanna hang out this weekend?
> Bobby: Sure. There's a party in Hillview. I'll text you the address.

Hillview was a town closer than where we worked at the movie theater and it was exactly what I needed. A night of partying to forget my life here and forget Will. Bobby could fuck just as good as Will, at least that was the lie I was going to tell myself.

CHAPTER 7

THE ARRANGEMENT

Will

Haley barely spoke to me when I walked into school behind her, but I couldn't take my eyes off her, and I hadn't wanted to.

What I'd wanted to do was drag her down to the basement and fuck her against the wall again. I still hated her, but it was a toss up if I hated her more than I wanted to fuck her, and after feeling her wrapped around me yesterday, I didn't want to hate her as much, but I couldn't help it after so many years hating her.

When she left me lying on the cold concrete of the floor, it took me five minutes to recover from the best sex of my life. Kissing her had felt electric, unlike kissing Mackenzie or any of the other girls I'd kissed where there was no spark, no feeling, no matter how into them I'd been at the time. And fuck, I'd never had a girl so aggressive—her hands around my throat had been so fucking sexy I thought I was going to come on the spot.

When I pushed myself off the floor, the panic set in because we'd fucked without a condom. My brain must have short-circuited with the fact that I'd been fucking Haley Winters, and I'd completely forgotten that condoms even existed.

I *always* used condoms.

And I'd finished inside her, not even thinking about pulling out, and she'd ridden me to climaxing with her, not even forcing me to pull out. She must have been too caught up in the moment, too.

That was the only explanation.

But then why all last night had she been the only thing I could think of?

At dinner, my mom fussed over me the entire time, checking my forehead to make sure I wasn't warm. I couldn't very well tell her that the reason I was acting so strange was because less than three hours before I'd had my dick buried in the girl my father had recently—very explicitly—told me to leave alone.

And I was, quite literally, probably risking my life. If Snake didn't kill me for fucking his girl, her dad surely would if he ever found out.

Nobody could ever find out, not her friends or parents, not my friends or parents. It was a one-time thing.

If that was true, why were the first few weeks of school all I'd thought about last night? The interactions we had? Seeing the bruise on her face made me so fucking angry. She didn't deserve whatever abuse she'd been receiving. I'd spent days wondering who it was, looking for all the signs. Why didn't she report it? Haley was as intimidating as most men I knew, who would she let beat her like that without fighting back? I knew she could fight back.

As I watched her disappear down the hallway to her second period class, I couldn't stop staring at her. I wanted her again. Forcing the feeling away, I walked to my own second period class, desperately trying not to think about what her ass had felt like in my hands yesterday. I'd always known she was hot. It was hard not to see. When she'd come in junior year with that nose ring, she'd been ten times hotter. My only regret from yesterday was that I hadn't taken the time to investigate her tattoo. Her body had felt so good against mine. She was soft, heavier than Mackenzie and felt so good pressed against me. I was getting hard again just thinking about it. Then I was thinking about the last few weeks again. Every time I'd see Haley, I'd wanted to interact with her, to talk to her. But why? In the years before senior year, whenever we'd spoken, it had been vile, hate spewed words. I talked shit about her criminal father and she talked shit about my dad. It was who we were. But somehow the interactions of the last weeks, although there'd been a lot of hate spewed, there was also concern, and that concern was mostly on my side for her.

How had I let it get this far?

I could blame my hormones, right? We learned in class that our brains didn't fully develop until well into our twenties. Therefore, I could not be held responsible for my actions. Right?

"What's with you?" Jordy asked when I ran into him in the hall.

"Sorry," I said.

"You good?" I only nodded as we walked together to our second period class.

Jordy was one of my best friends. He was a douche, but all of my friends were. "Yeah," I said. "I'm good."

"How was detention last night?" He asked. "The entire school is talking about it."

"Why?" I asked. Nobody actually knew what went down during detention.

"Only because it's looking like Potter actually grew some balls this year."

"Oh," I scoffed. "Yeah, right. I bailed early, and he hasn't said anything about it yet." I shrugged as I lied. I absolutely had not bailed early, staying until our designated time, finishing the task that Haley and I had been assigned to. I didn't want her to get in trouble.

"Where's Miss Winters?" Potter asked when he'd strolled down the steps precisely at five o'clock.

"She left just a few minutes ago. Her mom called to ask her to pick up her little sister," I lied smoothly. "I told her it was okay. Family comes first, after all."

"Very well," he nodded. I couldn't actually tell if he'd believed me or not. "Don't get sent to my office again, Mr. Roberts."

"Yes sir," I replied.

But if getting sent to the office again had the same consequences as yesterday, I couldn't wait to be sent again.

"Fuck," I cursed lowly under my breath. There it was, the thought I'd been desperately trying to avoid having. *I want to fuck her again*, more than I want to hate her. I wanted to fuck her again, and again, and again, all while still hating her.

Who knew hate sex was so damn hot?

"What?" Jordy asked.

"Nothing." Nobody could ever know. It would ruin my reputation with my own friends and family and would probably get me killed.

"You're weird."

"Maybe I should get back with Mackenzie," I said absentmindedly.

"You miss her?" He asked. "Whenever you two are together all you do is bitch about her."

He wasn't wrong.

"Yeah, you're right. Just an errant thought."

"Well, quit fucking thinking about her," he said.

He'd meant her as in Mackenzie, but I'd taken it to mean Haley and it worked.

Until lunch.

When the second best period of the day rolled around, I looked for her in the cafeteria, but couldn't find her. Snake and Sassy were sitting at the table they usually did with Haley, but the girl I couldn't stop thinking about was nowhere to be found.

And like a dumbass, instead of sitting at my table, ignoring the fact that she wasn't there, I went in search of her, tossing a lame excuse over my shoulder as Jordy and the others asked where I was going.

Walking straight past the library because she had no reason to be there, I walked down the corridor where the seniors spent their free periods in the secluded alcove. That was where I found her sitting with a book in her lap while her legs were crossed underneath her.

"Avoiding me?" I asked her.

Quickly, her eyes shot to mine before darting around the space, making sure we were actually alone.

"Go away, Will," she said. An involuntary shudder washed over me as she said my name, even in that exasperated tone.

"We need to talk," I told her.

"No, we don't."

"Just tell me you're on birth control," I said.

"Yes! How fucking irresponsible do you think I am?" She snapped at me, harshly closing the book she was reading.

"We were both a little... otherwise engaged," I offered. "Thinking with parts that are a little south of our brains."

"Exactly. We weren't thinking. Nothing happened. Nothing will *ever* happen again."

She spoke the words we were both desperate to say, but our bodies were not on board because as I was moving closer to her, she was moving closer to me.

"Ever," I repeated, my lips a breath from hers. But as I spoke, my hand grabbed her by the nape of her neck and dragged her forward, stealing her lips again. Haley melted into me and it felt so damn good, even better than yesterday. I bit harshly into her bottom lip in an attempt to gain the control she never willingly gave, but the action made her pull away.

"Ever. Go back to Mackenzie, Will."

With that she turned and let me standing there, my hard dick visible in my stupid khaki uniform pants.

I didn't want to go back to Mackenzie, and Haley wasn't an option. I needed a distraction. Pulling my phone from my pants, I texted Logan. He lived a few towns over, and our dads were friends, so we hung out during the summer and on breaks.

> Me: Anything happening this weekend?
> Logan: Yeah. Party in Hillview Saturday. Meet at my house, around nine?
> Me: Hell yeah.

That's exactly what I needed. A distraction.

THE REST OF THE WEEK, I DID MY BEST TO AVOID HALEY. THAT DIDN'T mean that I didn't still see her, speak to her, or exchange snarky words with her, but, each time I did, all I could think about was shoving her against the nearest surface, wrapping my hand around her throat and kissing her fucking senseless.

But that hadn't happened because both of us were finally thinking straight again.

I desperately needed this party with Logan. I needed to get Haley out of my system, and the best way to do that would be to put somebody else in it. Somebody who also wasn't Mackenzie because I didn't want to go back there either.

My parents trusted me, which was why when I told them I wouldn't be home until Sunday, they were fine with it.

I drove to Logan's house, the drive taking about thirty minutes. I spent most of that time avoiding thinking about Haley.

I wasn't successful.

"What's up?" Logan asked as he climbed into the truck. I hadn't even had time to climb out before he was sliding into my passenger seat.

"Same old shit," I told him. "You?"

"I broke up with Chelsea."

"And I broke up with Mackenzie."

"So we're both single for once? Nice." Logan punched my arm, fiddling with an app on his phone while he gave me directions.

"Whose party is this?" I asked.

"Some rich girl from Hillview. She just turned eighteen and her parents went out of town, but they bought all the booze and shit. House is isolated, no cops. Not that you have to worry about that. All you have to do is drop daddy's name and your indiscretions are forgiven."

Not all of them. I thought to myself.

By the time we got there, I already had to park about half a mile down the road. Cars of all makes, models and price classes lined both sides of the road. Music could be heard thumping even with how far away we still were. When the house came into view, my jaw dropped open. I lived on the rich side of town, but this house was a damn mansion, at least three times the size of mine. There were kids yelling, talking, and partying on the front lawn. Haley would hate the red solo cups littering the ground, hate the single use plastic and unnecessary waste.

Even at a party I couldn't stop thinking about her.

Before this last week, I'd never actually realized how much attention I'd been paying to her, how much I actually knew about her, like how she was an environmentalist.

Why had my brain chosen to hold on to all that information but barely give me enough room to remember anything about physics?

"Let's go," Logan said, walking into the house. The smell of beer and weed was pungent in the air. The living room furniture was all pushed against the wall, making a makeshift dance floor in the center. Bodies pushed together. Guy on girl, girl on girl, guy on guy, person on person. It was chaos—hot and sweaty chaos. Logan must have been here before because he navigated easily through the huge space, between the bodies and to the kitchen where the keg was. He got us both beers before leading us back to the living room.

He bailed three minutes in, already having his sights set on a pretty blonde that was dancing with her friends. She offered him a seductive smile before turning and pushing her ass into his groin. Shaking my head, I laughed at him. He looked like he was having the time of his life. I watched, listening to song after song come through the speakers. Some of them made the people on the dance floor lose their minds, jumping up and down, beer spilling from their cups and on to each other, but still, they pressed on. Logan already had his lips pushed against the blonde's, their tongues clashing violently for everyone to see.

"Shit," I cursed when someone bumped into me. She'd knocked me backward and my drink spilled.

"I'm so sorry." Looking down, I saw a cute redhead with freckles over her entire face and a button nose standing in front of me. "My friends." She gestured to the group of extremely intoxicated girls behind her.

"It's okay," I waved her off.

"Can I get you a refill?" She smiled at me, biting her lower lip.

"How about a dance instead?" I countered.

"Okay." She took my hand and pulled me into the chaos, not so deep that we had no chance of escaping, but not on the edge where anyone could see us either. "I'm Tara."

"Will," I shouted over the music. Tara turned, moving against me while I put my hands respectfully between her hips and waist. Not too low and not too high. She gyrated on me, her ass against my dick that didn't seem to want to come to life. Her hands covered my own, bringing them down to her hips. When she had them where she wanted them, she turned around, my hands now on the curve of her ass. "I think I might want that drink now," I said.

She smiled and separated herself from me. Following behind her, I walked to the kitchen. She didn't go for the beer, instead, she went for the liquor bottles and mixers on the counter. Tara was cute, just what I needed, and I was just about to see if she was enthusiastically willing to be that distraction when a head of brown hair and a body I could never forget walked by. There was a guy holding her hand, and she was pulling him outside. "I gotta go," I mumbled. I hadn't seen the girl's face, but it was Haley. I knew it was.

When I stepped outside, I finally saw her face. It was her. I didn't recognize who she was standing with, but the way he touched her was familiar, like he knew her body well. Was this her guy? The one she'd been talking about when she'd told me she'd had a real man? Was this the guy who'd put the bruises on her? I watched his hand wrap around her and pull her close.

Jealousy filled me, an emotion I wasn't familiar with.

No fucking way.

Hurriedly, I walked over to them. "Get your hands off of her," I growled.

"Will?" Haley asked, voice full of confusion as she looked up at me. Venom laced her voice, and anger radiated from her eyes when she realized that it really was me. "What are you doing?" She snapped.

"I'm not sure what this is," the guy said. "But I'm out. You know I don't do complicated."

With that, the douchebag walked away.

"Who do you think you are?" She seethed at me. "You have no right to tell him not to touch me."

Stepping closer, I forced her to the corner of the deck. "The fuck I don't!"

"I don't know what the fuck you think is going on, but I can guarantee you, it is not this." She'd been pissed at me thousands of times in our lives, but fuck, she was so livid, and unlike dancing with Tara, it was making me rock fucking hard for her.

"I'll show you what the fuck is going on," I bit out darkly. Grabbing her by her elbow, I tugged her with me, left her drink behind and pulled her through the crowd of people until I found my way to what I assumed was one of many bathrooms in this house. Pushing her in, I slammed and locked the door behind us. "Is he the one who bruised your face?"

"What? Bobby? No. Jesus, Will, just let it go."

"Who is he?"

"We work together and we fuck occasionally. I'm a big girl, I'm allowed to fuck who I want."

"No."

"No?" She scoffed before letting out a dark laugh. "Get over yourself, Will. It was a one-time thing. And it wasn't even that good."

"No? You've been able to stop thinking about the way my fingers felt inside you? How good my dick felt stretching your pussy. How fucking wet you got for me. I bet you're wet for me right now, aren't you, dollface?"

"No," she said, but her body betrayed her words, making them come out breathy.

"No?" I questioned.

Her tongue snuck out, licking her lips while she looked at me dead in the eyes and lied. "No."

But as soon as the words left her mouth, she was on me, her hands digging into my shirt and her lips on mine. Pulling me forward, my hands went to her ass, cupping her over the leather skirt she was wearing and pushing our hips together. Our tongues clashed, battling for dominance I knew she wouldn't easily give.

I liked that about her.

Her hands snuck up to my hair, gripping at the blonde strands I'd let grow too long and tugged my head back. "Fuck, Haley," I grunted. But she didn't stop. Her lips went to my neck, biting at the skin harshly and making me hiss. Lifting one hand from her ass, I spanked her once before wrapping my hand around her throat and using it for leverage to push her off of me.

I wasn't sure if she jumped onto the sink or if I helped her up, but she was sitting there, legs open and waiting for me. Dropping to my knees in front of her, I pushed her thick, gorgeous thighs apart and tugged her forward, forcing her skirt to ride up. I could already see a wet spot on her panties.

"Liar," I said before reaching under her skirt and pulling her panties down, letting them fall carelessly to the floor. "You're fucking soaked, dollface."

"Shut up," she said, voice full of a heady combination of lust and annoyance.

I chuckled before pushing her thighs even further apart and dropping my face to her pussy. I inhaled deeply, loving how she smelled and how wet she was for me. Wrapping my hands around her thighs, I licked at her, from her opening to her clit. "Mmm," she moaned when I lapped at her clit quickly, her hands going to my hair, holding me there.

Fuck, she tasted so damn good that it made me never want to stop.

The door rattled, someone trying to get into the bathroom.

"Go away!" She shouted. "Don't fucking stop," she growled at me.

I palmed myself through my pants and got back to work. Flattening my tongue, I licked through each of her folds, acquainting myself for the next time I was buried between her thighs.

Next time? Fuck.

Pointing my tongue, I fucked it into her needy, clenching hole, as far as I could manage. "Fuck!" She cried. Her hips lifted off the sink, nearly falling off, as I grabbed her leg and draped it over my shoulder before doing the same with the other. I pushed two fingers into her, feeling her squeeze down on me immediately. "Yes! Harder." I slammed my fingers into her slowly, making sure she could feel every inch of them inside her before wrapping my mouth around her clit and sucking it between my lips. "Don't stop. Oh god, Will! I'm going to come."

Her hands fisted in my hair, pulling so roughly it hurt, but it spurred me on. Her body bucked and despite the music from the party, people could probably hear her release as it spilled in my mouth.

And I didn't stop.

She writhed for me, crying out in pleasure as I continued to suck on her until she physically had to pull my head from her.

"My god," she said.

Standing, I pushed my pants down and stepped between her legs. One hand on her lower back and one on my dick, I pushed inside her. "You feel so fucking good," I said through gritted teeth.

"More," she begged.

How long was she going to let me have control?

I got my answer a moment later.

When I pushed on her hips, holding her still so I could slam myself into her, fucking her faster and faster, her hand left my shoulder and found its way to my throat. "Slower," she demanded.

"Fuck," I grunted in response.

I did what she asked, slowing my thrusts. I was rewarded with a loud, long moan pushing past her lips. "Harder. Keep your pace. But harder."

"You're fucking killing me, dollface. Fuck, your pussy feels too good. So fucking wet."

Again, I did what she asked, keeping the slow pace she'd set but slamming myself into her. "Just like that. Oh fuck, Will. You're gonna make me come."

That was a reward too.

"Come on my dick, Haley, let me feel it. Squeeze that pussy on me, dollface."

Her hand squeezed my throat, making me gasp despite her not cutting off the air supply. She came hard and fast, clamping down on my dick as she did. When she was coming down, she pushed me away from her until I stumbled into a sitting position on the closed toilet seat. Jumping down from the sink, she lifted her skirt again and straddled me, immediately sinking herself around my dick.

My hands went to her ass, lifting her up and pulling her perfect cheeks apart while I lifted myself into her. She ground against me, pushing her clit against me while she rode me.

This time, it was my hand that went to her throat, squeezing. "Faster, dollface. Ride my dick like a good little slut."

Her head fell back, giving me more access to the delicate column of her throat while she rode me faster and faster. Using my other hand, I pulled her flimsy, lace, gray crop top off. Fuck. How had I not immediately noticed how fucking sexy her outfit was? She looked phenomenal. Bending my head, I wrapped my lips around one of her straining nipples. She let out another loud moan, and I could feel her pussy clench around me as I did. Switching sides, I bit down harder. "Fuck Will." Her body was losing control as she bounced on me, bringing me to the brink of my own orgasm. "I'm gonna come again."

"Come for me, dollface."

I felt her pussy clamp down around my dick like a vise, squeezing me while her head fell back and she came again.

Before I could say anything, she was hopping off me and dropping to her knees. As soon as my dick hit the back of her throat, I came. Watching her swallow all of it made me want to fuck her again.

Taking a deep breath, she pushed herself to her feet before bending back over and picking up her panties. I watched her slide them back into place. "This can't happen again."

"You said that," I told her. I was still sitting, pants around my knees, watching her in the mirror. When she started adjusting her top, I finally got a glimpse of her tattoo. Standing, I quickly tucked myself back in before my hands were on her and I was spinning her, pushing her top up so I could see.

"What are you doing?"

"It's beautiful." It was a painting of the night sky, above a forest with a shooting star through it.

She smiled softly. I wanted her again, and my dick was already fully on board. Spinning her further, I pushed her crop top up this time instead of pulling it down. I was greeted by the sight of a nasty bruise, just beginning to color yellow and start to fade. If I had to guess, I would say it was about a week old.

"Haley," I bit out her name. "Who keeps beating you?"

"It doesn't matter," she said, pushing my hands away. "Leave it alone, Will."

"I can't."

"Why not? We're not friends."

"No, but we're apparently friends with benefits."

"Enemies with benefits is more like it," she scoffed.

"Do you need help?" I asked her.

"No."

Her eyes held mine firmly, leaving no room for doubt in her words. She must have believed her own lie. "I can help you."

"I don't need help. Actually, that's not true," she said. "I do need help."

"With what?"

"Sex."

"You don't need help with that," I said, my voice dropping and stepping closer to her. "You've got that all under control. Fucking fabulously."

"Obviously," she said with an eye roll. "Look. I hate you. You hate me. But apparently hate leads to some pretty fantastic fucking."

"Fabulous fucking."

"Yeah, whatever. Anyway, I don't do feelings. You won't ever develop feelings for me. It's the perfect way to get what I want. Nobody has to know."

"You want to use me for sex?"

"Don't act so offended."

"Enemies with benefits?" She nodded. "Deal," I said, shaking her hand. There was no risk of either of us developing feelings for the other.

"Put your number in my phone," she said, handing me hers. Grabbing it from her, I put in my contact information, assigning my contact as Golden Boy. "Golden Boy?" She asked when I handed it back. "More like asshole." I watched her change the name before sending me a text. I added her as Dollface.

"Is this an exclusive thing?" I asked quickly.

"Why?" She asked, furrowing her brows.

"Condoms."

"Oh. Shit. Fuck. We forgot again. And I never forget."

"Yeah, me either."

"I'm okay with being exclusive," she said. "As long as you are."

All I did was shoot her a wink before I left the bathroom, closing it behind me. I heard it lock again before I walked away.

Things were about to get really fucking interesting at Carver High.

CHAPTER 8

THE SUMMONING

Haley

What the fuck was I thinking? That was the only thing I could think on the drive home after the party.

Enemies with benefits?

Seriously, what the fuck?

It was a bad idea, and I should text him right now and put an end to it, but then I remembered the way he'd felt in the bathroom, and I didn't.

We needed to be more careful than we were tonight though. We'd been the only two people there from Carver High, but that didn't mean somebody didn't know someone who knew someone. I mean, I knew Bobby. I wasn't actually sure how Will ended up there—I hadn't asked. But clearly he'd known someone too, which meant someone else could know someone who could tell someone who could tell someone else. That was the way gossip went.

And neither of us could risk that.

We couldn't risk being outed.

Ever.

My dad would literally kill him.

After Will left me alone in the bathroom, I waited a few minutes, cleaning myself further before leaning with my hands against the sink he'd just fucked me on and stared at myself in the mirror. Insane, it was absolutely insane. But it also wasn't the worst idea. We hated each other equally, and the sex was surprisingly good.

My brain clearly couldn't decide if it was actually a good idea or not. When I thought about it too long, I knew it was ridiculous, but when I thought about how good the sex was and how I would never have to worry about catching feelings for him or vice versa, it was a fabulous idea.

Maybe I should sleep on it.

As I drove back into town, I drove through the rich neighborhood on the way to my own. I knew Will's house. In a town like this, everyone knew where everyone else lived. But Will's house was one that was burned into the back of my brain since I was five-years-old, and I couldn't help slowing down as I drove by, staring at the windows and wondering which room he was in. Was he even home? He should be. I hadn't seen him when I'd done my final lap at the party, looking for Bobby to say goodbye.

A smile played on my lips as I replayed my conversation with Bobby.

"So, uh?" He asked a bit awkwardly. "Who was that?"

"No one."

"Didn't seem like no one. I thought you were single. If I'd known you were with someone, I never would have asked you to hookup."

"I *am* single."

"Doesn't seem like it."

"It's a friends with benefits situation. No feelings at all. And it's new, like it just started after the last time we hooked up, kind of new."

"But still," he said. "It was fun, but I don't want to get in the middle of whatever that is. Because you can deny it, but there's *something* there."

I furrowed my brows at him. He must have been confusing hate for something else. That was the only explanation.

When I finally pulled up to my house, a scream flew out of my mouth when I saw Sassy sitting on the steps.

"What's wrong?" I asked as soon as I climbed out, closing the car door softly behind me in an effort not to wake anyone up.

"I did something so stupid," she said through a broken sob.

"Shh," I said, racing to her and wrapping my arms around her. Pulling her against me, I let her rest her head on my shoulders while I rocked her softly. She was still crying against me, her tears falling down my chest. "What happened?"

"I'm such an idiot." That still didn't tell me anything. With that explanation she could have done anything. "I told Snake how I feel."

Oh.

"And?" I asked. Which in hindsight maybe wasn't the best question, since she was sitting on my front steps crying.

"He rejected me," she whimpered.

I felt horrible. It was me who encouraged her to go for it, to tell him how she felt. "What did he say?"

"That I was his best friend, and that he didn't want to potentially hurt me, especially when in a year he's going to be married to you."

That didn't sound like a real rejection. In fact, it sounded like he cared about her… a lot.

"It's okay," I said, rocking her a little faster.

"I just ruined our friendship, too. He's not going to want to be around me knowing that I'm completely and totally, obsessively in love with him."

I didn't know if that was true or not. I was going to have to talk to Snake. What if Sassy was the girl he'd been talking about, the one he told me he had real feelings for? I had to find out.

"Where have you been?" She asked when she pulled herself away from me.

"A party in Hillview," I told her. "Bobby invited me."

"Are you guys a thing now?"

"No," I said, shaking my head. "He actually pulled the plug on our hookup relationship tonight."

"Why?"

"He's in love with someone else." That hadn't exactly been the reason, but it was true.

"And you're not upset?" She asked, like she couldn't believe I wasn't.

"Why would I be upset? I keep telling you I don't do feelings."

"Can you teach me how to do that? How not to feel."

"Why would you want to be as damaged as me?" I teased her.

"Because I'm done pining after Snake. It's time I lost my virginity. And I don't want feelings to get in the way of my mission."

I snorted as she called losing her virginity a mission. It wouldn't be a hard one. She could have her pick of guys.

"Maybe don't change who you are just because of Snake."

"Fine. But I still want to have sex."

"Well, if that's all you want, I can help."

"Please," she scoffed. "I couldn't handle you."

We burst out laughing together.

"Thanks," she said softly.

"For what?"

"Being my best friend. For making me smile when I'm sad."

"You'll always be my best friend," I told her, pulling her close again and kissing her forehead. I just hoped she would feel the same when I did the unthinkable and bailed on her.

Would she ever forgive me?

"I should go," she said. "I'll see you tomorrow."

"Night," I called after her as she walked towards the other side of the trailer park. Most people would be scared if they came around at night, not daring to walk by themselves, but truthfully, this was the safest part of town.

As quietly as possible, I opened the door with my keys and stepped into the trailer. All the lights were off, so I turned the flashlight feature on my phone on. A heavy sigh left me when I saw the beer bottles stacked everywhere, dirty dishes from dinner still on the stove. It was nearing one in the morning, but if I didn't clean now, my mother would drag me out of bed as soon as she was awake, beat me, and then demand I clean. So, I cleaned as quickly and quietly as I could, making the place spotless.

Twenty minutes later, I was checking on Chloe. Her soft, even breathing filled the room. I watched her roll over and mumble something in her dream state. I hoped those dreams never gave way to nightmares.

The next morning, I woke up to the sun pouring through the windows and the sounds of birds chirping. It wasn't cute like some damn animated movie but annoying as hell when all I wanted to do was stay asleep. "What time is it?" I mumbled into my pillow.

"Ten," Chloe answered me, nearly making me pee the bed. I hadn't noticed she was still in the room and thought I was mumbling to myself.

"You scared the shit out of me," I said, rolling over to look up at the ceiling. Leaning up, I saw her with an open textbook in her lap. "Have you had breakfast?"

"No," she said. "I'm surprised the yelling didn't wake you up."

"Yelling?"

"Mom and Dad are fighting again."

"What about this time?" I asked while rolling myself into a sitting position on my bed.

"Money? Drugs? Who knows?" She shrugged. "But I have to pee and I haven't dared leave the room."

My heart broke for her. If there was a person who didn't deserve to live like this, it was my sister.

"Get dressed," I told her.

"We can't go out there," she said, and right on cue, her words were punctuated by the sound of something in the living room breaking.

"We're not. Just get dressed."

Jumping out of bed, I pulled on a pair of joggers and a crew neck sweatshirt. I haphazardly tossed my hair into a bun on the top of my head and wiped the mascara remnants of last night from underneath my eyes. In two minutes, I was ready to go.

"I'm ready," Chloe said, standing next to me in leggings and an oversized hoodie.

Walking over to the window, I lifted it all the way before swinging one leg out and then the other, jumping the two feet to the ground. "Seriously?" My sister asked.

"What? It's not high," I told her.

She followed me, and we walked to my car. Sometimes, I was smart enough to bring my keys with me to bed, otherwise we would have been trapped with nowhere to go. I guess we could have gone for a walk or something, but that would be less fun.

"Sunday is my favorite day," she commented as we were pulling out of the trailer park and onto the main road.

"How come?" I asked her.

"We always spend them together."

"You're such a nerd," I teased her, uncomfortable with the affectionate words, even if they were coming from my baby sister.

"Where are we going anyway?"

"Not sure. How much money you got on you?"

"Isn't it your turn to treat?"

"Probably," I shrugged. I headed to McDonald's, the best place for cheap food.

"Yes!" Chloe said excitedly when I pulled in.

"What do you want to eat?"

"Everything." I didn't have time to roll my eyes at her ridiculousness before I was pulling into a parking spot and parking the car. "I need to pee first!" She shouted as she all but bolted from the car. I laughed, following her. But I had to pee pretty badly too.

How bad did your parents have to be to make you use a fast-food restaurant bathroom instead of feeling safe enough to pee in your own house first thing in the morning?

"Welcome to McDonald's, may I take your order?" The young cashier asked after we had peed and were standing at the counter.

"Yes, may I please have four hash browns, two sausage biscuits, two sausage McMuffins and two small orange juices?"

"Will that be all?"

"Yes."

"Here," Chloe said, handing me a twenty.

"It's my turn to pay."

"You've paid for enough."

"If I'd known you were paying, I would have ordered more."

"Exactly why I didn't tell you," she quipped.

Rolling my eyes, I took the money from her and handed it to the woman. "Here's your change," she said, handing me a receipt and a wad of cash and change. I passed it back to Chloe.

We moved to the side, waiting for our order number to be called.

"Order number twenty-one," a cute young cashier said, setting our bag of food and drinks on the counter. "Oh, hey Chloe."

"H-hi," my little sister stuttered out, a hint of red coloring her cheeks. My eyes widened, and she cleared her throat and spoke again. "Hey Mick." Her voice was steadier.

"See you in class tomorrow."

"Yeah. Bye," she said, grabbing the food, leaving me to grab the drinks and chase after her.

I was able to hold my laughter in until we were safely back in the car.

"So, who's Mick?" I asked her, wiggling my eyebrows up and down as I looked at her and pulled back onto the street.

"Focus on the road." I did, but I was silent, waiting for her to indulge me with an answer. "Ugh. Fine! He's in my social studies class. He's not from the rich side of town or from our side." Ahh. One of the few magical unicorn children who weren't from the good or bad part of town, but neutral territory. "He's cute I guess."

"So, do we need to go to the clinic?" I asked her.

"No!" She shouted at me. "And I already promised you that if I did, I'd tell you."

"Fair enough."

Letting the conversation go, I drove us to the park. It was on the rich side of town, but hopefully we were still early enough that none of the housewives would be there with their vodka filled coffee cups and pill bottles in their purses. As soon as we parked, I climbed out and Chloe followed suit.

"Let's go sit by the water," I told her. There was a little pond that housed ducks. It was fall, not spring, which meant there wouldn't be any cute little ducklings, but I made a mental note to bring Chloe back in the spring because she loved baby animals of all types, even snakes. She was weird. But she especially loved the ducklings, and I'd want to experience that again before I ran away from my shitty life in this shitty place.

"It's getting chilly," she said. "We should have gotten coffee, not orange juice."

"You're too young for coffee."

"I'm almost fifteen. Weren't you drinking it at like thirteen?"

"Yes. But if you're lucky, you may still have another growth spurt. You won't if you start drinking coffee."

"That's just an old wives' tale," she countered. I shrugged my shoulders, not knowing or caring if that was actually true or not. I just wanted to keep my little sister little for a bit longer. We sat in silence as we ate our breakfast. "We should have brought stale bread."

As soon as she said the words, a deep, male voice scared the crap out of me, making me nearly piss myself for the second time that day. "Here," the voice said. Turning, I couldn't hold the surprise in my expression back as Will stood there, a cocky smirk on his face. "You guys took my spot. Take the bread too."

Will came to feed the ducks?

That was adorable.

Quickly, I shook my head at the errant thoughts. Will was not adorable. He was a good lay. That was all.

"Thanks," Chloe said, taking it from him before I could tell her not to. While she turned back around and stood, walking to the edge of the water to break the bread into pieces and toss it to the ducks, I kept staring at Will.

"Hey dollface," he smirked. "I'll see you tomorrow." He shot me a wink before putting his headphones back in and taking off in a jog down the path.

Was Sunday the unofficial day of bumping into him?

I'd need to start staying home on Sundays.

Standing, I threw our garbage away before going and standing next to Chloe. She handed me a piece of bread and I absentmindedly tossed it to the ducks, but my eyes were on Will. He was running on the other side of the pond, his long, muscular legs the only thing on display, his upper half hidden under a sweatshirt, but last night it had been underneath my hands.

"You okay?" Chloe asked.

"Fine," I said, turning to look at her. She smiled at me, but didn't give anything away. I really needed to stop bumping into Will before she started to figure something out. She could not get caught up in our secret.

"Ready to go?" I asked her.

"Yeah."

When we pulled back into the trailer park, I parked in my usual spot. Instinctively, we both stood outside the front door, waiting to hear if there was any noise. When there wasn't, we felt safe enough to enter.

The scene was worse than usual when I walked in. There was blood on the coffee table and on the linoleum floor. There was broken glass everywhere. It shattered so bad I had no idea what it had even been. "Go to Buck's," I told her.

"Hilly," she protested.

"Go."

She sighed reluctantly, but did as I asked, turning on her heel and leaving. Stepping over the broken glass, I made my way to the small pantry where the cleaning supplies were kept. Hopefully, I'd be able to get everything cleaned before my parents showed their faces again.

Sweeping up the glass, I tossed it into the aluminium foil I'd laid out before balling it up gently, being careful not to cut myself and depositing it into the trash. Next I mopped up the blood. There wasn't a lot of it, but it had already dried, making it harder to clean off.

It took me nearly thirty minutes to get rid of all the evidence that something violent had happened. After I did, I finally got in the shower.

When I was done, I put the clothes I had gotten dressed in that morning back on and left, not wanting to be around when one of my parents finally decided to show up. I hadn't been planning on going to Snake's; I'd actually been planning on going to Sassy's, but somehow I'd ended up knocking on his door anyway.

"Hey," he said, opening the door and letting me inside. "What's up?"

"Sassy was sitting on my steps when I got home last night. Crying." A pained expression crossed his face. He just stared blankly at me. "It's her, isn't it, the girl you like but can't let yourself have?"

"Haley, leave it alone," he said.

"Why?" I asked.

"Because you're fucking right," he shouted at me. "It's Sassy. It's *always* been Sassy." He looked so sad. "She's beautiful, hilarious, and sweet."

"You're in love with her," I stated.

"I can't let myself be," he said, shaking his head. For the first time in the eighteen years that I'd known him, Snake was acting vulnerable. "I fucked half the town just to try and keep her away from me, and it still didn't work."

"You can be with her," I told him. "You *should* be with her."

"How? We're going to be married to each other in less than a year," he said. "I love you, but not like that."

"I know," I told him. Snake was like a brother to me. "But I can get us out of it."

"How?" He asked, his brows furrowed in disbelief. Flattening my lips into a hard line, I looked at him, debating on whether or not to tell him my plans to run away, but I couldn't. If anyone suspected he knew after I was gone, he'd end up beaten for it.

"I'm not sure yet," I admitted. "But I will. You should be with Sassy. You guys would be great together."

"And if we can't get out of it?"

"Then you have my permission to cheat on me with her." He barked out a laugh, not wanting to make light of our perilous situation. "Maybe we can be sister wives?" I continued joking. "But she'll get the goods," I said, glancing at his crotch and making him bark out another laugh. "And I'll just be the maid."

"What kind of life would that be for you? I know I don't love you like that, but you still deserve a full life, one full of sex." He wiggled his eyebrows at me dramatically while he spoke.

"If you get to cheat on me, I get to cheat on you."

"Fair," he conceded.

"But in all seriousness," I said, swallowing and changing the tune of the conversation again. "If you want to be with her, you should be. Whatever happens after that, we'll figure it out. Together."

"Thanks, Haley," he said. "Um. I think I'm gonna go talk to her."

"Just remember," I told him. "Our dads can't know."

"I know the drill."

Snake and I walked out of the trailer together, and since he was going to Sassy's that gave me no other choice but to go back to my own. When I walked in, my mom was standing there, her left eye bruised and dried blood on her lip.

"You missed a spot of blood," she seethed. With long, hard strides she walked over to me, pushing me roughly into the wall. "Worthless, good for nothing, brat," she barked.

Grabbing me by my hair, she dragged me a few paces to the living room before forcing me to my knees and pushing my face into the table. "See that?" She shouted. "Blood!" With that, she pulled my head back and slammed it into the coffee table. "Clean it again."

Releasing me, she snapped my head roughly forward before lighting a cigarette and walking out of the trailer. When I lifted my hand to my head, there was fresh blood there. Tears filled my eyes as I forced myself to my feet and to the bathroom. She was getting worse, becoming more violent and making it harder and harder for me to hide what was going on. In the bathroom, I rinsed the cut before applying Neosporin and a bandaid. Next, I carefully cleaned the fresh blood as well as the old blood, making sure I didn't miss a single spot.

When I was finished, I went to my room and opened my phone, looking for scholarships. Every Sunday I spent time with Chloe, I had second thoughts about leaving her behind to deal with this life alone. But then something would happen, my mom beating me or my dad beating my mom and I'd remember why I was desperate to leave.

So, steeling my nerves, I did what I'd been avoiding and looked for scholarships to apply to that would help me escape.

After I'd applied for four, I closed my phone and collapsed on my bed.

It beeped almost immediately.

Asshole: Tomorrow. First Period. The janitor's closet.

CHAPTER 9

THE RULES

Haley

When I woke up Monday morning for school, I rolled from my side onto my back. My head throbbed, and I was sure the spot where my mom slammed my head into the table was bruised. But all I could think about was Will. His text replayed over and over in my mind. Did I want to have sex with him? Yes. Absolutely, yes. What I didn't want was for him to think that I would be okay with being his booty call. Could that potentially fall into the definition of our enemies with benefits relationship? Maybe, but the point was that I was going to be in control, not him, so I wasn't going to meet him. Petty? Definitely, but I didn't care.

"Are you getting up first or am I?" I asked Chloe.

"You," she said, her voice coming out muffled since her face was still buried in the pillow.

"What do you want for breakfast?"

"Oatmeal."

Climbing out of bed, I grabbed my towel and made quick work of showering in the lukewarm water.

"All yours," I told Chloe when I was back in our room.

"You shower too quickly," she grumbled.

When she left, I put on a uniform, choosing a skirt that was still hanging in my closet from sophomore year that I should have passed on to Chloe. It was a size too small, and so short I was probably going to be cited for a dress code violation because of it, but teasing Will was absolutely going to make it worth it. Feeling extra brazen, I pulled out white knee highs and black Mary Janes, completing my innocent school girl look.

Hope you can keep it in your pants, Will. I thought smugly to myself as I examined my appearance in the mirror. Momentarily, I thought about braiding my hair into pigtails, but that may be just a tad over the top, even for me. Instead, I added a waterfall braid before heading to the kitchen to make breakfast. Strategically, I'd swept my hair sideways, making sure the new bruise wasn't visible. I didn't need Will asking anymore questions.

I made brownie batter flavored oatmeal, Chloe's favorite and the only way she ate the stuff. It was finished when she came out of the room. "You okay?" I asked her. "You look tired."

"I am," she said. "High school is hard. I'll be fine. I just need to have an early night tonight." I nodded at her, but my worry hadn't dissipated. "Thanks," she said, grabbing her oatmeal from the counter and making her way out of the trailer to where the bus stopped at the entrance. "Oh, hey Sassy," she said.

"Hi, Chloe," my best friend greeted her. Cutting up a banana, I added it to my oatmeal and waited for Sassy.

"I want to ditch first period," she said.

"Fine with me," I told her. "I don't have to be there on time anyway. What do you want to do?"

"Smoke," she said. "And tell you a story."

"You got stuff?"

"Yeah, bought it off Blane on my way here."

"Let's go."

Grabbing my oatmeal, I picked up my school bag and followed Sassy out of the trailer. We climbed into my car and I headed to the spot we always parked when we wanted to get high, which wasn't very often, but enough that we had our own spot for it. When we pulled into the parking lot of the Methodist Church, I backed my car into the spot between the bushes that kept us hidden from passing cars. The church was right next to the train tracks and was the dividing marker between the rich and poor side of town. My car would only be visible if someone walked out the backdoor of the church, and even then, they'd have to be looking for it.

I watched Sassy pack the bowl before she lit it, taking a long drag and blowing the smoke through a toilet paper roll with a dryer sheet to block some of the smell. Even if we showed up at school smelling like weed, a lot of kids did, so the school just stopped caring. "So?" I asked, as she handed me the bowl and I took a hit.

"Snake came to my house yesterday," she said.

"Oh?" I asked, but I had a smirk on my face and I knew she saw it.

"Yup," she said, taking another hit before she continued to speak. "He, uh," she started and stopped. "He said he was into me too."

"I'm not surprised," I told her. "Have you seen you? The only reason we're not together is because you keep shutting me down."

She rolled her eyes at me, but continued. "I don't know if we're like a couple or what. After he admitted that, we didn't talk much."

"Oh my god!" I squealed. "Did you bang with him?" As I asked, my phone vibrated in my pocket. When I snuck a glance, I saw *Asshole* pop up with a message. I ignored it; he could wait for me or not, but I was busy.

Sassy sighed at my use of the word bang. She hated it, which was why I used it a lot around her. "No," she said. "He said he wanted to take things slow."

"So why wasn't there a lot of talking?"

"We did other stuff. Or rather, he did other stuff to me."

"Like?" Sassy blushed. My poor, innocent best friend blushed.

"His hands. And his mouth."

"For the love of god, Sassy, say the words. Tell me he ate your pussy."

"Haley!" She said, slapping me lightly while I laughed at her embarrassment. "Fine, ugh. He ate me out."

"You still didn't say pussy. But I'll allow it."

"It was so fucking good." Sure. Fucking, she could say but not pussy. "You were wrong, by the way. I did not have to teach him a damn thing. He knew my body like he'd drawn it himself. I came so many times I thought I was going to die."

"Damn."

"I tried to reciprocate his attentions."

"You tried to blow him," I edited her words.

"Do you have to be so gruff?"

"A little." I winked at her.

"Anyway. I tried, but he stopped me. He said he wanted me to get used to being pleasured before I started giving." She let out a dreamy sigh, like she was replaying the memory in her head.

"And you were... pleasured?"

"Half a dozen times." I nearly choked on my oatmeal. Will was going to need to step his game up.

"Keep him."

I'd meant for the words to be playful, but Sassy suddenly looked sad. "I love him," she said. "I'm not stupid enough to tell him that yet. But I've always loved him. And I'm going to lose him to you. And that was okay when he hadn't touched me, when I hadn't felt his touch. But now that I have…" Hot, fat, salty tears streamed down her face as she let her sentence trail off. She sniffed and tried to fight them, but it didn't work.

"I'm going to figure it out," I told her. "I swear I don't want Snake. He wants you."

"But why? Since when? He never wanted me before, not until I tried, and failed, to seduce him."

"You need to talk to him about that," I told her.

"What do you know?" My lips flattened into a thin line as I looked at her. I'd never lied to Sassy, not in eighteen years of friendship. Me keeping quiet about leaving town and Will were not lies, they were omissions. If she ever asked me directly, I wouldn't be able to lie to her. "Haley," she said my name harshly.

"I didn't know he was talking about you," I told her. "But, last year, Snake told me there was one person he could never let himself have because he had to be with me, and he didn't want to hurt her because she was the one girl, the *only* girl, he could ever see himself really falling for."

"Me?"

"Yeah. I didn't know until yesterday, and then I sent him to you."

"How did you convince him?"

"I promised him I'd figure a way out of this bogus 1800s style arranged marriage our parents have us trapped in."

"And if you can't?"

"Sister wives. But I'll be the Cinderella wife, doing the cooking and cleaning while you're the service wife."

"If he services me like he did yesterday, I'm down." I laughed loudly before taking a final hit of the bowl and passing it back to Sassy.

"We should go," I told her. "I'm going to be late for creative writing."

"Can we ditch all day?" She asked.

"No, I have a chemistry test today," I said, shaking my head. Usually, I wouldn't mind as much, even missing school didn't prevent me from keeping my grades up. But I had to make sure Will saw me in the outfit. "We'll ditch next week sometime."

"Fine," she huffed. "But what was even the point of you taking AP chemistry if you're not going to learn how to blow up the school for us?"

"Honestly, Snake could do it without me having to teach you guys," I told her. Her head fell back against the seat as she laughed. And just like usual, I was actually scared that someday she just might actually burn the shithole to the ground.

"You know the homecoming dance is next week," she said.

"I had no idea." My answer wasn't sarcastic. I honestly had no clue. I didn't pay attention to stuff like that.

"Are we going?"

"Have we ever?"

"No, but I was thinking it might be nice to go with Snake. But then you'd have to go so we have a cover story."

I inhaled sharply through my nose. "I don't have a dress."

"You can borrow one of mine. My mom saved all hers from high school, and you know I can make vintage look brand new." She could. She was a miracle worker. Since her dad died, she had even less money than we did and all her mom's old clothes were what she was forced to wear.

"If you get Snake to agree, I'll go."

I was safe though. There was no way she was going to be able to get Snake to agree to go to a homecoming dance.

"Yay!"

I pulled into the last available parking spot in the back lot. Sassy and I were right on time for second period, but being right on time wasn't enough to make me miss walking past Will, who slid his body past mine, closer than necessary, tingles spreading over my body as he did. The hallways were so crowded that his actions went unnoticed by the rest of the students.

"Later, love muffin," Sassy called after me as I walked to the other side of the school. On my way, I finally pulled my phone out and read the messages from Will.

> Asshole: I'm here
> Asshole: Where are you?
> Asshole: Answer me, dollface.
> Asshole: Haley...

I decided to finally answer.

> Me: Sorry. Had an emergency.
> Me: And FYI, you don't summon me. I summon you.

A self-satisfied smirk crossed my face as I imagined the low groan he'd let out at the last message, the way he'd have to adjust himself in his jeans. I was having far too much fun playing with Will Roberts.

By the time lunch rolled around, I had gotten three more text messages from Will. Tone was challenging to assess through a handheld device, but I'd say he was begging. Especially when the last one read, *'please, Hales'*.

Part of me hoped Hales hadn't been a typo, that it had been a new and improved nickname from dollface.

"So," Sassy began when me, her, and Snake were all sitting at our usual lunch table. "The homecoming dance is next weekend."

"And?" Snake asked. He was sitting closer to her than usual, and the table was partially blocking my view, but it looked like he had his hand possessively on her thigh.

"Do you want to go?"

"To a school dance?" He scoffed.

"With me."

His tone and the look in his eyes changed when he looked at her. Fuck. They were both in love already, something they'd probably been fighting for years.

"Please."

"Sure."

And just to make sure I was absolutely certain that he loved her, Snake leaned across the space between them and pecked her lips delicately. I'd seen plenty of PDA from Snake, but it was usually in the form of rough ass grabs or shoving his tongue down the throat of whoever his flavor of the week was. I'd never seen him so sweet or intimate.

Sassy gave me an *I told you so* look.

"Okay. I'll go, too. We need to keep your cover."

"Thanks," Snake told me sincerely. It was the least I could do. I was going to leave them with a gigantic shit storm when I finally bailed out of this shithole.

"Come on. We need to buy tickets."

Snake opened his wallet and handed Sassy forty bucks, enough for both of their tickets. Shit. This little adventure was going to put another dent in my college savings plan.

When Sassy and I were walking across the cafeteria, to where the cheerleaders were selling tickets, I couldn't help but overhear Will's conversation at his table.

"Aren't you going to buy us tickets?" Mackenzie asked.

"Why would I buy *us* tickets to the dance?" He asked her.

"We're going together?"

"No, we're not. We're not a couple anymore, Mackenzie."

"That break-up was serious?"

"Christ." I watched him inhale sharply, his head falling back and his Adam's apple bobbing as he swallowed. "Yes. I don't want to date you. I've tried to be nice about it," he said. Truthfully, he hadn't tried all that hard to be nice about it, but still she couldn't take a hint.

I hid my snicker with a cough and continued to walk with Sassy. There were about ten people in line ahead of us while we waited. When my phone beeped, I wasn't expecting Will's name to pop up again.

> Asshole: You're going to the dance?
> Me: Sassy and Snake want to go. I have to keep cover and pretend we're a couple.
> Asshole: I'll buy your ticket.
> Me: Why? We're not a couple? And I can't be your date.
> Asshole: As if I'd ever date you anyway. But I am a gentleman, dollface. And since it's gonna be me you sneak off with in some dark, unoccupied corner of the school, and let me slide your dress up so I can fuck you, I'll buy your ticket.

My mouth fell open as I read his message. Shit. He was definitely starting to mess with my head. How did the golden boy have a mouth like that?

> Asshole: I'll buy two tickets later and slide one into your locker.
> Me: Okay.

He could buy my ticket if he wanted to. And he could certainly fuck me at the dance.

"Two please," Sassy said when we made it to the front of the line. The cheerleader who was sitting at the table, one of Mackenzie's best friends, Kinsley, snorted at her, but took her money regardless. "Thanks," Sassy said sarcastically when she turned to let me purchase mine.

"My cash is in the car," I told her. "And I don't feel like going to get it. I'll get one tomorrow during my free period." She looked at me disbelievingly. "I'm not gonna bail. I promise."

"You'll come over this weekend so we can make our dresses?"

"I can do Friday after school or Sunday, but Saturday I have to work."

"Friday. My mom has to work late."

***

BY THE TIME AP CALCULUS ROLLED AROUND, I WAS READY FOR THE DAY to be over. It was also the first time Will must have gotten a decent look at me in the outfit I put on specifically to torture him.

> Asshole: You ditch me this morning, and then show up in that?

He texted me in the middle of class and I wasn't discreet when I opened it.

"Miss Winters," Ms. Smalls snapped at me, making me tuck my phone back into my bag. "Would you like to share what's so riveting on your phone with the class?"

"No thank you."

"Come on, dollface," Will had the nerve to put his two cents in. "It can't be *that* interesting."

"It's not. It's actually rather small. And insignificant."

I saw his lip pull back into a sneer, and I felt a triumphant jolt of pleasure.

Jackass.

"I apologize, Ms. Smalls. It won't happen again."

She nodded at me before getting back to her lesson.

When my phone beeped again, I knew it was him. This time, I was more careful when I snuck a peek.

> Asshole: We both know it's not small, dollface.
> Me: Hm. We must have different definitions of big then. Or even average.

After that, I shut my phone off and really started to pay attention. My grade had slipped from an A to a B and I hated to admit that the reason for said slip was Will. I could only have my fun with him if it didn't affect my grades and potential for a scholarship.

When the final bell rang, I brushed past Will, pushing my ass against his groin as I turned, making his breath hitch, but he covered it with a yawn, complaining that practice was exhausting him.

"Hey!" Sassy said as she was waiting for me at my locker. "Snake is going to give me a ride home."

"Okay. And tomorrow morning?"

"I think I'll be riding in with him too."

"Or riding him," I smirked. She blushed before turning and walking away from me.

I dilly dallied around my locker, not wanting to run into Will. By the time I was done packing and unpacking books and notebooks from my backpack, I was the only one left in the hallway. Everyone else was either off to a sports practice, detention, or some other after school activity. I was involved in some of the clubs, but mostly I never went. I just signed up so that I could write them on my college application since nobody actually looked at their attendance records anyway.

About halfway down the hall, I was unexpectedly pulled into a janitor's closet. I knew right away that it was Will.

"Dollface," he husked in my ear. I couldn't see him since there was no light on in the confined space. "You wore that little outfit for me, didn't you?"

"Don't flatter yourself."

"This skirt is way too short for the dress code. Not that I'm complaining. Every time you walked today, I could see those little white panties sneaking out. Why did you blow me off this morning?"

He didn't give me time to answer before his lips were pushed against mine and one of his hands was on my leg, hitching it around his hip. Momentarily, I gave into the kiss, letting his tongue push its way into my mouth and have his taste of me. Choosing to let him have his fun, I ground my hips into his, feeling his hardening cock behind his khaki uniform pants as he rubbed himself against me.

How has this become my life? Since when did I dry hump Will Roberts in the janitor's closet?

When he tried to take it too far, sneaking his hand between my legs, I bit into his bottom lip, making him hiss. But the sound of pain turned into a moan when I sucked on his lip. Moving my hands up his body, I laced my fingers through the blonde strands of his hair, pulling on them and tilting his head roughly back.

"Let's get one thing straight Will, you don't summon me. I summon you." He gulped, but pushed his hips against mine rougher, proving how much he liked having me in control–just as much as he liked controlling me. "Meet me back here during first period tomorrow, and if you're a good boy, I'll get on my knees for you."

With that, I pushed him off of me, and walked out of the janitor's closet and out of the school.

CHAPTER 10

THE DANCE

Haley

The week leading up to the homecoming dance went by quickly. I studied, waited anxiously to hear from my college and scholarship applications even though I knew I wouldn't hear anything for at least another month, and I avoided more beatings from my mother. My only hope was the love bubble she and my father found themselves in didn't pop until after the dance tomorrow night. The bruise on my face finally healed, so I didn't have to sweep my hair in front of it anymore.

Will and I fooled around a handful of times in the janitor's closet and in one of the school bathrooms. The sex was amazing, a fact I'd have to stop denying it at some point because he knew my body well.

I was playing a dangerous game, and I knew it, but it was just for a little while because in less than a year, I'd be secretly loading up my car and sneaking away in the middle of the night and fleeing town.

After that, Will would be just a blip on my radar, a passing memory of a life that I'd once lead, one I would be desperate to forget as soon as I managed to pull my sister out of this life too.

Which was why I couldn't understand the words that were coming out of my mouth as I spoke to Sassy. "We should go to the football game tonight," I said while we were sitting at our usual lunch table. I looked at her as I spoke, but as soon as the words were out of my mouth, I snuck a glance at Will. He had his football jersey on—black with bright gold letters and number thirteen. Of course, he would like an unlucky number like thirteen. Why wouldn't he?

"We've never gone before."

"And we've never gone to a school dance before either. I just figured since you wanted to go to homecoming, we should have the entire experience."

In four years of high school, I'd never been to a single sporting event, never had a reason to, and I didn't have a reason to go now. Will was not a reason. I was just trying to have the experience. When I got to college, I wanted to be a normal girl, and normal girls went to high school football games. That way, if someone ever asked, I would have a story to tell.

"Can we bring booze?" She asked.

"Obviously." What high school story would be complete without sneaking booze into a game? That was like a rite of passage or something, wasn't it?

"Fine, we can go." I smiled at her, not wanting to give too much excitement away.

"Meet me at my house at six thirty," I told her. "And you can invite Snake."

"I will, but he's not going to come."

Sassy and Snake were an adorable couple. He'd been missing school the past two days, and I was sure it had to do with the gang. They were up to something, but I didn't know what. Snake told Sassy she didn't need to know, and I legitimately didn't want to know, so we were both left in the dark, and I knew whatever it was would have

Sheriff Roberts and his band of deputies rolling into the trailer park again soon.

"I can't believe you're making me do this," she said.

"And I can't believe you're making me go to a dance tomorrow," I deadpanned. "The things we do for friendship." I grinned as my sarcastic comment shut her up. "Love you lots, baby cakes. I'll see you tonight." As soon as I stood, the bell rang and I was off to my next class.

The rest of the day went by relatively quickly. When I finally got to AP statistics, I was annoyed with how good Will looked in his jersey, and that I couldn't stop looking at him. I listened to Ms. Smalls talk about statistical probability, then she had us do an assignment where we and a partner flipped a coin one hundred times. One of the partners wrote out heads or tails every time the coin was flipped while the other wrote down a series of random heads or tails. Ms. Smalls told us that with greater than ninety percent accuracy she would be able to tell which were the real answers and which were the falsified ones.

Kelly, the girl who sat next to me and was relatively nice for being from the rich side of town, asked to be my partner. Ms. Smalls left the room, but left the door open slightly, ensuring we would actually do the work and not just goof around for the next twenty minutes. "I'll do the real one," she said, pulling a coin from her bag. It took me three minutes to write down one hundred heads or tails in a random combination of whatever felt right.

"Here," I said when I was done, taking the paper from her. "You flip and I'll write down the answer. It'll be quicker that way."

Kelly and I were the first group done, so I pulled out my phone.

> Asshole: How about a good luck blowjob after class?
> Me: Aren't athletes not supposed to ejaculate before games? Doesn't that make them tired?
> Asshole: Old wives' tale. What do you say? Meet me in our spot.

Our spot. It sounded romantic, but it wasn't. It was just the janitor's closet.

Ms. Smalls walked back into the room, and I had to put the phone away before I could answer. I watched her walk around the room, standing in front of all the pairs of students. To my surprise, she got every single one right.

"How is that possible?" One of the students in the front row asked.

"Because," Ms. Smalls said, "I always choose the one that has the longest streak of heads or tails in a row. Statistically, the probability that a long sequence will occur is pretty high. It's because the same person flips the coin so the effort is the same. But the person writing the made up statistics always panics a little when they put too many heads or tails in a row and then switches it."

"Seems like bullshit," someone in the back called.

"But it's not." Her voice had a little sing-song style to it as she spoke with a smirk.

"Wait," I heard Will's voice. "This is AP calculus, why are we learning about statistics?"

"I was bored," she shrugged, making the class laugh. "With the football game and dance coming up, I knew none of you would be able to concentrate. Class dismissed. Have fun at the dance tomorrow and at the game tonight."

As everyone was packing up their belongings, Will walked discretely past me. To a passerby it would just look like he was trying to leave the room. "See you in a few minutes, dollface," he whispered as he walked by.

I was going to meet him all right, but I certainly wasn't going to be on my knees for him. I wasn't in the mood.

Ms. Smalls let us out early, and I waited until everyone from our class had disappeared from the hallway before walking to mine and Will's janitor's closet. When I opened the door, I could already sense his presence. "Thought you weren't coming." Even in the dark of the closet, I could sense the smirk on his face, the teasing tone of his voice that I was growing accustomed to.

"I'm not sucking your dick," I told him.

"I'll play so much better if you do," he whispered huskily in my ear. His body pressed against mine, and I could feel his cock, hot and hard for me against my lower stomach, the thin fabric of my uniform shirt and his pants doing nothing to hide it from me. Searching, his lips found mine and pushed against them softly, teasingly.

He was trying to seduce me.

"I'm going to the game," I mumbled.

"You've never been before."

"Maybe there's something I'm interested in seeing. Like this," I said, cupping him through his pants. "I've got to know if you stuff a sock in there to make him look bigger or if you let the real you be on display for all the girls to see."

"You and I both know I don't need a sock," he said gruffly.

"And you don't need a blow job. I don't want to drain you of all your energy and then be the reason you lose the first game I ever go to. What kind of supporter would that make me?"

"The best fucking kind," he said, his lips pushing against my neck softly in a barely there kiss.

"Instead, how about you think about tomorrow," I whispered, pulling his neck down so I could whisper in his ear. "What will my dress look like? Where are you going to meet me? Am I going to be wearing panties for you?"

"Fuck, dollface," he grunted.

"Good luck at the game, asshole," I said before sliding out of his arms and into the hallway. I'd timed it well because the bell rang and a flood of students pushed into the hallways.

With a smirk on my face, I collected the books I'd need for the weekend and headed to my car.

"I CAN'T BELIEVE WE'RE ACTUALLY GOING TO THIS," SASSY COMPLAINED while we were on our way to the football game. Chloe and Buck were in the back seat. The season was already half over, but neither of them had been to a game either, and when they found out we were going, they wanted to come with us.

"It'll be fun," I said.

"Yeah, yeah." She didn't believe me, but we had gotten coffee from the gas station and once we got to the game, we were going to fill them with whiskey.

"Snake's not coming?"

"He said he had business." She sighed. She may love him, but I worried his involvement in the gang that got her father killed was going to put an end to their relationship before it really even got started.

What are they up to?

All the parking spots were nearly full, and we still had a few minutes before kick off. Luckily, I managed to snag a spot in the teacher's lot. "Go ahead," I said to Chloe and Buck. "Meet us back here when the game is over. And come straight to the car."

"Okay," she agreed before she and Buck slipped out. Sassy reached under her seat and pulled out the bottle of cheap whiskey, and we filled our cups with it.

"All right, I'm ready now."

It was cold out in the almost mid-October weather. We were bundled up, jackets, hats, and gloves, but still the cold was piercing. Good thing we had booze to keep us warm. We paid the three-dollar admission fee, me paying for Sassy since I'd dragged her out. The bleachers were full with parents and the student spirit section. The student section all had black sweatshirts on with gold lettering, Carver High written on them and the sports teams written all over the back.

I didn't have that much school spirit and would never order one.

Instead, Sassy and I walked to the fence near the track, which surrounded the football field. The stadium lights were nearly blinding, but I found Will immediately. His number thirteen jersey didn't stand out since it looked like every other jersey our team was wearing, but my eyes knew where he would be. I watched as he ran up and down the field, sweat beading down his forehead despite the frigid temperature. Running down the field, he turned, putting his hands up as Jordy effortlessly threw the ball into his waiting hands.

I watched as his fingers flexed around the ball when he caught it. Images of those fingers on me and in me filled my mind, knowing exactly what they felt like, and suddenly, I found myself jealous of a football. As if sensing my eyes on him, Will turned and found me instantly. I watched his tongue lick across his lips, an innocent gesture to anyone else who might see, but I knew it was directed at me. Palming the football with one hand, he used the other to push his sweaty blonde hair out of his face before grabbing his helmet and pulling it on. I could still see his eyes on mine.

Warmth flooded me and it wasn't from the whiskey in my cup.

I watched as Will and Jordy walked to the middle of the field.

And that's when things got really fucking interesting because standing in the middle of the field for the other team was Bobby.

"Oh shit," I said under my breath.

"What?" Sassy asked, confused.

"Nothing," I said, shaking my head. "Coffee was just hotter than I'd imagined." Her attention was pulled away from me when the crowd was on their feet and yelling. Bobby and Will were in each other's faces, gripping each other by their shoulder pads. Will was taller, his face bent down as he yelled in Bobby's face. Bobby pushed him away, but Will was back on him in an instant. Whistles were blowing and yellow flags of nonsense were being thrown in the air.

What the fuck is happening?

The game hadn't even started yet. When they were finally pulled away from each other, I watched them both spit on the ground before being dragged to opposite sides of the field. Will's eyes burned holes into mine.

I'd seen Bobby at work last weekend, but we hadn't hooked up. He didn't have feelings for me and neither did Will, so I couldn't be sure what was going on. Maybe it actually had nothing to do with me?

Once the pre-game scuffle was forgotten, Bobby's team was kicking the ball towards ours. I had a basic understanding of football, but I didn't cheer as I paid attention. Thankfully, Bobby and Will managed to keep their tempers in check, and by the time it was halftime, there hadn't been a fight, and we were winning 10 to 7.

"Want a snack?" I asked Sassy.

"Yeah, I could use something warm." Our spiked coffees were long gone.

The line for the concession stand was super long, but what else did we have to do? I certainly wasn't going to watch Mackenzie and the cheerleaders perform their half time routine.

"I'll have two hot chocolates, a bag of m&ms, and nachos with cheese, please," I ordered when it was finally my turn.

I handed her a ten, and ridiculously received no change—almost as expensive as the movie theater snacks. "Thanks for supporting the Wildcats," the PTA mom smiled enthusiastically while she handed me our overpriced food. Chloe and I definitely wouldn't be able to go to the diner this week. I may also need to pick up an extra shift at the movie theater this week to make up for it, but at least I didn't have to buy my own ticket to the dance or a dress.

The second half was just getting started when Sassy and I were back in our spot, leaning against the fence. Will wasn't on the field for the kickoff this time, and when I found him, he was facing the crowd, helmet off, hands pulling against his pads, and his eyes found mine, holding eye contact while he ran his thumb across his bottom lip. The action forced me to push my legs together. Noting the reaction I had, I watched him smirk before turning around. The coach slapped him on the back and pushed him onto the field.

Even with my limited understanding of football, all I did was watch Will.

By the time the clock was winding down in the fourth quarter, Will scored another two touchdowns and the Wildcats were winning 24 to 10. When the buzzer finally rang, the crowd went wild with applause. I clapped too, even though Sassy looked at me like I'd grown a second head. "What?" I scoffed. "I can't pretend to have some school spirit?"

"Woohoo!" She yelled loudly, clapping her hands and making me laugh at her over the top enthusiasm. "Okay. That did feel good," she conceded. "Woohoo!"

Taking her hand, I held it as we weaved our way through the throngs of people and followed the path back to the car. Chloe and Buck were already waiting for us when we got back. "Can we come to the next game too?" Buck asked.

"No," Sassy said. "You can go if you want. But it's fucking freezing and I have no desire to come back and watch sweaty boys tackle each other. I don't get the draw."

I laughed at her. "How are we supposed to get there if we don't have a car?" Buck asked her.

"Pay me like a taxi and I'll take you," I told him.

"Deal."

***

It was close to midnight, and I was still awake, laying in my bed scrolling through my phone. We'd gotten back from the game almost two hours ago and I still couldn't sleep. When my phone beeped in my hands, I ignored the butterflies when Will's pet name popped up.

> Asshole: And to think I would have played better if I'd been able to have your lips around my dick before the game.
> Me: Sure.

Hopefully, my sarcasm translated through text.

> Asshole: I'll see you tomorrow dollface. Don't bother with panties.
> Me: I hate you
> Asshole: Not as much as I hate you.

Rolling my eyes, I tucked my phone under my pillow, but it beeped again. This time I had to suppress a smile at the thought of Will still texting me.

> Bobby: Your boyfriend is a dick.
> Me: He's not my boyfriend.
> Me: What did he do?

> Bobby: Asked me how it felt to have him steal my girl, told me to stay away from you and then about the bathroom at the party.
>
> Bobby: I told you I didn't do complicated because I don't. But the dude is a dick.
>
> Me: I know he is.
>
> Bobby: Do you?
>
> Me: Yes. It's not serious. Just don't tell anyone.
>
> Bobby: Sure. Just be careful. We're friends, Haley. I don't want to see you hurt.

I knew Bobby meant what he said because he was in love with his best friend's girl. He cared about me like a friend.

And now I was fucking livid with Will.

"Sassy, this dress is gorgeous," I told her. She'd taken my measurements and asked if I had any requests for the dress. My only request had been that it had pockets, and Sassy came through. It was by far the prettiest thing I'd ever put on. The green color wasn't something I'd ever choose for myself, but she'd turned the cheap satin into a beautiful garment. It was short with a little flare just above my knees, a strapless style that accentuated my chest nicely, and the embellishment around the waist made me feel like a damn princess. And it had pockets! I couldn't stop thinking about a dress with pockets. I fucking loved it, even if dresses weren't usually my style.

Even though my dress was gorgeous, Sassy's was on another level. Hers was a deep pink that fell all the way to the floor. It had two thin straps and a plunging neckline that showed off her chest with a crisscross of fabric on the back, revealing much more of her skin than would be deemed appropriate by the patriarchal society the school functioned under. But she looked absolutely stunning.

Our hair and makeup were much the same as they always were.

I was doing my best to put on a happy front, but I was still so pissed at Will. If Sassy wasn't my best friend and if she didn't desperately want to go to this dance with Snake, I would bail, but I wouldn't because I was a good friend.

But fuck if I was letting Will Roberts get his hands under my dress tonight. He had no right to say what he said to Bobby.

When there was a knock on the trailer door, Snake opened it up, dressed in an all black suit with a pink tie, looking like it was cut from Sassy's dress. That definitely wasn't going to give us away. It was fine at the dance, as long as our parents didn't see. "Baby girl," he said. "You look gorgeous." The ice surrounding my heart thawed just a little bit as I watched him kiss her sweetly and whisper something in her ear that made her giggle.

"You look great, Haley," he said when he pulled away from her. "We need to take some pictures," he said. "Make everything look good."

"Yeah, but you can't be wearing that tie in the pictures. It's clear your Sassy's date, not mine."

We were getting really bad at keeping up the appearances we'd worked so hard on over the years. Hopefully, our dads were too wrapped up in club business to notice.

"Right," he said.

"Wait," I stopped him. "Let me take some pictures of you guys first."

Our lives weren't like the movies and I'm sure the same as all the other kids getting ready for the dance. Our parents didn't care. Well, Sassy's mom probably did, but she had to work. She always worked doubles on the weekend, so she could work a little less during the week.

Using Sassy's phone, I snapped a few pictures of them, even one of them kissing before Snake and I swapped places. Sassy and I struck what felt like a million poses in the dresses she'd made beautifully. We were laughing, being young and carefree, and even if I was annoyed with Will, I was happy to be going to the dance, even if I was a third wheel with my two best friends.

With my phone and my ticket in the pocket of my dress, we all headed to the dance. When we got there, the sun was already setting, and crowds of well dressed students poured into the gym.

I didn't miss Will walking in with Jordy. He looked gorgeous in his black suit, with a dark gray shirt and a black tie hanging loosely around his neck.

He was a sure fit for homecoming King.

And Mackenzie would be his Queen.

And I wasn't jealous at all.

The gymnasium was transformed into a mediocre party. There were balloons and decorations everywhere, drinks and snacks. The DJ was set up in the corner and the music was pretty good, a mix of the usual top forty songs and stuff I actually enjoyed listening to—eighties and nineties rock.

Ridiculously, the three of us went to the center of the mass of dancing students. We'd been dancing for close to thirty minutes and I was sweating and laughing when I felt my phone buzz in my pocket.

> Asshole: After the king and queen dance. The bathroom on the second floor in the English wing.

I ignored it.

He wouldn't be getting anything from me, not after that stunt he pulled.

I held firmly onto that thought until Principal Potter was standing on the makeshift platform and tapping the microphone. "Welcome to the 2021 homecoming dance. It's time to announce our homecoming King and Queen." A roar of cheers went up. Everyone knew whose names were going to be called. "Our homecoming King is Will Roberts!" I clapped dutifully, but my body had a different reaction to watching him climb onto the podium.

My heart beat picked up and my palms started to sweat. He winked out into the crowd, but I knew it was directed at me, and it made me quiver in need. I hated that my body reacted to him—stupid fantastic sex.

Nobody was surprised when Principal Potter yelled "Mackenzie Richardson," as homecoming Queen.

The crowd cheered again. I did too, but less enthusiastically than I had for Will. Sassy eyed me curiously, but I ignored her. In cliché homecoming dance fashion, Will and Mackenzie walked to the center of the circle and we watched them dance. Will looked less pleased than she did about their dance.

I really hadn't been planning on meeting Will when and where he asked, not after what he did, but while he was slow dancing with Mackenzie, he'd kept his eyes locked on me the entire time. Blue pools filled with lust pulled me in, promising me endless orgasms if I just gave in to what I was feeling.

Jealousy.

That was what I was feeling. It was unfamiliar and unsettling because I'd never been jealous, but watching Will hold Mackenzie made me wish he could hold me like that.

Which was a completely normal thought to have about the person you were in an enemies with benefits relationship with and had absolutely nothing to do with romantic feelings. I didn't have those. The ice and barbed wire keeping my heart trapped were firmly in place, keeping me from doing something stupid like falling in love and deciding to stay in this shithole town.

I was jealous because I wanted him to be fucking me. Not dancing with her.

"I need to go to the bathroom," I whispered to Sassy.

"Okay, we'll be here when you get back."

As the song came to a close, I hurried out of the gym, dodging chaperones as I snuck up to the back stairwell and up to the bathrooms. Leaning against the wall between the girl's and boy's bathrooms, I waited. I could still hear the music from downstairs; the song changed into a faster, more upbeat one than the slow song it was. Will had to be getting close.

"Hey dollface," he said.

"Don't hey me, asshole."

"What did I do this time?" He asked frustratedly.

"Why did you and Bobby almost fight yesterday?" Something like possessiveness flared in his eyes, matching the flaring off his nostrils as I spoke. "What did you say to him?"

"I told him to stay away from you."

"Why? You have no claim on me." I tilted my chin up in defiance as I spoke the words.

"You. Are. Mine." He growled the words out through gritted teeth. "We agreed that this was exclusive. You are mine, and I don't fucking share, Hales." There it was, that goddamn nickname, not the ridiculous dollface, but the one nobody else ever called me, the one that made my insides melt for him.

"I belong to no one."

Quickly, he closed the distance between us and dragged me against him by the back of my neck. His strong fingers dug into the muscles, making me tilt my head back and look up at him. "We'll see about that."

With that, he crashed his lips against mine. We were a mess of limbs, hands roaming everywhere as we fought to control the other. Pulling me impossibly closer, not allowing enough room for even air to slide between our bodies, Will pulled me into the girl's bathroom, locking the door behind us. Once inside, he had my hands pinned above my head, holding them in an iron grip as his tongue dominated my own. When he pulled away, I leaned my head forward, chasing his lips. "Tell me you're mine, Hales." When he leaned back in, I sunk my teeth into his bottom lip roughly, making him hiss. "Bad girl, dollface."

"I hate you."

"Good 'cus I hate you too, but that doesn't mean this pussy doesn't belong to me," he whispered, running the hand that wasn't restraining me, down the front of my dress and beneath it, finding my soaked panties. Pushing them to the side, I felt his eyes study every wave of pleasure as it washed over my face. Spreading my legs, I gave him better access to me, the sound of my heels clanking against the tile as I did.

"More," I begged.

"Mm. Beg for me, dollface. I fucking love it."

"I wasn't begging," I denied. "It was an order. Give me more, Will." He chuckled against my ear before his fingers pushed into me.

"Always so fucking wet for me," he grunted. Roughly, he pushed two fingers in and out of me while I pushed my hips forward, still desperate for more. Finally releasing my hands he'd been restraining above my head, he pulled my dress down, letting my breasts spill out. Will licked a path from my chin down to my chest, covering me in his sloppy wet kisses and saliva, all while his fingers continued fucking me, curling and hitting the perfect spot with every thrust. Stopping intermittently along the way, he sucked on my exposed skin and I should have stopped him. There would be hickies, but I couldn't stop him, I didn't want to stop him. I was lost in the way he was touching me, making me submit like I never had. When his lips finally wrapped around one of my nipples, I looked down and saw his blue eyes trained on me, making me swallow harshly.

"I'm gonna come," I told him, breaking eye contact.

"Good girl. Soak me with it, dollface," he murmured against me. "I wanna feel your tight little cunt squeeze my fingers, hear your cries of pleasure echo off the walls."

"Will!" I screamed for him, granting both of his wishes.

I wasn't even recovered before he was dropping to his knees in his suit. This time, he pulled my underwear down to my ankles before his head completely disappeared under my dress. "Oh fuck, Will," I moaned when his hot mouth came into contact with my oversensitive pussy. He didn't even bother pushing my dress up, content to hide himself completely under it while his hands stayed on the outside, crawling up my body until they reached my chest, roughly pulling at my nipples. I whimpered for him, my head thrashing against the door. His tongue expertly flicked wicked circles against my clit. My hands went to where his head was lifting up my dress, holding on while his nose pushed against my clit and pointed his tongue and fucked it into me, changing tactics. Using one hand to hold his head, I looked for anything to grab on to so I didn't collapse into a puddle on the ground. Grabbing the closest thing to me—the automatic paper towel dispenser—I clutched it like it was my last lifeline. He'd started too quickly, not giving me enough time to recover, and my second orgasm was coming on too fast. It was going to break me. "Will! Will! Yes! Oh god." My body spasmed but nothing, no sound coming from my throat as I came, my release flooding from me. I pushed so hard against the paper towel dispenser that I actually broke it, disconnecting the top that opened for it to be refilled.

When Will finally reappeared, he slid back up my body, his face was covered in me. "That good, huh?" He asked smugly, pointing to the damage I'd done. Snapping my head away from the image, choosing to ignore him, my hands found their way to his belt, undoing it as I dropped to my knees. "We don't have time," he said, stopping my downward motions. "I need to be inside you before we have to get back."

"Right. People will start to miss the homecoming King."

"But he's right where he wants to be." With those words, he lifted me into his arms and pinned against the door again, his thick cock slamming into me. My legs wrapped around him and my hands clutched onto his shoulders as he pulled his hips back, pistoning himself into me. "Fuck, I love being inside you," he groaned in my ear.

"Less talking, more fucking." Will grunted in annoyance, but did as I told him, fucking me against the door. "Good boy." One of his hands held me against him by my lower back, my shoulders pushing into the door for leverage. But he used his other hand to roughly grab my hair, pulling it to the side and attacking my neck. I whined in pain and pleasure, my pussy clamping down on him as he plowed into me. "Fuck, Will."

"You love my dick, don't you, dollface?" He couldn't see, but I rolled my eyes. "Say it."

"Not on your life, asshole."

Will chuckled darkly in my ear, increasing his pace and making me moan for him. We both knew the real answer, the one I'd never speak.

"Are you gonna come for me, doll?"

"Yes," I cried with my arms wrapped tightly around his shoulders.

"Come on my dick," he grunted in my ear. "Come all over me so I can fill your tight little cunt. I wanna know that for the rest of your dance my cum will be spilling into your panties."

"Oh my god, Will. Fuck!"

My pussy spasmed around him, squeezing him and pulling his own orgasm from him. Will's lips pressed against my neck, lingering there while he stilled inside me and filled me. "Hales," I heard him say almost indiscernibly. When he finally pulled himself out of the crook of my neck, he released my legs, helping me drop elegantly to the ground. Breathing heavily, I bent over and pulled my panties up, already feeling the post sex drip pool in my panties, just like he wanted.

Moving to the sink, I started washing my hands wordlessly, rinsing my mouth and straightening my clothes and hair. When I opened my eyes, I found Will standing behind me. "You go first," he said. When he moved to stand next to me, he washed his hands and rinsed his mouth. "Later, Hales."

There was nothing left to say, so I walked out wordlessly. We'd fucked, gotten the benefits we both signed up for.

Checking around the corners, I made my way back to the gym where the dance was.

"Where's Snake?" I asked Sassy when I found her standing by herself.

"He went to get drinks." She eyed me suspiciously. "Where were you? What took you so long? And why do you look like you had sex?"

"You're still a virgin. How would you know what I looked like post sex?"

"I'm a virgin, not an idiot." I just looked at her. "Where were you? Who were you with?"

"Nobody." As soon as I spoke the words, Will walked into the gym–using the side door like a fucking idiot.

"Haley," Sassy said in disbelief. I shook my head at her. "No."

"Don't," I told her.

"Don't what?" Snake asked.

"Nothing," I said too quickly. "Just begging her not to make fun of me for how much I actually love this dress, and the dance, even though it's obviously a ridiculous high school cliche."

"Yeah, baby girl, don't tease her," Snake said, wrapping his arms around her. "She loves it too. Don't let her fool you," he told me. "Here, I'll go grab another," he said, handing us both a drink.

"Haley," she whispered, yelling at me when Snake was gone again.

"Not here," I told her. "Not here."

With a reluctant sigh, she dropped it.

But I knew the conversation was far from over.

CHAPTER 11

THE QUESTIONS

Haley

After the dance, Snake drove us home, and we walked back from dropping Sassy off together. She wasn't even inside ten seconds before my phone buzzed with the first text, but I ignored it while we walked slowly through the dark.

"Thanks for this," he said while we walked. "She really wanted to go."

"She deserves it."

"She does. I want to give her everything." Snake was in love.

"You will."

"How?"

"I'm working on it, okay?" Maybe I could tell them about my plan. They'd benefit from me bailing too. My dad couldn't force Snake to marry me if I wasn't here, and that would free him up to be with Sassy.

"Okay," he said, but I could tell he didn't believe me.

"I promise." He nodded once before kissing my cheek like he always did and walking to his door. When I walked into my house, I was pleasantly surprised to find it quiet.

Pulling my phone out, I read the messages I had from Sassy.

> Sassy: Will fucking Roberts?! Haley, you can't be serious.
> Sassy: How?
> Sassy: When?
> Sassy: Holy shit. What the fuck. I cannot. This is.
> Me: Breathe, Sas. Come over in the morning. Please just don't say anything to anyone. And delete these messages so no one finds them.
> Sassy: Okay. I love you. I'm just worried about you.
> Me: I know. I love you too.

I deleted our messages too before walking quietly to my room where Chloe slept peacefully on her bed, so I made my movements extra quiet. Stripping out of the dress, I tossed it carelessly in the direction of our hamper before putting on a t-shirt and a pair of shorts. Before climbing into bed, I plugged my phone into the charger and tucked it underneath my pillow. Just as I closed my eyes, I felt it vibrate again. Expecting another message from Sassy, I grabbed it and pulled up my messages, but it wasn't from her.

> Asshole: Next time I'll save you that dance you wanted too, not just a bathroom break.

I ignored it.

I hadn't wanted to dance with him. That wasn't what my feelings were telling me. I wasn't sure what they'd been telling me, but I knew, undoubtedly, that it wasn't that.

"WHAT?" I ASKED AS I WAS BEING SHAKEN AWAKE. "GO AWAY," I mumbled into my pillow.

"Sassy is here," Chloe's voice said.

"What time is it?"

"Almost eleven."

"Shit." Rolling to my back, I rubbed the sleep from my eyes and looked at my sister. "Are Mom and Dad here?"

"No, they were gone when I woke up."

"Let Sassy in."

Wordlessly, Chloe disappeared while I sat up in my bed. I had six text messages from Sassy, all in varying degrees of anger, asking me to answer her and when we were going to meet up.

"Hey," she said, walking into my room and closing the door.

"Hi." She handed me an iced coffee from the gas station down the street and I took a grateful sip.

"So?" She said, sitting on my bed and sipping her own iced coffee that was more sugar and milk than coffee.

"It's not a big deal."

"You're sleeping with Will Roberts!" She yelled, cutting me off.

"Shh. Not so loud!"

"Sorry," she mumbled. "I just don't get it. I thought you hated him."

"I *do* hate him."

"Does your vagina know that?"

I snorted at her. "Yes, which is why the sex is so fucking good."

"It's good?"

"Would I be repeatedly hooking up with him if it wasn't?"

It was her turn to snort. "How long?"

"Since we got detention."

"How many times?"

"I don't know. I haven't been counting."

"Do you like him?"

"No."

"Are you going to tell him I know?"

"Fuck no. That's none of his business."

"Does he understand that he's actually, quite literally, risking his life? Your dad will kill him, and that's not an exaggeratory euphemism for just threatening him. Viper will literally murder someone who gets in the way of his plans for you and Snake."

"So you're risking your life by being with Snake," I reminded her.

"But I love him. You and Will don't love each other."

"Never will."

"Then why? Is this why you told Snake to go for me?"

"Look," I told her. "I don't know why. If I did, it would probably be easier to stop, but I can't. I don't want to, and it's just sex, so there's no chance of us getting caught."

"I caught you."

"Nobody else could ever or would ever pay enough attention. I'll tell him to be more careful. If he wasn't a fucking idiot and had used the main entrance instead of the side one, not even you would have noticed."

"I just don't get it," she said. "How did it even happen?"

"We were in the basement where they keep the janitorial supplies. We'd been fighting. After your first fight with Snake, tell me how high the sexual tension is between you two."

"Shouldn't it have been just a one-time thing?"

"It was supposed to be, but then Bobby invited me to a party out in Hillview. Will, of all fucking people, was there. We're enemies with benefits, which is like friends with benefits except it needs a different name since we are not and will never be friends. We both just want to fuck."

"I don't know, Haley. This seems like a terrible idea."

"I've got everything under control," I told her.

"I'm not going to tell you what to do, but if I found out, other people are bound to find out too. It's not worth the risk, for him or for you."

"I hear you," I said while taking a sip of my coffee. "As long as you don't tell anyone, nobody else will find out."

"I'm not going to say anything," she promised. "I'm your best friend. I would never betray you."

I could tell there was more she wanted to say. Most if it was probably along the lines of telling me that I needed to stop before something bad happened. And I would stop. Eventually.

Before I left town.

"So was the dance with Snake as your date everything you were expecting it to be?" I asked, in desperate need of a subject change. I couldn't keep thinking about Will.

"It was magical," she said dreamily. I chuckled at the lovestruck look on her face. If I ever have that look on my face while thinking about a man, please slap me. "He's a surprisingly good dancer."

"You know what they say about men who are good dancers," I said while lifting my eyebrows up and down.

"What?" She asked completely seriously. She was so innocent, Snake was going to ruin her.

"That they're good at sex," I told her seriously.

"Oh." She blushed.

"So, when are you gonna do the deed?" I asked. She seemed to be content to let the subject change from me to her.

"As soon as he drops this goody-goody act he's got going on. You'd think he was the virgin, not me."

"He probably just wants it to be special for you."

"Your first time wasn't."

"No, but you cannot compare us," I told her. "You value sex and intimacy, which is one hundred percent your choice. I, however, did not grow up in a stable home. Sex is meaningless to me, simply a means to the endorphin release that comes with an orgasm, a perfectly acceptable opinion, just like your feelings about sex. Just don't compare the two. Yours are actually probably better."

"If it's just for orgasms, couldn't you do it with anyone? Does it have to be Will?"

"No, it doesn't. But you know that it's always been hard for me to find guys willing to sleep with the daughter of the leader of the Southside Gang. They all run scared. He doesn't."

"What about Bobby?"

"Bobby's good, but Will is better, and at school. Bobby I see once every few weeks. That's not enough to sustain me."

"You sure you're not a sex addict?" She teased.

"Positive, but by the time Snake is done with you though, you might be."

"Let's hope," she said, lifting her hands in a prayer position while tilting her head towards the ceiling. "I just love you and I want you to be careful."

"I am. I promise." She nodded her head at me, clearly thinking about Snake again as she started sipping her coffee again. "Speaking of being safe," I said. "Do I need to take you to the clinic?"

"I already called and made an appointment for tomorrow."

"Aw. Look at my baby girl all grown up," I cooed at her.

"Yeah, yeah," she tutted. "There is something I wanted to ask you." She was chewing on her lip nervously as she looked at me. Sassy had never in her life been nervous to ask me anything. "I, um, I. Well... you see."

"Sas. Spit it out."

"I want to give Snake a blowjob," she whispered. Sure, when we were talking about *my* illicit sex partners she could yell at the top of her lungs, but when it came to hers, she could whisper. "I know he's gotten lots from lots of other girls, and I want to blow his mind, give him the best of his life."

"And you want my help?"

"I'm assuming you know what you're doing."

"Bold assumption, but also an accurate one." She just rolled her eyes at me while I found myself hysterical as usual. "Have you felt him?" I asked. "Like cupped him or felt it against our leg while you've been making out or after he's feasted on you?"

"God, you're so vulgar."

"If you can't handle the word feasted, you're definitely not going to like how I teach you to do this."

"God, fine. Yes."

"Okay, come on." Hopping off my bed, I walked towards the kitchen. Chloe was sitting in front of the TV watching some random show I'd never seen before. "Chloe," I called. She didn't respond, too engrossed in her show. Satisfied she wasn't paying attention to us, I turned back to Sassy. "Grab a banana that closely represents his length and girth."

"You cannot be serious."

"Do you want my help or not?"

"I'm starting to rethink my answer." I rolled my eyes at her while she chose her banana and we walked back to my room.

Closing the door, I locked it to prevent Chloe from walking in and grabbed the banana from her so I could examine it. "Not bad." Sassy was already blushing, which didn't bode well for her getting through this lesson. "Let's start with the basics. Don't use your teeth. If you can't get your mouth around him without your teeth scraping him, tuck them behind your lips."

"Like this?" She asked before demonstrating.

"Yes. Now, how's your gag reflex?" She just shrugged. "Stick a finger down your throat and see how far you can get."

"Seriously?"

"You're going to have his dick in your mouth. It's gonna be back there." I watched her tentatively stick a finger into her mouth. She could go pretty far before she gagged. "Not bad," I said, impressed. "So if you can't take him to your throat, or you don't like it, you need to wrap your hand around him and squeeze somewhere between tight and gently, then just go to your own hand. Grab the banana and wrap your hand around it."

"You're not going to make me deep throat the banana, are you?"

"What? No, I'm not crazy." She gave me a look that clearly meant to relay how much she doubted that statement, but now was not the time for that discussion. "When it comes to blowjobs, wetter is better. Use your spit to make him nice and wet. If you're dribbling down your chin, you're doing it right."

"Jesus," she muttered under her breath.

"It's true." She inhaled sharply, content to continue with the lesson. "You're going to have to pay attention to him. His moaning, groaning, his hands fisting in your hair will let you know how much he's enjoying it. Use your tongue to lick the underside of him; along the veins is the best spot. And if your jaw gets tired, you can just use your tongue to work the head, lick it like it's a damn lollipop or ice cream cone. If you moan while you're doing it, it'll make him think that he's the best thing you've ever tasted. They love that shit."

"I didn't know I was going to have to take notes."

"If you want, you can try letting him do the work."

"How does that work?"

"You keep still and your mouth open and let him basically fuck your face."

"Oh my god."

"Guys love it."

"Do you let them?"

"Fuck no, I'm in charge. But, like I said, we're different."

"Do you think Snake would do that?"

"Yes, but you'll have to be relaxed and trust him. You don't want to end up throwing up all over him because he kept hitting your gag reflex."

"Is there a way to suppress your gag reflex?"

"There are some tricks online, squeezing your left thumb in your fist, but honestly, practice is the best one."

"Why did we need the banana?" She asked.

"We didn't really," I winked at her.

"You just wanted to embarrass me."

"I mean, you can use it to practice if you want. I won't judge you."

"I'm good."

"When are you going to jump him?" I asked.

"Hopefully tonight, my mom is working a double."

"Good luck."

"Thanks."

"Also, just google it," I told her. "There's so much information on the internet."

"I'll remember that next time."

"Are we good?" I asked her. "You seemed pretty mad last night."

"I was upset, but mostly just because you didn't trust me with your secret."

"It's not that I don't trust you. I trust you with my life."

"I know, and after last night, I calmed down and remembered that being your friend doesn't mean you're not entitled to your own secrets. But I'm still *worried.*"

"You don't need to be. I've got everything under control, but you can't tell anyone, not even Snake."

"I won't. He doesn't need to know. It'll only put him in a weird spot where he has to lie to your dad and his dad even more." Our iced coffees were finished, so I stood from the bed as Sassy followed me back into the living room. "I'm gonna ride with you to school in the morning so I can tell you all about my night."

"Deal."

"Love you."

"Love you too."

I was rummaging through the cereal boxes in the cabinet, looking for breakfast, when Chloe finally realized she wasn't alone anymore. "Do you want to go to the diner?"

"Not today, Squirt," I told her. "I've got lots of homework to do. But maybe we can order pizza for dinner?"

"Okay," she said. "The teacher I babysit for got a weekend job as a bartender every other weekend so I'm gonna start working every other Saturday for her. Can you take me and pick me up?"

"I have to work at the movie theater sometimes," I told her. "But I'll make sure Snake can pick you up."

"Okay."

"We'll figure it out," I promised her.

After I had breakfast, I went back to my room and sat on my bed. I was halfway through reading *The Great Gatsby*. I needed to finish the book and write an essay on it before next weekend, so I definitely needed to finish the book this weekend.

By the time I'd finished, it was past lunchtime. Just as I was standing to go find more food, my phone beeped.

> Asshole: Not at the diner today. Too bad. I was getting used to our weekly Sunday meetings. I was thinking that one of these days I'd make you follow me into the bathroom. That does seem to be your favorite place to fuck.

Me: You wish.

Asshole: Oh I do, dollface.

He didn't need a response.

"Do you want grilled cheese and tomato soup?" I asked Chloe who started her own homework at the table.

"Yum."

Grabbing a can of soup, I made it and quickly cooked us grilled cheese.

"This is nice too," she said when I set our food down. "You cook almost as good as the diner."

"I wish."

She smiled at me before eating her food. Her birthday was coming up in a few weeks—November third. "What do you want for your birthday?" I asked her.

"A sissy day," she said. "Where you're paying."

I laughed at her, nearly spilling soup all over myself as I did. "Fair. We'll go to the diner, ice cream, feed the ducks at the park, and then have pizza for dinner. Do you want to go to the movies too? I can get us free drinks and popcorn at the theater."

"Maybe. I'll have to wait and see what's playing."

"Okay."

Finished with our lunch, I collected our plates and set them in the sink. "I'll do the dishes," she offered.

"Thanks, Squirt." I kissed her forehead like she was still just a baby before heading back into my room.

Quickly, I made an outline for my essay, but since it wasn't due until next week, I switched to math homework. Math was my least favorite subject and not anything I intended to use in my life post college, but the dual AP Statistics and AP Calculus looked amazing on my college applications.

By the time I had finished all of my homework, it was time for dinner. "Pizza?" Was the only thing I said to Chloe when she came into our room.

"Yeah. You wanna go there and get slices? It's cheaper than needing to get a whole one delivered."

"Sure, let me just shower and change."

By the time I was done showering and had on a pair of joggers and a sweatshirt, Chloe was sitting on the couch, waiting for me. We were dressed nearly identical—black joggers, black sweatshirts.

"Go change," she whined.

"No. Let's go."

"I hope people think you're my mother and not my sister," she said.

"I hope they think you're older than me."

"As if."

"Stop watching clueless. The millennial obsession with that movie is ridiculous." I was starting the car as she was going on about the relevance of the movie today, as if either of us could ever relate to the spoiled brat that was Cher. By the time we pulled into the pizza place, she still wasn't done talking about it.

"I'm sorry I said anything," I muttered.

There wasn't anybody else in the restaurant, but the employees, made mostly up of the kids from Carver High school, were all busy working on to go orders. "Welcome to Lake's Pizza," the cashier, who I recognized from the homecoming dance, said. "What can I get you?"

"Can I have a slice of pepperoni and a slice of buffalo chicken and a side of blue cheese dressing? And whatever she wants."

"Can I have a veggie lover's and a meat lover's slice, please?"

"That'll be ten fifty, please." I handed him a ten and dug around in my pocket for some change. Damn blue cheese cost me fifty cents, what a ridiculous markup.

We went and sat in the booth in the corner while I watched our slices be tossed into the oven. Chloe was still playing with her phone, writing a very long text message, and I believed less and less that her life didn't have some type of romantic partner involved, or potential one at least. My heart clenched—she was still such a baby in my eyes.

"Hey, what's up, man?" The guy who'd taken our order asked as the bell dinged, alerting us that someone else entered the space. Looking up, I saw none other than Will.

It was like I could never escape him.

"Hey, here to pick up."

"Sorry, dude, we're slammed tonight. I just put your pizza in, it's gonna be at least ten minutes."

"No worries. I'll just hit the arcade." I watched them exchange fist bumps before Will turned and finally noticed me. When his ocean blue eyes found mine, they darkened instantly, a wicked smirk crossed his face, and his tongue snaked out and he licked across his lips. The last thing he did was shoot me a wink before walking out of the pizza place.

Ten seconds later, my phone buzzed.

Asshole: Bathroom.

I didn't even pretend like I didn't want to go.

"I've got to pee, I'll be right back." Chloe just nodded, eyes still glued to her phone.

There was only one bathroom in the building, and it was situated between the pizza place and the arcade. Turning the handle, I found it open. When I stepped inside, I was pulled to the side before being roughly pushed against the door. I heard the lock click.

"Miss me, dollface?"

"Never," I husked.

"Liar," he chuckled.

"We can't do this. Anybody could start a line outside waiting for us to come out."

"Where's your sense of adventure?"

"In places we can't get caught. In places being exposed wouldn't ruin both of us."

"Fair," he conceded, stepping away from me. I missed the warmth of his body pushing against mine. "But that's what this is about. There's a Halloween party at that girl's house in Hillview. We should go."

"Like as a date?"

"A sex date," he clarified. "But yeah. Nobody from our school will be there, nobody will be able to recognize us in our costumes. We can escape this world for a night."

"Fine, but I get to pick both of our costumes, and you have to pay for them."

"Deal." He kissed me, which was strange since we both knew it wasn't leading to sex. "Meet me tomorrow morning in the janitor's closet?"

"Not on your life, Will."

The handle to the door wiggled. "Haley," Chloe's voice called. "Our pizza is done, are you okay?"

"I'll be right out. Go sit down."

We were being way too reckless.

"I have to go," I whispered, pushing him away from me. "Later, asshole."

"Bye, dollface." I rolled my eyes at him before leaving the bathroom and heading back to my sister and our pizza.

CHAPTER 12

THE HALLOWEEN PARTY

Haley

In the days between homecoming and the Halloween party—exactly two weeks—I'd been sneaking off with Will every few days, the janitor's closet, the school bathrooms, anywhere we could find to squeeze in sex. They also weren't always rushed quickies, when we'd meet after school and nobody else was around, he'd take me for what felt like hours. The last time, just two days ago, I'd barely been able to walk straight when he finished with me. Snake gave Sassy those six orgasms, and I'd been jealous at the time, but when Will pushed me to eight—the eighth one forcing my soul to leave my damn body as I clamped down around him—my jealousy faded.

We ended up in Principal Potter's office again because Will picked a fight in calculus. He'd walked by me and whispered something about my dad getting arrested again. I snapped at him because he'd been pissing me off all day—he'd brush by me in the hallway, send me random text messages that would ding in the middle of class. He stared at me through the entire lunch period.

"You've been such a dick all day!" I whispered harshly at him when we were walking from calculus to Principal Potter's office.

"I know," he grinned stupidly at me. I hated that stupid grin and I hated how it made my insides turn to fucking mush.

Principal Potter hadn't spoken more than five words to us. "Again? Detention. Same as before." He pointed us to his door in dismissal. As soon as we got into the basement, Will pushed me against the wall, the same wall I'd been pushed up against the first time he'd kissed me.

"No way," I said, pushing him away. "You've been pissing me off all damn day."

"For a reason."

"What reason?"

"This one," he said, pushing his body flush against mine. "To get you back here to where it all started."

He stared at me, a pleading look in his eye that was far too adorable for the calculations he'd taken to piss me off to get us both detention, but it worked because I'd ridden him to orgasm like that first time, my hand around his throat while I called him a good boy.

After we were finished, he pulled the Halloween costume I'd told him to buy out of his backpack. Because I was me, I wanted a twist. When I searched for ideas, I'd come across pirates and mermaids, and chose that, except I was going to be the pirate, and Will was going to be a merman, shell bikini and all.

He didn't even protest. All he said was, "I'll be the sexiest merperson there."

Honestly, I'd been hoping to get a little resistance so I could belittle him about his patriarchal beliefs, but he surprised me at every turn, proving to be a feminist at heart.

Shocking.

Somehow, in a post orgasmic haze, he even got me to agree to drive there with him. I was going to park my car behind the church, where Sassy and I always went to smoke.

It was a horrible idea, but it was too late to back out now. The party was tonight.

"You sure you don't want to go to the Halloween party with us?" Sassy asked.

"I have to work," I told her.

"Do they even need you? It's Halloween weekend, they can't be that busy." I was lying to her. My secret with Will made me lie to her more in the last few weeks than I ever had in my life. I thought about telling her, but after our last conversation she said the less she knew, the better. It would feel less like lying if she had real, plausible deniability.

"There's a Hocus Pocus showing, and a Halloween marathon, and a bunch of old Disney channel Halloween movies."

"That actually does sound fun," she said.

"I know, and if it's not busy, I'll get my choice of movie." She laughed as I once again listed the only perk of my job, that, and free popcorn.

"But if I hear something about you in a couple's costume, I won't be surprised," she said, basically confirming she knew I was lying without saying the words.

"On Tuesday, Chloe and I are ditching school for her birthday. Do you want to ditch with us?" I asked her, effectively changing the subject.

"She said it was a sissy day."

"You're basically our sister."

"True. Yeah, I'm in need of a ditch day because there's no way I'll survive until Thanksgiving break without one."

"Did you guys do a couple's costume?"

"We couldn't be too conspicuous," she said. "We're going as a hotdog and a hamburger. Chloe and Buck are going as ketchup and mustard, so it just looks like a group costume when we're all standing together, but the pictures we'll take will be adorable of just the two of us."

"That's so cute. Send me pictures."

"I will."

"I gotta go get ready," she said. "I'll see you later."

"Bye," I waved her off.

As soon as she was gone, I pulled my costume out of the closet and started getting ready. It started with tight black pants that I'd be pairing with black, knee high, heeled boots. I added the peasant blouse over it, noticing it was skin tight as I put it on, and when I looked at the tag, I saw Will ordered a size smaller than I'd told him to. He was too damn predictable. Over the blouse, I added a red and black corset style top that had capped sleeves on the shoulders and ties up the front.

Will was going to have his work cut out for him if he wanted to get me naked.

I didn't really want to wear the eye patch, but, between that and the big hat, it would be harder to recognize me, which was the purpose—just in case. The last touch was a cross body holster for a toy gun. Assessing myself in the mirror, I was pleasantly pleased with my appearance. Lastly, I applied heavy, black-rimmed eyeliner, a dark smokey eye and dark purple lipstick.

The sun was already setting, so hopefully I'd be able to sneak out the back entrance to the trailer park, which was almost exclusively used by my dad's men to sneak in and out, but tonight, I'd be using it.

Chloe was already at Sassy and Buck's, and with any luck, I'd get out of the house without running into either of my parents, and for once in my life, luck was on my side because I made it out without passing anyone. By the time I pulled into the secluded church parking lot, it was dark, and I was five minutes early for Will's designated pickup time.

Like a gentleman, he arrived exactly on time. I could see him doing the same as me, assessing the surroundings to make sure nobody was around before I snuck out of my car and into his shiny new truck.

"Hey doll."

"Will," I said in greeting. He just grinned at me.

And I was surprised it took me that long to see what he was wearing. I expected him to at least have a jacket on since it was freezing, but he was wearing his seashell bra, and he had body glitter on, like everywhere I could see. And I could see a lot. He was naked from the waist up, except for his bra. The green mermaid tail was pulled above his knees so he could drive easier, his hair was pushed back out of his eyes with a seashell encrusted headband, and sitting on the seat between us was a stuffed crab.

"You look amazing," I told him, barely keeping my laughter in.

"Told you I'd be the best looking mer-person at the party." We laughed together while he pulled onto the country road that led us to Hillview. "You look gorgeous, Hales."

"Thanks," I said, feeling my cheeks color. Hopefully, in the darkness of the truck, he wouldn't be able to see it. I never blushed.

We'd been having sex for over a month, but I had no idea what to say to him, how to act around him when I didn't know for sure sex was on the table.

"Where did you tell your friends you were?" He asked.

"Working. You?"

"With my secret girlfriend at a party for her school."

I mean it was closer to the truth than what I'd said, but wait. "Girlfriend?"

"Couldn't exactly call you my enemy with benefits, that would definitely blow your cover."

"Can I ask you something?" I asked.

"Yeah."

"Why did you kiss me that first day?"

"Honest answers only?" He asked, his brows raised. I nodded. "Because I wanted to." I furrowed my brows at him. "It's that simple, Hales. You're fucking hot, I'd be an idiot to not have noticed it all these years. And despite the hate, there was too much sexual tension. My brain malfunctioned."

"Mine too," I admitted. "I thought it was just a one-time thing. That was my intention."

"Which is how you ended up at the last party in Hillview."

"Exactly."

"My turn," he said. "Who keeps putting all those bruises on your body?"

"Next."

"You have to answer."

"Next question, Will."

"If I guess correctly, would you tell me?"

"Probably not." He sighed. "I answered your question. It's my turn again."

"No you didn't."

"I told you I probably wouldn't tell you if you guessed. I answered." I paused, waiting for him to try and argue his way out of it, he didn't. "Why are you obsessed with my bruises? Why are you so convinced there's something sinister going on? Couldn't I just be clumsy?"

"Because I don't think any person should be a victim of whatever type of abuse you've been suffering from. It doesn't sit right with me, even if it's happening to someone I can't stand." So it wasn't because he maybe didn't completely hate me. I didn't have a response. "Is my dad a crooked cop?"

"What?" I asked quickly.

"I'm not an idiot," he said. "I know your dad has to be paying someone off. I don't know if it's him, Mackenzie's dad, a politician, one of the deputies, but based on how many times he's been arrested and never been taken to trial, I know he's got someone on his payroll. Is it my dad?"

"As far as I know, no, your dad isn't dirty." He let out a sigh of relief at that. I actually didn't know if he was. I only knew for sure that Mackenzie's judge father was dirty, but the way my dad spoke about Sheriff Roberts, I didn't think he was dirty.

"But you know who is?"

"It's not your turn to ask a question." He sighed again, but continued driving in silence, waiting for me to ask a question. "Do you really want to be the sheriff? Live here for the rest of your life?"

He was quiet, but I could feel his eyes glance at me, momentarily taking his eyes off the road as I stared forward out onto the dark road, illuminated by the lights of his truck.

"Some days yes, some days no."

And that would be the only explanation I got because he was parking the truck on the side of the road next to the house that had been the scene of the crime, the house where we'd agreed to this stupid enemies with benefits arrangement. I guess maybe you could look at it like the janitor's closet was the original scene of the crime, but that was where the momentary lapse in good judgment happened. When we climbed out of the truck, Will walked around the front, making me laugh as I watched him tuck his keys into his seashell bra. He pulled the bottom part of his costume down and was forced to waddle next to me as we walked into the house. The sight was exactly the same as last time: red solo cups everywhere, sexily dressed girls on the arms of boys, booze in hand.

The door was wide open as we walked in. The only difference versus last time was the Halloween costumes rather than the short skirts and tight jeans everyone wore last time. Will grabbed my hand. It was the second time in our entire lives that we'd held hands and I was immediately brought back to the feeling of his hand in mine in pre-kindergarten all those years ago. I didn't like it when he let go to pour us two beers from the keg. He handed me one before guiding me to an empty spot on the wall where we could stand and watch.

"Damn, Will," someone said, making me panic. "Who's your date?"

"This is Dolly." I looked at him and he grinned. Dollface. Doll. Dolly. This fucker. Seriously? "Dolly, this is Logan." Logan's face conveyed his disbelief. "Her parents are huge Dolly Parton fans."

"Hi," I greeted him, not bothering to tell him my real name. "Nice to meet you."

"Do you guys go to school together?"

"Used to," Will offered. "She had to drop out, horrible grades. She's a stripper now."

Logan's head fell back as he laughed, and I actually thought he might believe Will until he spoke again. "Keep your secrets, dude, I don't care. I'll catch you later." He took two steps away before turning back to us. "Oh, and Will, you make a sexy as fuck mermaid." Will shimmied his pecs, tried to anyway, and then turned, bending over and attempted to twerk.

He was ridiculous, but I found myself laughing before finishing my beer. He and Logan fist bumped before Logan finally walked away, wrapping his arms around a girl in a hot nurse costume.

"Wanna dance?" Will asked.

"Sure." He took our empty cups, setting them on a random table before pulling me to the makeshift dance floor. Some club song was coming through the speakers, nothing I usually listened to, but I found the beat and started swaying my hips to it. Will was behind me, hands low on my body, his groin pushing into my ass while he rocked with me. The flimsy fabric of his mermaid tail did nothing to prevent me from feeling his growing cock behind me. My costume was going to be covered in his body glitter with how close he had us pushed together.

The dance floor was nothing more than a mass of bodies, grinding together, hot, sweaty and sticky. Will's fingers moved up my body, pulling at the fabric of my peasant blouse. Slowly, he moved them higher and higher until they were resting on either side of my waist, his thumbs high enough they were on the outside of my breasts. My breath hitched as he rubbed softly, I could hear his breathing, hot and heavy in my ear.

The song changed, but the beat was the same. Turning me in his arms, Will pushed our fronts together, his hands traveling lower again until they were resting on my ass. He didn't let them rest long before he was grabbing fistfuls of my cheeks, pushing me against his growing erection. We were still dancing, grinding our hips together to the beat, and it sounded like the music was getting further and further away, just like everyone around us disappeared from view. I could feel my heartbeat in my ears as my breathing increased. Will's roaming hands were everywhere, up and down my back, the nape of my neck, my throat and back down to my ass while both of us panted heavily.

When the music changed again, it was a slow song. The world around me stopped being hazy, and I remembered watching Will dance with Mackenzie at homecoming. Except this time, it was me he was dancing with, it was me who was wrapped in his arms as his movements slowed and he pulled me impossibly closer.

There wasn't even room for a sheet of paper to pass between our bodies. No words were spoken, but the chemistry was electric; I could feel it pulsing through my veins, and the only thing I could hear was the music and the alarm bells in my head, the bells that were screaming danger. But I ignored them.

Despite the fact that my movements slowed, my heartbeat didn't and neither did my breathing. It was Will affecting me, making me dizzy, not the booze or the lack of air in the smoke filled room.

When his head pulled away, I chanced a glance up at him. Wasting no time, he bent his head down and pushed his lips against mine. His kiss was the same as always, rushed and urgent, and desperate. His hands around my lower back squeezed me, lifting my feet off the ground so he could turn my head and deepen the kiss, holding me suspended in the air, but it was me who was dominating his mouth, and he freely let me.

"Let's go," he said when the music stopped. Will pulled me from the dance floor hurriedly behind him. He walked away from the crowds, down the endless hallways until he finally found a door. When he opened it, it was already occupied. The occupants cursed at us, making Will laugh as he closed the door. We were laughing as we rushed through the house. Will finally found a door that led to the basement. Opening it, he called down. When no one answered, he pulled me inside, locking the door behind us. "Fucking finally," he said when we found a furnished basement. "A soft fucking surface to take you on."

"Still not a bed," I snorted.

"Soon," he whispered, and before I could ask what he meant by that statement, he pushed me onto the couch. "Be a good girl and take your clothes off for me."

"Nope," I said. Sitting on the couch, I leaned forward, elbows on my knees. "Strip, pretty boy."

"It's gonna take me two seconds to get out of this costume. Yours has layers."

"Get naked, Will."

He huffed, but finally played along. Turning so that his back was to me, he looked over his shoulder, winking before undoing the tie holding his bikini up. Removing it he tossed it to the floor, his keys landing somewhere too. When he turned to face me, he was cupping his pecs, making himself appear modest. Finally releasing himself, he pushed his skirt down, revealing his naked body. I had to suck in a breath. Leaning back, I lifted my arms, resting them on the back of the couch and waited for him. "Crawl to me, Will." His blue eyes darkened visibly. "Be a good boy for me," I mocked him, using his own words.

Doing as I asked, Will got on his knees and crawled to me. When he was close enough, I grabbed him roughly by his hair and tugged it back. "Take off my pants."

"I hate you," he growled.

"I hate you more."

Lies.

I watched as he unzipped my boots, tossing them aside before he peeled my pants off of me, taking my underwear and socks right with them. I was naked from the waist down. Without having to be told, he wrapped his hands around my legs, tugging me forward so I was at the edge of the couch, spread out for him like a buffet. Using his hands to push my thighs into the couch, spreading them even wider for him, he dropped his head and covered my pussy with his mouth.

"Fuck, doll," he groaned. "You're always so fucking wet for me." Grabbing his head, I pushed him back against me, moaning as he swept his tongue through my sopping wet folds. One of his hands reached up to my breasts, squeezing them before running his fingers down my body until he found the tie of the bodice I was wearing. His mouth worked against my pussy as he reached his other hand up, taking my clothes off while my body lifted against his. His tongue worked quick circles against my clit, building me up before he backed off and pointed his tongue, using it to fuck me.

"Please, Will. Stop teasing me." Releasing his head, I helped him get the bodice off of me before pulling my blouse off and then my bra. I was completely naked for him now. Using his thumbs, he held me open for him, his tongue lapping at me now instead of flicking against me. "Oh god," I moaned. Taking my hands, Will pulled them around my thighs, forcing me to hold myself open for him. "Don't stop, please. I'm so close."

"Who's begging now?" He asked, smugness lacing his voice. Somewhere in the midst of the pleasure, I'd forgotten that it was me who was supposed to be in charge.

Letting my legs fall, I sat up a little and grabbed him by his neck, squeezing lightly on the outside. His eyes dilated further, pleasure on his face as his smug smirk died. "Make me come." Releasing him, I laid back onto the couch again. Will groaned as he inhaled my scent. His lips wrapped around my clit, my orgasm building again rapidly. Roaming my hands over my body, I pinched my nipples, pulling at them like he usually did, looked down at his blonde head between my legs, and saw his eyes open, tilted up in my direction.

"That's right," he said. "Eyes on me while I eat this fucking cunt. Remember it's me, the man you hate, making your body feel like no one else ever has."

My eyes clenched shut before I snapped them open again, holding his blue eyes. Even with his mouth covering me, only the tip of his nose and his eyes visible, I could tell he was smirking against me. When he pulled my clit into his mouth and rolled it against his tongue, I exploded against him. "Fuck! Will!" I cried, my body convulsing for him as he licked my release from me.

"Sweetest tasting cunt I've ever had," he said as he licked his lips dramatically. Will climbed to his feet, using my post orgasm haze to his advantage and take control back. Lifting me, he spun me around, making my head lean over the arm of the couch, my throat extended as my pirate's hat fell to the ground by his feet. "Open up, doll," he said, straddling my face. His ass was almost against my chest, his balls against my chin as I opened for him and let him push his cock into my mouth. He slid all the way in before pulling back. "Just like that," he encouraged as I licked along the underside, paying attention to the large vein. "Fuck, doll." Grabbing my head, he held me still while he pushed himself in and out of my throat. Spit and slobber poured out of my mouth, down my cheeks and towards my eyes because of how I was tipped over. "You look like such a fucking mess," he grunted. "My fucking mess." *His.* I didn't have time to dwell on his meaning or why he kept claiming me as his when I wasn't. "Swallow. I want to feel your tight little throat squeeze around my dick, be a good girl, Hales."

Doing as he asked, I swallowed, ignoring my gag reflex. I gurgled on him while he grunted above me. When Will finally pulled out, I gasped for air, letting fresh oxygen fill my lungs. Still in control, he pulled me up and pushed my chest into the back of the couch. "So fucking wet for me," he grunted, repeating the same words he usually did as he slid easily in to me.

"Yes," I moaned as I felt his long, thick cock stretching me. His hips slapped against my ass as he pulled out and pushed back in. Grabbing my hair, he used it for leverage, wrapping it around his fist to pull me back as he shoved himself deeper and deeper inside of me. "Will," I groaned as my hands dug into the back of the leather couch, my knuckles turning white.

"I love how well you take my dick," he grunted. "You're a desperate slut for me." My face fell forward, resting on my hands as the truth of his words washed over me. I was desperate for him. But the opposite was also true.

I tried bucking him off of me, to take control back, but his grip was too tight. "Tell me how much you love when I'm in control," he demanded. "Fucking tell me, doll."

"I hate you," I said instead.

"I can tell," he laughed in my ear. "Fuck." Releasing my hair, he pushed his chest against my back, his lips against my ear. "Fucking admit it," he whispered before licking the shell. I moaned at the contact. His hand came around, wrapping around my throat. "Say it," he growled.

"Never." Turning, I pushed my lips against his. Using his surprise against him, I pulled away, breaking the kiss and turning so that he was sitting on the couch. I watched him situate himself as I stood. His cock was covered in me, long and thick, standing straight up while he leaned against the back of the couch, blue eyes glued to my naked form in front of him. Straddling him on the couch, I dropped down on his cock, enveloping him in my warm pussy and squeezed my walls around him.

"Who's in control now, Will?"

His hands were on my ass, lifting me and dropping me back down on him. "Me," he grunted in my ear. Reaching my hand between us, I wrapped my fingers around his neck, squeezing the outside, the way I always got him to submit and guaranteed to make him see stars as he came.

"Try again," I whispered. My hips moved on him. The sounds of him entering me filled the room. The music from the party, the beating of the bass could be heard around us, shaking the walls and making sure nobody knew what we were doing, not that anybody here knew who we were, knew that we shouldn't be doing this.

"Fuck, Hales," he grunted. "You. Always you."

"Good boy," I whispered. Moving my hands back to his shoulders, I scratched into him, guaranteeing I'd leave marks behind as I rode him. Our breathing was in sync, our heartbeats and bodies in sync as I rode him, chasing both of our orgasms.

He was so close, I could tell.

"I'm gonna come," I warned him.

"Come for me, doll. I wanna feel you soak me." Extending my arms, I held my grip on his shoulders but let my body fall back away from his. I could feel his eyes taking in each inch of my exposed skin, my extended neck, my heaving breasts. I could tell, could feel when they stopped and watched where his cock was disappearing inside of me. He groaned when I squeezed on him, my fingers leaving more marks behind on his skin and my body shaking above him.

I wasn't even done yet, my body still flying high when he had us moved and had me pinned beneath him. My legs wrapped around him, anchoring us together as he continued to thrust into me wildly.

There was no question who was in control now.

"Who's in control now?" He asked, anyway. "Tell me, doll, who's in charge," he commanded me when I didn't answer him quickly enough.

"Me," I said through my panting breaths.

"Fucking try again," he barked. His hand came to my throat, squeezing the way I did him. His thrusting slowed but got impossibly harder, slamming inside of me and making me see stars with every thrust. "Tell me, Hales. Who the fuck is in charge now?"

"You, Will. Fuck. Oh god, I'm going to come again."

With one hand on my thigh, squeezing hard enough to bruise my skin, the only type of bruise I actually welcomed, the other squeezed my neck. "Come for me again, Hales. Come all over my dick again. I'm dying to spill myself inside your perfect fucking pussy."

"Shit. Fuck."

I came again, soaking both of us with my release. Will grunted in my ear, whispering a soft, "doll," before he stilled and released inside me.

We were still connected when someone pounded on the basement door. "Cops! Cops! Get out."

"Fuck," I said, pushing him off of me.

We scrambled into our costumes. My body was covered in glitter, as was my costume. Will was dressed in seconds while I was still struggling into my pants. "Let me help," he offered. I let him help me pull my pants up my sweaty body. Between the two of us, we had me dressed again in under two minutes.

"This is Sheriff Parks!" Someone pounded on the door. "Open up."

"Fuck! Will, we cannot get caught together."

"Relax," he said, grabbing my face. "I'll take care of this. It's Logan's dad, he's friends with my dad. We'll be fine. He doesn't know who you are, just pull your hat down and fix your eyepatch."

Fuck, I'd actually let him fuck me with an eyepatch on.

Doing as he said, I followed him up the basement stairs. "Sheriff Parks," he greeted.

"Will," Sheriff Parks greeted with a shake of his head. "You and Logan. Christ, are you drunk?"

"No, sir."

"Who's your friend?"

"Just a friend," he said. "She rode with me and she's not drunk."

"I'm calling your dad, but get the hell out of here."

"Yes, sir."

Will took my hand and pulled me through the throngs of bodies of kids who had to call their parents to come get them. Having your daddy as the sheriff had its perks.

We were silent on the way home.

"What are you going to tell your parents?" I asked as we crossed the town line.

"The truth. I was at a party that got busted by the cops."

"What about me?"

"Random girl from a town over. They don't care as long as I tell them I'm being safe, which we are, since you're on birth control."

"We keep almost getting caught."

"That's half the fun," he said as he parked the truck behind the church. "Let me know when you get home," he said.

"Why?"

"Because I'm not a total asshole and it's late on Halloween. People are crazy."

"Bye, Will."

I climbed out of his truck and into my car.

My mind was racing on the drive home. The truth was right there in front of me. We were playing with fire, and I couldn't afford to get burned.

When I got home, I was thankful to be alone, not caring where my parents were. I knew Chloe was safe because she was with Snake and Sassy. I texted Will before climbing into the shower.

He texted me back, but I deleted it without reading it, getting rid of our entire message thread.

Whatever stupidity this had been, it was over.

I was cutting him off. Effective immediately.

CHAPTER 13

THE SISSY DAY

Haley

The day of my sister's birthday, when my alarm went off thirty minutes earlier than usual, I didn't bother attempting to wake Chloe. I was going to let her sleep in and surprise her with breakfast birthday pancakes, which were just regular pancakes with sprinkles in them and a lit candle. I'd made them for her every year since I was tall enough to stand at the stove, since our parents never did anything special for either of our birthdays: no presents, no celebrations, never a party. I'd taken the responsibility of making sure each of her birthdays was special.

Climbing out of bed, I tiptoed to the kitchen, stopping to look out the kitchen window, and saw my mom's car was gone, same as my dad's motorcycle. Had they even come home last night? The first time I remembered them not coming home I'd been eight, and Chloe had only been five, but it wouldn't surprise me to learn that it actually started much earlier. They probably didn't even remember that it was her birthday.

Grabbing the ingredients for pancakes, I made them quickly, having the recipe memorized. As I was mixing the batter, all I could think about was Will. I'd ended it only a few days ago, but he hadn't stopped texting me, refusing to give up. I'd been ignoring him and hiding in the library first period every day, so we didn't end up trapped somewhere together.

But I missed the sex. It kept getting better and better, and if I was being honest, I loved the give and take of power. Bobby, and the others I'd been with before, were content to give their power to me temporarily, and I loved it. Will was the first to challenge my sexual dominance, to wrap his hand around my throat the same way I did his, and although I'd never admit it to him, I fucking loved it.

It just wasn't worth the risk. Sassy had already caught us, and we'd almost gotten caught by Logan's dad. I couldn't risk it. Our relationship being exposed would end up with him dead by my father's hand and with me beaten black and blue, with probably more than a few broken bones.

Not worth it.

No matter how good the sex was.

Adding butter to the griddle, I waited for it to turn golden brown before adding the batter. After a few moments, I added the sprinkles. They were probably stale at this point, but buying new wasn't a luxury I could afford. While I waited for the little bubbles to pop up, indicating that it was time for them to flip, I grabbed my phone seeing I had four more messages from Will.

> Asshole: Come on Hales, meet me tomorrow.
> Asshole: Dollface, I know you miss the sex.

He wasn't wrong about that.

> Asshole: Please, Haley.

Fuck. I loved it when he begged.

> Asshole: We'll be more careful.

I deleted all of them without responding. As soon as Sassy got here, I'd be turning my phone off for the day, focusing on my sister and best friend—who was basically my sister. Once I'd plated the pancakes, I used my lighter to light the candle.

Walking into our bedroom, I flipped the light on, making Chloe grumble into the pillow. "Happy birthday," I said, holding the plate of pancakes out to her.

"Thanks, Hilly," she said gratefully when she finally rolled over and sat up. Taking the plate from me, she blew out the candle. "It smells delicious."

"They always do," I quipped at her. She rolled her eyes at me. How was she fifteen? In my mind it should be me getting older, and she should always stay my baby sister.

I watched her take a bite and swallow. "So good," she affirmed.

"Good." I leaned forward and kissed her forehead, attempting to pour some motherly love into her because she sure as hell wasn't getting it from ours. "I'm gonna shower, enjoy your breakfast."

Since our parents weren't home, I didn't have to worry about saving the hot water; so for once, I took my time showering. I shaved with warm water instead of cold and washed my hair while the steam filled the bathroom. It was amazing, and I wanted to stay longer, but it was Chloe's birthday, and she should definitely have hot water for her shower.

"Did you not make pancakes for yourself?" She asked when I walked back into our bedroom.

"No," I replied, shaking my head. We hadn't had enough ingredients for more than one serving, but I didn't want to tell her that. "I wasn't in the mood. I'm going to make myself a breakfast sandwich."

"Okay." She knew I was lying.

"Go shower," I told her. "Sassy should be here soon, and then we'll get our day started."

"What are we starting with?" She asked.

"Why ruin the surprise?"

"Fine," she huffed. Once she left the room and headed for the shower, I dressed in a pair of high-waisted jeans and paired it with a gray turtleneck that was skin tight. I wasn't in the mood to blow-dry my hair, so I braided it in two dutch braids. It would be curly tomorrow for school, which I'd like.

Will would probably like it too, except that didn't matter because we wouldn't be spending any more time together.

Once I was dressed, I walked back to the kitchen, Chloe's plate in hand. I was making my breakfast sandwich and cleaning up at the same time when there was a knock on the trailer door. Peeking out the window, I saw Sassy standing there, dressed almost identical to me.

"Hey," I said when I opened the door. The only difference in our outfits was that her jeans were dark and her sweater was a lighter gray.

"Great minds," she said, indicating our outfit. I nodded and laughed. For as different as we were, we were also very similar. "Where's the birthday girl?"

"Still in the shower. Did you eat?"

"Yeah, I had some cereal."

Sassy sat at the barstool on the other side of the kitchen while I finished cleaning and making my breakfast, sitting next to her to eat once I finished.

"How are things with Snake?"

"Good," she said without giving anything away.

"Eighteen years of friendship and those are the only dirty deets I get? Good? Spill. Did he bang you yet?"

"No," she said. "And I'm starting to think he doesn't want to."

"Why would you say that?"

"I've offered myself to him on a silver platter and he keeps turning me down. What kind of eighteen-year-old does that?" She paused and looked truly upset. "Do you think he thinks I'm desperate?" I went to answer her, but she was speaking again. "He still hasn't even let me blow him."

This was serious if she was using words like blow.

"I don't think he thinks you're desperate. I don't know what it is, maybe he just wants to make it special?"

"It'll be special because it's with him."

"Have you told him that?"

"No," she answered before she started chewing on the inside of her cheek again, a stress habit she'd had since we were in elementary school.

"I've never seen Snake act like he does with anyone but you. I think he's scared. Sure, he's banged his way through half the town, but it's never meant anything to him. *You* do." Offering me a soft smile, she stopped chewing on the insider of her cheek.

"What about you and Will?" She asked, whispering his name.

"I ended it," I told her. "Not worth the risk." She looked at me like she didn't exactly believe me, but it was true; I had ended it. "Now no more boy talk. It's sissy day."

"Sissy day!" Chloe said excitedly, coming into the kitchen.

"Is that my shirt?" I asked her.

"Yes." Well, at least she didn't lie to me. She was wearing a skirt and tights and, with them, the blouse I'd worn on Halloween. I couldn't tell her to take it off without a good reason, not on her birthday and because I didn't want to tell either of them that Will had torn it from my body before having his way with me, definitely couldn't admit that.

"What's first?" She asked.

"Grab the loaf of bread I opened last night. We're gonna go feed the ducks, but we're stopping somewhere first."

Chloe grabbed the bread before we all piled into my car. Usually when it was the three of us, Chloe sat in the back, but since it was her birthday, Sassy sat in the back, right in the middle, leaning forward so she could talk to us.

"Dunkin' Donuts?" Sassy asked when I pulled into the drive through line. "I thought we all already ate?"

"Coffee," I said. "What do you guys want?"

"Mocha latte," Sassy said.

"I thought I wasn't allowed coffee," Chloe said.

"It's your birthday. Now, what do you want?"

"Iced coffee with caramel swirl and cream."

"Iced coffee?" Sassy asked her. "It's like five degrees outside." That was a mild exaggeration. It was like forty, but still, I agreed it was too cold for iced coffee.

"I always see girls walking around with them," she said. "I want to try." She was probably just happy I wasn't making her get a hot chocolate like I usually did.

"Welcome to Dunkin' Donuts," the voice came through the speaker. "What can I get for you?"

"Hi, may I please have a small iced coffee with caramel swirl and cream, a medium mocha latte, and a medium hazelnut latte?"

"Anything else?"

"No thank you."

"I'll have your total at the window."

"Chloe, can you pull a twenty from my wallet?" Chloe handed me the cash, and I handed it to the cashier, taking my change without really hearing how much it had cost. I'd picked up two extra shifts to cover the costs for today's birthday celebration. I wouldn't be here for the next one, or the one after that. Hopefully, I could show up for her eighteenth and get her out of this town.

When we each had our drinks, I started driving towards the park.

"How's your first taste of coffee?" Sassy asked Chloe.

"Good," she said before taking another sip, making a slurping sound come from the already nearly empty cup.

When we pulled into the park, we climbed out, stale bread and coffees in hand. It was too cold for most of the moms, so there were only a few of them on the playground. There weren't a lot of ducks left either, most of them were already flying south for the winter and the ones that hadn't yet, would soon. I made a mental note to come back in the spring to see the ducklings with Chloe one more time. They were our favorite.

Sassy and I let Chloe do most of the feeding herself. She loved it. She was so smart and wise, smarter than even me, but she hadn't lost her childlike, innocent view of the world yet. I'd done my best to shield her from the harsh realities of the world, especially the one we were born into.

"Let's take a picture," she said once the bread was gone. Chloe held out her phone, snapping a bunch of selfies, some with us making goofy faces and others where we were just smiling happily at the camera.

"Here," I said, taking her phone from her. "Strike a couple of birthday poses." She laughed, being extra dramatic as she pretended to be a model.

"Go stand with her," Sassy said. Smiling, I went to stand next to Chloe, being just as dramatic as she was. We were in fits of giggles, and I was sure that the photos were going to be fantastic.

"You go stand with her," I told Sassy.

"She's not my sister."

"As good as," Chloe said. "Come on."

I was nearly peeing my pants as I took pictures of them. Chloe jumped on Sassy's back and Sassy accidentally dropped her. Thankfully, all parties were uninjured because I couldn't keep it together long enough to help them up. When I tried, I landed on the cold wood of the pier with them, laughing like maniacs. I knew the few judgemental moms were staring at us with disdain, but I didn't care. This was as good as I'd felt in a long time.

And it was the first time that I wasn't thinking about Will.

"THAT WAS SO MUCH FUN!" CHLOE EXCLAIMED AFTER OUR SECOND morning stop. We'd gone to the arcade. I'd given us each a five-dollar limit, but when the games were still twenty-five cents a piece, just like they were when our parents came here, we had hours' worth of fun. Sassy and I gave Chloe all of our tickets so she could choose the biggest prize. She'd ended up choosing a giant stuffed Pokemon called Squirtle, but I'd never been into Pokemon so I didn't get it. "Where are we off to now?" She asked.

"It's lunchtime. Let's go to the diner."

Piling back into my car, we drove the short ten minutes to the diner.

"Don't get too much," I warned her as we slid into our booth. "We're getting ice cream after this and then we're heading to the movie theater. My friend Bobby is working, so we'll get in free and get free drinks and snacks."

"You've never mentioned Bobby before," she said.

"He's just a work friend," I said.

Sassy was fighting a smirk. She knew Bobby had been more than that. He wasn't anymore, but now that Will and I weren't something anymore, maybe Bobby could scratch my itch.

"Shouldn't you all be in school?" Suzie asked us.

"No, it's Sissy day," Chloe told her with a dead serious look on her face.

Suzie cocked a brow at her, clearly not enjoying the joke like we all were. "What can I get you kids?"

"Do you guys want to share the platter? And get extra curly fries."

"Sounds good," Chloe said.

"Sure," Sassy answered.

"Coming right up," Suzie said. "What do you guys want to drink?"

"Sprite," Chloe ordered.

"Coke Zero," Sassy ordered.

"Coke for me."

Suzie didn't write anything down before she disappeared to get our drinks. It was the middle of the lunch rush and more than a few people recognized us, but nobody said anything about us ditching school.

"How am I ever going to fit ice cream and snacks into me?" Sassy groaned once we'd successfully eaten every last molecule of food off our platter.

"Use your dessert stomach," Chloe told her seriously, making Sassy burst into fits of giggles.

I ignored their antics and flagged Suzie down so I could pay. I handed her a twenty, telling her to keep the change. "Come on." I tried to corral my giggling sister and best friend. "We've got to get ice cream quickly or we won't make the movie."

Walking from the diner to the ice cream shop. "Sassy," Chloe began. "If it's too cold for iced coffee, why isn't it too cold for ice cream?"

"Smartass," Sassy said. "You take after your sister too much."

"Thank you," Chloe said proudly.

Chloe and I ordered our usual, her basic order of chocolate chip cookie dough and dark chocolate in a waffle cone and my superior one of salted caramel and butter pecan. But I got mine in a dish this time, so that I could eat and drive at the same time. Sassy ordered a cone with chocolate brownie batter and chocolate peanut butter in a chocolate dipped waffle cone. The girl loved chocolate.

When we were back in my car, I headed towards the movie theater, not caring about the extra gas it was going to cost. This was the best day I'd had in a while, and I was hardly thinking about Will.

"What movie are we seeing?" Sassy asked. "And do you have any napkins?"

"Chloe, the napkins are in the glove compartment. And my crazy sister is obsessed with horror movies, guess since she was almost a Halloween baby. So we're going to see some crappy horror movie that was released for the spooky season."

"Can I pass?"

"Nope," Chloe answered. "It's my birthday, so I choose. You can choose on your birthday." I drove, eating my ice cream and listening to them bicker about who had superior taste in movies and music. The point was moot. The answer to both of those questions was me, obviously. I parked in the employee parking lot even though I probably wasn't supposed to when I wasn't working, but I didn't care.

Bobby was standing behind the counter when we walked in. "Hey Haley," he called.

"Hey Bobby, this is my sister Chloe and my best friend Sassy."

"Nice to meet you," he said before handing us three tickets and walking with us to the concession stand.

"What can I get for you guys?"

"One large Coke," I said. "Do you guys want a different drink?"

Chloe shook her head no while Sassy said, "Water."

"A large popcorn with extra butter, peanut m&ms, sour patch kids and cookie dough bites." Bobby gave us a ridiculously large bucket of popcorn and gallon sized soda before grabbing our candy. "You guys go ahead," I told them. "I'll catch up." Sassy, very indiscreetly, wiggled her brows at me, making me roll my eyes at her.

"What's up?" He asked when it was just the two of us.

"Do you want to hang out soon?"

"What about your *friend*?"

"That's over," I said.

"Tell you what, if it's still over the next time we work together, you can come home with me."

"It will be."

"When do you work again?" He asked.

"Next Friday, then the Wednesday before Thanksgiving. Then I work the Saturday after."

"I've got a basketball tournament over Thanksgiving, but I'll be back Saturday to work part of the late shift."

"See you then." I winked before sauntering off.

Will and I were done, so I'd be spending time with Bobby after Thanksgiving. Trailers were still playing by the time I slid into the seat next to Chloe. "Everything okay?" She asked.

"Yeah." I smiled at her before turning my focus to the screen.

♡ ♡ ♡

"That movie was horrible!" Sassy shouted as we pushed our way out of the theater. Bobby was helping customers, so I waved at him as we left.

"It was so good!" Chloe gave her own opinion.

"So much blood," Sassy said with a shudder.

"It's a horror movie."

"Still. Too over the top and unrealistic."

"Didn't you read the credits? It was based on a true story."

"Don't tell me that."

"Enough," I said, cutting off their banter. "Everyone has different tastes. It's fine." They ignored me, continuing their ridiculous exchange until I pulled into the pizza place in town.

"What are we getting?" I asked.

"Pepperoni?" Sassy asked.

"Fine with me."

"Welcome to Lake's Pizza. What can I get you?"

"Medium pepperoni pizza to go."

"You sure you don't want to eat here?" Chloe asked tentatively. I knew what she was asking. Would it be better to eat here and avoid our parents?

"Yeah, we can do that if you want." The guy behind the counter nodded before taking the cash I offered. "We'll need drinks too. Just a pitcher of water," I said. We'd all had more than enough soda for today.

"Thanks so much for inviting me today," Sassy said.

"You're family," Chloe said. "And this is the best birthday I've ever had."

"Good," I said. "I had a great day, too."

I was exhausted. We'd been on the move all day and I couldn't wait to crawl into bed.

"We should do this more often," Chloe said.

"If you're paying."

"I'm going to be gone all weekend," she said. "I'm babysitting from Friday night until Sunday morning."

"That's a lot of responsibility," I said tentatively.

"They have a security system. I'll be fine, and the kid is so easy."

"Okay, but you'll call if anything goes wrong?"

"I will, and if it goes well, they want me for the weekend after Thanksgiving as well."

"Here you go," the same kid who took our order said, placing our pizza in front of us and three plates. "Enjoy."

"Can I get some blue cheese?"

"And Ranch?" Sassy asked. The kid rolled his eyes, probably thinking that we were trying to get out of the surcharge for sauces, but I'd forgotten since I thought we were taking the pizza to go.

"Sure," he said.

"I have no idea how we've eaten so much," Sassy said.

"It's so good," I said. Pizza was one of my favorite foods. I liked food too much to actually try to decide which one was my favorite. Depending on my mood, I wanted something different.

"I really had the best day," Chloe said again. "Thanks so much."

"I love you, Squirt."

"I love you, too."

"I love you both."

"And we love you," I said back.

After we'd finished our pizza, we drove back to the trailer park. My mom's car was back and so was my dad's bike.

Great.

"I'll see you tomorrow," Sassy said as she walked off.

"Do you need a ride?" I asked.

"I'll text you."

"Bye!" Chloe called to her. Sassy waved, not turning around, and I wondered if she was going to meet Snake.

Right before I opened the door to the trailer, I heard the sound of glass breaking. Shit. "When we get inside, go right to our room."

"Hilly," she protested.

"I'm serious, Chloe, go." She nodded her assent, even though she was unhappy about it.

Taking a deep breath, I opened the door. Glass was covering the floor; it looked like a beer bottle. "How fucking dumb are you?" My dad seethed at my mom. "It's not fucking rocket science, you dumb bitch. I give you money, you buy groceries. There's nothing to fucking eat."

He wasn't wrong about there not being anything to eat. Had she spent the grocery money on cocaine again? Chloe went to our room, and I tried to follow, but I was prevented from following her when my hair was yanked and I was pulled back into the living room.

"Where do you think you're going?" My mother seethed. "Someone has to clean this mess up."

I tried to pry her hand out of my hair, but I failed. She was always stronger when she was high.

"And why is there no food? Are you and your sister taking it all?"

"No," I said. She acted like it wasn't her responsibility to feed her children that lived in this house.

"Don't lie to me."

"I'm not."

She released me and roughly turned me to her. Grabbing my arm, she twisted in opposite directions, one hand moving my wrist clockwise while the other moved my forearm counterclockwise. "Don't lie to me!"

"I'm not lying! Chloe and I eat the bare minimum."

If she wasn't careful, she was going to break my arm.

"Go to the grocery store tomorrow," my father barked at me. He slid me a few bills. "I want a receipt."

"Yes, sir."

"Ungrateful bitches. Fucking all of you."

I held my tongue. He could say what he wanted about me and my mom, but Chloe did nothing wrong, ever.

My mom finally released me. "Clean this up."

Dad stormed out of the trailer while Mom went to the bedroom. I cleaned the glass, making sure not to miss a spot, before walking into the bedroom.

"I'm fine," I told Chloe before she could even ask. "It's been a long day. Let's go to bed." Changing into my pajamas, I turned off the light and turned my phone back on, ignoring all the dings of messages that could only be from Will.

CHAPTER 14

THE GIFT CARD

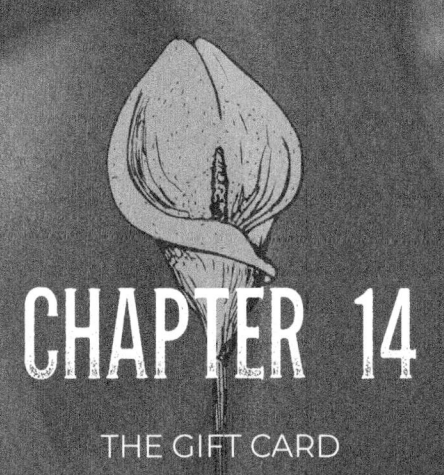

Will

Haley wasn't at school yesterday. It'd been less than a week since she'd cut me off, ending whatever frenemies with benefits relationship we had going.

And fuck if it wasn't driving me crazy. She was all I could think about. Going to the Halloween party with her almost made me feel like we were a real couple and dancing with her in my arms turned me on more than anything else in my life ever did. She was so fucking gorgeous. Her brown hair was lush and soft and I loved pulling on it. The tattoo and the nose ring, combined with the nearly permanent scowl that graced her pretty face, screamed not to fuck with her, but I loved pushing her buttons—all of them—and pushing her buttons, getting under her skin, led to fabulous sex.

And fuck me.

Somewhere along the way, caught up in the sex, I'd fallen for Haley fucking Winters.

How had I not seen it coming?

I wanted to protect her from whatever or whoever was hurting her. I knew her better than she thought I did, better than she'd ever admit to. I'd been watching her in AP calculus. People who didn't know her like I did wouldn't figure it out, but she was fucking smart, damn near a genius. How had no one ever noticed? By watching her, even when I wasn't in class with her, I'd seen her go into almost all the AP classes the school had. People just didn't pay attention to her, letting under the radar thanks to the protection of who her father was. Proving my suspicions, I'd strolled into Principal Potter's office after he'd left one day. The old man never locked his office. He was apathetic at best and didn't seem to take privacy seriously. It was easy enough for me to find the class rank list, and the number one spot—Haley. Number two was Mackenzie. Guess maybe I had a type. Except, having brains was the only thing they had in common. Mackenzie was a spoiled little rich girl with rich parents, too much money, access to the best tutors and would be able to afford any college she wanted to. Haley deserved that too. But how would she get out? She was betrothed to Snake like some mafia exchange.

Haley had no advantages in her life. She worked for everything she had. Even if she got into a good college, which she was guaranteed to do with her grades, would she be able to afford it? Not only that, but the more time I spent with her, the more of her I got to know, the harder I fell. Everything she accomplished, she did while being abused, while being Viper's daughter. The times I saw her out in town with her sister, she was so protective of her. The more I saw, the more I knew, and the more I knew, the more I liked. Her attitude, the hard shell, it was all an act to protect herself.

I'd never be able to tell her how I felt. She'd run. I knew her, she'd run. But that didn't mean that we couldn't still do what we'd been doing. We'd just need to be more careful. If it meant more time with her, I could be more discreet.

As I pulled into the front parking lot of the school, I couldn't even remember the drive, too consumed by thoughts of my girl. She hated that I called her dollface, didn't see it as a compliment, but the nickname stuck. It was doll or Hales more often than not now, but it originated because she looked like a doll. She had soft, smooth skin, like a doll, and her eyes were big, round and curious. In the moments right before I'd decided to kiss her for the first time, it felt fitting.

As I was walking into the school, my question about whether she would show up today or not was answered. I saw her, standing with the Southside crowd, a cigarette between her fingers. She never smoked when we were together. Was it just another part of her act? A part of the wall she'd built up around herself?

I was determined to get inside those walls.

"What's up?" Jordy asked, coming up next to me and pulling my attention away from my girl.

"Not a lot," I said, taking his offered hand and patting him on the back. Football season was over and we didn't win any championships. Jordy was a good quarterback, but the rest of us were just mediocre. The only benefit I'd gotten from playing football was the wide shoulders and muscles from the weight room.

Haley loved those muscles.

"You seem distracted lately."

"I know."

"Maybe you should get back with Mackenzie," he offered the worst advice in the history of our friendship.

"Fuck no," I said with a laugh. "She deserves someone who loves her. I don't."

"Love? It's fucking high school. Just bang her until she leaves for college."

"Don't be such a tool," I said, shoving his shoulder. "She deserves better than that."

And after having Haley, there was no way in hell I could ever go back to Mackenzie.

"Suit yourself. Why do you come in for first period? I sure as hell wouldn't if I had a free period."

For Haley.

"Because how could I possibly give up our romantic morning walks into the school?" I asked, fluttering my eyelashes at him. "Besides, during football season, it was required."

"Season's over."

"Habit." The bell rang as we were walking inside, and I headed to the office to sign in while Jordy made his way down the hall.

As I was walking in, Haley was walking out. "Hales," I whispered. Her body still reacted to mine, a shiver leaving her, but she kept her head down, refusing to meet my eyes.

"Good to see you two getting along," Principal Potter said.

"We're not. We just ignore each other." He looked at me disbelievingly, and I had a feeling he may have some idea about what suddenly changed between us.

It was his fault anyway. What did he expect when he put two headstrong teenagers in a contained space together?

By the time I'd signed in, Haley was gone from the hallway. I had no idea where she'd been hiding out during first period, and I'd looked all over the school for her, but never found her.

Maybe she went back to her car?

Deciding to check, I dumped my books in my locker before walking out the back door. There were still a few of the Southside kids hanging out, but she wasn't amongst them. Thankfully, they were mostly underclassmen who wouldn't pick a fight. I made a show of pulling out my phone, like I was taking a call and had reason to be out back as I weaved through the cars until I got to Haley's. She wasn't in it, so I made my way back to the front.

Pulling up our message thread on my phone, I reread the last few texts I'd sent her. They'd all gone unanswered.

> Me: We can be more careful.
> Me: Answer me, dollface.
> Me: Come on, Hales.

When I made it to the student lounge where most of the seniors hung out during their free periods, I sat on a chair and texted her again.

Me: Where are you, doll?

No answer.

I'd give her through the rest of the week and the weekend, but come Monday morning, I was going to find her hiding spot and I was going to get her back.

I half paid attention in most of my classes throughout the day, which was pretty much normal for me. But my day didn't perk up until AP calculus. Why was our school uniform so sexy on Haley? Did she dress like that to torture me? Probably not. She probably didn't even give me a second thought when she was getting dressed in the morning. She'd made it clear this was just sex for her, and it was for me, too. At least it had been until somehow I'd managed to fuck up and let myself fall for her.

Her hair was loose and wild around her face, the best look on her. Her uniform shirt hugged her chest tightly, and that skirt showed me her thick thighs, the ones I loved to have wrapped around me.

As she walked by me, her uniform shirt pulled up at the sleeve, revealing a fresh bruise on her arm.

It was a fucking handprint.

Anger radiated off of me. Her eyes caught mine, and I glanced down at her arm. Her eyes fell to it too, and she quickly covered it, tugging the sleeve down. After that, she refused to look at me.

Who the fuck was doing this to her? And why was she protecting them?

It had to be someone she cared about.

Grabbing my phone, I texted her before Ms. Smalls came into the class.

Me: Meet me in the janitor's closet after school.

I wasn't surprised when her phone beeped. Turning to look at her over my shoulder, I watched her read it. And then I watched her thumb swipe left and hit one single button, deleting it. I wasn't sure she even read it. All my messages over the past few days had probably just been deleted.

Fuck.

She really was trying to cut me off.

The only hope I had of getting her to speak to me was to get her alone.

I did my best to pay attention to Ms. Smalls as she lectured about limits or some shit. I couldn't even be sure how I ended up in this class because I wasn't a genius. This was the only AP class I took and the only one I had with Haley. Maybe that's what I was doing sitting here.

When class was dismissed, I took my time waiting for the hallways to be mostly empty before I slipped into our janitor's closet.

I waited nearly thirty minutes, lights off, staring at my phone before finally giving up.

She wasn't coming.

Grabbing my bag from my locker, I walked to my truck. I wasn't in the mood to go home, and now that football was over, I had way more time to kill. I'd been happy when the season was finally over, thinking I'd have more time to spend with Haley.

As I was buckling up, my phone started ringing in my pocket. Disappointment filled me as I saw my mom's name on the screen and not Haley's.

"Hey Mom," I said as I brought the phone to my ear.

"Hey sweetheart," she said. "Can you stop at the grocery store on your way home? I forgot a few things for dinner."

"What are we having?"

"Fajitas."

"Only because you're making my favorite this time."

"Of course." It was no secret that my mom and dad valued their relationship as the foundation of our family. For a while, I hated it, but after watching my friend's parents who put their kids above all else, including themselves and their relationship, I didn't have it so bad. Maybe my parents actually got it right. "I'll text you the list, and I transferred some money to your bank account."

"Thanks, Mom. I'm leaving school now, I'll be home soon."

"Drive safe. I love you, sweetie."

"I love you, too, Mom."

Tossing my phone into the passenger seat, I pulled out of the parking lot and headed to Ralph's grocery store. Mom always drove a few towns over to the Walmart to do her grocery shopping. She'd probably gotten distracted by the Christmas decorations that were already on all the shelves. She was a little spacey sometimes, but it was one of the things my dad loved most about her. She was a free spirit, a little wild, which didn't make sense to me since she was Suzy Homemaker when she was home. And if she was making my favorite for dinner, that also probably meant she was making my favorite dessert—chocolate chunk brownies.

When I pulled into the grocery store, I parked in the back, not wanting anyone to put a dent in my truck. My parents bought it gently used, basically new. Dad had an in at the bank and whenever a repossession came in, Dad got the chance to buy it. He'd only had to pay what the bank wanted for it, which was much less than its value.

Opening the text message from my mom, I read the list: hot sauce, guacamole, refried beans, ice cream. She hadn't specified an ice cream flavor, meaning I got to choose. Another message popped up.

Mom: Get yourself a snack too, sweetie. Chips or something.

Grabbing a small basket, I went to the produce section first, getting the guacamole. Not in a hurry to get home, I walked slowly up and down every aisle. I was debating what hot sauce to choose when I saw Haley coming down the aisle. She had her head down, focused on her phone, and she hadn't seen me yet.

Stepping back, I stood in the path of her cart, knowing she'd run into me since she wasn't paying attention. Ten seconds later, she bumped right into my legs.

"I'm so sorry!" She said before realizing who she'd bumped into. "Hales."

Her face went red. "Are you stalking me now?" She hissed.

"No. My mom sent me a grocery list."

Her cart didn't have a lot in it, but I noticed that it was full of only foods that were Ralph's brand and no fresh fruits or vegetables. Were they too expensive for her? Did she have to pay for food with her own money? Her parents were so shitty, they probably barely fed her and Chloe. Haley was eighteen, why hadn't she left yet? I was also surprised her parents hadn't kicked her out yet, or forced her to marry Snake yet. He was eighteen too, as far as I knew.

"Leave me alone, Will."

"I saw the bruise on your arm."

"It's not your concern."

"If it concerns you, it concerns me."

"We're not together, Will! And we're not sleeping together anymore."

It was a bad idea to be having this conversation here, but I couldn't bring myself to care, and apparently neither could she.

"You don't deserve the abuse."

"Goodbye Will." She turned her cart around and headed back in the direction she came from. If an old lady hadn't been coming down towards her, I would have chased after her. Instead, I grabbed hot sauce and refried beans before heading for the ice cream. As much as there was still shit I wanted to say to her, now wasn't the time or place.

I grabbed a gallon of butter pecan ice cream and headed for the checkout. I saw Haley walk by the ice cream aisle, her head looking up to read the signs so she could find whatever else was on her list.

As I was checking out, I saw the gift cards. She'd be pissed if she ever found out. "Can I ask you something?" I asked the cashier. She wasn't from town, making me feel like what I was about to do was safe. "If I put some money on this gift card, will you give it to the girl who comes through here? She's my age, has a hoop in her nose, brown hair, light brown eyes."

"Um, sure?"

"But she can't know it's from me. Tell her she's the hundredth customer of the day, or she got a secret item that triggered the gift card."

"Um. Maybe I should talk to my manager."

"Don't please. Look, I'm just trying to do something nice for someone who needs it, but she won't accept my help."

"Okay," she agreed reluctantly.

"I'll pay cash for the gift card and use my debit card for the groceries." I didn't pay attention to the total as she told me, just swiped my card. Next I had her put fifty bucks on the gift card and pulled a fifty from my wallet. "Thanks for your help," I told her.

"No problem," she smiled.

I took my one bag of groceries and left the store. If Haley saw me again and then got a gift card, she'd figure it out. I'd need luck on my side for her to not figure it out as it was.

"Thanks for the fajitas, Mom," I said when we were all sitting down to dinner.

"You're welcome."

"How's work, Dad?"

"Same old same old. Still trying to figure out what's going on with the Southside."

I wondered if Haley knew. She didn't seem that interested in anything to do with the gang, never even speaking about it.

I only nodded, taking a bite of the chicken fajitas Mom made.

"Can I ask you a question?" He nodded yes, waiting expectantly. "If you had a friend who needed help, but wouldn't let you help them, what would you do?"

"Depends on the situation. Is this person hurting themselves or someone else?"

"What if they were the person being hurt?"

"Do you need to tell me something?"

"Not yet," I told him. "I just need some advice."

"So, this friend, they're being hurt?"

"Yes."

"Do you know by whom?"

"They won't tell me."

Dad set his fork down, folding his hands in front of him. "How worried are you for her safety?" He guessed it was about a girl. He wasn't wrong.

"Very."

"Then I wouldn't give up. You can't force someone to accept your help, but if you didn't do everything you could do to help, how would you feel about yourself?"

"Pretty shitty."

"Language," my mother chastised me.

"Sorry," I said to appease her, even though I didn't mean it.

"You need to tread carefully," Dad warned me. "You don't want to make the situation worse. Mostly, you just need to make sure she knows she can count on you, and that when she's ready, you'll help her. And if it's bad, I'll help her too."

He would. It wouldn't matter to him that she was Viper's daughter. He'd help anyone regardless.

"Thanks, Dad."

He nodded at me and went back to eating his dinner.

After the dishes were cleaned, I took a brownie and went to my room, scrolling through all my old messages with Haley.

Monday. I'd wait until Monday, give her a little distance over the weekend and not see if I could accidentally run into her on Sunday. Those days, watching her with her sister, were some of my favorites. In the beginning, it really was an accident, randomly running into her. But once I figured out that she spent almost every Sunday with her little sister, I purposely went all over town until I ran into her. I'd just gotten lucky a few times. It was a small town; there weren't that many places for teenagers to hang out.

My mind raced trying to figure out where she could be hiding. I pulled everything I knew about her to the front of my mind. She was never in the gym or the wrestling or weight rooms. She wasn't ever in the student lounge.

It was the library.

Now that I knew how smart she was, it made perfect sense that she'd hide out there, hiding her work from prying eyes.

Come Monday, I'd find her in the library, and I'd make sure she knew she was mine.

CHAPTER 15

THE LIBRARY

Haley

Monday morning, I sat in the library, where I'd been hiding for the past week from Will. Ending it with him hadn't changed anything—I still wanted him.

I fucking missed him.

I'd thought about calling Bobby to try to get Will out of my system, but now that I'd had him, I didn't know if I could be with Bobby again—no matter what I'd said last time I'd seen him. It wasn't the same.

I was addicted to Will, but only in a sexual sense. I still hated him and his good-boy reputation and his daddy sheriff.

Which is why I'd cut myself off from him—cold fucking turkey. No more. After the Halloween party, it was an easy decision. We were playing with fire and I couldn't afford to get burnt before I blew out of this town.

I was leaving in a few short months anyway, but that didn't mean I wanted to be caught with him, and being caught was exactly what we were asking for, then the entire school would know. Hell, we'd almost been caught—once by my sister at the pizza place and then by Logan's dad at the party. Hell, Sassy *had* caught us. We were lucky nobody else from Lake View was at the party. Going to the party with him felt like a date. We'd danced, and I hadn't cared who'd seen. But I didn't want to think about what would happen if we were exposed.

It'd been over a week since the last time and each one of his texts went ignored. I wouldn't give in, but I missed his touch. Today was day ten without his touch. That should have been long enough to get him out of my system, but it wasn't.

I'd thought—hoped—he'd given up since I hadn't heard from him since running into him at the grocery store last week. But that was a lie, I hadn't been hoping to not hear from him. Truthfully, not having his attention on me was making things worse. I wanted him to want me, even though I wouldn't let him have me. Right on cue, my phone beeped.

> Asshole: where are you, Hales?

My core flooded with heat as I read the text, but I ignored it anyway. I would be strong.

> Asshole: you wanna play hide and seek dollface? You won't like what happens when I catch you.

Spasm.

Fuck.

And worst of fucking all was that nickname. It had grown on me to the point that I actually liked it. He used it sarcastically when other people were around, and it made me instantly wet for him. Even in his sarcastic tone, all I could hear was the husky way he whispered it in my ear when it was just the two of us. Recently it had been cut short to just doll most of the time or *Hales*. Hales was my favorite, nobody else ever called me that.

I wanted him to find me. But I didn't, and I did. But he never would. I was hiding in the furthest corner of the library. Not even the cleaners ever came back here; that's how much dust there was. Next time principal Potter wanted to give somebody detention and force them to clean, he should do it back here.

Asshole: you know how much I like games doll

He wouldn't find me here; he'd probably never even set foot in the library.

Ignoring the beeping of my phone, I focused on my creative writing essay. It was hard to come up with a story that wasn't cliche and hadn't been done before. My teacher said that cliches were fine, that it was the author who made each story unique. So I was writing a story about a girl who hated her life and grew up to find out she was adopted. She was searching for her birth mother because she wanted revenge, to know how her mother could have chosen to put her into the care of such abusive people.

It was only one of two creative writing projects for the entire semester. It had to be between 50,000 and 75,000 words. I was reaching the climax, and it was already 68,000 words. I may need to cut some scenes, but I could edit them back later.

"Told you I'd find you."

I nearly jumped out of my skin at Will's voice.

Fuck.

No way would I be able to resist him all alone. It was hard enough resisting him in the grocery store last week, and we'd been surrounded by people.

"Go away," I said, but my voice betrayed the meaning. I didn't mean the words. Ten days without him was too long.

"You've been avoiding me for days, doll."

"Can't take a hint?" I said in an annoyed voice. And I was officially one of those girls—one of the ones who told guys to leave them alone when all they really wanted was to keep being chased.

"We both know you don't want me to." I hated that he suddenly found me so easy to read. "Why don't I show you what happens when you ignore me," he said darkly.

My body hummed in anticipation.

I tried to fight it... I did, but I wasn't quick enough. The only way to tell him no was to keep enough space between us so he couldn't touch me because once he got his hands on me, I wouldn't say no. I wouldn't want to. I was trapped in the corner of the library with nowhere to go, making me easy prey.

Will caught me and pulled me to my feet. Roughly and wordlessly, he tugged on my hair, tilting my head back. His mouth descended on mine, capturing my lips in an urgent and dominating kiss. I let him have control... for now.

Quickly, he spun me around and lifted my skirt over my ass before moving my thong to the side.

"Will," I whispered needfully.

"Shh," he said. "Be a good girl and be quiet so we don't get caught." He squeezed my ass before I heard his zipper being undone. His fingers pushed through my folds, finding my soaking pussy.

"Your fucking soaked, dollface, just the anticipation is enough."

I was always wet and ready for him, a fact I hated. My body betrayed me when it came to him, and I couldn't control myself.

"Shut up!"

One hand on my hip and the other on digging into the back of my neck, Will slammed himself into me. No foreplay, but it didn't matter because like he'd said, I was soaked.

"Mmm," I moaned loudly.

"Quiet!" He said harshly in my ear. The hand on my neck moved to cover my mouth as he pounded into me. I moaned around him, already so close. I went to move my hand to my clit in an effort to get myself off quicker. "Don't," he snapped. Will grabbed both of my wrists and trapped them behind my back, pushing my breasts out and against the bookcase. With every thrust, my nipples got harder and harder, feeling the roughness of the shelf, even through my skimpy bra. "Bad girls don't get to come. But I do," he said darkly. "And I'm already so close. I never last inside your tight cunt, it's too fucking good."

Will fucked me in long, deep strokes, building the tension in my abdomen. His words hadn't fully registered, but they finally did when I was just about to come and he pulled out. I heard his sexy as hell groaning and moaning. Looking over my shoulder, I watched as he stroked himself to orgasm, coating my ass in his cum.

"Bad girls don't get to come," he repeated. "How long will it be before you have to sneak away to the bathroom and get yourself off?" He asked smugly. "You won't make it until lunch."

Before I could snap at him and tell him to hand me a tissue, he was moving my thong back in place and pulling my skirt down. He rubbed it against his release, making sure I'd spend my entire day covered in him—smelling like him.

"Later, dollface," he said before tucking himself back into his pants and finally retreating. My head spun. I hadn't even had an orgasm, and that was still better than anyone else I'd ever been with.

Sexually frustrated and annoyed as hell with Will, I gathered my stuff to head to the bathroom. Not that it mattered, my skirt and panties would be ruined.

But two could play at his game.

By fourth period, my sexual frustration was out of control. I couldn't focus in any of my classes and every time I passed Will in the hallway, all I wanted to do was slam him against a locker and force him to fuck me until I came.

By lunch period, I'd boiled over.

Phone in hand, I leaned against Will's brand new Silverado. It had four doors and all the luxurious upgrades. Of course, it did. Fucking rich kids.

> Me: meet me at your truck
> Me: Now, Will.

Five minutes later, I heard him. "What's up, doll?"

"Get in," I commanded him.

He looked at me before opening the truck and climbing into the back seat. I climbed in behind him and shut the door. I looked out to make sure nobody saw us and was thankful for the dark tinted windows.

"Wha-" he went to ask something, but before he could, I had my hands on his pants, unbuckling them and pulling his cock out. He was already hard for me. Thank God, because I was drenched, my pussy a sopping mess for him.

"I'm going to fuck you," I said.

"Your fingers not do it for you?" He asked with a laugh.

"Didn't use them. You weren't that good," I said, taunting him. But he was. Of course he fucking was, otherwise I wouldn't be sitting in the back of his truck about to mount him like he was a prized stallion.

I turned, facing away from him and straddled him. Pulling my panties to the side, I impaled myself on his cock. "Fuck, Haley," he groaned. His hands dug into my hips while I rode him. I wasn't wasting any time, still too turned on by the way he'd fucked me earlier. I leaned my back against his chest and flicked my clit while I rode him. "Just like that, Hales. I love how wet you always are for me." My pussy clenched as he whispered 'Hales' in my ear while I rode him. I also knew that he loved how wet I always was. He didn't need to tell me, but he was always smug about it, loving the effect he had on me.

Will pulled my shirt open, thankfully not ripping any buttons as he went. His hands pulled my bra down, letting my breasts spill out. His hands ran up my body until he cupped them. I moaned as he squeezed them roughly before pinching both of my nipples. My head fell back, resting against his shoulder, and I felt his teeth scrape at my neck.

"I'm so close," I whimpered. I was making myself sound needier than usual. I needed him to get me off before he was close to finishing. His hands pinched and pulled at my nipples more, making me ride him faster. "Yes! Yes! Yes!" I cried, my pussy spasming around him, my orgasm consuming me.

"Fuck," he cursed in my ear.

He was too close to his own release.

As soon as I came down from my very satisfying orgasm—maybe putting it off had been more rewarding—I climbed off of him.

"Where are you going?" He asked, dumbfounded.

I looked at his hard cock—it was glistening. I wanted to take him into my mouth, but he needed to be taught a lesson.

"Later, asshole," I said. "See if you can last longer than me before you go to the bathroom and finish yourself off."

With those words, I straightened my skirt and underwear, buttoned my shirt and climbed out of his truck. His truck would smell like me, smell like sex when he climbed into it after school. *Good.* Let him remember that I can play just as well as he can. I looked around, once again thankful there was nobody nearby.

Sated and completely smug, I walked back into the school.

I was feeling pretty good about myself by the time last period came and I walked into Ms. Small's class.

Will was seething and it only added to my glee. When he walked down the row, I could see the outline of his still hard cock in his pants. He'd flashed it at me by moving his strategically placed notebook, guess hadn't taken care of himself.

He was trying to win.

I wouldn't let him.

> Me: What's wrong?
> Asshole: I hate you so fucking much.
> Me: good thing your cock doesn't.

I turned my phone off after that.

When the bell rang and school was done for the day, I stayed in my seat. I had to hide from Will so he couldn't get his hands on me again. Ms. Smalls didn't even care and left me alone. I waited about thirty minutes, mindlessly trying to finish my creative writing assignment.

Finally, I packed up my stuff and headed out of the classroom and down the empty hallway.

I only made it to the next classroom before I was being pulled into the Chemistry lab. It had high black work stations and swivel chairs. The door slammed closed. I hadn't seen him yet, but I knew it was Will.

"I hate you so fucking much," he whispered. I didn't feel the need to reply as he dragged me to the corner closest to the wall where nobody would see us if they walked by and pushed me against the lab table before lifting me onto it and pushing my knees apart so he could step between them. His mouth descended on mine, but unlike in the library this morning, I didn't let him have control. I wrapped my fingers around his neck and squeezed, thrusting my tongue into his mouth, making him moan into my mouth.

God, this was so bad, anybody could walk in here and see us. We were getting less and less discreet, which was why I'd ended things. But I'd fallen back into his trap, and now, I didn't want to escape. Sex with him was the only thing helping me survive this year.

I sank my teeth into his bottom lip, hard enough to draw blood before pulling away.

"We can't do this here," I said. "Anybody could walk in. Don't the nerds have a club in here?"

"There's a Dungeons and Dragons tournament. They won't be here today." I wanted to ask how he knew that, but he was dropping to his knees. He pushed my skirt up and pulled my panties down, pushing them into his pocket.

Wordlessly, he licked through my core. "Yes," I groaned. My hand went to his head, holding him there as he fucked his tongue into me. "Will!"

Pulling away from me, he rubbed slow, torturous circles against my clit. "This is the third time I'll have been inside your tight little cunt today. I turned Haley Winters into my own personal slut."

"Shut up," I snapped at him. He chuckled before reattaching his mouth to me. Lifting my legs, I dug my heels into the desk and lifted my hips into his face. Will knew just how to touch me to make me lose my damn mind. He wrapped his lips around my clit and slid two fingers inside me, knowing it would push me over the edge in an instant. His fingers curled against my g-spot and his teeth grazed my sensitive clit as I saw stars. "Yes!"

Breathing heavily, I waited for him to stand back to his feet. I pushed him backwards, my hand in the center of his chest, and I dropped to my knees, my entire body shielded by the desk. Will braced his hands on the lab table while I unbuckled his pants. He was hard as steel for me. I tugged them down and pushed his shirt up before wrapping my lips around him and bobbing up and down on him. I didn't give him a teasing buildup, just swallowed around him.

He tasted like me.

With one hand on his balls, I jacked him off with the other while I bobbed up and down on him. His hands went to my hair, and I let him have his little moment of control, let him force me down and push my nose against him, making me gag before pulling back a little only to force me back down. Spit dripped out around my mouth and down my chin, soaking my shirt. When he was in the back of my throat again, I swallowed, loving the way he moaned for me. When he finally released me, I stood to my feet.

Will helped me back onto the desk and pushed my thighs open before sliding himself easily into me. "Harder," I begged immediately. I was so fucking desperate for him and I didn't know who I hated more for it—him or me.

He pinned his arms under my legs, making me bend my knees and lay my legs over his arms while he slammed into me, forcing me to bite my lip to silence myself. His cock pounded into me, the sounds of my wet pussy filling the science lab. I was worried someone would walk by and hear the unmistakable sounds of him slamming into me, the sounds of sex that couldn't be denied.

"I hate you so fucking much," he growled. "But I love this fucking cunt." He slammed into me. I was gripping the edge of the desk. When he released my legs, I wrapped my legs around his waist and tugged myself against him, our entire upper bodies pushing together. "You love it too. You're fucking obsessed with my dick."

"Fuck, I hate you so much."

"But you love my dick. Say it," he grunted in my ear.

"Fuck. I love it, Will. I love your cock. You're the biggest I've ever had, the best," I finally admitted the words we both already knew were true out loud. I'd been avoiding saying them for months. "I'm so close again," I moaned.

"Me too," he said through his own moaning. "I'm gonna fill you," he said.

I wrapped one hand around his neck, squeezing into it. "Beg for it. You wanna fill my pussy?" I asked. "Beg me for it, Will."

My fingers dug into his neck and his eyes rolled back in his head in pleasure.

"Haley, fuck. Let me come inside you," he said. "Please. Damn. I need to fill you."

"More," I commanded him, squeezing even tighter.

"Please," he pleaded. His eyes locked on mine as he looked at me, blue pools clouded with lust and need—for me. "Let me fill your perfect pussy. I'm begging, Haley."

"Fuck. Fuck. Fuck! Will!" His words and merciless thrusting pushed me over the edge. "Come inside me."

I squeezed his neck with both hands as he came, spilling himself inside me, coating my inner walls in his release. My body shuddered with aftershocks.

"I hate you, dollface," he said through his panting breath.

"Feelings still mutual, asshole," I said.

Will tucked himself back into his pants before leaving. He'd taken my panties with him and left me to clean up the desk and straighten myself out.

I hated him.

Without panties, our combined release was dripping down my legs. I grabbed a paper towel from the hand washing station and tucked it between my legs, hoping it would stay put at least long enough to get me out of the building without someone seeing the evidence of what we'd just been doing all over my legs.

Thankfully, nobody was around when I walked out of the classroom. I desperately needed a shower. And *fuck me*. Will Roberts had somehow become more than an enemy with benefits.

CHAPTER 16

THE MIRROR

Will

"What are you doing tomorrow night?" Jordy asked me when he sat down next to me at our usual lunch table. "Another party with your secret girlfriend?"

"Maybe." I smirked as thoughts of my girl filled my mind.

Haley had finally fucking caved. Hearing her admit I was the best and biggest she's ever had, did things to my ego. The last time we'd fucked, in the chemistry lab, was the best it had ever been, but she'd had too much damn control, and I was tired of not being able to take her on a damn bed. I wanted her beneath me, writhing and screaming my name. The Halloween party gave me a taste, but a couch was not the same as a bed, which was why I was planning on doing the most reckless thing I'd ever done.

Haley mentioned offhandedly that her little sister was going to be gone Saturday night babysitting, that meant she was going to have her room to herself. And it was time I showed her who was in control. Sneaking through the trailer park after dark was a surefire way to get myself shot at, but that's what fucking Haley had done to me—she made me lose all my damn sense and not be able to think about nothing but her, not even my own safety.

"When are you gonna let me meet her? Scared she'll like me more if you introduce us?"

"Not a fucking chance," I said. "Besides, it's not serious. It's just sex. No point introducing her to the family."

"Family?" Jordy said, fluttering his eyelashes and placing his hands over his heart like a damn idiot. I just rolled my eyes at him. I'd taken to sitting on the other side of the table, next to Jordy instead of across from him so I could look at Haley.

I was becoming obsessed with her and I couldn't figure out how to stop it. I didn't want to stop it. I was still staring when my phone buzzed on the table.

> Hales: Stop fucking staring. It's creepy.

Fuck. I was busted, but I couldn't let her see me flustered or feeling guilty.

> Me: Just thinking about how you told me I was the best and the biggest you ever had. Hurts doesn't it? Knowing the guy you hate will be the best you ever get.
> Hales: Comments made during sex are inadmissible

I chuckled to myself. Only Haley Winters would use the words inadmissible and sex in the same sentence.

> Me: Keep telling yourself that, Doll.

I watched her read the message and turn her phone over, not bothering to answer. And I didn't bother to stop staring at her. Instead, I texted her again.

> Me: Our spot. After school.
> Hales: Can't. I've got to work. Bobby has a game and I need to cover his shift.

I hated that she still worked with that asshole. It wasn't jealousy. He just wasn't good enough for her, and I didn't share.

Me: Right now then.

"I'll be back," I said to the table. Nobody even paid attention, all too engrossed in their own Thanksgiving and Winter break plans to focus.

I'd only been waiting about thirty seconds when the door to the janitor's closet opened. I could smell Haley's perfume; it was intoxicating, like my favorite drink. "What do you want?" She asked, her tone conveying all the annoyance she felt for me.

"What I always want, Hales." Reaching out for her, I pulled her close. The space was so confined that, even in the dark, I always knew where she was. I loved the way her breath hitched for me, unable to hide her reactions to me, as much as she tried to deny it.

"We don't have time," she whispered out breathily. She was trying to deny me, but it wasn't working. I loved when she took control, grabbed me by the throat and demanded me to fuck her harder or make her come on my tongue. But this—those few precious moments I got before her brain turned back on and she realized she didn't want to let me have my fun—was my favorite, and tomorrow night, I planned on taking and keeping control. She'd had her fun in the chemistry lab, and now it was my turn. She thought what I'd given to her in the library was teasing? I had bigger plans.

"Not for me," I whispered in her ear. My lips brushed against the shell of her ear as I spoke. Moving my lips down, I nipped at the lobe, making her turn her head to give me greater access. One hand pushed into her lower back, making her arch for me like I loved. With my other hand, I traced delicate circles up her legs, back and forth between both thighs. Out of instinct, she spread her legs for me. "Lace today?" I asked as my fingers brushed against the delicate fabric. "Did you wear these for me?"

"Yes," she whimpered. Usually she'd give me a defiant no, telling me she didn't dress for me. I'd figured out she was lying, and she didn't deny it anymore. I was already liking the direction this was going.

"Another pair to add to my collection." Her protest died on her pouty lips when I pushed them to the side and slid my fingers through her. Her head rolled back, digging into the wall, and her chest pushed out. Pushing my lips against her exposed throat, I bit softly into her creamy skin, making her moan louder for me. I rubbed quick, teasing circles against her clit, making her hand clutch the doorknob. She couldn't break that like she'd done the paper towel dispenser at homecoming. If she broke that, we'd be trapped in here together, and as appealing as that thought was, it would definitely lead to us getting caught.

"Will," she whimpered. I loved hearing her be all needy for me. Pulling away from her clit, I slid my fingers lower, toying with her entrance. "More, please," she begged. I didn't comment on the begging—every time I did, she snapped out of her trance, that wasn't what I wanted. Giving her what she'd so sweetly begged for, I pushed two fingers inside of her. I felt her squeeze around me. Pulling myself out of the crook of her neck, I watched her. She had her eyes closed, head lolled back and was sinking her teeth into her bottom lip in an effort to suppress her moans. I hated that ninety-five percent of the time we were fucking she had to be quiet to prevent us from getting caught.

When her eyes popped open, she caught me staring at her. I couldn't place the look on her face, but I ignored it and pushed my lips against hers. Haley's hand clutched at the back of my head, her fingers digging into the locks of my hair and making me hiss. For the first time, she submitted easily, letting me push my tongue into her mouth and sweep it against hers. I moaned into her mouth, exploring every inch while she tried to keep up. Our lips moved perfectly together, something I was all too aware of. When she whimpered into my mouth, I knew she was close, which was exactly why I pulled my fingers from her again. That was two. One more close call and I was going to walk out of the janitor's closet.

She groaned in frustration as I moved my fingers between her soaked folds up to her straining clit. "Tell me what a slut you are for me," I whispered in her ear. I felt her squirm against me. "Tell me, Hales."

"Fuck Will," she said frustratedly. "I'm a slut for you."

"My slut."

"Your slut. I'm your slut, Will."

"Good girl."

I pushed harder against her clit, and her hips rocked as she started chasing after the high she *thought* was coming.

It wasn't.

"Oh god. Will. Yes!"

And then I pulled my hand from her skirt.

"What?" She snapped.

"Too bad you can't meet me after school, so I can finish the job. Guess you were right. We don't have time."

When she went to speak again, I pushed the fingers I'd had inside her into her mouth. I half expected her to bite me, but it was worth the risk to watch as she licked them clean, her gaze turning even more heated as she did.

"See you Monday, Hales. First period."

"Fuck, I hate you."

"Hate you too, dollface. Later."

I slipped out of the janitor's closet and walked across the hall into the bathroom just in time for the bell to ring. When I came out of the bathroom, the hallways were filled with students, including Haley. She looked frustrated, and I had to stop myself from grinning.

The rest of the day was uneventful, until AP calculus.

I was already seated in my seat when Haley walked by my row to the back of the class for her usual seat. She flipped me the bird, not caring who saw it. Anybody who did would just think that we were having one of our usual fights and not that she was pissed at me for edging her and then denying her. I winked at her, pissing her off even more.

My phone beeped and I didn't need to look to know it was from her.

> Hales: Asshole
> Me: <3

I heard her slam her phone on her desk before sighing heavily.

By the time class ended, I was filled with glee, happy with the way my plan was going. When the bell rang, Haley was the first person out the door, despite sitting in the furthest corner of the room.

> Me: I know you won't make yourself come. You're too stubborn and too prideful. You'll be rewarded for that.
> Hales: Watch me.

We'd see about that. I'd know tomorrow night for sure if she'd touched herself or not.

I SPENT MOST OF THE DAY SATURDAY COUNTING DOWN THE MINUTES until it was dark enough that I could sneak over to Haley's. My parents were gone for the weekend, which meant I could have easily just asked her to sneak over here, but she wouldn't have. She wasn't there yet. Somewhere in the last two months of us sleeping together, I'd stupidly let myself fall for her. It wasn't love, obviously it wasn't love. I just didn't hate her anymore. That wasn't completely true either. I was confused, that was pretty much the only thing I knew. I also wasn't sure how or when it happened, but it had, and she'd fallen for me too, I thought anyway. But she was as stubborn as the day was long and would never admit it—not easily anyway—but I could be patient.

"I beat you again," Jordy said, pulling me away from my thoughts of Haley. "Where's your head at?" He came over in the afternoon to play video games.

"I'm good," I brushed him off.

"You're hiding something. It's this secret girl. Who is she?"

"It doesn't matter. I told you it's just sex."

"Then why are you spaced out all the time? Why do I catch you with a goofy fucking grin on your face whenever you're quiet? Because you're thinking about her."

"Thinking about the position I fucked her in, probably," I said gruffly. I cringed at my own words. Haley didn't deserve to be talked about like that, but I didn't know how else to get Jordy off my case.

"Your face is giving away your lie, and I know it's not Mackenzie. Who is it?"

"You don't know her."

"Dude. We've been best friends for our entire lives. I know when you're lying. I also know that you have a post sex glow half the time you're at school, so clearly I do know her."

"I'm not ready to tell you yet," I tried a different approach.

"Fine. But I'm right, aren't I?"

"Does it matter?"

"No, but you never keep things from me," he pouted. I just rolled my eyes at his dramatics. "But um, I've been asking because there's something I want to confess."

"Okay?"

"I'm dating Mackenzie."

My head fell back in a deep laugh, my body shaking. I tried to stop, but I couldn't. The harder I laughed, the worse it got, and Jordy looked at me like I had grown a second head. I went to talk, but choked on air because I was still laughing. Tears fell from my eyes with how hard I was laughing. That must be the reason he'd been asking if I wanted to get back together with her.

"I'm serious."

"I- kn-ow," I snorted out. When he slapped the back of my head, the laughing finally stopped. "I know you're serious," I said, wiping under my eyes. "You'd never joke about that."

"You're not pissed?"

"Fuck no."

"Bros before hoes?"

"Don't call your girl a hoe," I told him seriously. "I don't care because we're not together anymore, and I never loved her. She deserves that. She's not a bad person, just spoiled and naïve."

"Okay, well, I'm going to her place now."

"Don't get her pregnant."

Jordy flipped me the bird before walking out of my room and out of the house. It was still too early for me to go to Haley's, so I scrolled through social media for a bit while laying on my bed. Haley didn't have any social media, not even a private one. I wondered if that was a rule from her dad? Snake didn't have one either.

Finally, after I'd heated up the burritos Mom left me for dinner and ate, I got ready to go to my girl's.

It was dark outside, the moon barely visible through the clouds as I walked to my truck and climbed in. I drove to the methodist church, parking where Haley had when we'd gone to Hillview for the Halloween party. As I climbed out, I double checked my surroundings and made sure nobody saw me. Walking close to the tree line, I stayed hidden as I walked quickly towards the trailer park.

It took me nearly twenty minutes to walk there, but it was worth it. When I crept through the broken fence into the back of the trailer park, I didn't exactly know where to go. I wasn't sure which was hers, and I couldn't exactly ask her without giving myself away, so I looked for her car. With any luck, she'd be in the row closest to the back, so I didn't have to dart between trailers, exposing myself more. I could hear the rumbling of motorcycles and I crouched behind a bush, watching as the line of bikes rode out. There must have been close to twenty of them. Haley's dad was in the front, completely unmistakable with his height, the bandana he always wore and his beard that fell to his chest. I waited until the motorcycles were gone and headed further into the trailer park, looking at every car I walked past.

In the middle of the last row, I spotted Haley's car. Carefully, I checked my surroundings before creeping forward. There was a small window on the side with a light coming through it. Running to it as quickly and quietly as I could manage, I squatted under it.

Lifting my head up, I snuck a glance. Haley sat on her bed, legs crossed, school books open in front of her. She chewed on her pen with headphones in her ears. Her hair was piled into a messy knot on top of her head and she was in her pajamas already. I knocked twice quickly and stood in front of the window.

Her head snapped up, a look of bewilderment on her face. Squinting her eyes, she leaned forward. I could tell the exact moment she realized it was me standing there because she flew off the bed and pulled the window open. "What are you doing?" She whispered. "You can't be here!"

"Let me in. It's fucking freezing." Haley checked behind her before stepping back and letting me climb into the trailer. It wasn't much warmer inside than it was outside.

"What are you doing here?"

"I came to finish what I started yesterday. And to finally fuck you on a bed."

"My mom is home!" But she was closing the curtain. "She's asleep on the couch." Something about the way she said asleep seemed off, but I let it go. I didn't come to fight with her.

"Guess you'd better be quiet then." I sat on her bed only to find that it was the squeakiest fucking bed in the history of man. "Well, this isn't going to work."

"Will, you need to go." She was panicking.

"Relax, Hales," I said. Grabbing her wrist, I pulled her towards me, pulling her body between my knees. I ran my hands up the back of her legs until I got to her ass. Her hands found my shoulders. "Your mom is asleep, lock your door and be quiet." She looked down at me, her teeth nibbling on her bottom lip again. She was trying to figure out if it was worth it. I knew the risk. I knew what I was doing when I came over here. Stepping out of my hold, she walked to her door and locked it. "Good girl," I whispered when she was standing back in front of me.

Standing, I cupped her cheeks and pushed my lips to hers. I'd meant the kiss to be slow and building, but Haley had other ideas. Her tongue pushed into my mouth. She was trying to change the game, to take control and end this as quickly as possible, but I wanted to take my time. Reaching my hand between us, I grabbed her by the throat. Her tongue paused in my mouth, and her breath hitched, allowing me to take control back. I swirled my tongue along hers before retreating, only to push back in and repeat the process. She chased me every time, but I never let her catch me and kept control.

"Get on your knees, Hales," I said, pushing her away from me gently. Her nostrils flared at the command, but she didn't fight me on it. As she stepped back a little more and dropped to her knees, I noticed the gigantic full-length mirror next to her bed.

Fucking perfect.

I pulled my sweatshirt over my head and tossed it on the ground, my t-shirt quickly following. On her knees in front of me, Haley undid my pants and pulled them and my boxers down, letting my dick spring free. I watched in the mirror as she stroked my dick and brought it to her lips. When she kissed the tip of it, I thought I might combust. She'd never done that before. "Fuck, Hales," I groaned almost indiscernibly when she wrapped her lips around me and started to suck with her expert mouth. Nobody gave head like Haley. One hand on the top of her head, my other wrapped around her throat, pushing my hips forward and forcing more of myself into her throat. I felt her swallow around me. "Look at me," I said, moving my eyes away from the mirror and towards her. Leaning her head back, she let more of me slide into her throat. "Such a pretty mess," I said. Her eyes were watering already, spit poured out the corners of her mouth, and her throat swallowed around the head of my dick again.

Pulling her head back, she used her tongue to lick along the underside of me. I hissed in pleasure, my hand instinctively squeezing around her throat as she bobbed back down on me. She was enthusiastic in her movements, which only made her ten times hotter than she already was. Letting her work her mouth on me the way she wanted, I watched in the mirror. Something about seeing it from the side and not while I was looking down at her made the experience that much more erotic.

Her small hands reached around me, cupping my ass. Her fingernails dug into them painfully as I slammed myself into her throat. I would have nail prints there, but I didn't stop, didn't care. Haley kept one hand on my ass while the other reached underneath to my balls, cupping them and rolling them in her hand. I watched all her movements in the mirror, fighting off an orgasm. I didn't want it to end, but I couldn't stop. "I'm gonna come, don't spill a fucking drop, Haley," I warned her. Telling her I was close increased her enthusiasm. She moaned and hummed around me, slurping on my dick as she went. Moving my hand to the back of her head, I held her there, against the base, her nose pushing into my skin while I filled her throat.

When she pulled away, there was a line of spit attaching her mouth to my dick, and I reached out with my thumb and wiped it away. Haley stayed on her knees, trying to return her breathing to normal while I kicked my way out of my pants. Going to my knees in front of her, I pulled her pajama top over her head. "Nice pajamas, doll," I teased her. She was wearing a matching set with that little white kitten from the Disney movie I couldn't remember the name off the top of my head. It had a little pink bow on it and the matching flannel pants were covered in images of the cat.

"Shut up," she whispered.

She wasn't wearing a bra. Bending my head, I wrapped my mouth around one of her nipples, loving the way she reacted immediately by whimpering and squeezing her hand into my hair. "Will," she barely whispered my name loud enough for me to hear. Switching sides, I pinched the nipple I released, rolling it in my fingers. "Oh fuck." I smirked against her before sucking on her nipple again. Her hips pushed forward in an effort to touch me anywhere, to create pressure. "Please."

"Lay down."

Haley laid on her back, positioning herself in front of the mirror without me even having to tell her. Grabbing her hips, I pulled her to a better angle before taking her pants and tossing them into the pile with my clothes. She was wearing simple white cotton panties, and as much as I loved the lace she wore sometimes, these were my damn favorite. I couldn't explain it; they just were.

Pushing her legs open, I settled my shoulders between them. When she tried to snap her legs shut around my head, I held her open. "Be a good girl for me, doll, and hold your legs open."

"Why?" She asked breathlessly.

My face was in her pussy, nearly touching the wet folds as I prepared to have my fill of her. "Look in the mirror." With those words, I pushed my face against her, wrapping my entire mouth around her flooded pussy.

"What for?"

"Just do as you're told for once." Licking through her, I felt her abdomen clench as she lifted her head towards the mirror.

"Oh, fuck."

"You like that?" I asked before wrapping my lips around her clit. She only moaned softly in response. Sucking lightly on her clit, I lifted my eyes up and saw her eyes glued to the mirror, watching me eat her cunt. I watched her as she watched the mirror, unable to take my eyes away from the way her honey-colored ones were glowing with lust. The hand she'd placed on my head dug into my hair, tugging while she tried to lift her hips and hump into my face.

"Will. That's so good. Please don't stop."

She said *please*. I fucking loved to hear her beg. Her body writhed beneath me and as much as I wanted to finally take her on a bed tonight, having her in front of her mirror was a really good replacement. I had so many ideas, so many positions I wanted to take her in, wanted to force her to watch as I pounded my dick into her. Her eyes were still focused on the mirror. "That's right, watch me eat your pretty little pussy." She moaned again, but kept her eyes on the mirror as if she was entranced by what I was doing to her.

One hand reached up to pinch her straining nipple while the other pushed between her folds, finding her pussy sopping wet. "You're dripping all over your carpet, Haley," I told her, my voice filled with arrogance. I was the one doing this to her. "Sopping wet for me." My fingers slid easily into her. I pleasured her body with every part of me I could—a hand on her perfect tits, rolling and pinching her nipples, my mouth around her clit, flicking it quickly with my tongue like I knew she loved, and two fingers inside her, curled to that perfect spot. "I had you like this yesterday," I mumbled. I gave her another few flicks of my tongue before continuing. "And you didn't get to come. Did you touch yourself, doll?"

"No," she said immediately, her head shaking rapidly.

"Good girl." Wrapping my lips around her clit, I sucked it lightly again while releasing her nipple and sliding my hand to her throat. I put pressure on the outside of both sides with my thumb and fingers. Her moans got louder, but just barely, both of us too aware that we couldn't get caught.

Sliding my hand further up her body, I covered her mouth, unwilling to take any chances. "Come for me, Haley." I felt her mouth open against my hand, but the sounds came out muffled as I felt her shake beneath me. I moaned as she came on my tongue, but I didn't stop. Haley bucked underneath me, both hands in my hair as I continued touching her body.

"Will!" I could understand her screaming my name behind my hand, even when barely any sound came out. Her legs were still shaking, both her heels on the floor now as she lifted her hips up into my face when she came a second time.

When I pulled away, Haley laid a minute longer on the floor, still coming down. "Hands and knees, Hales, face the mirror." She complied instantly. Part of me wished she was always this submissive when we messed around, but the other part of me couldn't wait for her to exact whatever revenge she'd definitely need the next time we were together. "Eyes open." We locked eyes in the mirror as I settled myself behind her. Her ass looked so fucking good high in the air and waiting for me. My hands were itching to spank her, but that would definitely get us caught. I watched in the mirror as her eyes rolled back in her head while I pushed inside her. Taking my time, I watched each expression she made until she finally sighed, and I was all the way inside her.

Her eyes snapped closed when I slammed into her, only for a moment before she forced them back open. "Good fucking girl," I told her. I loved that she knew what I wanted without me even having to tell her. Pounding myself into her, I watched her tits sway in the mirror, her entire body shaking. She kept her lips tightly closed, swallowing all the moans that wanted to bubble out. Releasing one of my hands on her hips, I moved it to her neck, holding it there and using her for leverage while I picked up my rhythm. "Hear how wet you are for me?"

She nodded her head. If we got caught, it was going to be from the sounds her sloppy wet pussy was making as I pushed in and out of her. Her head bowed back between her shoulders and I knew she was close to coming. "Be quiet!" I reminded her. I felt her clamp down around me, her mouth falling open but no sound coming out as I slowed my pace to fuck her through her orgasm.

After she'd come down, her body still shaking slightly, I reached under her shoulders, and pulled her up, making her look at her entirely naked body in the mirror. "You're so sexy," I husked in her ear before biting down on the lobe. "Look at these tits bounce while I fuck you." To punctuate my words, I pulled back and snapped my hips roughly back into her, making them jiggle. "And this fucking cunt—so good." Her eyes held mine, my chin pushing into her shoulder as I had one hand wrapped completely around her waist and the other between her folds, rubbing her clit while I set a slow and hard pace.

"Fuck," she cursed lowly before biting her cheek in an effort to keep quiet.

"Look at you." Her entire body was flushed, nipples hard and straining. A light layer of sweat covered her. Her eyes roamed up and down the mirror, taking in every inch of herself. When she finished, I watched her eyes fixate on where she could see my fingers rubbing her clit.

"Too much," she cried.

"Do you want me to stop?" I asked while increasing the pressure against her.

"No, please, don't stop."

"Such a good girl." Her nostrils didn't even flare when I called her a good girl that time. Her body softened against mine, letting me do what I wanted with her. I loved her like this.

Pulling out of her, I sat back against her bed, legs spread out in front of me. "Come ride me." She turned, straddling me and settled herself on top of me. She couldn't see the mirror anymore, but I had a prime view of watching her ride me.

She buried her face in the crook of my neck, moaning against me. I could feel her hot breath along my neck and it made me shudder. "Ride my dick, Hales. Come on, faster." Her ass filled my hands and I wanted to spank her again, but I settled for squeezing while I watched her pick up her pace in the mirror. Lifting herself off her knees, she planted her feet on the ground on the outside of my hips, squatting on my dick. Her pussy clamped around me like a vise and I fought the urge to come, still not having had my fill of her.

"I'm going to come again," she whispered. Her hands dug into my shoulders, nails breaking skin as she rode me, taking what she wanted from me. When her body stopped, we still weren't done.

"Turn around," I told her. Her breathing was still heavy when she slid herself off of me. Turning around, she settled herself back on top of me, head bowed as she watched my dick disappear inside her again. "Put your feet on my thighs, spread them for me." When she'd done what I asked, I grabbed her chin, forcing her eyes to the mirror. I rocked subtly into her, watching my dick pull out of her slightly before sliding back in. "Watch me fuck you in the mirror, Hales, watch me take what's mine." Her hands rested on her legs, eyes finding mine in the mirror. "Look at how well I fit inside you." I could see every goddamn inch of her cunt in the position she was in.

"Fuck, Will."

I rocked steadily into her, watching as her face contorted in pleasure. She'd come so many times, but I needed one more from her before I finally filled her. I couldn't take my eyes off of the mirror, watching as I fucked her, took her, claimed her. "You feel so good, Hales—always so fucking wet for me, soaking my dick."

Her body shook, and I knew she was close to coming again. "Will, I'm going to come again."

"I know, doll. I can tell. I can always fucking tell. I'm gonna come too."

"Fill me, please."

I took the opportunity to make her beg for it like she'd made me beg to fill her in the chemistry lab. "You want me to come inside you?"

"Yes," she hissed. Sneaking my hand between her folds, I rubbed her clit.

"Beg for it, doll. Beg me to fill your cunt. Beg for me to claim what we both know is *mine*."

"Will!" She cried softly. This was the quietest we'd ever been during sex. Something about potentially getting caught made everything that much hotter. "Please, fill me. Come inside me. I need it."

"Are you desperate for it?"

"Yes, so desperate. I need it. Fuck, Will I need it so bad. Please."

Pushing my fingers against her clit, I pushed her over the edge, feeling her clamp down on me while I finally released myself inside of her, coating her insides. "Yesssss," she moaned, long and quiet.

"Damn, Hales," I said.

Somehow, fucking her on her bedroom floor turned out better than I'd ever imagined. I was going to have to find more places to fuck her in front of a mirror.

"You need to go," she said. "This was stupid and reckless."

"And fucking amazing."

"Yes, but you still need to go." She climbed off of me, already putting her pajamas back on. I watched her visibly panic when her front door could be heard slamming shut. She tossed my clothes to me, already going to open the window. But I'd already heard what she didn't want me to hear. Her dad was back and he was yelling. His voice boomed through the house like thunder. Haley's panic only increased. "Go! Quickly." I barely had my sweatshirt on when I heard glass break.

"I can't leave you here with this," I protested.

"Go. Now. Please, Will," she begged with tears in my eyes.

Everything was starting to make sense.

"Haley!" I heard her mother's voice screech. Haley was pushing me out the window. She just had it closed behind me when there was a pounding on her bedroom door. "Open this mother fucking door right now you little bitch!"

Her mother spoke to her like that?

"What's wrong?" She asked, opening the door, her voice softer than I'd ever heard it.

"You were supposed to clean the bathroom today."

"I did."

"No you didn't." I was crouching below the window, listening, when I heard Haley cry out in pain, and I lifted my eyes above the windowsill just in time to see Haley's mom backhand her across the face. Rage flashed through me. I couldn't move. The entire scene looked like it played out in slow motion. Haley's mom grabbed her by her hair. It was messier now than when I'd arrived. It was the hair I'd just been running my hands through. I watched as she pulled her daughter's head back and slammed it forward into a wall. Haley fell to the ground, and I saw her mom's leg move, most likely kicking her.

"Ungrateful bitch," her mom spat at her before finally leaving. After long moments, Haley pushed herself off the floor, leaning against her bed with her forearms on it. Her eyes met mine, tears of shame filling them.

"Go," she mouthed at me. "Go."

I hated leaving her, but I knew her dad was home, and I also knew Viper was stacked to the teeth with weapons. If I went in there recklessly, I'd end up getting us both killed.

I needed to protect her. And the best way to do that right now was to walk away, but it was the hardest fucking thing I'd ever had to do.

She couldn't hide the truth from me anymore. It was staring me in the face the entire time, but it took seeing it with my own eyes to believe it.

How was I going to help her?

Would she let me help her?

I wasn't about to give her a choice.

The entire time I walked back to my car all I thought about was what I saw. *Her mom's the one who beats her.* Everything suddenly made so much sense. The reason she doesn't stand up for herself, the way she's so protective of her sister, everything fell into place. And it only made me want to protect her more.

CHAPTER 17

THE CAGES

Haley

When I woke up, my head was throbbing in pain. Rolling from my side to my back, I pushed my hand against my forehead and almost had to cry out at the intense level of pain, knowing my entire face was probably bruised. My mom was getting more and more reckless in her abuse, which could only mean she was using more and more drugs, caring less and less about anything that wasn't her high.

I groaned in pain while rummaging around my bed to find my cell phone.

"Morning," I heard Chloe's voice call when my door opened. She must have just gotten home from her babysitting job, that probably meant I overslept. I'd probably get another beating for that perceived indiscretion.

I tried to hide my face from her, but I was too late. "Hilly. Oh my god, what happened to your face?"

"Nothing," I said, attempting to play off the bruise that, based on her reaction, must be horrible.

"Mom?" She asked. Walking towards my bed, she sat on the edge with me, and pushed the hair out of my face, a gesture more motherly than anything our mother ever touched either of us with.

"What happened?"

"I don't even know." Truthfully, everything just kind of blurred together—hearing my dad come home, begging Will to leave, my mom pounding on my bedroom door, the beating.

He'd seen.

Fuck.

He must have had some idea before, but now he knew for sure, and him being who he was, he would want to talk about it.

"Maybe whenever I'm not home, try to find somewhere else to stay?" She suggested gently. I'd never had that option before, which was why the thought hadn't crossed my mind yet.

"That would probably just make things worse for both of us when we were home."

"It's not fair. Why doesn't she hit me too? I wish I could take some of it for you."

"Don't ever say that," I snapped harshly, not meaning for my tone to be so sharp, but I took the beatings for her... all of them. "I will take as many as I need to take, as long as you never have to. You're my baby sister. It's my job to protect you."

"And who protects you?" She asked.

Will.

That thought came out of nowhere, but it was probably true. If I let him, he'd definitely protect me, probably even use his dad to do it, and as good as it would feel to have someone to lean on, finally, to feel safe and protected with, I couldn't let that happen because if I did, they'd take Chloe and put her in the foster care system. And even though things were shitty here, she wasn't being beaten, and she wasn't being molested, something I couldn't guarantee if she ended up in the system.

What I would do was make sure that when I was gone, fled from this shitty town and life that Will had her back, that he'd make sure she was safe. Instinctively, I just knew that he would do that for me if I asked.

"Do you want to go to the diner? It's almost lunchtime."

"I can't go anywhere today," I told her. "Not with my face as bad as it is."

"I'm gonna go get you some ice, see if that helps with the swelling."

"Thanks, Squirt." Chloe closed the door behind her when she left our bedroom. It was another act of protection on her part, but it wouldn't keep the monster that was my mother out if she really wanted to get in.

Rolling to my side again, I searched for my phone, blindly patting my night stand until I found it. I ripped it from its charging cable and opened my messages, finding half a dozen from Will starting from as soon as he'd probably gotten home last night, randomly throughout the night and one from just a few minutes ago. He must not have slept... could he not sleep because he was busy worrying about me?

> Asshole: Christ, doll...
> Asshole: Hales..
> Asshole: I don't know what to say.
> Asshole: Haley. I. Shit.
> Asshole: Your mom? She's the one who's been doing this to you? Haley...
> Asshole: Can we meet?

I could feel his torment coming through the phone.

I hated that he'd seen it, especially after the sex last night. It had been... amazing, the best time yet. He'd taken control of me, and, for the first time, I hadn't wanted to take it back... ever. The way he'd made me watch in the mirror as his cock slammed into me repeatedly was like nothing I'd ever experienced, and my body flushed from head to toe at the memory. I told him my mom was sleeping, but really she'd been passed out from the drugs, but we still had to be so quiet so we didn't get caught. And we had been—all the moans and groans were needy and quiet—*desperate*. The way he'd said Hales when he finally spilled himself inside me... I, god, there were no words. Another message popped up.

> Asshole: Meet me at the park. Please?
> Me: I can't.
> Asshole: We have to talk, Hales. Meet me before school tomorrow behind the Methodist Church. Where we met for Halloween.
> Me: Okay.

I'd have to get it over with, eventually.

"They're not home," Chloe said when she came back into the room, holding a plastic baggie filled with ice wrapped in a cloth in her hand. She handed it to me and I pushed it against my forehead, where I'd taken most of the blow last night, but my ribs hurt also, and I didn't need to lift my shirt to know they would be bruised too.

"How bad is it?" I asked her.

"It's worse than I've ever seen it," she admitted reluctantly. Her words didn't surprise me.

"How did you get home?" I asked, not wanting to face the reality of my face or get out of bed to look at the evidence.

"Mrs. Scott brought me home. She always does when you can't pick me up."

"She doesn't mind?" Most people from that side of town didn't like crossing the railroad tracks to our side, risking getting caught or stranded with the criminals.

"I have her drop me off outside the park and walk in."

"She seems to really like you."

"She does. I was her favorite student. She treats me well. I get real meals and can have all the snacks I want when I'm there."

How horrifying was it that basic human decency being extended to my sister was all it took for her to believe someone was a good person? The bar was so low because those basic, bare bones, necessities that should be normal to her, something she received in her home, weren't.

Maybe Mrs. Scott could take her in after I left?

I made a mental note to explore that option, a different way to keep her safe after I'd left.

"You should take a cool shower," she told me when the ice finally began melting. "It'll help too. And take some Tylenol. Why don't you get in the shower and I'll make us lunch?"

"Thanks," I smiled at her. She was so grown up, more grown up than I'd given her credit for.

"What do you want to eat?" She asked, standing from my bed.

"Sandwiches are fine. Chips if we have them."

Which we did.

I'd won a fifty-dollar gift card at the grocery store, but I had a sneaking suspicion that Will was behind the "win" even if I couldn't prove it. The girl at the register had been insistent that it was a real thing and completely random.

I hadn't asked Will about it because I didn't really want to know the answer, to be confronted with the implications of what him doing something like that for me meant. Him doing something nice for me would mean this was more than just sex when it couldn't be. Even if I was developing feelings far, far away and out of my mind, it could only ever be just sex.

Chloe went to the kitchen while I went to the bathroom. I kept my eyes closed and my head bent down while I stood in front of the mirror. Hands on the sink, I took a deep breath before looking up.

There was an enormous bruise across my entire forehead, and a bit of dried blood where my forehead opened. Shit, it looked so bad there was no way makeup alone was going to be enough to cover it up for school tomorrow. I was going to have to cut my hair and give myself bangs. Grabbing my phone, I googled how to cut your own bangs. I watched two tutorials before coming across a thread that said: *'Don't cut your own bangs! Read this first'*. Opening the link, I found a video about how to put your hair into a ponytail and make the ends look like you had cut bangs without actually having cut them.

That was probably a better solution, so I saved the link before climbing into the shower.

The water hurt my face when I accidentally let the spray come directly at me. Turning, I let it wash over my back and looked down for the first time, finding a bruise in the shape of a foot spread out across my abdomen, right below my boobs. Taking a deep breath hurt, and I bit my cheek at the pain.

Once I was clean, I stepped out and applied arnica ointment to my face and stomach. The ointment hadn't been cheap, taking a sizable chunk out of my college savings, but with the amount of times my skin was covered in bruises, it was a necessity.

Walking back to my room, I dressed in leggings and an oversized hoodie before going to the kitchen. Chloe was sitting at the table with two sandwiches and a bag of chips in front of her.

"Thanks," I said, sitting next to her and grabbing a chip.

"You take care of me all the time. Let me take care of you sometimes, too."

Leaning across the space between us, I hugged her, hoping she knew that even though I couldn't stay here after graduation, I would still make sure she was always protected.

When I woke up Monday, both of my parents still weren't home and there was no evidence they'd come home at all on Sunday. Could we be lucky enough that they'd abandoned us, that my dad finally did something he wouldn't be able to talk or buy his way out of? Probably not. And if he did have to run, I highly doubted he would take my mother with him.

While Chloe was in the shower, I did my hair according to the tutorial and decided it was a good thing that I hadn't actually cut bangs—they didn't suit me.

Once I was in my uniform, I headed to make breakfast. It felt like there was a block of nervous energy in my stomach. I knew Will would have a lot to say, and I didn't know what I was going to tell him, so instead of making a breakfast sandwich like I usually did, I just made toast and covered it in butter and cinnamon sugar, hoping the sweetness would settle my stomach a little, but I still made Chloe an egg sandwich.

"I gotta go a little early," I said to her when she came into the kitchen. I wanted to beat Will to the church so that it would be my car that was hidden, ensuring nobody would ask questions. The golden boy at the local church wouldn't raise suspicions like me being there would.

"Okay. I'm taking the bus."

I handed Chloe her breakfast sandwich before walking out of the trailer.

The parking lot at the church was empty when I got there. I backed into the small clearing and waited, playing with my phone, spinning it in my fingers anxiously until I saw his truck pull in. He parked by the back of the building before hopping out and walking towards me as I unlocked the doors to let him climb inside.

"You cut your hair," was the first thing he said.

"I didn't, just styled it like this."

His large hand reached across the car so he could touch me. Gently, his feather light touch pushed the bangs up, his jaw ticking in anger as he took in the damage. "Christ, Hales." His fingers danced over the bruise, like he was studying it. "Fuck," he cursed lowly when I winced in pain. "Why didn't you tell me?"

"Because there's nothing you can do."

"I can tell my dad."

"No," I blurted out. "I'm eighteen. But they'll take Chloe away and put her into the foster care system. I might never see her again, and at my house, she's safe. They don't beat her, just me."

That knowledge didn't seem to make him any more relaxed.

"They can keep her safe."

"No offense, Will, but you've got no idea what the foster system is like. She might need to change schools. She might end up in a place where people only want to collect the check and she gets abused or assaulted." My voice cracked and tears sprang into my eyes at the slightest thought of something happening to her.

"You're eighteen, you could take custody."

"While I'm still in school? How am I going to support us? Those are all questions a judge will have. Trust me, I've thought about it, googled everything I could about the laws."

"You're not safe there," he said. There was so much concern, genuine concern for my safety in his voice, that I started to tear up again. What was happening to me? I was the ice queen and had a remarkable ability to keep my emotions at bay at all times. Slowly, Will broke down my walls and pushed his way inside—so slowly I didn't even realize he did it.

"I have to keep her safe."

"Let me help you."

I wanted to say yes; I did. But Will was getting too close for my comfort level, inserting himself into more areas of my life than just the sex portion. I needed him to get back in his lane.

"Let me see your stomach."

"Will, no."

"Please," he begged softly. His voice was so different from the dominant, commanding tones he'd used on me while he'd fucked me into oblivion last night. Sighing, I undid the buttons of my school blouse and pulled the tank top I had on underneath up. His hand moved to me again, his hand splaying out across the bruise. My stomach clenched involuntarily at the touch, making me cry out in pain.

"Let me help you," he pleaded again.

"How, Will? Tell me realistically how you can help me?" I wasn't trying to be a bitch. Secretly, I loved knowing that he cared about me enough to want to help, but I'd been trying for years to help myself. He wouldn't be able to just swoop in and change my entire life.

"We can tell my dad."

"No," I said immediately. "That'll just lead to the same outcome, Chloe in foster care."

"Maybe not. He might have another solution."

"Your idea of helping is running to your daddy?"

"Fuck, Haley. I'm out of my depth here too, but all I know is that you aren't safe there. What if it escalates again? What if she kills you?"

I never thought it could get that far out of hand.

"You need to come up with something else."

"If Chloe is home, are the beatings milder?"

"Yes," I said. I didn't know if it was because of witnesses, but it always seemed to be just a little better if Chloe was home.

"My parents go out of town all the time on the weekends," he said. "They like to camp. I'm home alone at least three weekends a month." That was new information. "If your sister is gone, babysitting for her teacher or whatever, don't stay there. Stay with me."

"Seriously?"

"Seriously," he said. "You can park your car here, hide it. I'll pick you up." I bit my lip, contemplating if it was worth the risk.

"What if I have to work?"

"I'll take you."

"And waste your gas money?"

"If it'll keep you safe."

"I'll think about it." It was the only thing I could agree to right now.

"Thank you." We sat there quietly. We'd have to leave soon to get to school on time for second period.

"By the way," he spoke. "Last night, Hales… I don't have words." He looked almost shy as he spoke, a slight brush creeping over his cheeks.

"It was amazing," I admitted, mirroring his own shy demeanor. We stared at each other for a minute until he leaned across the seat and kissed my forehead gently, his lips lingering warmly like we weren't just enemies with benefits. His lips moved down my face until he planted a kiss that could only be described as sweet to my lips before pulling away. A wink and a smile later, he was climbing out of my car, and my stomach did that annoying thing where it flipped nervously because of him.

I didn't wait for him to get back to his truck before I was pulling out of the parking lot and heading towards the school.

"New hairstyle?" Sassy asked when I sat across from her at lunch, finally seeing her for the first time since last week.

"No," I said, shaking my head. I glanced around to make sure nobody was paying attention to us before lifting my bangs slightly.

"Haley!" She shouted. Lowering her voice, she spoke again, "It's getting so much worse."

"I know."

"Does Will know?" She didn't say his name aloud, but mouthed it.

"He was there."

"What. The. Hell!"

"Shh," I told her. "He snuck over and we had sex. My mom was passed out from too many lines, and my dad came home pissed off. He snuck back out just in time for us to not get caught, but he saw."

"You're being so reckless. It's not just sex anymore, is it?"

Before I could answer, nearly admitting to her what I couldn't yet admit to myself, Snake was walking towards the table. "I got a text. There's a meeting tonight. We're both expected to attend."

"Great," I said sarcastically.

By the time school was over, my head was throbbing in pain, the Tylenol I'd taken before worn off. Sassy rode with me back to the trailer park and I told her I didn't want to talk about Will. She knew me as well as I knew myself, meaning she also knew when not to push it.

"Be safe at the meeting tonight," she said before walking towards her own trailer.

"I will."

Going straight to my room, I worked on as much homework as I could until the sun set. Around eight, I was starving and forgot to eat dinner. Thankfully, Chloe walked in with McDonald's bags.

"How'd you get the food?" I asked her.

"Mick." She had this glassy look in her eyes when she said his name. My little sister had her first real crush. "He brought me home."

"Are you being safe?" I asked her when she handed me a bag of what I presumed was my dinner.

"It's not like that."

"Not yet. But do you want it to be?"

"Maybe."

"We're going to the clinic."

"Okay." She definitely wanted it to be like that because she didn't even put up a fight.

I'd just finished my cheeseburger and was still working on the chicken nuggets and french fries when my phone beeped. I was expecting it to be Will, but it was Snake.

Snake: I'm outside.

"Thanks, Chloe. I'll be back." I shoved a handful of fries into my mouth, chewing quickly while I grabbed my thick coat and tugged my boots on. When I got outside, Snake was standing next to his motorcycle, leaning against it with two helmets in his hand.

"Ready?" He asked.

"For the meeting or the show we'll have to put on?"

"Both."

"Yes." I took a helmet, put it on and climbed onto his bike with him. The wind in my face was freezing as Snake buzzed through the town, heading all the way to the town limits before turning onto a dirt road and heading up the mountain.

We were the last to arrive apparently because the line of bikes was long outside the storage unit that looked completely out of place.

I climbed off, handed Snake my helmet, and fluffed my hair. Taking my hand, he squeezed it, readying for the show as we walked towards where the noise was coming from. Holding his hand didn't feel anything like holding Will's hand.

The crowd cleared as we arrived. The sounds were confusing and a little overwhelming because I heard the men, but something else sounded distinctly animalistic. After being blinded by the lights above my head, I figured out why.

We were surrounded by cages filled with wild animals.

Snake's hand squeezed mine tighter, and I knew he was just as surprised by the sight as I was. Turning, I took it all in. There were all manner of exotic looking birds, a few snakes, a tortoise, monkeys. And the loud roar I heard pulled me to the sight of a fucking tiger cub scratching at its confinement.

"This," my dad spoke proudly. "This is how we're finally going to make some real goddamn money."

"Animals?" Snake asked.

"Exotic animals. Rich bastards pay so much money for illegal pets, and we've just cornered the market in the Pacific Northwest."

Holy shit.

CHAPTER 18

THE LEFTOVERS

Haley

Three days after the revelation that my father moved the Southside Gang into the territory of illegal exotic animal distribution, it was Thanksgiving, and my head was still reeling from the discovery. Snake and I were forced to stay and listen to my father's ridiculous plan, detailing how the animals would be imported from Asia somewhere on cargo ships. Someone from the gang would meet the ship at the port, collect the animals on a truck, and bring them to the warehouse. Members would take turns doing the security detail, making sure no hikers strayed too far from the path and discovered the animals.

He'd gone on and on about how it was so much less risky than trafficking guns, drugs, or people. I'd nearly vomited at how casually he mentioned human trafficking, as if that wasn't one of the worst things a person could be involved in. People were trafficked for sex or into modern day slavery. Snake looked just as horrified as I had, but he'd quickly put his mask on, standing stoically and nodding, taking it all in like a good soldier.

When we'd finally been dismissed, there were cheers and applause for the brilliance of my father's idea.

Snake didn't take us straight to the trailer park. Instead, he stopped at the park on the rich side of town. That late at night, we'd had the place all to ourselves.

"What the fuck?" Those were the first words he spoke after climbing off of his bike.

"He cannot be serious."

"You saw them. They're so fucking serious. If the cops don't catch us and throw us all in jail, we'll die at the hands of a poisonous snake or get mauled by a fucking tiger. A tiger. Did you see that? Was I hallucinating?" Snake was nearly hysterical as he'd spoken. "What the fuck are we going to do?"

"I don't know."

"Even when he finally puts me in charge, I don't know that I'll be able to get us out of this. The deal will be done. Whoever he's working for won't take lightly to us pulling out." In his frustration, he'd kicked one of the cylinder parking blocks. The steel toes of his boots protected him from doing any damage to himself, but I'd never seen him so pissed.

The longer things went on, the more I realized, at some point, spilling my plan might be the best thing for everyone involved—just not yet.

After Snake ranted more to himself than to me, we climbed back onto his bike and rode back to the trailer park. His dad and mine were standing outside my trailer as we'd pulled up with cigars between their fat fingers. There were disgusting comments about us taking the long way home and all that it implied. Snake played his role perfectly and not countered them or disagreed with anything, even making a show of dramatically licking his lips before he'd kissed my cheek and wished me goodnight while I'd gone inside.

Even three days later, I still couldn't wrap my head around it.

Laying on my bed, I remembered it was Thanksgiving. But for Chloe and me, and Snake, Sassy, and Buck, today was just another normal day. Sassy and Buck's mom had to work a double, so there wouldn't be a Thanksgiving dinner for them either. Snake's mom took off long ago and his dad was with my dad doing whatever manner of illegal activity they had planned for the day. My mom was nowhere to be seen, probably high somewhere and had no idea what day it was, let alone that it was a holiday.

A fake holiday.

But still.

"Happy Thanksgiving," Chloe said.

"Happy Thanksgiving." I felt guilty celebrating something that had such a horrible history and whitewashed society's history. So, I focused on the being thankful aspect and not the rest. And I was thankful for my sister and how neither of our parents were anywhere to be seen.

"We're going to the diner later, right?"

"Yes."

Chloe, Sassy, Buck, Snake, and I had been going to the diner on Thanksgiving for as long as I could remember. When we were younger, we'd walk there, but this would be the third year we'd be able to drive. They had a Thanksgiving buffet every year. It was cheap, only six bucks a person, including drinks.

"I'll shower first," Chloe said as she climbed out of bed.

When I was alone, I grabbed my phone. As usual, there was a text from Will.

> Asshole: Happy Thanksgiving, Hales.
> Me: Happy Thanksgiving
> Asshole: I'm sorry you'll have to be alone this weekend.
> Me: I'll be fine.
> Asshole: Text me. I'll come get you if you need me too and figure out what to tell my parents.

Since it was a holiday weekend, Will's parents were staying home, and I wouldn't be able to go over there this weekend, even though Chloe was going to be babysitting. I'd picked up shifts on

Friday, Saturday, and Sunday to try to get out of the house as much as possible, but I still had to come home to sleep.

Will and I hadn't had sex since he'd snuck into my house last weekend, but after Monday, I'd spent Tuesday and Wednesday first period in the janitor's closet with him. We'd made out and ground ourselves against each other, but neither of us took it a step further. It was like something had changed, but I couldn't figure out what—or I was still denying it because denial was safe, admitting it wasn't.

Once Chloe was out of the shower, I went and took my turn. My mom was home less and less these days, which meant I got to take more and more showers with hot water.

After my shower, I inspected my bruises in the mirror. The one on my head was turning yellow and could finally be covered up with makeup. The one on my stomach hadn't changed color yet.

I applied makeup to my face, covering the bruise before getting dressed in black mom jeans and a baggy sweater.

When I walked into the kitchen, it smelled like the French toast Chloe was making. "Do you want to tell me more about Mick?" I asked her as she flipped the bread. Her movements faltered.

"He's a year older than me," she said. "A sophomore."

"Is he your boyfriend? Or are you guys just hanging out? Friends?" I inquired further.

"I really like him," she said. "He's so sweet. He walks me to my classes and carries my books, and he's kind to literally everyone, even the customers from the rich side of town who treat him like garbage when they go to McDonald's."

"I thought they were all too good to eat fast food."

"They probably think they are, which is why they treat him so poorly, but anybody who says they don't like McDonald's is a liar." I laughed at her. "In my opinion, anyway."

"Tell me more about him."

"He's pretty smart. Not like a genius and could be a doctor smart, but definitely smart enough to go to college. He wants to be a teacher."

"That's great."

"He asks before touching me, every single time."

"Consent is important, but that makes me want to ask how he's touching you." I quirked a brow at her while I asked.

"We haven't even kissed." She sounded disappointed. "He just holds my hand or puts his arm around me."

"I'll call the clinic Monday and make you an appointment."

"There's no rush."

"It's better to be safe than sorry."

She sighed, but didn't argue as she plated our French toast.

After breakfast, I cleaned the kitchen while Chloe watched TV. I spent the rest of the morning working on my creative writing project. I'd finished writing my story, but it needed to be edited and it was about five thousand words too long. That should be easy enough to cut down, hopefully.

While I was editing, my phone beeped.

> Asshole: Can you meet?
> Me: Not right now.
> Asshole: Later?
> Me: When?
> Asshole: 7
> Me: Where?
> Asshole: Our spot.

He wasn't talking about our spot in the school, but behind the church.

> Me: I'll be there.

Around noon, Chloe came into the bedroom and changed from her lounge around the house outfit to jeans and a sweatshirt to wear to the diner.

"Ready?"

"Yeah," I said, putting away my editing. I just had my shoes pulled on when there was a knock on the trailer door. Chloe opened it, letting Sassy and Buck in, and a few minutes later, Snake walked in, not bothering to knock.

"I'll drive," I said. Sassy sat next to me in the front seat while Snake grumbled about having to sit in the back, even though he was the biggest in the car.

Sassy was fed up with him not giving in and sleeping with her. Her mom had to work a double on Saturday again, and Buck would be out at a friend's house all day for some type of video game tournament. In her words, she was going to "pounce him." I laughed when she told me, but when she'd gone into detail about the lingerie she bought for the occasion, I knew she was finally going to be successful.

When we walked into the diner, we went to the corner booth first. Snake grumbled yet again when Sassy and I got a side to ourselves and he had to sit with Buck and Chloe. For some reason, his complaint died quickly on his lips and a strange look crossed his face. My eyes darted down under the table, seeing Sassy's foot rubbing up against his leg.

Her touch calmed him.

"Hey kids," Suzie greeted us. "Buffet I'm assuming?"

"Yes ma'am," Buck answered for us all.

"What to drink?"

"Orange soda," Buck said.

"Sprite," Chloe ordered.

"Coke," Snake said.

"For me too," I replied

"And I'll have a coke zero," Sassy ordered.

"Help yourself to the buffet," she said.

"You guys go first," Snake said, stepping out of the booth to let Buck and Chloe go.

While we were alone, Snake reached across the table and squeezed Sassy's hand a few times before retreating to his side.

I didn't know if he told her about the animals, I hadn't. It wasn't something she needed to know. Not telling her would keep her safe, and I was sure he knew that, too, but we needed to come up with a plan, and soon. Graduation was in six months. We would be married right after that if my plan somehow failed.

I need to stop spending so much time with Will and focus on my future again. I was back to straight A's in all my classes, and when report cards came out just before the Christmas break, I was confident that my number one spot in the class would be secure, but just because that was secure didn't mean my future and college enrollment were. I still needed to pay for it, somehow, still needed an escape plan, and most importantly, I still needed a plan to keep Chloe safe after I left.

When our younger siblings came back to the table, we stood and made our way to the buffet line. It was full of Thanksgiving staples. I piled my plate with turkey, mashed potatoes, sweet potatoes, stuffing, two dinner rolls, creamed corn, macaroni and cheese, gravy, Brussel sprouts and green beans.

I'd have a second plate and then also go back for at least one dessert plate, but probably two. When we got back to the table, our drinks were already there, and Buck had already cleared his plate. He stood up to go back for seconds before letting Snake sit down.

"I think he's having a growth spurt," Sassy commented.

By the time I'd gone back to the buffet three more times, once for regular food and two more times for dessert, I nearly had to unbutton my pants.

"Roll me home," I groaned.

"I'm gonna be sick," Buck moaned, and if that wasn't the genuine spirit of the American Thanksgiving, and the holiday season in general—over indulgence.

After we paid the bill and piled back in the car, we drove around town for a while. None of us felt like going home to our empty houses, but we also didn't actually have the luxury of all hanging out together. None of our parents would be happy to come home to a house full of teenagers.

I drove past the park and all the way to the town line before turning back around and taking the backroads to the trailer park.

"I really won't see you until Monday?" Sassy asked.

"Yeah. Thanksgiving weekend and the week of Christmas are the busiest weeks at the movie theater. I picked up extra shifts."

When she hugged me, she whispered in my ear. "Are you seeing him?"

I knew she meant Will. "No. I swear." When she pulled away, she gave me a look that told me she actually believed me. "I'm driving you to school Monday," I told her. She blushed and knew exactly why. I was going to want the dirty details.

Chloe and I walked into the trailer, thankfully finding it still empty and quiet.

"Want to watch a Christmas movie?" She asked. "Don't give me that look," she said before I could even actually give her one. "Thanksgiving is over. We've eaten the meal. It's Santa's time now."

"All right. I'll make us some hot chocolate."

Chloe dug through the old DVDs we had, that were mostly stolen, but we weren't the ones who stole them. "I'm picking," she shouted. I hadn't expected anything different.

When I walked into the living room with two mugs of hot chocolate, she was curled under a blanket and had the opening credits of Elf paused. It was her favorite Christmas movie. I found it baffling, but I always indulged her and watched it.

She snuggled against me while she laughed at the TV. I cherished these moments. In a few months, I wouldn't have any of them at all anymore, and I was going to miss them. Tears welled in my eyes as I realized how much I was going to miss her.

I had to keep her safe, even after I left.

It was too soon to ask Will for his help, or even Mrs. Scott, if it came to that. It would give away that I was planning on leaving town right after I gave my scathing commencement speech. I couldn't have that secret outed until I was ready, and I wouldn't be ready until I was standing at the podium watching the shock on people's faces when they realized I was the valedictorian of our class.

Somehow, the timing worked out well, and the movie ended just as I needed to leave to go meet Will at our spot.

I cleaned the mugs and the pan that I'd used to make the hot chocolate in. "I'm going out for a little. Will you be okay?"

"Yeah."

"Later Squirt."

The trailer park was eerily quiet as I pulled out of it and onto the road. Somehow, living in a trailer park was always harder during the holidays. It seemed like we had more family drama than the other side of town, but maybe they were just better at hiding it.

The entire town was actually eerily quiet as I drove the familiar road to the church. Will's truck was already there when I pulled in, but he'd left the secluded spot between the trees open for me to back my car into. I'd just put the car in park when he was opening the door and climbing in. I didn't notice until he was seated that he had a plate covered in foil in his hand, a couple of them stacked on top of each other, actually.

"Hey Hales," he said. He greeted me with a kiss, a new habit. Before this last week, we'd only ever kissed a few times without knowing it wasn't leading to sex, but now, it was almost like it was second nature for him to want to push his lips against mine, even when we weren't planning on slipping into the back seat.

"Hi," I said when he pulled away.

"We had a bunch of leftovers, so I brought you some." My stomach fluttered at the gesture. "Mom always cooks everything from scratch, and it's so good." I had no words. The thoughtfulness was a reason for the confusing feelings I kept denying. "I even brought you four different slices of homemade pie: pumpkin, pecan, apple, and Mississippi mud pie."

My mouth watered.

"Will, that's," I started and stopped my words, unsure of what to say. "Thank you."

"I remember pre-kindergarten," he said. That was the first time either of us mentioned it. "Sharing one of my mom's cookies with you the first day, how much you liked it, well, she still bakes with love."

"Thank you," I said again, my voice coming out breathier than I'd intended it to.

"No need. I can't stay. My grandparents are here and I'm expected at family game night."

"That sounds fun, but where did you tell them you were taking the food?"

"To a friend in need," he said. "They trust me, Hales. They know that if I need help, I'll ask them, and as long as they don't believe I'm lying, they don't ask questions. Remember that next time I offer to help you." I could only blink at him, my voice lost for any type of words. "Bye, Hales." Will climbed out of the car, taking the food with him only to set it on the passenger seat, lean across and kiss me again. I was so shell-shocked that he had already backed out of his parking spot and pulled out of the church's driveway while I was still sitting there completely dumbfounded.

Thanksgiving break was almost over, and I was absolutely exhausted. Working two ten-hour days in a row at the theater had wrecked me. And I still had half my third shift to go. Chloe and I binged on the food Will brought me all weekend. When he said he'd brought four slices of pie, each piece had been half a pie. I'd hidden the food in the drawer of the fridge where the fruits and vegetables were because I knew my parents would never look there, keeping it safe.

Chloe asked questions about how I'd gotten the food, but I'd just brushed her off. Will's mom could cook. It was some of the best food I'd ever tasted, the perfect amount of spice on everything, giving it an amazing flavor.

"We hardly got to see each other at all yesterday," Bobby said. We had a small lull in traffic since there wasn't a new movie starting for thirty minutes.

"I know. We were slammed all day."

"Do you still want to come over after our shift?" He asked.

"Um," I began.

"You got back with him, didn't you?"

"I did."

"I figured. What do you see in him?"

"It's complicated," I admitted. "There's a lot of history, and most of it's not friendly, or good. We were both shitty to each other."

"Are you in love with him?"

"No," I answered, but probably way too quickly.

Bobby just gave me a look that said he didn't believe me. "Speak of the devil."

Turning my head, I looked over my shoulder and saw Will walking in all by himself. When he was close enough that I could see his features, I saw his face clouded with jealousy. Bobby took a step away, putting more space between our bodies.

"Hales," Will said when he was standing at the register.

"Hey," I said, trying to be casual, but the truth was that interacting with him like this, so casually in front of Bobby, was making my heart race.

"I'd like one ticket."

"Which movie?"

"Whichever one starts next."

"It's a kid's one."

"I love kid's movies." I rang him up, and he swiped his debit card. "Do you have time for a break?"

"No."

"Go," Bobby said. "I'll cover for you." I offered him a generous smile as a thank you and made my way out of the booth and towards the back, pulling Will towards the break room. I shouldn't have brought him there, but nobody was scheduled to be on a break for at least another fifteen minutes.

"What are you doing here?"

"Wanted to see you," he shrugged as if it was that simple for him.

"This is dangerous. People from Lake City come to this theater, people from our high school."

"And I'm one of those people." I sighed. "I haven't seen you in a few days." Was he trying to tell me he missed me without actually saying the words? It seemed like it. "Not next weekend, but the one after that, my parents are going out of town again. Does your sister have to babysit?"

"I think so."

"Come stay with me." I bit my lip. It might be nice to be in a house alone with him. "Do you have to work?"

"No."

"Then stay with me."

"Okay."

"We'll figure out the details next week. I'll see you tomorrow, Hales, first period, our spot."

Closing the small space between us, he cupped my face and kissed me deeply, ending it too quickly for my liking and retreating out of the break room. I stood at the entrance watching him walk towards the theater on his ticket and right into the kid's movies.

"Thanks," I said to Bobby when I got back. I could see a bunch of cars pulling into the parking lot. It was going to get busy again.

"You might say you don't love him. But he loves you."

Before I could process his remark and tell him how far off base he was, customers flooded the lobby, ending all conversation.

CHAPTER 19

THE CUDDLING

Haley

Nervously, I stuffed three day's worth of clothes into my duffel bag. Somehow, spending the night with Will seemed like an even more reckless idea than when he'd shown up at my trailer. He'd wanted me to come over yesterday evening since his parents had left after dinner, but Chloe didn't start babysitting until Saturday mornings, and I wasn't about to let her spend a night in this trailer alone with my parents, not while I was still there, and hadn't figured out how to protect her once I was gone. After I dropped her off at her teacher's, I was going right to the Methodist church.

I had two pairs of joggers, a couple t-shirts, and a bathing suit. Will had a hot tub, and I planned on using it.

I was zipping up my suitcase when my phone vibrated.

Asshole: Let me know when you've dropped your sister off
Asshole: Oh, and Hales...

Asshole: Don't bother bringing any clothes, you won't be needing them.

He could forget about it. Just because he'd invited me over didn't mean I had to sleep with him, or even be naked in his presence if I didn't want to. The problem was that I absolutely wanted to.

"Ready to go?" Chloe asked, walking back into our room. She was speaking to me, but she was staring at her phone, presumably texting Mick. I'd gotten her to the clinic, and she started her first month of birth control. The woman from the clinic sat with both of us, the same woman who'd helped me three years ago when I'd gone after turning fifteen. Chloe paid attention, asked questions, and I was proud of her when we walked out.

"Yeah, let's go." Chloe kept her eyes glued to her phone, typing away anytime she got a message while I drove.

The last two weeks were eventful. Sassy finally had sex with Snake. When she'd come over, we'd grabbed all the snacks we could carry and sat on my bed while she gave me a detailed play-by-play. She'd been fucking glowing. "I told him I loved him," she said when she'd finished telling the last part of the story.

"What did he say?"

"'That's good because I love you too.'" She stuck her hands on her hips and shook her head and made her voice deep in a ridiculous attempt to mimic him.

"I'm so happy for you, Sas," I said and hugged her.

"You were right. I am going to be addicted to it."

"Atta girl."

She'd laughed and thrown a pillow at me.

Now, more than ever, I was certain I had to figure out a way out of this sham of a marriage my father expected to happen. I would not be marrying the man my best friend was in love with.

Things for Will and I had been more or less the same, hooking up wherever and whenever we could, argued all the damn time because he was an asshole and then had more sex.

"Thanks for driving me," Chloe said when I parked the car in front of her teacher's house.

"No problem, just text me if anything comes up."

"I will."

I waited until she'd gone inside, turning to wave back at me before texting Will.

Me: Leaving now.

The Methodist church was only a few minutes away.

Once I pulled into the parking spot, I pulled a baseball cap low on my head and put sunglasses on. The other times I'd been in Will's truck, it was after dark. With the tinted windows, nobody would have been able to see me. Even in the light, it was hard to see through them, but I wasn't taking any chances, especially when we had to drive through the heart of the town to get to his place.

While I waited, I reached in the back seat and pulled my bag into the front, wanting to get from my car to his as quickly as possible. My heart was becoming as big a traitor as my body because it fluttered when I saw his truck pull into the parking lot, pulling in and completely blocking me from the view of the road. When the door swung open, I saw Will leaning across the seat, a wide grin on his face. He had aviators on and looked sexier than he had any right to. "Hey Hales," he greeted me sweetly as I climbed in, closing the door behind me. Surprisingly, it didn't shock me when he kissed me chastely. "Nice disguise."

"Thanks," I mumbled out.

Why was I nervous?

We'd had sex countless times in countless places. Actually, the places weren't countless. The list was pretty limited—his truck, the janitor's closet, the school bathroom, that house in Hillview, the supply closet in the school's basement, and my house. Oh, and the library and the chemistry lab. The number of places we'd fucked was longer than I'd expected, and pretty creative considering our circumstances.

"What's with the duffel bag? I told you not to bring clothes."

"If you think I'm spending all weekend naked," I let my sentence trail off.

"That's where you're confused, doll, I don't think—I know."

We arrived at his house, and he pulled his truck into the garage. I waited until the garage door completely closed behind us before I dared climb out of his truck. Will grabbed my duffel bag, and I wasn't sure if he was doing it to be a gentleman or if he was doing it to hide it, so I would have to be naked for the next two days.

His house was as pristine as I'd always imagined it to be. "Do you want a tour?" He asked.

"No thanks," I said. All I needed to know was where the bathroom was. Tossing my bag at the bottom of the stairs, he pulled me to the couch.

"Let's watch a movie."

This was all too fucking normal, and it was making me itchy on the inside, anxious. I didn't like it, but I didn't protest when Will pulled me down so that I was resting my head on his chest, cuddling me while he held the remote. He put on some cheesy Christmas movie that looked like a Hallmark channel reject.

His arm wrapped around me with my head on his chest all felt so normal. Cuddling. Will and I were cuddling, and I was enjoying it. His body heat radiated into me, making me feel warm and fuzzy, and my heart raced erratically in my chest. It was so loud he could probably hear it, feel it against his own ribs.

Yeah, it was definitely his body heat making me feel that way, not that we were snuggling like a normal couple.

His arm bent at the elbow, and he ran his fingers through my hair. I shivered under his touch, ignoring the warm, tingly feeling that spread through my body.

Cuddling. We were cuddling.

It warranted repeating in my mind because I didn't understand it.

Will grabbed my hand, the one I had resting on his chest. He played with my fingers and bent down to kiss my head. I didn't know if I wanted to run or sink further against him.

Luckily, I didn't have to decide because we were only ten minutes in when he repositioned us, moving his head down to capture my lips. I didn't object. It felt like all we should do was have sex while I was there, not snuggling on his couch or fucking talking. We weren't in a relationship; we were in a mutually beneficial relationship without feelings. I was just here to avoid being at my house, no other reason.

Will's hand cupped my face as he deepened the kiss. Laying me on my back, he pushed himself between my legs. "I can't believe I've got a whole damn house full of beds and I'm still about to fuck you on a couch," he said before moving his lips to my neck, sucking harsh enough that it would leave a mark, and for the first time, I didn't want to stop him.

"We can go upstairs," I told him, turning my neck at the same time to give him more access to my neck.

"No time." His words were punctuated by thrusting against me, his already hard cock pushing against me with the layers of our clothes between us.

"Oh god," I moaned. Will sank his teeth into my neck harshly, making my body buck off the couch. There would be teeth marks in that goddamn hickey he was leaving on my body.

But that was a bruise I didn't mind having.

Sitting back on his knees, he pulled his sweater over his head, allowing me to sit up slightly and undo his belt and shove my hand in his pants. I grabbed his cock, stroking him as his hips pumped forward, thrusting into my hand. Leaning back over me, he pushed our lips together again, sweeping his tongue into my mouth all while I continued to stroke him. His kiss was heated and reckless, with his teeth nipping and sucking on my lips and tongue. My legs wrapped around his hips, lifting in an attempt to feel more of him, but I was still wearing too many clothes. "Fuck, Hales," he grunted in my ear. I was still stroking him, rubbing the drops of pre-cum along his head, making him hiss when he pushed my sweatshirt up and forced me to release him. My bra quickly followed. Taking my hand, Will put it back on his cock while he dropped his mouth to my chest, wrapping his lips around one of my straining nipples.

"Will!" I cried when he used his teeth.

"I love when you scream my name."

For what felt like the first time, we weren't fighting for dominance, just touching how the other loved.

Will switched sides, giving my other nipple the same attention. With one hand still stroking his cock, loving the way he hissed against me, my other hand held his head, clenching into the strands of his hair. When he started kissing his way down my stomach, I had to pull my hand from his pants. He stood from the couch, taking my jeans and panties down with him. I watched as he took his own pants off, leaving us both finally naked. "Stand up." I didn't even protest at his command.

Once the couch was free, Will laid down on it. "Come sit on my face, doll." That was a new position. Maybe we should fuck in his empty house more often. "Face the other way," he said when I tried climbing on him.

I settled on top of him, my face towards his feet. I couldn't see any of his head from between my legs. "Suck my dick while I eat your pretty cunt." The words came out mumbled, his mouth against me as he spoke, but I still understood him.

I leaned my body across his own, my chest against his lower stomach, while I took him into my mouth. I'd only had him in my mouth a moment when I shot back up, moaning from his tongue against me. Lifting his hand, he let it fall against my ass. "Every time you stop, I'm going to stop."

"Fuck, Will."

"Be a good girl for me, and I'll be a good boy for you."

What a compromise.

Leaning back over his body, I wrapped my lips around his cock, not letting myself shoot back up as he licked through me again. Sloppily, letting all the spit I needed fall from my mouth, I bobbed up and down on his cock, moaning around it as his tongue touched every inch of my pussy before circling my clit.

His big hands held my ass cheeks open, forcing me to fall further onto his face.

I was mildly worried he'd suffocate, or drown in me, but he didn't seem to mind.

"Just like that doll," he groaned, sliding two fingers into me. As I took him to the back of my throat, he lifted his hips, and pushed further in and made me choke on him. "I love hearing you choke on my dick, Hales."

I hummed around his cock, pulling back slightly before taking him further. "Fuck," he grunted, his hips lifting again. "Come for me, Hales." He slammed his fingers into me, making me gush, and wrapped his lips around my clit. The angles were different from usual, adding a new sensation and making me come. When I did, I shot straight up again, grinding on his face while my hands dug into the back of the couch next to me, holding myself up.

When my orgasm finally finished, Will pushed me off of him and slid out from under my body. I landed on my stomach with my head against the opposite armrest with Will on top of me in an instant, his thick cock slamming into me from behind and his weight pushing me into the leather of the couch. My clit rubbed against the leather, stimulating me without even trying.

"Harder, Will. Please." I was begging him and didn't care anymore. Nobody ever touched me the way he did, or made me feel the things he did.

"Push your legs together."

"Oh god." He filled me so much better like that, stretching me more, making me feel tighter for both of us.

"Good girl," he whispered. Pulling back, he slammed himself into me, making me scream into the couch. His hand fisted into my hair, wrapping it around his fist and tugging on it. My neck snapped back, and I cried out. Using the position, he tilted my head back roughly, making me hiss in pain and pleasure while he sealed his lips over mine. His rhythm never faltered as he thrust his tongue into my mouth, the same way he was thrusting his dick into my pussy. When he released me, he let his weight fall back on me. "Tell me how much of a slut you are, Haley—my slut."

"Fuck," I cried as I lifted my hips, meeting this thrusts before he pushed me back down, my clit straining against the couch. "Will, I'm a slut for you. Your personal slut."

"Good fucking girl." Will released me, laid on his back, and held his cock up for me. "Come ride my dick." I straddled him, impaling himself on his cock, and his hand went to my throat, squeezing both sides. "Fucking faster, Haley."

Tired of letting him be the one in control, I wrapped my hand around his throat. "Tell me what a slut you are for me," I said wickedly while I squeezed. His eyes rolled back in his head. "Tell me Will. You want me to ride you faster? Be a good boy and tell me how much of a slut you are for my pussy." He didn't answer. "What? It's 2021, baby, boys are sluts now too."

"I'm a slut for your pussy, Hales."

"Good boy," I said condescendingly before finally giving him what he wanted. With my hand still on his throat, I placed a foot on the floor, giving myself more leverage to ride him hard and fast, like he wanted. Releasing my throat, both his hands went to my chest, alternating between squeezing and pinching my nipples.

"Come for me, Hales. I can tell you're close."

Rolling my hips as I let myself fall down on him, my head fell back and my hand squeezed around his throat tighter. "Will! Yes!" I cried as I came, my pussy clamping down on him. Will grunted, his back arching as he came too, spilling himself inside me.

We were both breathing heavy, trying to catch our breaths while he ran his hands softly up my back, almost tenderly while we came down. Lifting off of him, I let myself fall between his legs, facing him.

"I'll be right back," he said.

I laid there naked, my legs still open as I waited for him. When he came back, he had a wet towel for me and a bottle of water, along with one of his t-shirts in his hands. He handed me the towel before pulling on his sweater and jeans while I cleaned myself up. "Here," he said, handing me the t-shirt. I slipped it on and watched as his eyes flashed with possessiveness seeing me in his clothes for the first time.

"Come on, I'll make us lunch."

Will was strangely quiet as he made us sandwiches with chips and homemade cookies.

"These are just as good as I remember," I told him offhandedly when I took a bite of the cookie. He offered me a smile full of an emotion I couldn't place.

We ate in silence even though there were so many things I wanted to say, things I didn't know how to say.

"Honest answers only?" He asked, just like he had on Halloween.

"Okay."

"Why have you been sending me birthday cards all these years?"

"When did you find out?" I asked, truly shocked that he'd figured it out.

"You can ask that when it's your turn. Why?"

"I guess I just thought... I don't know Will. I really don't. When we were younger, it was because I felt bad that you had a summer birthday, figuring you probably didn't get to celebrate either, but then we got older and I figured out you probably got to celebrate. I didn't because of who my parents are, not because of when my birthday is. But it was a habit by that point."

"I figured it out junior year. I saw one of your homework assignments and recognized the handwriting."

"That doesn't count as your answer because I didn't ask."

"I know."

"What did you mean on Halloween when I asked you if you wanted to be the sheriff and you said 'some days yes and some days no'?"

"Some days, I can't imagine my life any other way, always living here, following in my dad's footsteps, trying to better the town. And then there are days when I think that's not the life I want. Sometimes I dream of going to college far away, majoring in business or economics and starting my own company in some high rise in a major city. And other times I imagine..." But he didn't finish his second thought. And I couldn't ask a follow-up question. "How come nobody knows you're valedictorian?" My mouth fell open. "And before you ask, I'm not going to tell you how I found out unless you use it as a question. You only get one freebie."

It took me a moment to gather my thoughts and collect myself before I could answer. I didn't know how he'd figured that out. "Because I want it to be a shock. Nobody really knows me. Hell, Sassy has been my best friend my entire life and there are still parts of me I hide from her, like that. I want people to be shocked. Nobody believes that I'm smart. They see me and all they see is my dad, similar to you, fair or not. I want everyone in the town's jaws to be on the lawn at graduation when they see me being called up to give my speech."

"You always surprise me," he said. It was a compliment that made me blush slightly before he closed the distance and kissed me again. "You've got one more question before I drag you up to the shower and fuck you in there," he said, his voice turning dark and smokey as he spoke.

"Did you apply to colleges other than where everyone thinks you're going?"

"Yes."

And that was all the detail I got before Will swept into his arms and carried me up to his bathroom.

That was how the day went—we'd fuck, then eat, and then we'd fuck again. Then we'd eat again. And in between, we'd cuddle.

"Your mom is such an amazing cook," I exclaimed when we were eating the dinner he'd warmed in the oven. "It's so spicy, but so good."

"Fajitas are my favorite."

"I love Mexican food, too."

"She left my favorite dessert too—chocolate chunk brownies."

"Those sound delicious."

Will cleared our plates when we finished, putting everything into the dishwasher. When he came back to the table, he had two bowls with brownies already in them. I watched him set the bowls on the table before going back to the kitchen, and this time, when he came back, he had butter pecan ice cream, chocolate sauce, whipped cream, and sprinkles.

"How did you know butter pecan was my favorite?"

"Is it really? It's mine too."

I was finding out we had more and more in common. Will scooped ice cream into both bowls before sliding me the whipped cream and chocolate sauce, letting me completely make my sundae before beginning on his own.

"What?" I asked him. He'd spaced out completely. He was done with the whipped cream, but still had the can in his hand and the chocolate sauce in the other.

"I'm just imagining a much better use for these," he said. "Like covering you in them." And it was another very rare occasion where he'd stunned me into silence. "But that might have to wait until tomorrow, I've got other plans for you tonight. Eat up, doll, because after this, we're getting in the hot tub. And don't even bother putting on a bikini."

After we finished dessert, Will grabbed me a robe and a towel. He was already dressed in his own robe when he came down, and I knew he was naked under it. Keeping my eyes locked on his, I pulled the t-shirt I was still wearing over my head. His eyes held fire when he looked at me naked and slowly handed me the robe. I shrugged it on and closed it, tying it off and hiding my body from his prying eyes. He'd kept the curtains closed the entire day, so we'd been able to have sex anywhere in his house without the risk of being caught, but somehow, we still hadn't made it to his bed. We'd made it to his shower, the couch once more and the kitchen counter, but still not a bed.

Will led the way out to the backyard. It was pitch black out and his closest neighbors were about a quarter mile away. The hot tub was nestled close to the house on one side, protecting us from the wind and the peering eyes of his neighbors, but that didn't mean we couldn't be heard. The stars lit up the night sky above us as I watched Will take the top off, folding it over the side. He wasn't shy at all as he shrugged his robe off and hung it and his towel on the rack attached to the staircase. His cock was already half hard for me as he climbed into the warm water.

"Come on in, Haley, the water's fine." I laughed at his lame line. Turning my back to him, I pulled the robe off and hung it on the hook next to his, setting my towel on top of it. The air was freezing, making my nipples harden instantly. Will's eyes were clouded with lust as he watched me climb into the hot tub. The bubbles were on and the hot water instantly made me forget how cold the air was.

Immediately, Will pulled me right to him, without buildup, no pretense of climbing in to relax. He'd brought me in with him to fuck.

Hands around my waist, he held me to him, his erect cock pushing into my thigh. Seductively, he ran his nose along the side of my neck, up along my jaw. Turning my head with his hands, he tilted it, pushing his lips against mine. Reaching between us, I stroked his cock under the water, making him moan into my mouth.

"You know," I said while still stroking him. "Hot tub sex isn't nearly as sexy as you think it is."

"Way to kill the mood, Hales," he said, still kissing along my neck as I spoke again.

"It's pretty much guaranteed to give me a urinary tract infection. And the chlorine will make it feel like everything is dry, and I know how much you like things *wet*."

"You're the problem solver, Miss Valedictorian. And you like to be in charge." His hands moved up my waist to my breasts, squeezing them. "Tell me what to do."

"Keep kissing me," I whispered. Will groaned, pushing his lips back against mine while I stroked him under the water, making him moan loudly into the kiss. His hips lifted, thrusting into my hand and making my tits bounce against his hand. Taking control of the kiss, I rolled my tongue along his, making him chase me before I pushed back in. My teeth nipped at his lips before I sucked on his tongue. His hands dug into me harder, more sexy moans falling from his mouth and into my own.

I was going to regret what I was about to ask him to do because it was fucking freezing, but I definitely wanted to add a hot tub to the list of places we'd fucked.

Pulling away, I sat on the opposite edge from where we'd been, keeping my legs in the water and cupping handfuls of water and running them over my body in an attempt to keep me warm.

"Get to work," I commanded, opening my legs for him. Will half swam, half walked to me, his hands wrapping around my thighs before his mouth descended on me. He'd had his mouth on my pussy four times already today. I'd only had his cock in my mouth once—the first time. The other times had been all about me.

"Damn doll, you taste better every fucking time I have you."

The December air was numbing, hardening my nipples further, but I didn't care that I was probably going to catch the worst cold of my life like this. All I cared about was Will's wicked tongue working against me, the whispered words I couldn't understand because they were mumbled against me as he flicked his tongue against my clit again and again.

"Scream for me Haley, come on. Come on my tongue, baby."

I'd slipped and called him baby twice earlier. That was the first time he'd called me that. Shockingly, I much preferred doll or Hales falling from his lips.

"Will! Fuck." My hands fisted in his hair as his entire mouth covered my pussy. His tongue thrust inside while his upper lip rubbed against my clit, bringing me higher and higher. My legs clamped around his head as I came, squeezing him in a death grip while I cried out.

When Will pulled away from me, his mouth was covered in my release. My pussy spasmed when he licked his lips, blue eyes locked on mine. Quickly, I turned, leaning over the edge with my ass high in the air.

Will stood in the hot tub, lining himself up with me. Hands on my hips, he pushed into me slowly. I felt every inch of him stretching me for the fifth time today. My body would be so sore tomorrow. I'd never had this much sex at once. I didn't think he had either.

"God, I love being inside you. I love how warm and wet you are, the way you feel wrapped around me; it's fucking addicting, doll."

I spasmed around him again when he whispered 'doll'.

"Harder, Will. Please, baby."

"Fuck, again." He punctuated his words by raising his hand and slapping it against my ass, spanking me. I moaned before speaking.

"Harder!"

"The other," he barked.

"Baby," I whispered, my entire body shaking as I spoke the word. "Harder, please, baby, I need it harder."

Will let out a guttural groan before pulling out and slamming himself inside of me. He paused momentarily before pulling back and repeating the process. My knuckles were white as I clung to the edge of the hot tub and my breasts swayed wildly with each one of his rough thrusts.

"Yes!" I cried. "Will, I'm going to come again."

"How many is that today?" He asked, smugly. I couldn't even remember—at least twelve. I might not even wake up in the morning. "Come on my dick, doll, soak me with it."

My pussy clamped down on him, squeezing while I came all over him. "God, that's the sexiest fucking thing," he groaned.

Pulling away, Will pulled me into the water. "We're not done yet," he whispered. "But I can't have you freezing to death on me." Turning me in his arms, he put my knees on either side of his hips. I could feel his dick poking at my entrance, but he didn't try to slip it inside; he wouldn't, not after telling him what I told him. He respected me.

Instead, he kissed me again. He tasted like me, and I moaned into his mouth. His hands roamed up and down my back, touching me all over, warming me with his hands just as much as the water was warming my cold skin again. I didn't know how long he kissed me for, but I was breathless when he finally pulled away. His lips moved to the other side of my neck, leaving a matching hickey to the one he'd left earlier.

"Fuck me. Please," I whined, needy for him. Will stood, lifting me straight out of the water with him, and walked us to the corner. Laying me across it, he lifted my ankles to his shoulders, slamming himself back into me.

"This has to be quick, doll. Play with your clit for me."

I watched Will's eyes darken and follow the path my hand took as I slid it down my body between my folds. His arms wrapped around the tops of my thighs, holding me still while he pushed himself faster and faster inside me. My clit was straining and over sensitive from being touched too much with the two orgasms I'd already had.

"I'm so close, baby."

"Come for me, Haley. Let me feel it."

"Come inside me," I begged. "I need it, Will, so fucking bad."

He growled, releasing my legs and letting them fall. His body covered mine, making the cold seem less harsh. His face pushed into the corner of my neck, his thrusting becoming wild as the water from the hot tub splashed out around us.

I pinched my clit and made myself come as his cock pushed against my g-spot, sending me into an intense orgasm. My voice cried out into the night, not caring that it could definitely be heard. Will moaned, long and low as I felt him spill himself inside me.

"Haley," he said my name like he was in awe when he'd finally stopped.

Pulling out, he dragged us back into the hot tub. Both of our teeth were chattering. His arms wrapped around me tightly with my face tucked into his neck, snuggling again. His embrace made me feel safe from more than just the cold as we held onto each other, not daring to speak.

CHAPTER 20

THE BED

Will

Sunday morning, I woke up in the middle of the night with Haley still wrapped in my arms, just like how we'd fallen asleep. As carefully as I could, without waking her, I untangled us and walked to the bathroom.

When I got back to my room, she was curled into herself, seeking the warmth she'd been getting from me. I climbed back into bed, pulling her close, and her body immediately relaxed into mine, a soft, happy sigh leaving her slightly parted lips.

I'm a goner.

When I woke up again, I was in a lucid dream state, images of Saturday filling my mind. I'd taken Haley half a dozen times over the entire house—except for my damn bed. After the hot tub, we'd been too tired to have sex another time. It was late, and we'd been fucking all day. It seemed like every time with Haley got better and better, but despite that, her bedroom was still my favorite. Yesterday, she didn't have to quiet her moaning, bite her lip or have me cover her mouth with my hand, able to cry out as loud as she wanted, and she did, the sound like music to my ears every time she came for me.

The only thing on today's list was to finally fucking take her on a bed.

Last night, when we went to sleep, she hadn't protested when I wrapped my arms around her and fell asleep holding her close to me.

How long before she figured out what I couldn't deny anymore?

I'm in love with Haley Winters.

Admitting that, along with dreaming about her lips wrapped around me made me think I could actually feel her lips around me as I woke. Blinking my eyes open, I realized there was a reason for that.

My blanket was pulled down over my hips and resting between my legs was Haley, the blanket wrapped around her shoulders while she slobbered all over my dick. "Fuck, Hales," I grunted, hands going to her hair and fisting the long strands. "You're fucking perfect." She either didn't hear me, or chose to ignore me, either was plausible.

Wordlessly, she grabbed my hands and pulled them off of her head, pinning them to the mattress as she continued to bob up and down on me, sucking on me hard and using her tongue along the underside of my dick. When I lifted my hips, forcing her to take more of me, she pulled away, hands still pinning mine to the mattress, and she grazed her teeth—just barely—along the head, making me lose my mind. When her mouth was finally free of me, she looked me dead in the eyes and let a wad of spit fall from her mouth to the head of my dick. "Hold still like a good little boy or I'm going to stop."

"Haley, please," I begged her.

"Be a good boy for me, Will."

Her grip on my wrists was nearly painful as she dug her nails into them, but the pain added to my pleasure. Her wet mouth soaked me completely, covering my thighs and running down my balls. I could feel her everywhere, and I wanted to wake up like this every single fucking day for forever.

"Fuck, doll, I'm gonna come." She moaned, taking me all the way to her throat and hummed, making me see stars as I clenched my eyes closed and came down her throat. "What a fucking wake up call," I murmured when she pulled off of me. She had a self-satisfied smirk on her face, knowing how worked up she'd had me, but now it was my turn.

Grabbing her under her arms, I lifted her off of me and threw her to her back. "Will," she said breathily, the sound making my wilted dick already come back to life.

"Be a good little girl for me." I mirrored her words, making her gulp as I laid her flat on the bed and pushed her thighs apart, finding her already sopping wet for me. "Did you get this wet from sucking my dick, or did you wake up like this? Were you dreaming about all the things I did to you yesterday? In the kitchen, the shower, on the couch, and finally the fucking hot tub."

"Yes," she admitted easily. She was relinquishing control to me, and I wanted to keep it. I finally had her in a fucking bed, and there was no way I was letting this moment slip without doing what I wanted to her. I had her right where I wanted her. Settling my shoulders between her spread thighs, I used my thumbs to hold her pussy lips open, and held still, staring right at her. "W-W-Will," she stuttered out.

"Shh," I shushed her words and movements as she squirmed beneath me, her ass wiggling and her hands clutching into the sheets.

"Please," she whined.

Finally, I gave her what we both wanted and licked her from her dripping opening up to her straining clit. Her back bowed, and she struggled against me, trying to get me to do more to her, to give her what she wanted and not do to her what I wanted. I circled her clit a few times with my tongue, building her pleasure before retreating and sucking on each of her puffy little lips. "Fuck," she cursed. Opening my eyes, I looked up at her, trying to memorize every moment of pleasure that washed over her face, every moment I was giving her.

"Eyes on me, doll," I said. Her light-brown eyes opened, completely clouded over with lust, as she looked down at me. Slowly, making sure she could see my every action, I licked her again from her hole to her clit. Her nostrils flared, and she clenched her eyes shut before snapping them back open. "Good girl," I praised her. Keeping my eyes tilted up at her, I licked around her clit, flicking it quickly like I knew she loved, her body tightening like a spring, ready to pop back open as her orgasm built. She was so close, and I wasn't going to deny her. I wrapped my lips around her, sucking her into my mouth and flicked my tongue against her.

"Will! Will! Ah!" She moaned long and loud, her back arching and her release flooding my mouth as I brought her over the edge, but I still wasn't done.

Pulling my mouth away, I slid two fingers inside of her, watching as her orgasm slowed and her body stopped shaking. When I curled my fingers, she snapped her eyes open, confusion on her face. "W-what?"

"I can't fucking get enough of you, Hales." Her back arched again while I hit the spot inside of her that was guaranteed to make her see stars. She spread her legs even wider, giving me more access to slide a third finger in. Her hips lifted, humping my fingers desperately. "You're such a slut, doll. You just came and you want another."

"Only for you, Will."

Her words were dangerously close to admitting she felt the same for me that I did for her.

"My what, Hales?"

"I'm your slut, baby. You made me your personal slut."

The baby pet name slipped out in a moment of passion, but she'd kept using it and I fucking loved it. It was so much better than her calling me asshole.

Curling my fingers inside her, I rubbed her g-spot and watched as her mouth fell open and her eyes closed, head lolling back as she got close to another orgasm.

"Will," she breathed out my name, and it was the sexiest thing I'd ever heard fall from her pretty lips.

She came, covering my fingers in another release while no sound came out of her. I watched, mesmerized, as her body tensed and released. Her eyes opened again, staring at me in awe, and I pulled my fingers from her, bringing all three to my mouth and sucking them clean. Sliding up her body, I lined my dick up with her pussy, settling on top of her and easing inside inch by inch. Usually we were rushed, but I wanted to take my time with her for once, but she had other plans, wrapping her legs around me and pulling me in. "Naughty girl," I whispered. "So damn greedy for my dick." She didn't say anything, didn't protest, but anchored her legs tighter around me and held me inside her, buried to the hilt. "You feel so fucking good wrapped around me, so tight, so wet and warm." She moaned in my ear and ran her hands down my back until they got to my ass, digging her nails in and making me hiss. I pulled my hips back slowly and slid back in, feeling her clench around me. Burying my face in her neck, I felt her warm breath against my skin and her soft panting in my ear. I kept my body as close to her as I could while I fucked her in long, slow, deliberate strokes, building her up slowly, and it was driving my girl absolutely crazy. Her hands slid from my ass up my back to my neck, and I pulled my face out from the crook of her neck, looking down at her.

What I saw there had my slow rhythm faltering.

She loves me too, I'm absolutely fucking sure.

Her hand slid to my neck, and I grabbed it, interlocking our fingers and pinning it by her head while I kept my slow and steady pace. Haley's tits heaved, her hard nipples scraping against my chest while I rocked above her. "Faster, please," she whined.

"No," I told her defiantly. I was in control, and it seemed like she was going to let me stay there.

"Will," she begged.

Ignoring her, I kept my pace, letting her feel every inch of me as I stretched her pussy. She fit around me so perfectly. Her moaning got louder and the sounds her sopping pussy was making for me got louder too, absolutely gushing for me while my hips slapped against hers, while I rolled them just enough to rub against her clit with every thrust. "Just like that," she whimpered. "Will, I'm going to come again."

"I know, Hales, come for me. I'm nowhere near fucking close to being done with you yet. Let me hear you, doll."

The hand that was holding mine dug into it painfully as her body tightened even tighter than the first two times and she spasmed beneath me, soaking me again.

"I love how fucking hard you come for me, Hales," I whispered, fucking her through her orgasm. When she finally stilled, I pulled out of her, sitting on my knees, and lifted her leg around my body before rolling her to her stomach.

"I don't think so," she said before quickly scrambling away from me. She pushed me to my back, and my dick back inside her before I even realized what was happening. Her hands braced on my chest, nails digging into my skin while she set a rhythm that had to be five times faster than the one I'd just taken her with. She wanted control, but I still wasn't ready to give it up. Her tits bounced in my face and I grabbed them, palming them before lifting my head and sucking one into my mouth, licking around the taught bud. "Yes!" She hissed. I switched sides, bringing her more pleasure while she ground herself on me. While she was distracted, I sat up, pushing our fronts together, forcing her legs to shift and wrap around me while I crossed mine underneath her, in a lotus position, bringing us impossibly closer.

If she hadn't realized it yet, I wasn't fucking her, I was making love to her.

She must know.

She had to know how I felt about her at this point.

I'd do anything for her.

We rocked against each other, barely thrusting, but it was so fucking good.

"Haley," I whispered.

"I know. Fuck, Will, I know. Don't stop. Please, you're going to make me come again." Her head was pushed next to my own while she clung to my shoulders and I roamed my hands all over her back. Her pussy clamped around my dick, telling me she was close again.

"I'm gonna come," I whispered in her ear. "Come for me, doll. Let's go over together."

"Will!" She cried, her head tilting back while she clamped down around me.

"Haley, fuck," I grunted, as I finally spilled myself inside her.

We shook in each other's arms as our orgasms rolled through our bodies. And when we were done, we stayed like that, still connected, breathing heavily, just clinging to the other.

How the fuck had I let myself fall in love with her?

"Damn," she whispered before pulling her sweat covered body away from mine and untangling our bodies.

"Let's shower," I told her. I was scared that if I said anything else, I'd blurt out the words, and as much as I wished she was, I knew she wasn't ready for them.

"Are you hungry?" I asked her when we finally made it out of the shower and to the kitchen.

"Starving. You've barely fed me all weekend."

"Not true. I've fed you plenty."

"Your cock doesn't count," she smirked.

"I've fed you real food too, doll." She laughed at me. "You've just been burning it off quicker than usual." She blushed, and I fucking loved it.

"I might be broken. I've never had this much sex in two days."

Now it was my turn to laugh at her.

"We'll see how you feel after I feed you again." A moment of silence passed between us and again, I was tempted to blurt out the words. "Sit," I said, pointing to the barstools. "I hope you like pancakes."

"Do you have chocolate chips?"

"Do you ever eat vegetables?" I asked.

"With pancakes?" She quipped, her nose scrunching up cutely.

"Not with pancakes, just ever."

"Sometimes, but I didn't exactly have suitable role models for home-cooked meals."

I immediately felt guilty for my question. She'd turned out amazing, no thanks to her parents.

"Yes, I have chocolate chips." She smiled widely at me, and it only got brighter when I set a cup of coffee in front of her. "What time do you have to pick up your sister?" I asked while I was mixing the batter.

"Noon."

"We'll leave at eleven forty-five. I'll drop you back off at your car."

"Thanks." She took an awkward pause, contemplating her next words. "And thanks for… this," she said, her hand doing a circle in the air. Translation from Haley language to regular language—thanks for letting me stay here this weekend. The ice queen said thanks, even if it was in her own way. "I haven't felt safe like this in a long time."

Safe.

She felt safe with me.

"Can I have another cup of coffee?" She asked when I was pouring batter onto the griddle.

"Yeah, go ahead and grab it."

Haley sat at the breakfast bar, texting on her phone, most likely with Sassy, but I didn't ask. "Here," I said, sliding her a plate of pancakes and setting one where I would sit next to her. I grabbed the butter and syrup and set them next to her too. "Do you want something else to drink?"

"Milk?"

"Sure." I smiled at her. Unsure-Haley was a new version, one I could get used to.

This all felt so normal. When was she finally going to admit that we weren't just enemies with benefits anymore? Hell, we were barely even enemies anymore. This felt like we were a couple, and I knew she knew that, but I also knew that she was too damn stubborn to ever admit it. I needed to tread carefully, otherwise she was going to bolt.

Not yet, I chide myself. Don't tell her yet.

We ate in silence, and Haley cleared her plate in record time. "That was so good."

"My mom taught me to cook. It's important to her that I know how to cook and clean, that way my future wife doesn't have to mother me."

Her eyes blinked quickly as I said the word wife, and I'd officially just made this awkward, even though I hadn't meant to. Before things could get too out of hand, I grabbed our plates and brought them to the sink.

"What's that?" She asked when a rumbling noise sounded through the house.

"Shit," I cursed. "My parents, they're early."

"What!" She shrieked at me. "Will, we cannot get caught together!"

"It's too late," I said, just as the door from the garage was opening. My parents walked in and found Haley looking terrified, looking for anywhere to run, like a wild animal, panicking once they realized they were cornered.

"You're early," I said casually.

"Yeah," my dad said, but he was looking at a wide-eyed Haley. "Ms. Winters," he greeted her politely.

"Sheriff," she said, her voice terrified. "I should go," she blurted out.

"I'll take you."

"I'm fine," she protested.

"Hales," I said her name and her scared eyes flashed to mine. "I'll take you."

"Okay," she agreed reluctantly.

"It was nice to see you, Haley," my mom told her.

"You too, and you Sheriff." My dad nodded at her before turning to me.

"Come straight home."

Fuck.

"Yes, sir." Haley was already moving out of the kitchen. "Go get in the truck, I'll grab your bag."

She didn't reply as she hurried out the door.

"Haley Winters?" My dad all but shouted at me.

"Ian, please," my mom said, trying to calm him.

"We can talk about this when I get back. Just let me get her out of here. She's terrified."

"Fine," my dad sighed. "Come straight home," he warned again, but he didn't need to warn me a second time.

Racing up the stairs, I grabbed Haley's bag, making sure I stuffed everything back into it before heading to my truck. My parents were whispering when I walked through the kitchen, and I was dreading the conversation to come.

"Haley," I said when I climbed into the truck.

"Don't Will," she said. "Your parents know."

"And they won't say anything. I swear our secret is safe."

"But are the rest of mine?"

"Yes," I told her, hoping she couldn't see through the lie.

"This was reckless."

"Maybe it's better they know. All they care about is that we're being safe, and they know who your dad is; they won't say anything to anyone."

She bit her bottom lip, unsure if she believed me or not. She'd pulled the hood of her sweatshirt up in an effort to camouflage herself.

"Please, don't worry about this. We had such a good weekend, and next time they're gone, I'll just tell them you're coming over, and if they know, you can come when they're home too, whenever your sister is gone, even if I'm not alone."

"I don't know. They didn't seem happy I was there."

"They were surprised." She went to say something, and I was terrified she was going to run again. "Haley, I promise you, it's fine. Just relax."

"Okay," she agreed reluctantly.

I pulled into the parking lot of the church and put the truck in park. "Will you meet me in the morning?"

"I wasn't lying when I said I'm broken," she said.

Her words made me laugh. "Not for sex. I might need a break too. I'll tell you what happened with my parents."

"Okay, I'll see you in the morning."

Leaning across the cab, I kissed her, letting my lips linger. "Later, doll."

"Bye, Will."

I watched her go until she was safely inside her car before I pulled away and headed home.

My parents were sitting at the table, holding hands, a cup of coffee in front of them and a plate of cookies. Mom never had serious conversations without some sort of sweet treat in front of her.

"Sit," my dad commanded. I gulped but did as he said. "Haley Winters, Will. Are you serious?"

"Do you know what will happen to you if her dad finds out?" My mom asked.

"Yes," I answered both of them at the same time.

"Is she your friend who's in trouble?"

"Yes."

"I want to know everything."

"I promised her I wouldn't tell."

"I don't give a shit," he barked, and my mom squeezed his hand.

"Her mom beats her, and it's bad. Her sister wasn't home this weekend and the beatings are worse when she's not home, so I told her she could stay here."

"But you're sleeping with her. She's the girl from the party in Hillview."

"She is."

"How long has this been going on?" My mom asked.

"Since the start of school."

"And you're being safe?"

"We are."

"Let's go back to her being abused," my dad said.

"She's eighteen, but her sister is only fifteen. She doesn't want her to end up in the system. Her mom only beats her, not Chloe."

"I can help."

"I told her that, but she says it'll only end up with Chloe in the system and her not knowing if her sister is safe or not." Dad inhaled deeply, and I could tell he was thinking. "You can't do anything with this information. She'll kill me if she finds out I told you."

"You're in love with her."

My mom's words caught me off guard. Was it really that obvious?

"I am. How could I not be? She's damn near a genius, smarter than I could ever hope to be. She's been through more than anyone our age should have ever been through, and does everything she can to protect her little sister. She's vulnerable with me, even if she doesn't realize she's doing it yet. I love how she drives me crazy on purpose. She gets under my skin like no one else, and she sees me—to my core."

My mom looked at me with something like pride. "Does she know?"

"No, she'll run. She's a flight risk, and I need to protect her. That's more important than telling her right now."

"How are you protecting her?" Dad asked.

"However I can, letting her come here, keeping her secrets."

"I don't like this," he said. "This is dangerous. Viper is a psychopath."

"I know. That's why we're being careful. Nobody knows, and nobody is going to know."

My dad just shook his head. "You're eighteen, legally an adult, but I'm telling you, you're playing with fire."

"I know."

And for Haley, I was prepared to get burned.

CHAPTER 21

THE DRAWINGS

Haley

The weeks after Will and I got caught by his parents passed the same as before they knew. We hooked up at school and in his truck, but I hadn't been back to his house, despite him saying that his parents were fine with it. It felt too awkward, even though he assured me his parents weren't going to say anything. Their only concern was my dad not finding out, which was a concern we all shared because my dad could absolutely not find out. It would lead to at least one of us dead, probably both of us.

I should have ended it then, but whatever was going on between Will and me, I didn't want to end it.

His parents were going out of town for New Year's Eve, headed up to Oregon, where his aunt lived and celebrating there. Usually Will would go with them, but he wanted to spend New Year's Eve together, and I definitely wanted to kiss him at midnight and, since Chloe had to babysit, it worked out perfectly.

I just still had to tell Sassy I wouldn't be spending it with her this year, which was fine considering she was probably going to be with Snake anyway.

"Merry Christmas," Sassy said when she let me into her trailer. It was freezing out, and I was frozen from the short walk between our trailers.

"It's only Christmas Eve."

"Don't be such a grinch."

"I'm always a bitch, you don't have to switch it to grinch just because it's Christmas."

"Shut up and close the door. It's freezing."

Sassy and I walked to her couch, climbing under a blanket and huddling together. "What did you get Snake for Christmas?"

"He didn't want to exchange gifts since neither of us has any money." I nodded at her. "But I got a sexy red lingerie set. It's just from the cheap section of the dollar store, but it fits me well."

"He'll love it, and he'll get to unwrap you like a present."

"Did you get Will something?"

"Why would I get Will anything? We're not a couple."

"You've been exclusively sleeping together for the entire year."

"And that doesn't make a couple. There're no feelings, it's just sex."

And she knew, just like I knew, I was lying. Did I have very confusing feelings for Will? Yes. Was I going to do anything about said feelings? Ignoring and pushing them down was all I could do because having feelings for Will Roberts was absolutely not something I could allow myself to do. I couldn't think about how I liked it when he made me laugh more than when he made me come. I couldn't think about how being with him made me feel safe for the first time in my life, and I certainly couldn't think about how attracted I was to his personality—even more than his handsome face. His cocky smugness came off as confidence in everything he did, and there was nothing more attractive than confidence. No, I couldn't think about that because it would lead to disaster, and we were already flirting dangerously with that line. I could only imagine it felt like living on the east coast and seeing a hurricane rolling in days before disaster was going to strike, but telling yourself it wasn't going to be as bad as they predicted, but then, when it finally hit land, it was so much worse. I was going to drown in the hurricane that was Will Roberts and I wasn't even attempting to flee the wreckage guaranteed to be left in his wake.

"You can lie to yourself all you want, but when you're ready to stop lying to me, I'm here to listen."

I did not deserve her. The closer the date of my departure got, the more I wanted to tell her, and I would, eventually, but not yet.

"Come on," she said. "I'll make us hot chocolate and we can watch one of those stupid Christmas movies where the guy from the big city falls for the small town country girl. We can compare the men to our men."

Nobody compared to Will, but I agreed anyway. "Sure."

Sassy and I watched two ridiculously cliche movies. The plot was virtually the same, only the actors and the town were different, but it all added up to the same thing—a big city executive or lawyer hated Christmas, but somehow managed to end up at a small town Inn for the Holiday and fall for the inexplicably young woman who somehow had inherited an Inn from a family member and was obsessed with Christmas.

"Is Will anything like these guys?" Sassy asked.

"Not even a little," I laughed. "He's a little bit of a simp though," I admitted. "Everywhere except the bedroom."

"Have you two even had sex on a bed?" She asked.

"Just once."

I couldn't tell her he'd been making love to me in his bed. There was no other way to describe what happened between us at his house. It was slow, gentle, and so fucking tender that I thought I might die. He hadn't seen the tears that fell after the last orgasm. Maybe he hadn't realized what we'd been doing?

"At your house?"

"No, my bed was too squeaky."

"You've been to his house, then?"

"Yeah," I sighed, not sure how much detail I actually wanted to give her about what happened that weekend.

"You're being reckless."

"I know, Sassy, trust me."

"You wouldn't be this reckless if it was just sex."

"For amazing sex? The hell I wouldn't." She looked like she wanted to say more, but I cut her off. "How's Snake in the sack anyway? You addicted yet?"

"I have no idea if it's like it is with us for everyone, but my god, Haley, he knows exactly how to touch me, when to be rough and when to be gentle. He takes me like I'm a sex worker, degrading me and then praising me for how well I take it and then when we're finished, he pulls me next to him and whispers how much he loves me."

Tears of happiness filled my eyes. They were so good for each other. If I believed in soulmates, I would say that was what they were, but I didn't.

"You guys are perfect for each other."

"I'm going to be broken when it ends."

"Why would it end?"

"He has to marry you."

"I told you. I'm working on getting us out of that."

"How?" She asked again.

"Just trust me. As soon as I have a solid plan, I'll let both of you know. Okay?"

"Okay."

"I've got to go home. Chloe is waiting for me. I'm gonna have to suffer through more Christmas movies."

"At least you'll get more hot chocolate."

"Have a good Christmas."

"You too, I'll see you at New Year's."

"Oh, about that."

"You're going with Will?"

"Yes."

"Okay."

"Are you mad?"

"No, of course not. Just be careful, Haley. Please. I'm worried about you."

"I've got it under control, I promise."

I kissed her cheek before climbing off of her couch and heading back to my own trailer. While I was on my way, my phone beeped.

> Baby: Can you meet me?
> Me: Not right now.
> Baby: Ten? Our spot.
> Me: Okay.

I tucked my phone back into my pocket after deleting the messages. I'd been high, smoking with Sassy, when I'd changed his name in my phone, but even sober me couldn't change it back. I called him baby too fucking often now, but it was a habit I couldn't break.

"Hey Chloe," I said to my sister, who was cuddled up on the couch. She was on her phone, FaceTiming someone. "Who's that?"

"Mick."

She was always on the phone with him and I was worried she was in love. I didn't want her to get hurt. "I have to go, too."

"Merry Christmas, babe," he said.

Babe?

"Merry Christmas. I'll call you in a few days. Have fun with your grandparents."

"Bye." She waved and smiled goofily at the camera.

"So?" I asked her.

"So, what?"

"Are you guys a couple now?"

"Yes."

"And have you?"

"No, not yet."

"But you're taking your birth control like they told you to?"

"Yes, at the same time every night, and just because I'm on birth control doesn't mean he doesn't have to use a condom."

I was glad she thought that because once you started to sleep with someone without them, it was hard to go back. She was only fifteen, and I wanted to tell her she was too young to be having sex, but that would be hypocritical of me. I'd been fifteen, and the average was around sixteen or something. I wasn't going to try to talk her out of it. I'd given her all the tools she needed to be safe, and Mick genuinely seemed to be good to her.

"Did you come home to watch a movie with me?"

"As long as it's not *Elf*," I told her.

"Fine, make the hot chocolate."

"Okay, bossy." She rolled her eyes at me but turned the TV on. The only thing on today and tomorrow would be Christmas movies, so it wouldn't be hard for her to find one. When I got back to the couch, two mugs in my hand, the opening credits were rolling. "What's this?"

"Christmas Chronicles."

We sat on the couch, sipping hot chocolate and watching the movie. It was a kid's movie, but it was definitely better than the ones I'd watched with Sassy.

"I need to go out for a little while," I told her.

"I'm hungry," she said. "We forgot to eat dinner."

"I'll swing by McDonald's."

Because it was winter and she was babysitting more often, we didn't go to the diner nearly as much, so my college fund was back to its previous amount.

"Double cheeseburger, nuggets, fries and lots of sauce."

"I know," I smiled at her. "I'll be back, Squirt."

I left the trailer, hoping my parents wouldn't be back before I was and climbed in my car, heading to meet Will.

His truck was parked behind the church when I pulled in. I hid my car in the clearing, just like always. Will was opening the door before I'd even put the car in park. "Hey Hales," he greeted me, leaning in for a kiss. He was always kissing me these days. Sassy's words echoed in my mind, but I pushed them down, ignoring them at all costs.

"Why did you want to meet?" I asked. We never had sex here. Since his parents found out, we'd been only slightly more cautious.

"I have something for you, a Christmas gift."

"Will, no." Enemies with benefits didn't get each other gifts, and sure, maybe we had moved into the friends with benefits territory, but gifts were still not on the list of things we exchanged.

"I didn't spend any money on you."

"Just when you rig a fake prize at the grocery store and give me a fifty-dollar gift card."

His eyes widened, but he didn't seem surprised that I knew. "Take it," he said, handing me a present that looked to be the size of a picture frame. He watched me with eager eyes as I unwrapped it.

"Will," I breathed his name. I was holding a piece of art, and I was the subject. Staring back at me was my own image—my own naked image.

Is this how he sees me? I thought to myself.

In the colored drawing, I was on my back, and the details were wildly intricate. You could see everything from the tattoo he'd drawn from memory on my side to the scar on my left hip my mom left from one of her beatings when I was younger. My eyes were drawn in the exact shade they were. My breasts were completely proportioned to my body. He hadn't drawn the image explicitly but with my legs crossed. It was a breathtaking drawing.

"Did you draw this?"

"Yes."

How had I been spending so much time with him and not noticed that he was an artist?

"Is this what you actually want to do?"

"Sometimes."

"It's beautiful, Will, you're so talented."

"I had a good subject." He brushed off the compliment with a shrug. Modest Will wasn't a version I was used to, but I liked it just as much as the cocky version. I couldn't stop looking at it. He'd captured my smile too, and it looked true and genuine, which must be how I smiled at him when we were together.

"Thank you, I love it."

"Something tells me you don't usually get a lot of Christmas gifts, but you should." He tucked a piece of hair behind my ear while I offered him a soft smile. "I need to get back. I'll see you in a few days. Merry Christmas, Hales."

"Merry Christmas, Will." He kissed me again before he was climbing out of my car and back to his truck. It took me a few minutes to collect myself and stop staring at the drawing in my hands. He must have spent a little money because it was framed.

Feeling more confused than ever, I set it on the passenger seat and pulled out, heading towards McDonald's.

The week between Christmas and New Year's Eve was always strange. I never knew what day it was, but I spent a lot of time with Chloe and Sassy. Snake was given a lot of shifts watching the wild animals. Apparently there'd been two more shipments since the first, and product was moving well. That meant the club was finally making money. Not that making money changed how my dad treated any of us; he still yelled at my mom for spending too much. I'd only had one beating all break, and it was a quick one, just a backhand across the face, and it hadn't even bruised. I worked Christmas Day, the movie theater's busiest day of the year, and a bunch of shifts after that, making as much money as I could.

I hadn't seen Will at all. He'd been spending time with his grandparents who were in town, and his dad took the week off. I'd never admit it to him or anyone else, but I missed him, and not just the sex. Every time I was at the movie theater, I'd hoped he'd show up like he did the one-time, but he never did. Bobby was on vacation, so I didn't see him either, not that things between us had changed. I was only hooking up with Will, but Bobby was the one person who knew me without knowing my entire sordid history and about my dad, and it felt good to be treated normally by a friend once in a while.

"Are you almost ready to go?" Chloe asked. "We need to leave soon."

"Yeah, I am." I grabbed the duffel bag that had two days' worth of clothes in it and slung it over my shoulder.

"I'm picking you up the day after New Year's Day?" I double checked.

"Yes, Mrs. Scott is going to party tonight and then on the first she's got a double shift at the bar she works at, so she'll come home to sleep and then go as soon as she's awake."

"Are you going to have Mick over while she's gone?"

Chloe looked like a deer in headlights. It was the oldest trick in the book; babysitting was the easiest gig in the world if the kids slept well, and it was easier to sneak around when parents weren't home; I would know.

"Yes," she admitted.

"Be safe," was the only thing I said to her. She nodded and walked away. She was definitely ready to take the next step with him, at least she thought she was. I wasn't sure if she actually was, but she thought she was, and I wouldn't be able to talk her out of it. I hated how fast she was growing up. I would always feel the need to protect her.

My phone beeped as I was walking to the car behind my sister.

> Baby: Text me when you drop your sister off. See you soon, doll.

I smiled stupidly at my phone before tucking it into my pocket.

"Have a good time," I told Chloe when I dropped her off outside Mrs. Scott's house.

"You too."

She climbed out, and like always, I waited until she was inside before I drove away, but not before texting Will.

Just like the last time we'd done this, I parked my car in the clearing as he pulled his truck completely in front of it, blocking me from view as I pulled a hood on and put sunglasses on my face.

"Hey Hales," he smiled at me. It was me who initiated the kiss this time, leaning across the space between us and pushing my lips against his.

"How's your break been?" He asked. It seemed like an innocent enough question, but I knew he was asking if he was going to find a bruise on me when he got my clothes off.

"It's been okay. I've worked a lot and not been home too much." I didn't tell him about the beating because there was no evidence of it.

He nodded at me, but I didn't miss the way his hand tightened around the steering wheel; he knew I was dancing around the truth, but he didn't call me on it.

When we got to his house, he pulled his truck into the driveway like last time and closed it behind us before I climbed out. "Are you hungry?" He asked. It was right around lunchtime. "I don't want to be accused of not feeding you enough again," he teased. I smiled at him, unable to help myself.

"Will, we've been doing this for long enough now that you should know I'm always hungry."

He laughed at me, and I relished the sound. "Come on. I'll make us lunch. Mac and cheese okay?"

"Sure."

I watched Will make macaroni and cheese from scratch on the stovetop. He really could cook, he didn't even use Velveeta.

"This is amazing," I said when I finally took the first bite.

"I told you I could cook."

We ate in comfortable silence, and when we were done, Will cleaned up. "Honest answers only?" He asked me.

"Okay," I nodded.

"Have you really never been with Snake?" He asked. That wasn't the question I'd been expecting. He seemed... jealous and a little self-conscious.

"No, I'm not into Snake. I never was." He nodded, content with my answer. "The drawing you gave me, was that the only one you've ever drawn of me?"

"No."

"Can I see the others?"

"It's not your turn, doll." He offered me a teasing grin, making me roll my eyes at him. "What are your plans after graduation?"

"Undecided." It technically wasn't a lie because I still hadn't heard from any of the schools I'd applied to.

"Are you gonna ask the question you just asked?" I nodded. "Yes, you can see them. Come on."

I followed Will upstairs to his bedroom, the bed a reminder of what happened last time I'd been there. Walking to his desk, he pulled a notebook out of the bottom drawer and opened it. I flipped through dozens of drawings, all of me. Some of them were even more erotic than the one he'd gifted me, but others were of just my lips and eyes, or me in clothes and smiling back at him.

He drew me in so much detail that I felt my heart clench at it.

Will saw me—truly saw me.

While I was flipping through a stack of cards came out, birthday cards, and they were all from me. "You kept them? All these years, you kept them?"

"Yeah," he said. He blushed and his hand went to the back of his neck, his nervous gesture. I didn't know what to say, so I kissed him. He caught me by my waist and held me still while I worked my lips against his, but he pulled away before I could deepen it. "Come on, let's get in the hot tub."

"We are not having hot tub sex again. I almost lost my nipples to frostbite last time."

"That would be a tragedy. I know how much you like having your nipples played with." Now it was my turn to blush. "Not for sex, just to relax. Come on."

We changed in front of each other, unashamed of our nakedness.

Will was right, the hot tub was relaxing and by the time we'd been in there for almost ninety minutes, switching between talking and making out and dry humping each other, I was completely content. Back in his room, we changed into joggers and sweatshirts while Will pulled me to the couch.

He had pizza delivered for dinner and we sat on the couch, cuddling, not having sex… just cuddling until it was time for the New Year's Eve countdown to start.

Somehow, this day had been better than all the other days we'd spent having wild sex.

"I can't wait to kiss you at midnight," he whispered. We were still snuggled on the couch, my head in his lap. We'd even spooned, my head resting on his arm. It was all so normal, so intimate. With his words, he turned me so we were laying down, facing each other.

"Ten," Will whispered in my ear. "Nine…" Kiss to my forehead. "Eight…" Kiss to my cheek. "Seven…" Kiss to my other cheek. "Six…" Kiss the corner of my mouth. "Five…" Kiss to the opposite corner. "Four…" Kiss to my chin. "Three…" Kiss to my nose. "Two…" Kiss to my lips. "One…" he breathed before sealing his lips against mine, finally. He'd spent so much time building me up. His hand went to my cheek, cupping while his tongue delved into my mouth. My hand was on his chest, clutching into his shirt and pulling him closer. Will wrapped one of his legs around mine and pulled me closer. I could feel him, hot and hard behind his joggers as his kiss made me dizzy.

"Happy New Year, Hales," he said, breaking the kiss so we could catch our breath.

"Happy New Year, Will," I whispered back.

"I love you."

He looked like he wanted to take the words back as soon as he said them, panic set in his eyes I knew, without a doubt, reflected my own.

In an instant, I was off the couch, putting as much distance between us as I could manage. I heard my heartbeat in my ears, pounding wildly at his unexpected words.

"Hales," he said, arms out like he was approaching a wild animal.

"I have to go."

"Haley!"

"I have to go!"

"Don't run. I know you feel this too."

I did.

I loved him too, which was why the only thing I could do was run.

"This is over."

With those words I raced out the back of his house and into the tree line, running the entire way back to my car.

CHAPTER 22

THE LAST SEMESTER

Haley

"Are you ready?" Sassy asked from where she stood next to my car in the frigid January air. It seemed like only yesterday when she'd asked me virtually the same thing and we'd climbed into my car for the last first day of high school. Now it was the last first day of our last semester. Four and a half months until graduation, and then I was out of here for good.

Four and a half months I would need to spend avoiding Will.

He'd texted me twice since telling me he loved me, but I'd ignored them. I had nothing to say, there was nothing I could say. The entire thing with him—enemies with benefits—had been the stupidest idea I'd ever had. It was time to focus on finalizing my plans to get the hell out of town, and those plans did not in any way involve Will Roberts.

"Can't wait," I said sarcastically.

"Are you okay?"

"Yes."

She sighed heavily. I hadn't told her what had led to the demise of my relationship with Will, just that it was over. I couldn't tell her he'd told me he loved me because if I did, she'd asked if I loved him back. She'd be able to see right through the lie. When we drove by the front parking lot, I couldn't help but notice that Will's truck wasn't there. That was unusual. Maybe he'd start skipping first period to avoid me.

I wasn't even sure why I'd come in on time. I needed to avoid him, and he knew all my hiding spots. The only choice I had was to sit where the rest of the seniors sat, a place he couldn't try to get me alone. Alone, I was powerless to stop him. That was why I'd run on New Year's Eve. I couldn't stay and talk it out with him. If I had, my own dedication of love would have fallen from my lips and I couldn't have that. He could never know how I truly felt about him.

"How are things with Snake?" I asked, changing the subject as I pulled into a parking spot. She was always happy to talk about Snake.

"I haven't seen him in a few days. He's been busy with club stuff. There's something going on and I know both of you know, but neither of you is telling me."

Okay, so maybe Snake wasn't the safe conversation topic he usually was.

"If Snake isn't telling you something, he's probably doing it to protect you."

She sighed before climbing out of the car.

Once I'd climbed out, I straightened my skirt and tightened my jacket around my torso. When I closed the door and looked up, I saw Will climbing out of his truck. His head turned in my direction, but he was too far away for me to see if he was actually looking at me or not, but it didn't matter because I was looking at him. I shouldn't be, but I was. I watched as he ducked his head down and made his way into the building.

"You coming?"

"Yeah." I shook my head, pushing thoughts of Will out of my mind, but that never worked. All I could think about was the last four months we'd been together. How had it turned into love? I'd had plenty of good sex. Sure, not as good as with Will, but Bobby was decent and Tucker, the guy before him, had been good too, and I'd had a string of assorted hookups that had all gotten me there, but Will. It was like Will was made to know my body, to know exactly how to touch me, when I needed him to let me have control and when he could take it from me and keep it. I'd never let a man be dominant with me in bed. It was me who did the choking, me who made the demands, me who took the lead, but with Will, I'd wanted to give him my submission.

And Haley Winters did not submit.

I signed myself in at the office, thankful not to run into Will. Once I finished signing in, I walked to the student lounge. I never went there. It was filled with kids from my class doing all kinds of fuckery in the early morning hours: playing cards, being loud, smoking, some even drinking. I couldn't go to the library because last time Will cornered me alone when I'd been trying to quit him, and I'd ended up right back playing his games.

It had only been three days since he'd told me how he felt about me. New Year's Day had fallen on a Friday, so we'd gotten an extra long break. I'd spent the weekend with Chloe, watching movies and just hanging out. I was going to miss doing that with her when I left.

Thankfully, when I got to the student lounge, there was a free spot with a desk in the corner. A group of students sat around a table, playing cards. They didn't do anything other than seem surprised that I was there. I sat with my back facing everyone, not wanting to see Will if he walked in. I had no idea where he'd spent his morning free period before we started meeting in the janitor's closet, but his friend Jordy was there. He had more than that, but in all the stories he'd told me in our months together, Jordy was the most consistent character. What surprised me was that Mackenzie was sitting in Jordy's lap. There went my hope that Will would get back together with her and make it easier for me to forget him.

It wasn't until break I realized I hadn't heard from my college admission applications. With early admission, I should have heard something already. When I googled it, I found a link that said to check your spam mailbox in your email. Why hadn't I thought of that? Will. Will was the reason I hadn't thought of that. I'd been too busy thinking of him to focus on getting into college and out of this town.

Nervously, I opened the spam box to my email and scrolled down. And there they were, all in a row. East Carolina University gave my admission away with the title, *Congratulations*! I'd gotten in. Opening it, I read the acceptance letter and that I'd received a ninety percent scholarship that covered tuition and housing. If I wanted to cover the other ten percent and offset book costs, I could do a work study for eight hours a week in the library, cafeteria or the school's gym.

Giddy.

I hadn't felt happiness in three days, not since I'd walked out on Will. It had been pure fucking bliss, magical, ridiculous bliss laying with him on the couch, his arms around me and him planting sweet kisses all over my face while the countdown to midnight played around us.

I love you.

I could hear the words on repeat, every time I went to sleep, or when it was too quiet in my head, and I always answered the same.

I love you, too.

But he couldn't know. It would ruin him if he knew, would ruin my plans for escape and the future, possibly get us both killed.

Moving the email from ECU to my inbox, I clicked on the one from The University of Richmond. The first line congratulated me on my acceptance. Two out of three, not a terrible start. I only got a seventy-five percent scholarship, but I could take out student loans for what remained, and I still had scholarships pending.

I moved the email to my inbox like the other before finding the email from Dartmouth, the one I really wanted—my dream school.

Taking a deep breath, I opened the email, letting my eyes scan over it quickly.

Waitlist.

Shit.

It wasn't an outright rejection, but it still wasn't what I wanted. Reading the email, it said I'd be going into the second round of selections and would hear by mid-February if I was admitted or not, or even still on the waitlist. An appeal of my waitlist status could be made via email.

How did you go about appealing a status? I'd already written an essay, submitted my grades and SAT scores. Before I could google what to do, the bell rang, and it was time for me to move to second period. When I turned, I came face to face with Will. My breath caught. He looked like shit, like he hadn't slept in days. His uniform was unkempt, his tie not even tied and just hanging off of his neck. There was a hickey on his neck, and I knew it was from me; that was how faded it was. Selfishly, I felt relieved. I didn't want him to have a hickey from anyone else. Not now, not ever.

Fuck.

Ducking my head, I walked past him hurriedly, ignoring the pull in my stomach that told me to go to him.

"Hales," I heard him whisper under his breath, barely audible to me, let alone anyone around us. He sounded so broken, and my heart shattered. Will finally melted all the ice around it, burnt down every damn wall surrounding it, and wiggled his way inside, and that was exactly why I ignored him and kept walking. There was no room for love in my life, not when I was leaving, and definitely not when it would get him killed.

I couldn't risk his life like that. Love makes people reckless.

BY LUNCH TIME, I WAS HOLDING BACK A FLOOD OF TEARS. I SAW WILL between each one of my classes, and as the day went on, he looked more and more desperate to get to me.

Usually, I sat on the other side of the lunch table, facing him, letting my eyes wander to him every once in a while. I always found him staring back at me. I'd texted him a few times, telling him to cut it out, but secretly, I loved it. I could always feel when he was watching, which was why, today, I sat with my back to him. I couldn't keep it together if I looked at him the entire time.

"Are you okay?" Sassy asked when she sat down next to me.

"Yeah," I said, offering her a fake smile.

"Look, Haley," she began. She had her serious voice sounding more motherly to me than anyone else in my life ever had. "I don't know what happened, but it's clear that something happened between you two. He looks awful and so do you. You can talk to me about it."

"Where's Snake?" I asked.

"Running an errand for the club. He said he'll be back before the next period starts."

I didn't even want to think about what type of errand he was running or if it involved any poisonous or lethal animals.

"Come on. Let's go eat in my car."

We grabbed our food and walked out the back door, freezing without our coats. It was so cold we ran the last half of the parking lot.

"It's freezing!" Sassy said, putting her hands up to the air vent as she spoke, rubbing them together and letting the heat warm them. "What happened?" She asked when her teeth finally stopped chattering.

"He told me he loved me."

"Holy shit." Her eyes went wide in disbelief as she absorbed the words.

"Do you love him?"

"Yes," I said, the tears I'd been trying so hard to fight finally falling free. "I don't know when it happened, maybe slowly, but I fell for him, Sas."

"Oh, Haley." She set her food on the dashboard and leaned towards me, wrapping me in a hug. I sobbed against her, all the emotions I'd been fighting off finally breaking free. "How did this happen? You don't do feelings."

"I don't know," I said, sniffling against her. "It happened so slowly that I didn't even realize it was happening. One day I just woke up and I couldn't deny it anymore. I can be myself with him. I love his smug arrogance, even though I shouldn't. I love that he sees me. I love that I *let* him see me. I love how he makes me laugh. I love his happy, carefree attitude, and that he never takes anything too seriously, even himself, except me and my safety." When it came to the abuse, that was the only time he was serious. "And then he said it out loud. I knew it and he knew it, too, but we never said it because not saying it was safe, but he ruined everything by speaking it into the world."

"Did you tell him you loved him back?"

"No, I ran. I ended it. It's not safe for him to love me. I'm doing it to protect him from my father."

She bit her lip, and I knew she had something to say, and I knew I wouldn't like it.

"It's not safe for Snake and I either, but we still let ourselves love each other. Are you sure you're not just protecting yourself?"

I hated when she did that.

"It doesn't matter, ending it was the right thing."

"I know I was a bitch about it when I first found out, but you don't even see how much you've changed this year."

"Changed?" I scoffed.

"You don't smoke anymore and you've only cut school once and that was for Chloe's birthday. You don't pick fights, almost like you feel an inner peace that you never did before. If he gives you peace, he's worth keeping around."

"But I can't give him that back. I can only hurt him. He can only get hurt by loving me. I have to protect him."

I knew she was contemplating what to say next. I didn't want to hear it, didn't want to know she was actually right. If I didn't admit it, then it wasn't true.

"We should get back inside before lunch is over."

"I'm here if you want to talk."

"I know."

"I love you, Haley."

"I love you too, Sassy."

We climbed out of my car, finishing our lunches as we walked. We'd just gotten back inside when the bell rang.

The rest of the day was uneventful, and I seriously thought about ditching, skipping calculus so I didn't have to see Will, but if I wanted to turn my Dartmouth waitlist into an acceptance, having poor attendance wasn't the way to do it.

I listened half-heartedly, taking notes as Ms. Smalls went over the syllabus for the rest of the school year, when our AP exam would be, and what we could expect from it.

When the bell finally rang, I didn't rush out of the room. Instead, I stayed in my seat, pulling out my notebook and starting to doodle.

"Miss Winters," Ms. Smalls said when it was just the two of us. I distracted myself so well that I hadn't even seen Will leave.

"Yes?"

She glanced at the door that was still open, and walked to it, closing it before walking back to me and taking a seat in front of me. "Have you heard from your college applications?" Ms. Smalls had written my letter of recommendation.

"I got into two. Dartmouth put me on a waitlist, going into the second round of early decision. I'll hear next month if I got in or am still wait-listed."

"How are you going to get off the waitlist?" She asked.

"I'm not sure."

"You could write another essay?"

"You read my essay. It was excellent."

"It was," she admitted. "But that was about your love for your sister, an admirable topic for sure, but there's more to your life than that, and we both know it. Something has changed you profoundly this year."

That was the second time today someone had mentioned I'd changed.

"I have no idea what you're talking about."

"I'm the youngest teacher here, barely even eight years older than most of my students, still in my mid-twenties. I remember high school like it was yesterday, unlike the other dinosaurs who went to high school in the eighties." I laughed at her and she smiled at me. "I'm more attune to what happens between students. You and Mr. Roberts seem to be getting along much better."

Her words were only filled with innuendo. She knew we'd been together.

"I don't know what you're talking about," I denied her words.

"Your secret is safe with me. But it's changed you, profoundly, Haley. Love changes us." There it was again—love. That stupid four letter word that turned my entire life upside down. I went to speak, but she held her hand up, making me wait for her to finish. "Love is the thing that connects us most with other people—familial love, romantic love, platonic love. Everywhere in the world, someone has felt that type of love. But true love, not everyone gets to experience that, a love so profound that it changes us from the inside out, helping us reach our goals instead of holding us back, turning us into who we always wanted to be but never thought we could be, a love that simultaneously turns your world upside down while making everything fall into place. That type of love is rare, especially between two eighteen-year-olds trapped in the chaos of high school, who have completely different upbringings and family lives."

I had tears in my eyes.

"Don't worry. The rest of your classmates are as oblivious as the teachers. Your secret is safe with me."

"Thank you, Ms. Smalls."

"No problem. I'm here if you need to talk."

I nodded at her and smiled while putting away my belongings. The hallways were empty when I walked into them. On my way to my locker, I passed the janitor's closet—our spot. I had an urge to check if he was there, but I pushed it down and kept walking. I didn't want to know if he was hiding, secretly waiting for me.

I hurried home and trapped myself in my room. Laptop open, I started typing a story about profound change and unrelenting love.

CHAPTER 23

THE SHOCK

Will

I t'd been over seven weeks since New Year's Eve, seven weeks since I did the stupidest thing I'd ever done and admitted my feelings to Haley—seven weeks since she ran out of my house into the freezing night.

I love you.

She could tell I wanted to take them back as soon as I spoke them, not because they weren't true, but because we both knew she wasn't ready to hear them. I'd begged her to stay, trying to be calm while she panicked, but it didn't help me; she still ran.

Seeing her every day at school was torture. Life was so much easier when I hated her. But had I ever really hated her? I wasn't sure anymore. I may have always loved her—since that very first day of pre-kindergarten.

VIOLET BLOOM

It was the Friday before Valentine's Day and I was just trying to survive another day at school, where her presence tortured me. Her skirts weren't any shorter than before, but to me, they were shorter than ever, constantly teasing me and reminding me what was hiding beneath them. Her smile seemed brighter, her laughter seemed lighter, but I knew her so well at this point—I knew the sadness behind her eyes. I could tell every morning when she came in if she'd been at the end of a beating the night before, I could tell by the way she itched at her clothes or when her body was sore. Sometimes she would wince when she stood or sat.

Irritation didn't cover what I felt whenever I saw that. Rage barely even covered it, and my anger at her parents was growing by the day. I wanted to kill Viper myself for what he did to his daughter, what he allowed his wife to do to her. I wouldn't call her Haley's mom; she wasn't worthy of that title.

"Dude," Jordy said at lunch. I was staring at Haley again, not even trying to hide it.

"What?" I asked, my voice filled with annoyance.

"You've got to snap the hell out of it."

Whatever else Jordy was going to say was cut off by Mackenzie coming to sit on his lap and planting a sloppy kiss on his face. Mackenzie seemed to think that my shitty mood lately was because she was dating Jordy. She thought I missed her, and I had to prevent myself from laughing whenever I thought about it. At least she was offering me some sort of comic relief. There was no comparison between Mackenzie and Haley.

Haley was the only thing in the world that mattered to me, and Mackenzie was just a blip on the radar that was my high school history. Haley was the one I wanted for the rest of high school, college, and the rest of my life.

Frustrated and on the verge of tears again, I stood from the lunchroom table and headed out of the cafeteria. Haley's back was to me, just like it always was these days. Her posture was different, like she never relaxed anymore.

Why was she doing this? Why was she putting both of us through this torture? She loved me. I fucking knew she did. I also knew that she thought she was doing the right thing, protecting her heart, protecting both of us from her parents, but it wasn't the right thing.

Being without her would never be the right thing.

"Will!" Jordy shouted at me as I walked into the locker room. "The fuck, dude?"

I blinked back the tears. It seemed like I'd been getting more and more in touch with my emotional side since Haley broke my heart. I could never stop crying, and I wasn't ashamed of it. Men could cry too, should cry, it was healthy.

"Let's go."

"Where?" I asked.

"We're ditching the rest of the day."

I didn't even try to argue.

"We're taking your truck. I rode with Mackenzie this morning."

I tossed him my keys, not interested in driving.

Jordy shook his head, and I knew there was no way I was getting out of whatever he wanted to talk about. Maybe I should just tell him what was going on. I climbed into the passenger seat of my truck, and it still smelled like Haley. Nobody but me had been in the truck since Haley was in there with me.

Jordy drove in silence and I wasn't paying enough attention because I didn't realize he wasn't going to either of our houses until we were by the river. It was still freezing in February. He put the truck in park but didn't climb out.

"You need to tell me what the hell is going on with you. I'm worried."

I just stared out the front, not saying anything.

"It's obvious you and whoever the girl was are done, and that you're torn up about it. Who is she?"

I took a heavy breath, trying to control my tears.

"Is it that scandalous?" He asked. His voice nearly laughed as he said the words, but he had no idea. He'd be shocked when I told him. "You can trust me, I won't tell anyone, not even Kenzie."

Nobody ever called Mackenzie, Kenzie, and the fact that he was allowed to, spoke volumes about how much she liked him, way more than she ever liked me, which was fine. We weren't good for each other.

"Even if I tell you who it is, you'd never believe me."

"Just tell me. You're so depressed, it might help to talk about it."

Now he sounded like my parents. Both my mom and dad tried to get me to talk about what happened, but I never could, never wanted to. Hell, I still didn't want to, but I couldn't keep it in anymore. Haley would kill me if she knew I was about to spill our secret to Jordy, but I could trust him.

"It's Haley."

"Haleigh Sudder?"

"No," I said, shaking my head. Haleigh Sudder was a year behind us, a junior, unpopular, a little nerdy, but generally a nice girl. "Haley Winters."

I glanced at Jordy, trying to gauge his reaction. His mouth was hanging open, and he was staring right at me.

"Did you just say Haley Winters?"

"Yes."

He let out a low, long whistle and shifted in his seat.

"As in the daughter of Viper? As in the girl you've hated since we were five?"

"Yes, that Haley."

"I have so many questions. How? When?"

"Do you really wanna gossip like we're girls?"

"Yes! Guys can gossip, too. Don't be so sexist."

I laughed, despite myself. Jordy tossed words back to me I'd said to him countless times. It was the first time I'd laughed heartily in a long time, and it felt good.

"It started when we got detention together."

"That was months ago. You've been keeping this from me for months?"

"Yes," I sighed. Jordy was quiet, waiting eagerly for me to continue. "You can't tell anyone. Viper would kill me if anyone finds out."

"I'm not interested in seeing you dead. I won't say shit."

"It started out as just sex—enemies with benefits—and then somehow, I fell for her. I didn't even realize it, and then once I knew, I knew I couldn't tell her. Fuck, dude, she's… everything. I love how smart she is. I love that she gives as good as she gets, and always has. I love how sweet she is with her sister. I love knowing her 'don't fuck with me' attitude is just an act to protect herself. I love how she sees me for who I am, not just the sheriff's son."

"You've got it bad, dude. And you told her, anyway?"

"It just slipped out. She came over New Year's Eve, and after I kissed her at midnight, it just slipped out. I told her I loved her."

"Shit."

"She ran, and it's been over since."

"You've got it bad," he said.

"I fucking know it."

"So what's the plan?"

"Plan?"

"To get her back."

"There isn't one."

"What do you mean, there isn't one? You've got to get your girl back."

"It's better for everyone if I just forget her. We were playing with fire, anyway. My parents found out."

"Mama and Papa Roberts knew?"

"Yeah, they came home early one weekend while she was at the house."

"Daddy sheriff didn't lose his mind?"

"He did, but I'm eighteen. He can't forbid me from doing anything."

"I wish my parents subscribed to that same philosophy. Mackenzie thinks you're depressed because you're still in love with her and you're jealous that I'm with her."

I snorted out a laugh. "Let her keep thinking that. It'll keep her from sniffing around. I know she's your girl and you love her, but you can't try to convince me that she can keep a secret."

"Yeah, she can't," he agreed easily, making me laugh again. "But for real, dude, I won't tell anyone."

"Thanks, man."

"But for what it's worth, I think you should try to get her back."

I wanted to, but I didn't even know where to begin. She ignored all my texts, wouldn't even look at me in class or when I walked by her in the hall. For weeks after our breakup, I came to school with blood-shot eyes and bags under them. She saw, she knew, but still she let us both hurt, both because I could tell she was hurting, too. When I saw her laugh or smile, it wasn't the same as it had been during the months when we were together.

"I blew it," I said, shaking my head.

"But you love her."

"I do." I let out a heavy sigh as I spoke, effectively ending the conversation. There was nothing else to say.

"Come on. Let's go get a burger."

I let Jordy drive my truck to the diner, feeling a little better after having told him.

But I wouldn't be better, not completely, until I had Haley back.

Valentine's day fell on a Sunday, and my parents were gone again for a romantic weekend getaway, leaving me home alone. When I was younger, I thought it was weird how often they went away together, and then as I got older, I knew it was important for their relationship, but thought it was weird for a different reason. How could my dad, the sheriff, go away two or three weekends a month?

The answer was that there was almost no crime in Lake City. The only crime came from the Southside gang and occasionally some kids vandalizing the overpasses and tunnels.

So, I was all alone on Valentine's Day, still wallowing in my feelings for Haley.

Telling Jordy made me feel better for about three hours before I was back to missing her, desperately wishing that she'd show up at my door and tell me how stupid she'd been to walk out on me, that she missed me the way I missed her and how we'd figure out a way to be together, a way to get around her dad and the gang.

I'd been planning her Valentine's Day gift since Christmas. She loved the drawing I'd given her, and I had dozens more. She'd seen most of them on New Year's Eve, but even though she'd left me, I hadn't stopped drawing her. I couldn't. She consumed every waking thought I had and nearly all of my dreams. They were always filled with her, and they weren't even all sexual. Most of them were just the two of us hanging out, laughing together, bickering like we loved to do, and just holding each other. Cuddling with Haley quickly became my favorite activity to do with her.

She'd turned me into a sap.

Her present sat on my desk, wrapped neatly in bright red wrapping paper with a white bow on it. It was a morse code necklace, so that she could wear it with no one else being able to read it. It was one necklace with three layers. The first layer spelled 'Hales', the second layer spelled 'Will', and the third layer spelled 'not enemies', a little inside joke just for the two of us.

I'd thought about slipping it into her locker at school on Friday, but if I was going to give it to her, I wanted it to be in person. She would be pissed that I spent money on her, but she was worth all the money in the world—her happiness, her safety, were worth everything.

And I knew her well enough to know that she was trying to keep me safe. She didn't run because she didn't love me. I knew it was the opposite. She ran because she loved me. My girl wasn't stupid either—she must know I knew that.

How long before one of us, or both of us, caved?

Jordy was right. I should try to get her back, but I was trying to be some form of a good guy. I'd always been a good guy, the boy next door, the gentleman, and the guy all the fathers felt good about letting their daughters date.

Everyone except Viper.

I left Haley's Valentine's Day gift on my desk, sitting next to another drawing I wanted to give her. This one was of the two of us. It wasn't explicit, although I had a few of those too, and I knew she'd want to see them, but they wouldn't be for a gift. I had plans for them that involved watching her touch herself to the erotic images, but that dream had been put on the back burner for now, until she came back to me. This one was just of us sitting together, both of us facing forward and smiling together.

Was I being a fool for still thinking she'd come back to me after all these weeks?

Maybe.

But I couldn't give up hope she would because I missed her so fucking much. Seeing her every day at school wasn't the same.

I'd had so many plans for Valentine's Day with Haley. I was going to invite her over since we'd be alone. I wanted to make love to her in my bed again; I wanted to wash her in the shower gently again before pinning her against the wall; I wanted to hold her on the couch while we watched movies and watch her scrunch her nose up adorably when I offered her vegetables for dinner. I just wanted all of her.

Downstairs, I pulled open the fridge and found dinner left by my mom—chicken parmigiana. There was also salad, garlic bread and dessert—enough for two—and it was because she was still hoping Haley would come back to me.

In the beginning, she was even more unsure of my relationship with Haley than my dad was, mostly out of concern for my safety, but seeing me so broken-hearted hadn't made her hate Haley like a lot of moms would. It had made her love Haley. She could tell how much I loved her and after telling her story after story of us together—when she'd pried the words out of me in my sadness—she knew, just like I did, that Haley loved me too and she broke my heart to protect me.

Turning the oven on, I put the chicken dish and the garlic bread in the oven and wandered towards the living room to put on a movie. I needed to avoid anything romantic, not that it would help. I'd still end up thinking about Haley, regardless.

While dinner cooked, I scrolled through the TV guide, not surprised to find only stupid romantic comedies on every channel. Valentine's Day would be just as good a night for a horror movie marathon as Halloween. Not finding anything on regular cable, I pulled up a streaming service and browsed through. Finally, I settled on some horror movie, just like I'd wanted.

I'd only been settled on the couch for about ten minutes when the doorbell rang, catching me completely off guard. My parents, even if they were coming home, wouldn't use the doorbell. Jordy was with Mackenzie, and there was nobody else who would randomly stop by my house on a Sunday night.

When I opened the door, I couldn't breathe.

Shock.

Anger.

Fear.

Those were the dominating emotions, but what was more, was hope because my girl was standing in front of me again.

Haley.

She was standing in the glow of the front porch light, but I barely recognized my girl. There was blood everywhere. Her lip was split open and her eyebrow was bleeding. There was blood stained below her nose. Her cheeks were stained with tears mixed with her makeup and blood, giving her a hysterical appearance. It covered her shirt, which was ripped, it was on her pants. Her arms were wrapped tightly around herself and her teeth chattered; she wasn't wearing a coat, and it was actually freezing outside. And her car wasn't anywhere on the road.

Had she walked here?

"Hales," I whispered, reaching out to touch her, hardly believing she was actually standing there in front of me.

"Will," she whispered, her voice broken as she collapsed against me.

CHAPTER 24

THE TRUTH REVEALED

Haley

Valentine's Day was a joke of 'holiday'. It was a made-up commercial day where women forgot how horrible their partners treated them for one night of flowers, dinner, and a lame romantic movie.

Even though I knew that was true, it didn't stop me from wanting to celebrate with Will. It hadn't stopped me from spending some of my hard earned money—my escape money—on a present for him.

I got him a leather bound sketch book and had it inscribed with his name on the front, and on the back I had *Enemies* written on it with a stripe drawn through it. It came with a set of colored pencils, his preferred medium.

We weren't enemies anymore, and we hadn't been for a long time, and even though we would never be again, we still weren't speaking, and it was all my fault. I was the one who'd burned us to the ground and fled from the ashes. I missed him so damn much.

I was doing this for him. We weren't together because it was the only way I could protect him.

Running my fingers over the leather-bound book, I imagined the drawings of me Will would have filled the journal with if I'd been able to give it to him. I'd thought about sneaking it into his locker, but that would just be confusing for both of us. I didn't want him to think we had another chance.

We didn't.

We couldn't.

I was spending the day all by myself. Sassy was with Snake, Chloe was with Mick, and I didn't know where my parents were, but it probably wasn't with each other.

Snake and I did have duty at the wild animal warehouse later. I wasn't sure why my dad was putting more and more responsibility on me, especially since Snake made it clear to him that after we were married, he'd protect me by not having me involved in any of the business. *Business*, I scoffed to myself. What a joke of a word for the illegal exotic animal trade and drug business they were in.

Either way, it was mine and Snake's turn on duty, just for a few hours, while the other members of the gang did something else, probably something worse. Snake's stress level tripled when Dad said the wedding would take place right after graduation, which was only three and a half months away now, and he was feeling the pressure. He was head over heels in love with Sassy and he wouldn't be separated from her.

Soon I was going to tell them about my escape plan, then I could ask them to watch out for Chloe until she was eighteen and I could get her out of Lake City.

The best thing Will did for me was remind me it was okay to ask for help, even though I couldn't ask it of him, unable to risk his life like that, but I could follow his advice. Missing him was killing me, and needing him safe was the only thing keeping me from crawling back to him, from uttering the same words he'd whispered to me.

I love you.

I loved him so fucking much.

Somehow I fell for the ridiculous man-child who was always too damn happy and too fucking sweet everywhere but in bed or wherever he was taking me. He was a good boy, from a nice family, with a bright future.

I wouldn't be the reason he lost that.

But Will had left a mark on my life and ruined me for anyone else—ever. Whoever came into my life after him would never hold a candle to the way Will made me feel, made me fall in love with him, the way he touched me, treated me, loved me.

A knock on the trailer door pulled me out of my spiraling thoughts and away from Will. Wiping under my eyes, I sniffed back the tears and walked towards the door. Snake was standing there, bundled in his lined leather jacket, a beanie on his head and gloves on his hands.

"Are you ready?"

"Yeah. I just need to put my shoes on," I told him. If he could tell I had been crying, he didn't say anything about it. Sassy never told him about Will, but he'd mentioned offhandedly to her he thought I was seeing someone, too. Sassy refused to confirm or deny, but he could obviously read her well. Thankfully, he didn't push her for a name, respecting both of our boundaries.

I grabbed my boots and tugged them on, thankful for the faux fur lining that would keep me warm. The warehouse didn't have heat, which was ridiculous and dangerous. The club should take better care of the animals if they wanted to sell them for top dollar, especially because plenty of them were used to much warmer climates than the one they currently lived in. I shrugged on a puffy jacket and grabbed my cell phone and was ready to go.

"I'll drive."

"My bike is quicker."

"It's negative one thousand and one degrees out here," I complained. "I'm not getting on the bike."

Snake grumbled in protest, but climbed into my car anyway.

"Are you okay?" He asked.

"Yeah," I lied easily. "I'm fine." That was my answer for everything these days. I wasn't fine, I was about as far from fine as I could get. I was trapped in my own mind, desperately trying to and yet unable to forget Will.

He was it for me, even at eighteen, I knew that.

And I also knew I couldn't ever have him again.

Thankfully, Snake was quiet on the rest of the drive up the mountain to the dirt road which would lead us to the warehouse. When I parked the car next to the line of bikes, there were only four there, and none of them were my dad's.

"Ready?" He asked.

"Yeah," I sighed. Snake took my hand, interlocking our fingers and walking me into the warehouse. Snake's hand felt familiar in mine, much the way Sassy's did—like a friend.

"There they are." Bull was the first to greet us. The rest of them nodded at us, but remained wordless. "Animals have been fed. We'll be back in three hours."

"No problem."

Bull left three guns on the table, two shotguns, and a handgun. "Just in case."

Just in case what? I wanted to ask. Was this operation already on the sheriff's radar? Or worse, was it already on the radar of one of the federal bureaus? I suppressed a sigh, waiting until we were alone to speak.

But before I could, Snake was wrapping me in a hug. "Shh," he whispered in my ear. His lips pushed against my cheek and lingered, confusing me. "Hug me back, there're cameras," he whispered. "Whatever you want to say, don't." I wrapped my arms around him and pushed my face into his neck, acting as best I could. It was easier than I thought, imaging him as Will. Once I pretended he was Will, I let myself sink against him, and my imagination was so effective that he even smelled like Will, the scent calming and familiar.

Fuck. I missed him so much.

"Better?"

"Thank you," I whispered.

"No problem, babe." Babe was a teasing name from him and it made me smile.

We spent the next few hours walking around the warehouse. The amount of wild animals had increased tenfold. There was an entire family of tigers and two new lion cubs. The reptiles seemed to have multiplied. If one of those monster snakes—I didn't even know what type they were, just that they were huge—got out, Snake and I would be dead.

I chuckled to myself, Snake being killed by a snake. It wasn't funny, but I laughed anyway, and Snake just looked at me like I was crazy.

There were wolves now too, and as adorable as they were, as much as they looked like little puppies, I knew they were dangerous. The birds were loud, and they stank. My father and his men were not taking care of their cages; I'd be surprised if they were even feeding the animals appropriately. It must be expensive to feed all these animals, but they seemed to be moving their product quickly.

"Your dad said we could pick out an animal for our wedding present," he said. I stopped dead in my tracks to look at him.

"We don't want one."

"That's what I told him."

"Glad we can agree on at least one thing. Good groundwork for our marriage."

Snake squeezed my hand and laughed, making it more dramatic for the cameras that were clearly watching us.

Snake and I would never be married. We both knew that. At least I did, and I'd told him enough that he finally believed it, even if he didn't know how it was possible to get out of it.

After we walked around the warehouse, we sat at the table where the guns were and just waited for Bull and the rest of my dad's minions to come back.

When we heard the rumble of the bikes approaching, we stood, interlocking our hands again.

"Trouble?" Bull asked as soon as he walked in the door.

"No," Snake said.

"Good. Have a good rest of your Valentine's Day." Bull's words were spoken with open innuendo.

Gross.

Snake chuckled good-naturedly and pulled me out of the warehouse. When we were finally in the car, I let out a shudder.

"Get me out of here," I groaned.

"You've got the keys."

I turned on the radio and let the music drown out my thoughts—thoughts that were still consumed by Will.

"You can talk to me about it, you know."

"About what?" I asked.

"This guy that's got you all torn up, the one who broke your heart."

"I broke my own heart," I said. "It wasn't his fault."

And that was the truth. I broke my heart, and Will's, at the same time.

"You can still talk to me about it."

"I appreciate it, but I'm good."

I wasn't. But it wasn't the right time yet to bring Snake into the fold. I'd sit him and Sassy down a month before graduation and tell them my plan.

When we pulled up outside my trailer, my mom's car was there, but my dad's bike was still nowhere to be seen.

"Go back to Sassy," I told him quietly. "She'll be happy you're back."

"You'll be okay by yourself?"

"Yeah," I tried to convince him and myself.

But I never was, not when I was alone with my mom.

In the last seven weeks since the new year, I'd been home way more, and gotten more beatings than ever before. Chloe was babysitting almost every weekend and when she wasn't, she was out with Mick. And I was happy about that. It meant she was hardly ever in the line of fire anymore.

I waved goodbye to Snake and walked into the trailer. My mom was sitting on the couch, body leaned forward while she snorted a line of cocaine off of the counter.

Fuck.

"Well, well, well, look who's finally fucking home." I hung my coat on the rack while she spit her hateful words at me.

"I was doing club stuff for dad." It wasn't a lie.

"Club stuff," she snorted before snorting another line—the second one in two minutes. She was really going at it today.

"Sure." I went to walk away, but her hand wrapped around my wrist and pulled me back. "Don't walk away from me, you little bitch." I took a deep breath, pushing away the urge to fight back. It wouldn't help anything. I pulled my hand from her and went to walk away again. "You're fucking worthless. I wish I'd never had you. I wish Chloe was my only child."

Those words hurt so badly, I knew she hated me. I'd always known she hated me and that Chloe was the favorite. I was also happy about that. It meant that Chloe would never be on the receiving end of one of her beatings. She was safe.

But I finally snapped.

"Why?" I shouted at her, turning to face her again. The years of abuse finally bubbled over, and I lost my mind, demanding to know why she hated me so much. She slapped me across the face quicker than I could ever react to, bringing me to my knees. Her ridiculous fake rings were turned towards her palm and one caught me right on the eyebrow. I could feel the blood trickling down my face. "Why did you have me then?"

"Your father," she spat. "Thank God I only had one of his children."

Before I could ask anymore questions, she punched me in the mouth, making me bleed more. The warm blood trickled down my lip to my chin while I cried from the pain.

"Only you are a product of that fucking monster!" She shouted. "Viper only got me pregnant once."

The drugs made her loose lipped. Dad wasn't Chloe's dad? Did he know? There was no way he could actually know. He would have killed my mom.

"Who is Chloe's dad?"

"Hound."

What. The. Fuck.

Hound?

Sassy's dad was Chloe's dad? Sassy and Chloe were sisters, too?

"What?" I managed to get out. Instead of answering me with words, she pushed me to the ground and kicked me in the stomach.

"He was the love of my life."

My head was throbbing, and my nose was bleeding now, too. Lifting my hands, I went to shield my face as she continued her assault. I needed to get up off the floor if I had a chance to escape. Would this be the night she finally killed me?

"He should have been the leader of the Southside. Your father stole it from him, forced me to marry him. Forced my father to force me to marry him."

This story sounded too familiar, and momentarily, I felt sorry for my mom. She never loved my father, never wanted to be with him, but she'd been made to marry him, anyway. And unlike Snake, who would never force me into his bed, my father was an actual monster. The sympathy was brief because it still didn't excuse the abuse.

"And when your father found out we were planning on running away together, him leaving his wife and kids and me leaving you with your father, he killed Hound."

I'd always suspected my dad killed Sassy's dad, but if I had one thousand guesses, I would have never correctly guessed the reason.

My head pounded from the combination, from the beating, and from the new information.

Sassy, still to this day, believed her parents had been ridiculously in love. That was the way her mom talked about their relationship.

Did Sassy's mom know her husband had an affair with my mom?

The beating was almost over, my mom's movements slowing down, and she was getting tired, but she was also sobbing in a way that I'd never heard her cry before. She was sobbing from the death of the love of her life, the man she wanted to be with, the father of the only child she really loved.

Would that be me with Will? Would I spend the rest of my life in a state of perpetual sadness because I missed him so much, unable to ever move on, and never living fully, drowning myself in booze and drugs to forget?

I couldn't let that be my life.

With one final sob, my mom kicked me in the stomach one more time before collapsing onto the couch.

I laid still for a few minutes, trying to steady the spinning in my head, unsure if I was actually safe yet or not. When I heard her snore, I finally attempted to get up slowly.

Everything hurt: my head, my heart, my face, my stomach, my entire body.

Could my mother be lying? Chloe and Sassy looked nothing alike. But Chloe looked just like our mother, and Sassy looked just like her own. Neither of them had features from Hound, at least not obvious ones.

Why would she lie about something like that?

It must be true.

Will.

After my brain fog cleared, I only had one thought in my head, and that thought was Will. I needed him, needed to get to him. I couldn't run from him anymore, run from us. He was the only hope I had for keeping it together and getting out of Lake City alive.

I'd probably end up on the end of another beating for leaving my blood all over the house, but I left it, walking out of the trailer.

I climbed into my car and headed towards the church. I'd have to walk to his house in the cold.

Tears continued to fall as I drove. I needed Will.

When I made it to the church, I hid my car like I usually did and climbed out, tripping in my hurry. It was only then that I realized I hadn't grabbed my jacket on the way out and it was freezing in the middle of February.

Ignoring the chattering of my teeth, I half walked, half ran as best I could with the pain in my ribs and stomach until I was in Will's neighborhood. I didn't even care that his parents might be home. He'd told me I could come over when they were there. I just couldn't risk my car being seen outside, not yet.

I felt frozen to the bone by the time I knocked on his front door.

The porch light flicked on before the door opened, nearly blinding me.

Will was speechless when he opened the front door. His eyes flicked over my entire body and I could see the anger written in them.

"Hales," he breathed my name, and his voice was full of love and anguish.

"Will," I managed to speak out through a strangled cry before I threw myself into his arms, collapsing into his warmth and safety.

CHAPTER 25

THE LOVE

Will

As she fell into my arms, I thought she'd passed out, but when I heard her sobbing into my chest and felt her little hands clutch into my sweatshirt, I knew that wasn't the case.

Pulling her body close, I dragged her into the house, quickly slamming and locking the door behind us. I didn't know if someone was following her.

"Haley," I whispered into her hair. All of her weight was on me and I wrapped my arms around her lower back, lifting her so I didn't have to drag her. Her sobs got louder. "I got you, doll, I'm right here. You're safe now."

Moving us to the couch, I situated her on my lap and rocked her back and forth. I tried pulling away, so I could look at her face, to check her injuries, but she kept her face buried in my neck, clinging to me and refusing to let go.

"Haley, I need to look at your face. I need to see if you need stitches."

She sobbed one more time, her voice breaking before she stilled against me. Using all my strength, I pulled her face out of the crook of my neck. Her eyes were closed, but she let me touch her face, running my hands over the cuts that were still bleeding.

Dad raised me to never hit a woman, but I could make an exception for Haley's birth giver.

I put one arm under her legs and one around her waist and stood with her in my arms. My first stop was the kitchen, turning off the oven, so I didn't burn the house down. She let out a little mewl, like a kitten, when I adjusted her in my arms before settling against me. I carried her to the bathroom and set her on the sink. "Haley, I need to wash your cuts." Her head tilted up, and she looked at me with usually bright or angry eyes looking so broken my heart cracked. "I can't tell where all you're bleeding from. It might be your stomach and legs too. I need to take off your clothes and get you in the shower. Can I do that?"

She nodded her head at me.

I stepped away, but she grabbed me, refusing to let me go. "I'm just going to turn on the water. I'm not going anywhere. I'm right here, baby." Reluctantly, she let me go, but I stayed as close to her as possible while I leaned into the shower and turned on the water.

When I got back in front of her, I lifted the hem of her shirt slowly, making sure she didn't protest. My jaw ticked when I saw her in just her bra. She was already bruising, and the angry purple marks covered most of her stomach. Gently, I reached around her and unclasped her bra, letting it fall from her shoulders.

In all the years I'd known her, Haley Winters had never been this quiet.

"Can you stand for me, doll?" She nodded her head slowly, as if it hurt her. I helped her off the counter and unsnapped her pants before kneeling in front of her to untie her worn-out boots and slide them from her feet, followed by her socks.

In all the times we'd been naked together, I'd never been able to undress her like this, taking my time, delicately, like I was about to worship her body, and I would always hate the first time I didn't urgently strip her was after something so vile.

Once her bare feet dug into the carpet, I pulled her jeans down, followed by her underwear, finding bruises on her legs too, but from what I could tell, only her face was covered in cuts. I wanted to plant delicate kisses all over her, kissing each bruise and cut, to take away her pain, but she was too fragile.

I stood in front of her, eyes still assessing her and desperate to touch her, but I didn't want to take advantage of the situation. I didn't know if she'd come to me because she missed me or only because she felt safe here and knew I'd protect her, regardless of if we got back together or not.

Quicker than I'd stripped her, I took my own clothes off and stood in front of her naked. Taking her hand, I pulled her with me to the shower, stepping in first and turning to face her, seeing how she moved as if her body hurt, and it must. I adjusted the water, making it cool before grabbing a fresh washcloth from the rack settled in the window and wet it before pushing it against her face. She hissed but didn't pull away. "Sorry," I told her. Haley's hands wrapped around my arms, holding on to me and bringing our bodies closer together.

"Will?" She whispered as I cleaned her lip. That was the second time she'd said my name, speaking no other words the entire time she'd been here.

"Yeah, doll?"

"I love you, too." My motions against her lip stopped. "I should have told you on New Year's Eve, I loved you then. I love you still, baby. I'm so sorry." She cried out again, the sound broken and loud, like it was coming all the way from her toes.

"Shh. It's okay, it's okay. I know, and I knew then."

Her arms wrapped around me, and her head pushed into my chest. I held her tight, feeling her wet, naked body against me and willing myself not to get hard. Now was not the time.

"Tell me again," she begged.

Cupping her cheeks in my hand, I tilted her head back and looked into her bloodshot eyes. "I love you, Haley Winters."

"I love you too, Will Roberts." As soon as she finished speaking, she pushed her lips against mine, catching me completely off guard and making me stumble back. "Ouch," she hissed. Her hand went to her lip, where it was open. "Sorry."

I shook my head and smiled down at her.

I finally had her back.

"It's fine. Don't hurt yourself." For the first time since she'd shown up on my door again, I saw a flash of the real Haley, my girl, in her eyes. "Come on, I need to finish cleaning your cuts and get some ointment on them. It looks like you're just bleeding from your face. Everywhere else is just bruised."

I finished cleaning the cuts on her face and turned off the water, but now that I knew she loved me, there was something else I wanted to do. I turned the water back on and dropped to my knees in front of her. Haley's breath hitched, and she waited. I ran my hands up and down her wet legs before leaning forward and kissing the bruises.

Slowly, I took my time to kiss each bruise—up her legs, across her stomach and ribs. When I stood in front of her again, wet tears stained her beautiful face. I kissed each cut and bruise on her face before finally turning off the water. Haley was my only priority, so I dried her completely before drying myself.

"I'll be right back." I kissed her forehead and left her alone to go grab clothes. When I came back, I handed her a pair of boxers, a t-shirt and a sweatshirt before tugging on joggers and a t-shirt myself.

"Sit here," I said, closing the toilet lid.

"Are you going to ask?" She asked as she sat where I told her to.

"No, I want to get you cleaned up first." She held completely still while I put antibiotic cream and bandages on her cheek and eyebrow that, thankfully, didn't need stitches. Her lip couldn't be bandaged, so I just rubbed some ointment on it with my thumb.

"Come," I said, tugging on her hand. I clutched her hand the entire time I walked with her to the kitchen, terrified that if I let go, she'd run again. With one long squeeze of her hand, I pointed to the bar stool she always sat on before going to the stove. "Tea or hot chocolate?"

I didn't really need to ask.

"Hot chocolate."

I was already making my mom's recipe before she answered. A melted chocolate bar, whole milk, cocoa powder, vanilla, and some cinnamon later, I poured the drink into mugs and covered it in mini marshmallows before handing one to her and sitting next to her at the breakfast bar.

"What happened, doll?"

"My mom." I'd worked that part out myself, but kept my mouth shut. "She was high when I got home. She yelled at me and I just snapped, demanding to know why Chloe was her favorite. I'm glad Chloe is, that she doesn't have to face the abuse, but I still wanted to know why she hated me so much, and she finally told me." Haley stuttered over the last few words, taking a deep breath before continuing. "She told me that Chloe isn't my dad's kid, her dad is Sassy's dad."

"Holy shit."

"It gets worse. She said my dad killed Sassy's dad. I always assumed he did, club business or whatever, but it was because my mom was going to run away with him."

"Fuck."

"There's so much I need to tell you, baby," she whispered. "So much I should have told you from the beginning." I waited for her to continue. "Last time we played honest answers only, you asked me what I was planning after graduation."

"You said undecided."

"That was because I didn't know if I got into any of the colleges I'd applied to or not. But I did. I got into the University of Richmond, and East Carolina University." I wasn't surprised. She was basically a genius. "I was waitlisted at Dartmouth."

"Damn," I whistled, interrupting her.

"But Ms. Smalls told me to write another essay to change their minds. And it worked. I got accepted; I found out a few days ago."

"That's amazing, Haley."

"I wrote about you."

"About me?" I asked in shock.

"About loving you." I had no words. "Did I have my phone when I came in?"

"I think you dropped it by the door. I'll go grab it."

I left her alone and went to grab her cell phone. When I handed it back to her, she unlocked it and started scrolling through it.

"It's titled *Profound*."

I sipped my hot chocolate and settled into the chair, waiting for her to start reading.

"If you asked me six months ago if true love existed, if soul mates existed, I would have laughed in your face. Of course not. I've only ever loved two people in my life, and until a few months ago, only two people have ever loved me back—my sister and my best friend who I love like a sister. In my first essay, I wrote about the love I have for my sister, the need to protect her from the rough life I've lived.

Something changed in the last six months, and I experienced a new type of love. True love, the type of love I can only equate to what someone feels for a soulmate. I fell in love with an eighteen-year-old I've known my entire life, someone who isn't quite a man, but is also no longer a boy. I thought I hated him, thought I'd always hate him, but if I look back at our interactions over the years, starting from our very first day of pre-kindergarten, I've always loved him.

He's the first person ever to see me vulnerable, the first person ever to make me feel truly safe, and the only person to love me with no regard for what loving me could do to his own life.

It took me losing him, through no fault of his, for me to realize how much I love him, and what his love has done to my life. People, especially teenagers, tend to say that love shouldn't change you, and if it does, it's the wrong type of love. I disagree. Love changes us all, but the determination whether that's good or bad is on how it changes us.

Loving Will has changed me for the better. I'm lighter, happier, freer, safer, and loved like I've never been loved."

She wasn't done, but she had to pause because I was crying, and it wasn't quiet. Haley reached her hand out and squeezed my leg, her honey-colored eyes boring into mine as she read the essay that poured her feelings out to me. I knew she loved me, but she'd called it profound.

"I love him because he's got an artist's soul, even if I'm the only one who gets to see it. I love him because he's always happy and carefree, bringing out the same in me. He's honest and true to himself and those he loves. I love him because even when we fight, he's the only person I want to fight with."

I snorted out a choked laugh through my tears at her words.

"I love him because he makes me feel invincible. I love how just hearing his voice whisper my name brings a sense of calm into the turbulent parts of my soul."

Fucking profound, I thought.

"Loving him makes me believe in God and makes me feel like I'm capable of achieving all my dreams. And he's who I want with me when I finally do.

There are quotes about love in the Bible, the Quran, the Torah, and manuscripts from other major world religions—Hinduism, Buddhism, and Taoism—just to name a few. Songs are written about it, but no one understands it until they feel it for themselves. I certainly didn't.

Even still, living in the middle of it, I barely understand it.

What I do know is that his love, and loving him, has matured and enriched my life in ways I never knew possible, especially at just eighteen-years-old. My life is fuller, my laughter louder, my smile broader, and my hope higher. Hope and knowledge that whatever the future brings, whatever challenges life puts in my path, I'll conquer them all as long as I'm loving him and he's loving me. It's a deep love, a love that can quell the storm in my soul, my instincts to run; it's a love that soothes and fills the cracks in my heart and fills me with optimism for the life we can create together.

A love so profound that it rights all the wrongs in my world. And his."

By the time she finished, we were both crying.

"That's how I love you, Will, with my entire soul."

I stood from the barstool I was sitting on and pushed my way between her knees. Her thighs wrapped around me while I engulfed her in my arms and held her tightly to my chest. It must have hurt with the bruises, but she didn't protest. "I want to kiss you so fucking bad," I whispered into her hair. "But I don't want to hurt your lip."

"Just be gentle," she whispered, pulling away to tilt her head up at me. Using one of my hands, I pushed the hair out of her face and cupped her cheeks before pressing my lips delicately to hers, letting them linger without deepening the kiss. She needed to heal before I did all the things I'd been imagining doing to her for the last seven weeks.

"I love you the same way, doll." She smiled and pecked me one more time before pulling away. "So, you're going to college?" I had a lot more questions, but I figured she'd explain everything.

"I've always planned on going to college, knowing it was my only escape from the trailer park, but I have no way to pay for it, which was why I was so focused on getting good grades. Ivy leagues don't do scholarships, but I'm going to Dartmouth. I found out last week I was awarded a scholarship, covering full room and board, tuition and the cost of books for four years. It's contingent on me maintaining my valedictorian status through graduation and a 3.7 g.p.a. all four years of college."

"Hales, that's fucking amazing!"

"Thank you." She blushed and looked shy as I complimented her. "But the thing I've always been concerned about is leaving Chloe behind. My plan has always been to sneak away in the middle of the night, right after graduation, leaving my phone and everyone else behind."

"You were going to leave me?" I asked, unable to hide the hurt.

"You changed all my plans. I couldn't just sneak away from you in the middle of the night. I could do it to Sassy and Snake, and even Chloe, but not you."

"Now that you know the truth about your mom and Sassy's dad, the reason she won't ever be abused, do you feel better about leaving her?"

"Yes and no." I furrowed my brows at her, waiting for her to continue speaking. "I have to tell Sassy what I know, and I'm dreading that conversation. I don't want her to hate me because my dad murdered hers."

"Don't you think she already knows, though?"

"Yes, but the reason is wildly different from either of us ever imagined, and I have to tell her that her dad was cheating on her mom. Even if the love affair was only in my mom's head and she was just a side piece, she still has a sister, and her dad was still unfaithful."

"I can be there when you tell her—if you want."

"I would like that. I need to tell Chloe too, but I don't know how she's going to handle it."

"I can help you with that too."

We were still clinging to each other.

"I need help to get out, I know that. You helped me see that, so I want to tell Snake and Sassy my plans, and Sassy knows about us."

"Seriously, you told her?"

"You got us caught." I smiled sheepishly.

"How?"

"At the homecoming dance, when you used the side door to the gym."

"Oops."

"Oops," she mocked me.

"Um, I told Jordy."

"Will!" She shouted at me.

"He won't say anything, if only because he knows your dad will kill me and he can't live without me." She looked at me like she didn't believe the words. "I swear, our secret is safe."

"Okay," she sighed reluctantly.

"Is there anything else I need to know tonight?"

"No," she said. Even if there was, she might not be able to remember after the trauma she'd had today.

"I've missed you so fucking much, this month and a half nearly killed me, doll."

"I'm so sorry I ran. I should have stayed."

"We're together now, no more friends with benefits, no more enemies with benefits. Love, doll. We're in love and that makes you my woman. My girl."

"And you're mine."

"Gladly." She pulled me in again and pushed her head against my chest as I kissed the top of her head.

"Come on, you need a painkiller and some rest. Do you think you might have a concussion?"

"No," she shook her head. "I've had enough to know."

"As long as you're sure." I was probably going to wake her up a few times in the night, anyway, just to ease my mind. "I have a Valentine's Day gift for you upstairs."

"Yours is still at my house."

"You got me something?"

"I did. I love you, idiot."

"Ah yes, true love only uses terms of endearment like idiot and asshole."

"I call you baby, too."

I laughed at her before sweeping her into my arms, leaving our cups behind and carrying her up to my bedroom. I laid her on the bed before walking to the bathroom to get her Tylenol and some water. "Here, doll," I said, handing them to her. "You're safe now."

"I know," she murmured. While she took her pills, I went to my desk and grabbed her present. I sat on the bed next to her and handed it to her, watching her open the necklace first. "What does it mean?" She asked, running her fingers across the beads.

"Hales," I said, feeling along the first layer. "Will," I answered, running my hands along the second layer. "Not enemies," I whispered the last part as I touched the third layer.

She laughed lightly before clutching her stomach in pain from the action.

"I love it."

"There's more."

I knew she was going to protest, so I silenced her with a chaste kiss before grabbing the most recent drawing and handing it to her.

"Will, you're so talented. This is beautiful." She looked down at it, a goofy smile on her face. "Thank you. We really are stupid in love, aren't we?" I nodded at her. We were.

"You're welcome." I took both presents from her and set them back on the desk, and turned off the light. "You need sleep, doll."

I climbed into bed and pulled her against me, her head resting on my chest. When her soft little snores filled my room, I used my free hand to grab my phone and looked up colleges in New Hampshire, close to Dartmouth.

CHAPTER 26

THE LUNCH

Haley

When I woke up the day after Valentine's Day, I was hornier than I'd ever been in my entire life. Waking up wrapped in Will's arms, his long cock hard and hot against me after so long without sex with him was making me crazy.

Will woke me up twice in the night to make sure I didn't actually have a concussion, and I was so thankful for that. I wanted to show him how thankful I was for him. His arms around me tightened and pulled me closer. His cock pushed against my ass, and I wiggled it in an attempt to wake him.

It didn't work.

The hand he had on my hip squeezed on probably the only part of me not bruised.

"Will," I whispered, but he just squeezed tighter.

I pushed my hand inside the boxers he'd leant me, finding myself soaked.

Seven weeks without him was too long.

"Will," I moaned as I stroked my clit. "Will," I moaned louder. I heard him groan in my ear as I wiggled my hips against him. "I'm touching myself, baby, wake up."

"Haley," he groaned in my ear.

"I'm so wet."

"Fuck, doll. Are you touching yourself?" His groggy, sleep laced voice was smokey in my ear.

"You wouldn't wake up, so I had to do it myself."

"I don't want to hurt you."

"I'll tell you if I'm in pain, I promise. It's been too long," I whined. Will pulled the covers off of us, shoved the boxers down my body and pulled the shirt I wore over my breasts.

"We're going to be late for school."

"We have a free first period."

"And we can go have sex in the janitor's closet," he whispered teasingly in my ear.

"Would you rather have me in a closet or in a bed?"

"Bed. Definitely a bed. Let me see you touch yourself."

With the covers gone, Will rested his chin on my shoulder, eyes trailing down my body to where my fingers strummed my clit.

"Did you touch yourself while we were apart? Did you think about me?"

"Yes," I answered in a whine.

His hand pulled my top leg away, opening me up with a gentle touch to not hurt me, so he could see what I was doing. "Did you think about things I'd already done to you or what you wanted me to do to you?"

"Yes."

"Tell me," he demanded before biting lightly into my shoulder, making me moan louder.

"I thought about my house, in front of the mirror."

"You fucking loved that, didn't you, doll? Loved watching my dick disappear in your tight little cunt, watching me stretch and pound you."

"Yes, yes! I loved it."

"What else did you think about?"

"Last time we were together in this bed."

He hummed a noise of appreciation in my ear. "And what was so special about that?"

He was going to make me say it, force me to name what we both knew it was.

"For the first time, you didn't fuck me."

"No, I didn't. What did I do to you then, baby?"

"You made love to me."

"And you loved that too, didn't you?"

"So much I cried. You didn't see it, but I cried because that's when I knew I couldn't deny anymore that I'm in love with you."

"Yet you still made me wait over two months until you admitted it. Tell me again, Hales."

God. All three of my nicknames in three sentences. He was pulling no punches today.

"I love you, Will."

"Then come for me. Let me see what you looked like during our time apart, how my name fell from those pouty lips." I moaned and stroked myself faster. His voice in my ear and the images of him in my mind, all the things he'd done to me, had me hurtling towards an orgasm.

"You look so sexy like this," he whispered. "Body tight like a coil. I can tell how close you are."

"Will!" I went to snap my legs together again, but he held me tightly, preventing me from moving. "Oh god. Will!"

"Come for me, Hales. Soak your fingers for me." My head fell back, pushing into Will while I cried out his name. Will took my hand and brought it to his lips, licking me clean. "It's been too long since I've tasted you." Adjusting us both, Will laid on his stomach, head between my legs. "If I hurt you, grab you too tight somewhere, tell me to stop."

"You won't hurt me." I cupped his face as I spoke, and he leaned into it, kissing my palm before focusing back on my pussy. "Please, Will. Eat me."

With a groan coming deep from his throat, he held me open and attached his mouth to me. My hands shot to his hair, holding on to him while he poured all his love into touching me. His big hands held my thighs open, pinning them to the mattress while his wicked tongue flicked against my clit.

"Tell me, doll," he said, making me whine at the loss of contact. "What else did you think about?"

"Will, don't stop. Please!"

"Tell me!" He slapped four fingers against my pussy, making me buck. The bucking action hurt, but I was too far gone to care.

"Oh god." His mouth was on me again, his tongue fucking me. "You. Will. I-I-I." I could barely speak. The memories I'd conjured of him doing this while we'd been apart didn't do him justice. He knew my body better than I did. His fingers replaced his tongue inside me and his mouth wrapped around my clit. I needed to make a sentence come out soon, or he was going to stop again.

And he couldn't stop.

I was so close.

"The Hillview party, in the basement, the first time you had me on a soft surface and not against a wall or the hard ground."

Will groaned before slamming his fingers inside me and pushing them against my g-spot. His lips sucked on my clit, making me come.

"Will!" I cried to the ceiling as I came undone for him for the first time in too damn long.

"You've got to get on top," he said as he laid next to me on the bed. "I don't want to hurt you."

"Okay."

Will helped me straddle his hips and settle myself on top of him. When his cock slipped easily into me, we both moaned loudly.

"Fuck. You're squeezing me so tight. I missed being inside you." Will's hands squeezed my hips gently, avoiding the bruises while I bounced on him. "I love watching your tits bounce for me. They're perfect." His hands cupped my tits, squeezing while I bounced faster on him, and my hands covered his own, squeezing while he squeezed me.

My pussy gushed, making sopping wet noises.

"I can't believe I went seven weeks without you," I whimpered. My head fell back, my throat extending. Once again, neither of us was fighting for dominance, just bringing the other pleasure.

"Never again," he grunted. His hands abandoned my chest and ran down my back carefully, still gentle and worried about the bruises and pain. When he got to my hips, he ran his right hand around my body, across my soft stomach, and down between my folds. "Don't stop." I opened my eyes and watched him push his fingers through my folds, coating them in my wetness. When he reached around and pushed a wet finger against my ass, I stopped. "I said don't stop, doll. You're not the only one who imagined things while we were apart. Let me touch you here, doll." His finger pushed gently against my ass as he spoke.

"Will," I breathed his name.

"Tell me if you want me to stop."

"Don't stop. Do it," I encouraged him, nearly begging.

His finger danced around my back entrance, coaxing me to relax for him. When I finally did, he slid his finger slowly into me. My bouncing on top of him still forced it all the way in.

"Oh my god!"

"Yeah?" He asked. "You like that?"

"More," I begged. Will fingerfucked my ass while I rode him. I forced my eyes open to fixate on his blue ones, watching the pupils blown wide as they took in all of me. "I'm so close," I told him.

"Me too, doll, I'm gonna fill your tight little pussy."

"Yes! Baby. Oh god!" My body tightened before releasing and I exploded around him; my pussy clamped down on his cock, squeezing and milking his release until my insides were covered in him.

"Haley," he moaned one last time before pulling his finger from me. My head fell to his chest and his arms wrapped around me.

I shook like a leaf on top of him and planted kisses all across his chest while he did the same to my head. Delicately, he rolled us over so that I was on my back. After he climbed off of me, I watched his naked ass disappear into the bathroom.

My body ached. Part of it was from yesterday's beating, but some of it was also from having sex for the first time in so long. I grabbed my phone and opened it, seeing a message from Sassy.

Sassy: snow day! Wanna hang?

We got a snow day?

Me: can't. I'm with him...

She would know who he was.

Sassy: I'll ditch first period tomorrow so you can fill me in. I've clearly missed something.
Me: deal.

I set my phone back on the nightstand just as Will came back into his bedroom.

"We should go or we'll be late for second period."

"We got a snow day."

"Seriously?"

"Check your phone."

Will grabbed his phone and scrolled through it. "Hell yes!" I laughed at his enthusiasm. He was such a child sometimes still. "Here," he said when he'd stopped being so excited. He handed me a washcloth and then a glass of water. "How are you feeling?"

"A little sore."

"We can get in the hot tub."

"Feed me first."

"Do you love me more or food more?"

"Don't ask questions you don't want to know the answer to, baby."

Will chuckled at me before bending down and reappearing with his clothes from last night and mine. I hadn't even realized he'd got naked while we had sex.

"Do you want to tell Sassy and Snake today?" He asked when we were in the kitchen.

"Not today. I want to enjoy this," I said, motioning between the two of us, "just a little longer before everyone knows."

"I like that."

Will kissed me chastely again before going to the fridge.

"Bacon and eggs, okay?"

"Perfect."

I watched him work greedily, not commenting on the food he took out of the oven and tossed into the trashcan while reminding myself that the last seven weeks I hadn't been able to do this were my fault.

"Will?"

"Hm?" He called. His back was to me as he flipped bacon in a frying pan.

"I'm sorry."

"For what?"

"Running out on you. Denying you. Denying us."

Will set the spatula down and turned towards me. His blue eyes flashed to mine, full of questions. In two giant steps, he was standing in front of me. "Look at me," he said, grabbing my chin and tilting it up. "There's nothing to be sorry about. We're together now, and that's the only thing I want to focus on. Whatever happens tomorrow, we'll worry about tomorrow. Whatever happens after graduation, we'll worry about tomorrow too. I know we need a plan, that whatever happens moving forward won't be easy, but those worries are for tomorrow. Today's a snow day. We're together and in love. That's the only thing I'm worried about. Spending seven weeks without you was miserable; I barely recognized myself half the time, but this, right here, right now, you and me, that's the only thing that matters. And if it took being away from me for seven weeks to finally admit how you feel about me, they were worth it."

"You're smart sometimes."

"I know," he scoffed. Will kissed me before turning back to his cooking duties. "Do you need more painkillers?"

"No, I'm okay."

"Just let me know if you do."

"I will. Do you want coffee?"

"Yeah, that'd be great." While Will cooked our breakfast, I used the Keurig to make two cups of coffee. I handed Will's to him black and stood next to him, watching him cook us breakfast. "You're staring," he said.

"I like the view."

Will blushed, and I loved it.

"Go sit down, crazy girl." I winked at him, but took my coffee and sat at the breakfast bar. "You're still staring."

He wasn't even looking at me, but could tell.

"I'm willing you to cook faster because I'm starving. I haven't eaten since lunch yesterday."

"Why didn't you say anything?" He asked, turning to me, clearly angry at my admission.

"I was distracted."

"You need to eat, doll."

"I usually do."

He nodded and went back to our breakfast. By the time he was finished, I had two over easy eggs, a pile of bacon, two pieces of toast and cut up mixed berries.

"Thank you."

"You know I'd do anything for you, right?"

"I do."

He nodded. "Good."

We spent the rest of breakfast eating in silence, and even though it was quiet, I missed this, spending time with him.

"Hot tub?" He asked as he cleaned up our dishes and the mess.

"Sure."

Will disappeared into the mudroom and came back with the robes we'd worn last time and two towels. "Get naked, doll."

I rolled my eyes at him. "You had me naked this morning."

"If I had my way, you'd always be naked. Even when we're not fooling around, you'd be naked while I cooked, while we cuddled, while we did the most mundane things."

"Naked while you cook bacon?" I shuddered. Will laughed and closed the distance between us. His arms wrapped gently around me and kissed the top of my head.

"I've never had a boyfriend before," I mumbled into his chest.

"No?"

"Nope, you're the first."

"Good."

I rolled my eyes at his ridiculous sarcasm.

Being in love with him wasn't all that bad. We stripped out of our clothes and Will brought them to the mudroom while I wrapped the robe around myself. Will's new habit seemed to be constantly holding my hand, unable or unwilling to let it go, and I didn't mind. He held my hand the entire time we walked outside until he couldn't because he needed two hands to open the hot tub. It was the middle of the morning, but nobody could see us as we took our robes off and climbed in.

Will pulled me against him immediately and just held me.

"I was so scared when you showed up covered in blood," he whispered, his voice nearly breaking. "And I felt bad because it wasn't me going through any of it. It was you, and I was scared."

"But you were scared for me."

"I hate that you live there."

"So do I."

"Can you move out?"

"Where would I go? I can't live here."

"My parents would let you."

"We'd get caught. My dad would find out."

"Sassy?"

"Her trailer is barely big enough for her and her brother."

Will huffed against me, unhappy with my answers. "Whenever your sister isn't home, you're with me," he demanded.

"Okay," I agreed. I didn't mind spending time with him, and being with him would be better than being at my house.

Will and I made out, but stuck to my new no hot tub sex rule while we snuggled and laughed together.

How had I ever denied him?

By the time I was hungry again, it was nearly lunchtime, and we'd been in the hot tub for way too long. As we walked back into the house, Will held my hand. We were laughing when I heard the rumbling of the garage door again. "Relax," he whispered. "It's fine. They don't know you're here, but it's fine. Don't freak out, please don't run, doll."

"I'm not," I promised, but by the way he squeezed my hand tighter, I knew he didn't believe me.

"Haley," Mrs. Roberts said, surprised to see me. "It's lovely to see you again."

"You too, Mrs. Roberts," I said, smiling timidly at her. "You too, Sheriff."

"Miss Winters." Neither of them commented on my face—telling me all I needed to know. Will had told them about the abuse, but also respected my wishes enough not to have them intervene.

His dad didn't look nearly as happy to see me as his mom did, but I understood it was out of worry for his son. "Will you be joining us for lunch and dinner?"

"Yes," Will answered for me. "You said your sister was babysitting tonight again, and her teacher is taking her to school tomorrow."

"That's right."

"Stay with me again tonight. I-I." He stuttered over his words and I knew he didn't want me going back to my parents alone.

"If it's okay with your parents, I'll stay."

"We'd be happy to have you."

"In the guest room," Sheriff Roberts said.

"Dad. Where do you think she slept last night? We're eighteen, don't be so ridiculous." I felt awkward at the exchange, but his dad sighed and clearly conceded.

"Why don't you kids go change, and I'll make us lunch. Soup and grilled cheese, okay?"

"That would be great," I said.

"Come on, Hales." I followed Will up the stairs, embarrassed that I was naked underneath the robe. But his parents had no way of knowing that. A bikini could have easily been hidden by the robe I wore. "Are you okay?" He asked.

"I think so."

"Just think of it like meeting any boyfriend's parents."

"You're my first boyfriend!"

"I know," he grinned. There it was, that magnetic personality that made me fall for him.

"What about school tomorrow? I need to go home and get a uniform."

"Can you have Sassy bring you something?"

"Probably."

"If you can't, I'll bring you to your car early enough that you can run home and change."

Will handed me a pair of joggers and a clean sweatshirt to change into. I did, drowning in his clothes, but I didn't have any of my own. The only ones I had were covered in blood.

"Ready?"

"I think so."

Will held my hand again as we made our way back into the living room towards the kitchen.

"Have a seat," his mom said. "Water okay?"

"Yes," I answered.

The silence was a little awkward as Will's mom continued to cook and his dad worked on a laptop next to us at the table. "Are you looking forward to graduation?" She asked me while she set a high pile of grilled cheese sandwiches on the table.

"I am."

"Any plans for after?"

"I'm still undecided," I replied. I didn't want to tell any more people than necessary about my plans.

"Any plans for spring break?" She asked.

Spring break was only four weeks away, which seemed like a while, but most people already had their plans finalized.

"I was actually thinking of asking her if she wanted to stay the week at grandma's beach house," Will said.

"Really?" I asked.

"Yeah." He offered me one of his charming smiles as he answered. "I was also thinking maybe we could invite your friends."

I knew he meant Sassy and Snake.

"You're amazing, you know."

"I know."

I laughed, and so did his mom.

"You guys are adorable. I'm glad you've finally decided to come back to the house."

"Me too," I told her. She set a bowl of soup in front of me and closed the sheriff's laptop while he was still typing.

"Yes ma'am," he said.

"You have an open invitation to our home," Sheriff Roberts said.

"Thank you."

While we ate lunch, Will's mom told me stories about his childhood, making me laugh and him grumble. And after lunch, she showed me how to make those chocolate chip cookies she'd been making forever, the ones from our first day of pre-kindergarten.

As she shared the recipe with me, I knew I'd make them for Will whenever he wanted, baking them with love, too.

CHAPTER 27

THE TALK

Haley

Tuesday morning, we weren't lucky enough to have another snow day. We rarely ever got them, so yesterday had definitely been a fluke, but I still felt lucky because I woke up in Will's bed, his arm draped over my stomach and his face pushed into the crook of my neck. It was cold in his room, how he preferred it when he slept, but his body heat kept me plenty warm. "Morning," he mumbled. "What time is it?"

"Six, the alarm is gonna go off in just a few minutes."

"Don't move," he said, pulling me closer and sighed into my neck.

It had only been about thirty-six hours since we got back together, but it was like nothing had changed, except for us finally admitting we loved each other. I still couldn't believe it, but laying in his bed with him—snug and warm—I *felt* safe. The feeling was still foreign, but I liked it. My face was bruised ugly, and I didn't have any makeup with me at his house, and I didn't want to go home before school, which meant I'd be sporting bruises at school today.

"Sassy is bringing you a uniform?"

"Yeah."

When the alarm sounded, Will cut it off quickly, but he didn't pull away. "We need to get up or we're going to be late."

"We don't need to go to first period."

"Sassy is skipping first period to meet me."

"And you're gonna tell her?"

"About her dad? Not yet. I was hoping they could… maybe come over after school and we could tell them together. I'll make sure Sassy keeps Snake under control, but I know he won't care if we're together. He'll just be shocked."

"Okay." Will finally rolled away from me. "Shower with me?"

"Let me just go to the bathroom first."

"Watching you pee isn't a problem."

"Gross, Will, I love you, but I have some limits. You're not into water sports, are you?" My tone teased him, but still I worried he might have a kink I wanted nothing to do with. There weren't a lot of things I wasn't willing to try, but that was one of them.

"Hales, no, come on, doll. All I'm saying is. I mean… look." He was so damn adorable sometimes, especially when he was flustered, and I could hardly stand it. "My parents pee in front of each other?"

"You're too fucking cute."

"Stop," he chastised me. I kissed his cheek before slipping into the bathroom, closing and locking the door behind me. I heard the doorknob rattle while he tried to get in, and he muttered something I couldn't understand. When I finished, I flushed, washed my hands and unlocked the door. "I'm peeing with you in here, so if you don't want to see it, get your ass in the shower." I didn't necessarily care, but I didn't need to watch either. While he walked to the toilet, I stripped and climbed into the shower.

The memories of him washing me after I'd shown up beaten and bloody on his door flashed through my mind. He'd been so tender, so gentle and loving. When he'd kissed each of the marks and bruises on my body, the ones inflicted with so much hatred by the woman who was supposed to love me, I cried, unable to hold back the tears. It was the most intimate thing we'd ever done together.

Reaching my hand out to touch the water I'd turned on, I felt it warm against my skin and stepped underneath it. As soon as my hair was wet, I heard the door open and Will walked in. "You're gonna have to use my shampoo and body wash," he said, desire lacing his voice, "and I'm going to love knowing you smell like me all day." I grinned at him. Something changed inside Will when I showed up at his door. It was more than just him seeing me so hurt. It changed when I told him I loved him.

I wondered how long he'd been waiting to tell me before New Year's, not that it mattered, but knowing I loved him too allowed him to let his guard down. It had only been a day and a half, but he laughed more, smiled brighter, and was more relaxed, like a weight had been lifted off of his shoulders.

"Can I wash your hair?" When I nodded in response, Will grabbed his shampoo and poured a generous amount into his hands before rubbing them together. I sighed when his fingers brushed along my scalp and he lathered it into my hair, the woodsy scent—distinctly and traditionally masculine—filling my nostrils. His fingers dug into my scalp, massaging more than gently, but not too hard, the perfect amount of pressure, and I sighed again, leaning my body against his. When he finished, he rinsed his hands under the water. "Tilt your head back for me, doll."

Once my hair was rinsed, I looked at him again, seeing a look of peace on his face. Using his hands, he washed my body from my neck to my toes, and everywhere between, not turning it into anything sexual.

"Can I wash you, too?" I asked when he finished.

"I'd love that, but not today. I know you need to get to Sassy, and if you touch me, I won't be able to control myself any longer."

I also didn't love the idea of having sex while his parents were home. "Next time," I said, kissing him before sliding behind him so I could climb out of the shower.

"You can get dressed and go downstairs. You don't need to wait for me."

I swallowed nervously, even though his mom had been nothing but nice to me. While Will showered, I towel dried my hair, avoiding the mirror. I didn't actually want to know how bad the bruising was. My face didn't hurt as bad as it did yesterday, and Will said my cuts were healing nicely, but still, I didn't want to look. I wasn't looking forward to seeing Chloe today, either. I hadn't seen her, and I knew she'd freak out seeing my face.

After I dried, I pulled on a fresh pair of Will's boxers, joggers and a sweatshirt. The shower was still on, so I chose to be brave and walk down to the kitchen.

"Good morning, Haley," Mrs. Roberts greeted me happily. She stood at the stove, an apron tied around her waist. "Sleep well?"

"I did. Thank you for letting me stay."

"Ian was serious yesterday. You have an open invitation into our home."

"Thank you."

"Stop thanking me," she said, a bright smile plastered on her face. "Do you like pancakes?"

"Yes."

"Have a seat, breakfast is almost done." I sat at the breakfast bar. "Would you like a cup of coffee?"

"Yes, please." She left the pancakes to bubble on the stove and moved to the coffeemaker, pouring me a cup from the pot instead of the Keurig side, and slid it to me, setting creamer and sugar in front of me. "Thanks."

"I made you lunch, too, and I slid an extra cookie in it for you. Don't tell Will, he only got one."

My mouth fell open as I looked at her. She made me lunch? I couldn't remember the last time my own mother made me lunch.

I'd had to fend for myself even at four when my earliest memories started. "I-I." I couldn't get any words out.

"Oh, honey," she said, fussing over me and coming around the breakfast bar. "Can I give you a hug?" I nodded and let her embrace me, finally knowing what a loving hug from a mother felt like. "My son loves you, and that means I love you, too—no questions asked. Whatever you need, Haley, I'm here for you."

I blubbered a little and squeezed her tighter before she pulled away, offering me the softest smile, and walked back to the pancakes, piling them high on a plate.

"Good morning," Will said, coming into the kitchen right on time, walking to me and kissing my head before grabbing a cup of coffee for himself.

"Morning, honey, sleep well?"

"Best I've slept in weeks." His words made me blush while he snuck a glance at me.

Was being in love always like this? Sweet whispered words, long, lingering glances, and a combination of peace in being with the other person and anxiousness low in your belly for the next kiss or the next whispered word, certain that it would come.

"Morning," Sheriff Roberts said, coming into the kitchen just after Will.

"Morning, love." They exchanged a kiss while he stroked her back lovingly. Suddenly, it made sense why Will was so affectionate. He'd actually had a decent example of how an actual relationship looked.

I turned to look at Will while he sipped his coffee. When I pulled my attention away from him, a pile of pancakes was set in front of me with a side of bacon and some fruit. "This looks great."

"You didn't ask for chocolate chips?" Will asked, and I could see the smirk on his kissable lips even without looking at him, hearing it in his voice.

"I don't always need them."

He laughed at me before digging in. His parents ate at the table while Will and I ate at the breakfast bar, one of his hands on my leg the entire time.

"We should go if you want to meet Sassy." Will grabbed our empty plates and set them in the sink. "We'll be back after school." *We*. "I'll pull the truck into the garage."

"Thanks."

Will grabbed his backpack before walking out the front door and I walked across the kitchen and said a soft goodbye to his parents. I really liked his mom, and I didn't dislike his dad, but I felt nervous around him. When I heard the rumble of Will's truck in the garage, I left the house.

While we drove to the church, Will held my hand the entire time. Sassy was already there when we pulled in. Snake must have dropped her off, and I was glad she got him to leave her alone. I wasn't ready for him to know. He would by the end of the day, but I needed the day. Undeterred by Sassy staring at us, he still leaned across the cab of the truck and kissed me. "I'll see you at school. Meet me here after? Snake, Sassy, and I will ride to your house with you."

"You sure you want to tell them today?"

"I can't keep this from Sassy. Leaving I could, but not what my mom said about her dad."

"Okay, I'll be here."

"Holy shit," Sassy said, waving back at Will, who waved at her while he drove off. "Your face. What happened?"

"I'll tell you about it this afternoon. Can you and Snake come to Will's after school?"

"Seriously?"

"There's a lot I need to tell you, and I don't want to have to repeat it, but Snake needs to hear some of it, too."

"I'll make sure he comes with us after school."

"You don't have to tell him it's Will. He can find that out when Will meets us here."

"Deal."

"Wanna grab breakfast? We can go to McDonald's and I can change in the bathroom."

"Sure, oh, and I brought you this."

She handed me the sketchbook I bought for Will. "Where did you find it?"

"In your room, I went over there when both your parents' cars were gone."

"Why were you at my desk?"

"Looking for your school stuff." She held up my backpack next, and I grabbed it from her. "You love him."

"I do, and he loves me." Sassy didn't say anything, but just hugged me. "Come on, I'm starving."

"Didn't Will feed you?"

"His mom made me breakfast… and lunch," I said, holding up the brown paper bag.

"But you're still hungry?"

"I'll just get a coffee… and maybe a hash brown… and maybe a sausage biscuit." Sassy laughed and rolled her eyes at me while we walked to my car.

"Are you going to tell me what's going on?" Snake asked as he climbed into my car after school.

"Yes," I said. Sassy sat quietly in the passenger seat next to me, but let me do all the talking. "We're going to go park somewhere, and someone is going to pick us up."

"Who?"

"It might be best if I don't tell you, seeing is believing, after all."

"Am I being murdered?"

"No," I said, trying not to laugh, but given his lifestyle, the one we were both forced into, it was a fair question. "I just need you to trust me. Once we get where we're going, you can ask as many questions as you want. There are some things I need to tell both of you."

I glanced at Sassy, who shrugged her shoulders at me. Neither one of us had any idea how Snake was going to take seeing Will pick us up. Once we got to the church, I backed into my usual hiding spot, leaving the car hidden behind the bushes. When Will's truck pulled up, I grabbed his Valentine's Day gift and climbed out.

"Seriously?" Snake asked, but Sassy shushed him and climbed into the back of the truck while I climbed into the front seat.

"Hey baby," I said.

"Hi, doll," he replied, leaning over to kiss me.

"Holy shit," Snake said.

"Sassy, Snake, nice to see you."

"I have so many questions."

"They'll all be answered," I promised.

Will put his hand on my leg as we drove through town. I was less concerned with being caught, but I still kept my head ducked down, letting my hair hide my face, even though the chance of someone recognizing me through the dark tinted glass was unlikely.

When we arrived at his house, Will pulled the truck into the garage, and once the garage door closed behind me, I climbed out, prompting Sassy and Snake to do the same. Neither of his parents' cars were in the driveway when we pulled in.

They followed us into the house, and I could feel the waves of uncertainty coming off of Snake.

"Do you want something to drink?" Will asked.

"I feel like I need alcohol for whatever's about to happen," Snake said. Will laughed, but I was sure Snake was serious. Will set a bunch of sodas and waters on the counter, letting them choose.

Will and I sat next to each other at the table while Sassy and Snake sat across from us.

"So, you're a couple?" Snake asked. "How long has this been going on?"

"September twenty-second," Will answered, easily. I gawked at him. He remembered the day? I didn't even remember the day.

"Don't look so shocked, doll."

"We were just enemies with benefits. I ended it on New Year's, but we got back together this weekend. We're together, now, yes." They both nodded and took sips of their sodas. "What I'm about to tell you is long, and I need both of you not to interrupt me. What I'm going to tell you is shocking and sad, and I need you to stay calm, especially you, Sassy."

"What's going on?"

"I'm going to college… in New Hampshire." Both of them looked shocked, but I held up my hand to prevent her from cutting me off. "I'm also our class valedictorian."

"Holy shit," Snake said again.

"I've always been planning on going to college, and I was never planning on telling anyone. I was going to sneak away in the middle of the night. It's not because I don't love you, but because I knew it was my only chance of escaping my parents. I was going to leave you and Chloe and run away."

"Haley," Sassy said, clearly sad by the revelation.

"I know I can't do that now. I need help to get out, but the one thing that was always holding me back was Chloe, not knowing if she'd be safe once I was gone. Will helped me realize I needed help, and I love you both. It's not fair to just disappear on you."

"Wow."

"There's more, and this is the hard part."

"Sunday, after we got home from our club stuff, my mom was high, snorting lines in the living room. She came after me, did this to my face. While she was hitting me, I asked her why Chloe was her favorite. I don't care that she is. I'm happy she is because it means she'll never be a target for the abuse, but what she told me is… shit." Will squeezed my hand, and I took a deep breath. "She told me that my dad isn't Chloe's dad."

"Who's her dad?" Sassy asked.

"She said… she said her dad is Hound."

I didn't dare look up at her, scared of what I'd see on her face.

"What? That can't be true," she said in disbelief.

"She said they were in love, that my dad killed yours because they were going to run away together, leave us and Buck behind and take Chloe." Sassy started to cry, and Snake pulled her chair to him, pulling her out of it and into his lap while he tried to comfort her. "I'm so sorry."

Sassy didn't say anything, just cried against Snake. Tears filled my own eyes as I watched my best friend break because of what I just told her. "Sassy," I whispered. She looked up at me, eyes and cheeks already puffy and stained red. Climbing off of Snake's lap, she walked towards me. Tentatively, I stood, walking towards her until she wrapped her arms around me and pulled me into a hug. We stood in my boyfriend's kitchen, sobbing against each other and clinging to each other. "We can send some DNA off to compare you and her. My mom is crazy. Maybe she's lying?"

"Does Chloe know?"

"Not yet. I only found out on Sunday."

"Let's not tell her until we're sure, until we get the DNA test."

"Okay."

"What the fuck?" Snake said. "You've been planning on leaving this entire time." He was pissed, his eyes and posture radiating anger.

"Yes, I told you Sassy and you could be together."

"Your dad will kill me."

"That's another reason you're here," I said. "We need to figure out what to do with my dad."

"Turn him in," Snake said immediately, and my eyes shot up. I hadn't been expecting that. "I don't want this life, but I can't get out. I'm not smart enough for college. Sassy and I don't have a lot of money because your dad isn't giving me a fair cut."

"You want to turn him in?"

"Do you not want to turn him in?"

"No, I do, but I wasn't sure you did."

"Can your dad give me immunity for potential crimes?"

"Yeah," Will said automatically.

"We need to wait, though," Sassy said.

"Why?"

"Chloe. We can't leave her with your mom. We'll take care of her, right?" She asked Snake.

"Of course."

I always knew Sassy would look after her if I left.

"It'll be easier to get custody of her if we're graduated and have jobs," Sassy explained further.

"If we strategize before we speak to my dad, we can time it right and have him arrested right after graduation."

"Thank you," I said, finally walking away from Sassy and back into my man's arms while Sassy did the same with Snake.

We sat at the table, snuggling with our loves for long minutes, until Will finally murmured that he'd take us all back to my car.

I hated not being able to be together out in the open, but someday soon we could be, after my father was out of the picture.

CHAPTER 28

THE SISTERS

Haley

Will and I had been back together for two weeks—two amazing weeks. The only problem was trying to keep things under wraps at school. Sassy and Snake both knew, and so did Jordy, but that didn't mean that everyone else could know. The members of the Southside gang who were still in high school were more loyal to Snake than to my dad, and that was why he'd been able to sleep around so much without either of our parents finding out. We'd had them convinced that we both wanted to be free before finally settling down with each other. Most everyone knew Sassy and Snake were messing around, but not how they were in love, and nobody knew I was with Will. We couldn't take the risk.

Chloe spent more and more time with Mick and even more time babysitting, which meant Will and I were spending almost all of our time together too—at his house. His dad was stoic, and Will told me it had nothing to do with me, that he was always like that, even with his mom, who it was very clear he loved immensely. It was his personality. His mom, on the other hand, was amazing, with a bubbly, loving, gracious, and giving personality. She fed me almost every night, taught me to bake cookies, brownies, and was teaching me how to cook a few more complex dishes, improving my basic cooking skills.

I found myself drawn to her and loving her like a mother. My feelings were mixed about it, and it made me wonder how different my life would be if I actually had a decent mother. Will and I probably would have been together our entire lives already. Still, I couldn't regret the way things had developed between us. It all felt like it was always supposed to be.

"Hey," Sassy said, sitting down across from me at our lunch table.

"Hey." I smiled at her, taking a bite of my homemade lunch—turkey and cheese on whole wheat. Will and I met almost every morning during first period, and he always brought lunch his mom made for me.

"Did you get the results yet?"

"No, but I haven't checked since this morning."

The same day I'd told Sassy about our parents' affair, I'd bought a DNA test kit and collected a sample from her, swabbing her cheek. Chloe's sample was harder to get, but I'd stolen her toothbrush and replaced it, sending it in. For good measure, I also sent my DNA to have it tested against Sassy's. I didn't believe for a second my mom ever stopped sleeping with Hound, even at the beginning of my parents' 'relationship'. The company said the results would come in two to four weeks, but I didn't know if any of us could actually handle a four week wait.

Sandwich in one hand, I grabbed my phone with the other and opened my email. "Oh god, I have them."

"Have what?" Snake asked, sitting between Sassy and I.

"The DNA results."

I saw him grab Sassy's hand under the table and squeeze it.

"I'm ready," she said, but her words didn't sound confident.

I set my sandwich down, taking a deep breath. We both wanted my mom to be lying, not that I wanted Viper to be Chloe's dad, too, but I wanted to preserve Sassy's image of her dad—he was her hero.

I opened the email and read it.

Shit.

"You're siblings," I said. I kept reading, but Sassy and I weren't siblings, which was better since I didn't tell her I had myself tested too.

Sassy blinked a few times, holding her breath before taking a deep one and blowing it out quickly.

"Are you okay?" Snake asked her.

"I don't know. I think I need to go."

"Okay," he said. "I'll take you wherever you want to go, baby girl."

"I'm so sorry."

Part of me still believed she was going to blow up at me.

"We've talked about this. It's not your fault, it's our parents' fault."

"We need to tell Chloe."

"Can we do it at…" Her question trailed off, but I knew she meant Will's.

"Meet me behind the church after school time. I'll bring Chloe and have him pick us up."

"Okay." They both stood from the table and walked out of the cafeteria.

My phone beeped, and I knew immediately it was Will.

> Baby: Everything okay?
> Me: I got the DNA results. Chloe and Sassy are siblings. Can we come over after school to tell Chloe?
> Baby: You don't even have to ask doll. I'll meet you at the church. Are you okay?
> Me: I don't know yet
> Baby: I love you, I'm here if you need me
> Me: I love you, too
> Baby: Wanna meet at our spot?
> Me: Yes
> Baby: 5 minutes

I finished my sandwich quickly and saved the cookie for later, putting it in my bag before standing and walking to our spot.

Will wasn't in the janitor's closet when I got there, so I waited, but not long, less than a minute before the door opened again. "Come here," he said, pulling me close and wrapping me in a hug. We didn't need to fool around in the school anymore since we had alone time whenever we wanted, but we still used it during school for stolen moments like this. His lips lingered against my forehead, and the feeling of peace that only came when I was with him lingered with it.

"I'm okay," I said.

"Are you sure?"

"It was what I was expecting." It was too dark to see him, but I could feel him nod against me.

"Are you nervous about telling Chloe?"

"Terrified." She was so young and so fragile.

"It'll be okay. My mom will be home, though."

"I think Chloe will really like your mom."

"My mom loves you, you know."

"I do, she's amazing."

"I know I'm lucky." It was sad that having a great mom made us both believe he was lucky, something that should be the standard, not a rarity. "I'll see you in calculus." Will tilted my chin up and planted a sweet kiss on my lips before pulling away and leaving me alone in the janitor's closet.

Fuck, I loved that stupid boy so much.

With a stupid smile on my face, I walked out of the janitor's closet in search of Chloe. I liked to give her space during school. She flew under the radar and was more popular than I was because apparently, being the second daughter of the leader of the Southside wasn't as interesting as being the first, not that she was actually his kid anyway, but nobody knew that.

When I got to the cafeteria, I found her sitting with Mick and some kids I didn't know.

"Hey," she smiled at me, a little surprised.

"Can we talk for a second?"

"Sure, is everything okay?"

"Yeah." We walked away from the table and towards the back of the cafeteria. "You're not babysitting today, are you?"

"No."

"I need you to come with me after school."

"I have plans with Mick."

"I'll take you to him after, if you want to, but you need to come with me."

"Something's wrong."

"Not wrong, but I need to tell you something."

"You're making me nervous."

"Everything is fine, Chloe, I promise. It's almost the end of the day and I wouldn't have told you at all, but I didn't want you to be upset when I told you not to go with Mick later."

"Okay, I'll meet you at your locker."

"See you."

"What are we doing here?" Chloe asked when I parked in my usual hiding spot behind the church.

"I need you to trust me."

"Okay?"

"Sassy and Snake are meeting us here, and someone is picking us all up. We're gonna go with him, and then we'll talk." She looked so confused, and it was only going to get worse for her as the afternoon went on. Sassy and Snake pulled up on Snake's motorcycle and he parked it right next to my car. Will's truck appeared shortly after. "Let's go."

"Hey doll," Will greeted me with a sweet voice and a chaste kiss when the four of us climbed into his truck.

"What?" Chloe asked.

"Chloe, this is Will, my boyfriend, Will, my sister, Chloe."

"Nice to meet you," he said.

"You too?"

More confusion.

An awkward silence fell over the car, and it had everything to do with Chloe. Snake, Sassy, Will, and I hung out a handful of times in the last two weeks, even having a game night and hanging out in the hot tub while his parents were gone for another weekend.

They went away a lot, but Will said it wasn't until this year that he was left alone without them. It seemed to work for them because they were the happiest couple I'd ever seen that were together for years.

Will and Snake got along surprisingly well, considering how different they were, something Sassy and I giggled about, even though we loved how close they were. The only thing they seemed to have in common was a love of sports, specifically hockey, and they bonded over it.

Will's mom's car was in the driveway when we arrived at his house.

"This is insane," Chloe muttered, and I couldn't fault her because she was right.

When the garage door closed behind us, we all climbed out.

"Haley," Chloe hissed at me. "What the hell is going on?"

"Let's go inside."

Will interlocked our fingers. He always held my hand whenever he could, but he didn't squeeze like he used to, finally secure in the fact that I wasn't going to run from him.

"Hey kids," Will's mom greeted us.

"Hey Mrs. Roberts," Sassy greeted her.

"We've talked about this," she chastised her lightly. "Call me Linda."

"Hi, Linda," Sassy corrected herself.

"You must be Chloe."

"Hi," Chloe responded to Linda a little shyly.

"It's nice to meet you, and just like everyone else, you've got an open invitation to our home. Whatever you need, don't hesitate to ask me."

"Thank you," Chloe said, surprised.

"Will told me you were coming, so I made some snacks. I'll be upstairs if anyone needs me." I looked at the table and saw cheese and crackers, some cut up fruit and vegetables, bottles of water, cans of soda, and of course—cookies.

"Thanks, Mom."

She smiled at me and squeezed my shoulder as she walked by. Will, Sassy, Snake, and I sat in the same chairs we sat in when I'd told Sassy the news. Chloe sat between us, eyes trained on me. I looked at my sister, knowing I was about to turn her entire world upside down. Because of the way we were raised—or not raised more accurately—we were resilient, and she'd be fine, but I was still unsettled.

"What's going on? How long have you been together?"

"Since the beginning of the school year, but that's not what's important."

"Just tell me."

"Do you remember the last beating I got from Mom?"

"Yes, how could I forget? You looked horrible."

"While she hit and kicked me, I asked her why she hates me, why you're the favorite. Don't misunderstand me, I'd take every beating I've ever gotten ten times over if it meant keeping you safe from her, but I still had to know. She told me she hates me because of dad."

"But-"

"Let me finish," I cut her off. "She was high, and loose lipped, she told me that dad wasn't supposed to lead the Southside. She said she loved someone else, but that her dad and dad forced her to marry him. She said that you're the favorite because you aren't dad's."

"What?"

"She said that someone else is your dad."

"Who?"

"Hound."

"Sassy and Buck's dad?"

"I had a DNA test done, it's true."

"Sassy is my sister, too?"

"Yes." Wordlessly, Chloe stood and walked over to Sassy. I watched them embrace and cry softly. Will wrapped me in his arms and held me close, not blocking my view of their embrace. "I've always loved you like a sister," Chloe said, her voice breaking a little.

"Me too." They were both crying while we watched them embrace.

When they finally pulled apart, they both sat back down. "So what now?"

"There's more." She nodded her head and opened a bottle of water. Chloe always needed a drink or food when she was nervous. "I'm going to college, Chloe… in New Hampshire."

"You're leaving?"

"You know I have to."

"I know, but I'm going to miss you."

"You're the reason I wanted to stay, but you know why I can't. You know I can't stay here; I can't keep going through what I go through, but I didn't want to leave you alone with them either."

"So what now?" If you looked at her, you wouldn't know it based on her appearance, but she was panicking. I could tell by the tiny shake of her hand, the way the pitch of her voice changed, the way she looked at me. She was worried.

"We're going to turn Dad in."

"Really?" She looked at Snake now, knowing he was going to take over the gang.

"Yes," he nodded at her. "It's not the life I want. He's done too much damage, and it needs to stop. You and both your sisters need to be safe."

"You're a couple?" She asked.

"We are," Sassy said while Snake wrapped his arm around her.

"What about Mom?" She asked.

"What about her?" I asked.

"She needs to go to jail for everything she did to you, and I don't want to stay with her."

"You're going to move in with us," Sassy said.

"She still needs to go to jail."

"It's her word against mine," I told Chloe.

"No, it's not. I've seen multiple beatings, plus I have pictures."

"What?"

"I took pictures."

"You what?" Will's hand squeezed my own, helping me calm down.

"I took pictures. Sometimes while you were sleeping, sometimes while you were getting changed." While she spoke, she opened her phone and pulled up a photo album and slid the phone across the table to me. Scrolling through the album, I found hundreds of pictures of my bruised and beaten body. Will looked through them with me and I heard him inhale through his nostrils, knowing they were flaring. His hand squeezed my own as his anger built.

I turned to glance at him and saw his jaw tick. "I'm okay," I whispered. He nodded once, but stopped looking at the pictures.

"She needs jail, too."

"When we talk to Sheriff Roberts, I'll tell him about the abuse."

"Thank you."

Chloe stood from the table and walked to me. I stood too, hugging her and kissing her cheek. She'd grown a lot since the start of school and was nearly as tall as I was.

"You know you can't say anything to anyone," Snake said. "Not even your boyfriend."

"I can keep a secret. When are you guys planning on telling someone?"

"A little before graduation."

"And when are you leaving for school? Where are you going?"

"Dartmouth."

"Wow, Hilly, you got into Dartmouth?"

"I did, and I was planning on leaving right after graduation, but then I was planning on staying for the summer." I turned to look at Will again. I couldn't resist the idea of a romantic once in a lifetime summer with him. Unfortunately, that wouldn't happen. "But the scholarship I got is contingent on a few things, and the fine print is a summer job every year for four years, starting the summer before school starts. So I have to go before the start of the summer semester and work in the campus bookstore."

Will was really upset when I'd told him we'd only have about ten days together before I had to leave for the east coast. He wasn't ready for me to leave, and I wasn't either. It didn't matter though, we were staying together. We were in love and a few thousand miles wouldn't change that.

"That's so soon." I only nodded at her. "This is so much information." She leaned forward with her head in her hands on the table, trying to absorb everything.

"You're taking this all surprisingly well," I commented.

"Are you kidding? I'm thrilled. I gained a sister and a brother today and lost a psychopath for a father."

"Our dad was no saint," Sassy snorted. "But yeah, he was better than Viper."

"I won't say anything to anyone, not even Mick, I swear."

"Things could get really dangerous," Snake said.

"We'll keep you safe," I said.

"Who keeps you safe?" She asked me.

"I do," Will said immediately.

I turned to look at him, and without hesitating, he leaned in to kiss me. I accepted it eagerly, feeling tingly when his lips lingered on mine.

"Also, you can't let anyone know you know Dad isn't really your dad."

"For how long?"

"Until this is over," Snake said. "And nobody knows Sassy and I are together and not just hooking up."

"Or that I'm with Haley."

"Do you love him?" Chloe asked me.

"I do."

"And I love her."

"Good. I might be little, but if you hurt her, I'll kill you."

Snake and Sassy laughed while Will just shook his head.

For as tense as the conversation had been, this was my family, my real family, and Chloe took all the tension away.

"I'm gonna go to Mick's," Chloe said. "He's already on his way to get me."

"That's fine," I said. "Just remember, you can't tell him anything."

"I won't."

When I climbed out of the car, Sassy was already walking towards me. "Snake has club business, wanna hangout?"

"Sure, your place?"

"Yeah." I locked my car and walked with Sassy to her house. "Things with you and Will good?" She asked.

"Amazing." I couldn't help but grin at her. "With Snake?"

"Also good." But something about her response seemed off. "Did you ever think this year was going to end like this?"

"With me falling in love?"

"With the sheriff's son," she whispered as we walked into her house.

"Not a chance, not even a little bit."

"I've been hoping for this for forever, being with Snake."

"I'm glad it finally worked out for you."

"And I'm glad he doesn't have to marry you."

"You and me both."

Once we were inside her trailer, we sat on the couch. "I've been holding this in because these past two weeks have been crazy, but I'm freaking out."

"What's wrong?" I asked.

"I'm late."

"Late?"

"My period."

"Sassy!"

"I know, I know."

"How late?"

"Two weeks."

I took a deep breath.

"Weren't you guys safe?"

"I'm on the pill."

"But no condoms?"

"Do you use condoms with Will?"

"We're not talking about me!" She had a point though. Tears filled her eyes. "I'm sorry, I shouldn't have shouted at you. Do you have a test?"

"Yes, but I've been too afraid to take it."

"Come on."

"No."

"You need to know."

Sassy followed me into the bathroom. It was too small for the two of us together, but we made it work. I listened to her pee, not caring like I had with Will. We'd been to the bathroom countless times together. "Two minutes," she said, making me set the timer on my phone.

We didn't speak at all as we waited. Sassy looked terrified.

The annoying timer went off as Sassy took a deep breath. "I can't do it, you look."

I grabbed the stick and looked down at it.

One line.

"You're not pregnant."

Sassy exhaled audibly.

"Thank God."

"You're using the pill correctly, right? Same time, every day?"

"Yes."

"Maybe you should think about an alternate form? An IUD maybe? I've been thinking about one too."

"That's not a bad idea. Can you make us appointments at the clinic?"

"I will."

"Have you not been late, ever?"

"Never. I take my pill religiously, and I have a withdrawal bleed every four weeks."

"How are we sure the test is right?"

"Some people don't bleed on the pill." She nodded. "What would you have done?"

"I don't know," she answered truthfully. "But I'm not ready to be a mom."

"Me either."

"You're not pregnant, so let's have a drink."

"Stash is in my bedroom."

Sassy and I made hot chocolate with whiskey and watched a movie.

The day could have gone a lot worse. Sassy could have been pregnant, Chloe could have taken the news way worse.

But it felt like things were finally falling into place.

CHAPTER 29

THE REMINDER

Will

It had been a week since we'd all sat in my kitchen watching Haley tell her little sister that Sassy was also her sister, who'd taken the news much better than I'd expected. I'd been so worried for Haley. She already had shitty parents, and I didn't want her to lose her sister over this or Sassy. Surprisingly, we'd been spending a lot of time with Snake and Sassy, and even more surprisingly, I got along really well with Snake. I guess I should have assumed I'd get along with him. Haley loved us both—in very different ways—but I knew she wouldn't be such good friends with Snake if he wasn't a decent guy.

Whenever Haley wasn't working at the movie theater or with Chloe, she was with me. It wasn't my proudest moment, but I'd had a jealous fit one night when I'd gone to pick her up and found her waiting with Bobby. As she smiled at him, waved goodbye, and climbed into my truck, I'd been squeezing the wheel so hard that my knuckles turned white.

"What's wrong, baby?" She asked. My jaw ticked while I turned to look at her. "Will, come on, you're not jealous, are you?" She could read me so damn easily.

"I hate him."

"Why?"

"Because he's fucked you."

"Then you've got a long list of guys to hate."

My jaw ticked again.

Angrily, I'd pulled the car into an abandoned parking spot and pulled her to me. Since we'd gotten back together, the sex was incredible, instinctively just knowing what the other wanted, when we could be dominant with each other, or when the other needed us to submit. I'd needed to dominate her in the front seat of my car and she'd let me, riding me until we were both coming with my hand squeezing around her neck and her reminding me how much she loved me, that I was the best she'd ever had, the only one she wanted.

"You don't ever need to be jealous," she whispered before kissing me and climbing off of me. "I love you."

As I remembered how great that night was, my girl walked into our calculus class. She had a soft smile on her face while she looked at me. We were less and less discreet, and it made me nervous because we still couldn't get caught, considering we had another two and a half months of school to get through before graduation.

When she sat down in her seat and pulled her phone out, I grabbed mine, knowing she was texting me.

> Hales: I have an appointment at the clinic with Sassy after school. I'll text you when you can pick me up.
> Me: For her or you?
> Hales: Both
> Hales: Don't freak out, I'm not pregnant.

I let out a sigh of relief and I knew her eyes were on me. She took her pill religiously; I'd seen it more than once, but I was aware of how stupid we were to not be using condoms. The first few times I'd legitimately forgotten, too caught up in the fact I was fucking Haley Winters, and after that, when we'd become enemies with benefits, I just didn't want to anymore, and neither did she.

What would I do if she was pregnant?

Stop, I said, shaking my head at myself. She was it for me, the woman for the rest of my life, but I knew from my parents that having kids at eighteen wasn't a good idea. We'd get there… eventually, when we were much older.

> Me: I wasn't freaking out. Just let me know when I need to come get you.

Haley spent almost all of her time at my house. The only thing she didn't do was sleep there, leaving at about ten o'clock every night, going to pick up her sister from either babysitting or her boyfriend's, and then home to sleep. The schedule seemed to work because she hadn't had a beating since Valentine's Day. I couldn't wait until her mother was behind bars where she belonged and I hoped like hell someone on the inside would do to her everything she'd done to Haley for my girl's entire life.

"No Haley?" my mom asked, both surprised and disappointed when I walked into the house alone.

"She'll be by later."

"Your dad's coming home early."

"Oh, good, because there's something I wanted to talk to you both about."

"What's that?" My dad asked, coming into the kitchen. I sat down at the kitchen table and waited for them to do the same. "She's not pregnant, is she?"

"No, god," I grumbled, shaking my head.

"Sorry," my dad said. "This just feels exactly like how we told your grandparents your mother was pregnant with you."

"She's not. Haley is going to college in New Hampshire, to Dartmouth."

"That's exceptional. How's she leaving her family?" Dad asked.

"You'll hear that story eventually," I said, a little cryptically. "But I want to go out there with her." Neither of my parents spoke, only stared at me. There was no way they'd ever thought I'd want to go so far away for school. "But," I continued, before they had a chance to say anything. "She didn't tell me until a few weeks ago, and I missed all the application deadlines for fall semester. I can apply for next spring, but I'm not going to be without her." It wasn't that I couldn't be without her. I didn't *want* to be. "There are a bunch of job openings, construction, a few painting companies, landscaping, stuff I don't need more than my high school diploma for. So, when she leaves, I'm going with her." *If she'll have me*, I thought to myself. But there was no reason she wouldn't. She didn't want to be without me, either.

"That's a huge decision to make for someone when you're only eighteen."

"You two have been together since you were sixteen. Is it really so hard to believe that I can have that type of love, too?"

"No, it's not," my mom said.

"Dad?"

"I'm still worried about Viper."

"We are, too, but we love each other and we want to be together."

"We'll help anyway we can," my mom said, squeezing my dad's hand and looking at him while she spoke to me.

"I'm proud of you, Son." My dad's words had me feeling emotional. "You love that girl, and it's clear she loves you, too, and despite the risks of being together, her family, her history, you love her enough to not fear it."

I wouldn't go that far. I was terrified of Viper finding out about us, of what he'd do to me if he found out his daughter was planning on skipping town and doing it with me. He'd kill all of us, Snake and Sassy included.

"Haley will be here for dinner?"

"Yeah, she should be calling me anytime to go get her."

"I'll make macaroni and cheese, roasted broccoli, and sloppy joes."

"You love her more than us, don't you?" My dad asked.

I laughed at the pout on his face.

"You know I always wanted a daughter, too," my mom quipped at him.

"You're only thirty-seven, love. Wanna try again?" He wiggled his eyebrows at her and that was my cue to leave.

"And I'm out."

I walked into the living room, but I could still hear them whispering to each other. I had no idea another kid was even on their radar. Mom asked Dad if he really wanted to do the baby stage again, and not retire when he was forty-five. He replied it would be worth it to give her everything she wanted, including another child.

I flipped on ESPN and watched the sports news until my phone beeped.

Hales: I'm on my way to the church.
Me: On my way.

"You leaving, sweetie?" My mom asked as I walked to the garage.

"Yeah."

"Your father and I are going out to dinner. Yours and Haley's is in the oven. Broccoli will be done in forty minutes, same time as the macaroni and cheese. I've got the timer set. And the sloppy joes are in the crock pot keeping warm."

"Thanks, Mom."

Dad was nowhere to be found, presumably in his workshop outback cleaning his gun or working on a case. Most of the cases he couldn't break involved Viper.

The drive to the church was quick and, as usual, Haley's car was already hiding in her usual parking spot.

"What did you need to go to the clinic for?" I asked when she got back into the car.

"I got an IUD."

"A what?"

"An intrauterine device. It's birth control that's good for like five years."

"No more pills?"

"Nope."

"And I can still fuck you raw?"

"You're so crude," she mumbled. "But yes, it's effective right away, except, no sex for twenty-four hours."

"Dammit, and we're going to have the house all to ourselves."

"You'll survive," she mumbled.

"I wouldn't be so sure," I said teasingly. I grinned at her as we sat at the red light. "I'm addicted to you, Haley Winters."

"Poor taste, addictions are never healthy, baby."

"This one is."

Before she could come up with a witty retort, the rumble of a motorcycle pulling up next to us had us both panicking. Haley quickly pulled her hoody over her head, tucking her hair behind it, and leaned against the opposite window. I didn't dare look, but I had to.

Viper. He was unmistakable.

"It's your dad," I whispered, focusing my attention back on the road.

"Fuck," she whispered, her voice distraught. I wanted to reach over and comfort her, but I didn't dare move, not wanting to attract his attention to us.

"Breathe, baby."

When the light turned green, I waited a moment, letting him pull away first. Slowly, I followed behind him, until the rumble of more motorcycles could be heard behind us. Glancing in the rearview mirror, I saw three more bikes behind us.

"Fuck," Haley whispered again.

"I need to get off the road."

I had no idea if we were being followed or if all of this was just a horrible coincidence.

"The McDonald's is right up the road."

I checked my mirrors before getting into the left turn lane made just for the McDonald's. When I pulled in, the motorcycles kept going, paying no attention to us. I pulled into a parking spot and finally felt like my lungs could breathe again. "We're okay," I said, unbuckling her seatbelt and pulling her to me. Her tears hit my neck, where she pushed her face into me and I rocked her back and forth. "You're safe. I won't ever let anything happen to you," I whispered soothingly into her hair. I meant every word. I'd do anything to keep her safe, no matter the sacrifice. "Look at me." She pulled her face out of my neck and looked at me, blinking away her tears. "I will never let him hurt you again." She nodded at me and kissed me sweetly before snuggling back into me, knowing I'd hold her as long as she needed, until she decided to pull away.

For her entire life, Haley built so many walls around her heart, but I'd broken them down and made a place for myself there, but that meant when she was feeling emotional, it took a long time for her to come down; she wasn't used to feeling so much. She needed to feel safe, and the best way for me to give that to her was to let her have her control when she did show me her emotions.

After she'd been clinging to me for about ten minutes, she pulled away. "Do you want to get food?" I asked her.

"Did your mom cook?"

"Yeah."

"Then no."

I grinned at her and kissed her nose, making her cheeks turn a deep red before she finally climbed back across the cab and into her seat.

"Come on, let's go home."

"My sister is babysitting tonight," she said. "Last minute."

"Are you staying the night?"

"If you'll have me."

"Always."

The next morning, Haley and I woke up in bed together. I snuggled closer to her, pulling our bodies together. "I'm hungry," she mumbled.

"You're always hungry."

"So are you."

"Yes, but I'm always hungry for something else," I whispered, rotating my hips so she could feel me pressed into her ass.

"Twenty-four hours aren't up yet," she whispered, her voice teasing and light, nearly carefree. Haley had multiple sides: serious, funny, and a decidedly don't fuck with me side. But this side of her, the one I only got to see when it was just the two of us and we were laying in my bed, loving each other, that was the best version of her. That was the version that reminded me no matter what she'd been through, we were both just eighteen, and we had our entire future together as soon as we got out of this town.

"Fine, then I'll feed you, but when those twenty-four hours are up, you're mine."

She rolled towards me, looking in my eyes while she trailed her hand up my body. The little minx squeezed my hard dick, making me groan as she trailed her other hand up further until she got to my throat. She squeezed and the familiarity of the touch had my eyes rolling in my head. "Try again, Will," she said, her voice sultry and seductive, but I couldn't answer her. Her touch and her words had all my blood rushing south, making me unable to think, let alone speak. "Try again, Will," she demanded, her voice darker this time.

I knew exactly what she wanted me to say, exactly what she needed to happen later.

"When the twenty-four hours are up, I'm yours."

"Good boy."

She released my neck, kissed me and rolled away, climbing out of bed and leaving me there dumbfounded. I laid a few more minutes, willing my dick to deflate. When it finally did, I climbed out of bed and followed Haley into the bathroom where I found her brushing her teeth.

"Want me to cook breakfast?" She asked.

"My mom's probably cooking."

"They're gone for today, remember?"

"Oh yeah, I forgot."

When we got home last night, we passed my parents and they said they'd be home late, and gone early in the morning. They were driving down to the coast to spend the day at the beach.

"Don't burn the house down," I whispered teasingly.

"I can cook."

"I know," I grinned at her before turning on the shower and stripping.

When I got to the kitchen after my shower, I found my girl singing to the radio, a spatula in her hand, doing the most uncharacteristically Haley thing ever—using said spatula as a microphone. She was jamming to Meat Loaf, banging her head around while she twirled, probably burning the sausage.

I stood there, watching her as she screeched more than she sang, falling more and more in love with her. There was no doubt Haley had changed this school year.

"And maybe I'm crazy/ oh it's crazy, and it's true/ I know you can save me/ no one else can save me now but you."

I knew every word of this song too. It was one of my mom's favorites. I never understood it. *'I would do anything for love, but I won't do that'*. What did that even mean? Because watching my girl dance in the kitchen, cooking our breakfast, I couldn't think of a single thing I wouldn't do for her and her love.

"Who sings that song?" I asked her.

"Meat Loaf," she replied, turning and looking at me. Her cheeks flushed pink again.

"Maybe let them sing it."

Her eyes widened, and I laughed loudly at her expression.

"Asshole. Make yourself breakfast." She turned her back to me, but I could see the smile with the way her cheeks were turned up.

"I missed you calling me that, doll." I kissed her cheek while I wrapped my arms around her from behind.

"Keep it up and that's all I'll call you." She shook her head, but turned to kiss me. "Breakfast is ready."

I looked and saw breakfast sausage and scrambled cheesy eggs.

After breakfast, Haley and I cuddled on the couch, watching movies and intermittently making out.

Sometime in the afternoon, after we'd had lunch and too much junk food, Haley leaned against me and whispered in my ear. "It's been twenty-four hours." And before I could get my hands on her, she was off the couch and running up the stairs, leaving me to chase her.

When I got into my room, Haley was nowhere to be found. "Hales," I called out. No answer. "You wanna play doll? Remember what happened the last time we played hide and seek? I got my hands on you in the library, and you didn't get to come."

I heard footsteps in the hallway and chased them, running into the guest room. The closet door was open, and it never was. Slowly, I crept towards it and flung it open. Haley stood there, a grin on her face, and lust in her eyes as she looked at me.

"Caught you," I whispered as I took a step towards her, but she ducked under my arm and sprinted past me. I should have known she wouldn't make it easy for me.

I chased her down the hall and back to my bedroom. When I got there, she was sitting on the chair in the corner, hands on her knees, legs spread slightly. Instantly, the image brought me back to Halloween. It was the same position she had been in at the Hillview party.

"Be a good boy for me, Will."

Those few words were enough to have me rock hard for her.

"What do you want?"

"You," she said, voice full of confidence. "Take off your clothes for me."

She didn't tell me to strip, so I chose to get naked as quickly as possible. Her honey-colored eyes were hooded with desire as they raked greedily up and down my body. Once I was naked, she stood and took long, confident strides towards me. "Sit down," she said.

I sat on the bed and waited for her. "Be a good boy and keep your hands to yourself," she said. "No touching." I gulped, absolutely hating this game. "You're not going to listen, are you?" She asked, a perfectly shaped brow quirked at me. I shook my head no. "Sit on your hands." I compiled and was instantly rewarded with her perfect mouth wrapped around my dick. I clenched my hands underneath me to prevent myself from grabbing her head.

She needed the control.

"Fuck, doll," I groaned when she swallowed on me, taking me to the back of her throat. Her spit glistened on me as I watched her head bob up and down. My thighs flexed and so did my stomach as I fought my orgasm. "Hales," I moaned. She hummed around my dick, adding to the sensations she was already giving me, and tugged on my balls like she knew I loved. My head fell back and my throat bobbed and I swallowed as her movements increased against me. "Fuck," I grunted, making her release my balls and slide her hand up to my throat, squeezing lightly. I loved letting her control me. "Fuck, Haley. I love you so fucking much, your mouth, everything about you is perfect." My words spurred her on and she sucked me harder, hallowing her cheeks and loving the underside of me with her tongue. "I'm going to come."

Her hand squeezed the outside of my throat, while the other jacked me off in time with her bobbing, bringing me closer and closer to the edge. I wanted to lift my hips, but I knew she would stop if I did. "You're killing me, Hales." Her eyes tilted up to look at me while she milked my dick, forcing me to come in her throat and watch as she swallowed all of it. When she finally released me, she had a self-satisfied smirk on her face.

"What else do you want?" I asked her, still giving her the submission she needed.

"Make me come," she demanded.

"How?"

"However you can."

With a groan, I stood again and brought her to me, capturing her lips. I opened my mouth immediately, letting her take what she needed while I pushed the joggers she wore down her legs and cupped her pussy. Her hips pushed out, demanding more from me while she pulled her sweatshirt off, broke the kiss and stood naked in front of me. With her lips back on mine, I swept my fingers through her wet folds. She moaned into my mouth while I rubbed her clit slowly, immediately rewarded with her sweet whimpers, but I didn't comment on it. Roughly, she pushed me away from her, forcing me to plop down on the bed. Haley took what she wanted and climbed up my body, sitting her pussy on my face. Groaning, I wrapped my arms around her thighs and pulled her even closer, burying my face completely in her. She smelled and tasted so fucking sweet.

Her hips rocked on me, humping my face while I licked through her. "My clit, Will," she demanded when I ignored the straining bud. "Yes!" She yelled when I wrapped my lips around it. Her hands dug into my hair and tugged harshly. My head pulled back, and I looked up at her. Her eyes were closed, and she was lost in pleasure as she chased her orgasm, writhing on top of me faster and soaking my face as she did. I could barely keep up with the wetness pouring from her cunt. I moaned against her, but the sound was barely audible between her folds.

"Yes!" I grabbed her hips, trying to hold her still so I could get to her the way I wanted, but she was too wild on top of me. She palmed her tits roughly, squeezing her nipples while she rode my face. "Fuck! Oh god. Will, I'm going to come."

I groaned again, begging her to come all over my face.

Her body finally stilled on top of me and she cried out, long and loud, as she covered my face in her release.

She rolled off of me, panting for breath, and I wiped my face. "Fuck, baby," she moaned, her body still shaking from her orgasm. My dick was hard again, desperate to be inside of her.

I laid on my back in the middle of the bed and watched her straddle me. Her eyes and hair were wild as she sank down on me. Grabbing my hands, she pulled them to her tits, squeezing my hands as I squeezed her. "Harder," she demanded. I squeezed her tits as hard as I could, and she bounced harder on me. "Like that. Fuck Will, just like that." Her feet were flat on my mattress as she squatted up and down on my dick.

"Fuck, Hales, you're strangling my dick."

She didn't stop, just bounced on me, whimpering and whining the entire time. Her hand finally came to my throat, just like I knew it would. "You're such a good boy, my good boy."

"Yours," I said. She changed positions slightly, planting her knees on the outside of my hips and leaned forward while she rode me. Her clit ground against my pubic bone and her hand squeezed around my throat tighter, making my eyes roll back in my head.

"I love your cock so fucking much."

"I love your cunt," I told her. "And these tits, and your ass. Fuck, Haley, get there, baby, I can't last much longer."

Her body bucked on top of me as she chased her orgasm. Her fingers dug into my neck, cutting off my airflow but not my blood flow. I came instantly, uncontrollably spilling myself inside her while her pussy clamped down around me and her body shook while she came at the same time.

"Will!" She shouted.

"Haley," I groaned as we both finally stilled.

She collapsed on top of me as I wrapped my arms around her, knowing that we'd get to do this for the rest of our lives.

CHAPTER 30

THE ROAD TRIP

Haley

"I can't believe we're really doing this," Sassy said as we shoved our suitcases into the back of my car.

"It's only possible because Snake and Will are basically bros."

"Who knew they'd get along so well?"

"Not me." I closed the trunk and climbed into the driver's seat while Sassy climbed into the passenger.

Will and Snake were already together. That's right. They'd gotten up early to drive to the Walmart a few towns over and get snacks and groceries for the week. They'd wanted to do it together and they could only do that in what was basically still the middle of the night.

Like I said—they were bros.

"What's Chloe doing this week?" Sassy asked.

Despite knowing they were sisters, not a lot about their relationship changed, and I hadn't expected it to. It would take time for them to be as close as Chloe and I were, and if they never got there, it was okay. They just needed to know.

"Babysitting all week. Her teacher picked up like six double shifts in a row."

"It's sad she's a teacher and still needs to supplement her income."

"It is, but I'm thankful for it, anyway, because it keeps Chloe out of the house. So have you given any more thought to telling your mom and Buck about her?"

"No. Buck deserves to know, and I know my mom does too. She still hasn't moved on from my dad, despite him apparently being a shitty husband."

"Maybe tell Buck first and make the choice together?"

"That's not a bad idea."

"I'm full of good ideas. Text Snake and tell him we're getting breakfast for them."

When we'd all talked about taking this trip together, Will was adamant that he pay for everything: groceries, gas, our meals and activities. Snake and Sassy protested, but ultimately, they'd lost. I was at least going to buy breakfast for us before we got on the road.

I rolled the car to a stop at the McDonald's drive through. "Welcome to McDonald's. Can I take your order?"

"Hi. Can I get four sausage biscuits, two sausage McMuffins, two sausage McGriddles, also four bacon, egg and cheese biscuits, and eight hash browns?"

"Will that be all?"

"Yes."

"I'll have your total at the window." It was still early enough that just the second window was open.

"Oh hey, Haley," Mick said when I pulled up.

"Hey, Mick, how's it going?"

"Good, and you?"

"Good."

"Your total is $8.99."

"What?"

"Employee discount," he winked.

I handed him a ten. If he wanted to give me discounted food, I wouldn't argue with him. I knew where the owner of this franchise lived; he could miss a few bucks.

Sassy typed on her phone, most likely to Snake, while we waited for our food to be done. "There you go," Mick said, handing me two full bags.

"Thanks! Have a good break." I heard him saying you too as I drove away.

Five minutes later, we were pulling into the parking lot of the church, where Will's truck was already idling.

Snake and Will jumped out of the truck, looking around to make sure we were alone, even though we were mostly hidden from the road, and if Pastor Jenkins saw us from inside, he wouldn't say anything. He was the only man in town who truly could keep a secret.

"Hey doll," Will said, kissing me before walking to the back of my car and opening the trunk. He and Snake carried our suitcases, setting them in the bed of the truck, then Snake climbed into my seat… the front passenger seat.

"Um, excuse you?"

"Yeah?" He asked, window rolled down and head leaning out.

"Wow," I muttered. Sassy laughed as we were forced to climb into the back of the truck. I'd never sat back there before, only had sex on the seats. Them being bros wasn't working in my favor.

"We thought you might like some girl time," Will said, turning to look over his shoulder at me, that big stupid grin on his face.

"Yeah, yeah, just drive, asshole."

"Ah, the good old days."

I rolled my eyes at him. "We got you coffees," Snake said, handing them to us.

"Oh, we forgot to get you guys breakfast," I mumbled. Sassy laughed at me. I had no idea why I was pouting so badly from being forced to sit in the back of the truck, especially when Sassy and I would have so much fun on the three-hour drive to the beach house.

"Stop pouting, doll," Will said. "And I can smell breakfast. Hand it over, Winters."

Leaning forward between the two seats, I kissed Will's cheek, making dramatic lip smacking noises against him before pulling away and sliding him one bag. "You're lucky I love you."

"Luckiest guy in the world."

He was so damn sweet and cheesy at times it made me nauseated, but I'd be lying if I said I didn't also love it. Snake and Will seemed to pick up right where they left off with whatever conversation they were having before Sassy and I got to the church.

"You're wrong!" Snake shouted. "I'm telling you, Chicago stands no chance next season."

"Rikers had over a dozen hat tricks this season."

"Yes, but that's not enough to win the cup, which is exactly why they didn't make it past the first round of the play-offs."

Sassy rolled her eyes at me and took a bite of her breakfast.

Bros.

"What's Buck doing over break?" I asked her. "And what did you tell your mom, actually?"

"Buck is going to do nothing but play video games and eat. I told my mom you and I were going on a road trip."

"Did she not ask how we were paying for it?"

"Nope, I think she thought the fewer questions she asked, the better. She just wants a text every night telling her I'm alive." I laughed. "What did you say?"

I swallowed awkwardly. "Um," I began.

"We said we were going on a pre-wedding honeymoon," Snake said.

Will's eyes flashed to mine in the rear-view mirror, jealousy clouding his features.

"That's a good cover."

Sassy's words must have calmed Will.

We didn't have to worry about her mom finding out I'd given my parents a different story than she'd given hers because they never spoke, and the reason was so much clearer.

There was a lull in the chatter after that, and I knew Will's mind was going a mile a minute. After finishing my second breakfast sandwich, I leaned forward again. "I love you," I whispered in his ear while wrapping my arm around his chest. The hand not on the steering wheel came up and wrapped around my arm.

"I love you too."

As if all he needed was to hear those words, he relaxed and started talking to Snake again. Sassy and I exchanged a look and started eavesdropping. They weren't discussing anything interesting to us, just sports and cars, but they talked like they'd always been best friends, tossing around words men used when they liked each other: dumbass, fuck face, fucker.

Sassy and I watched them go back-and-forth, heads moving left to right as we watched the exchange. "Wow," she mouthed at me, making me laugh silently.

As cute as it was watching them become besties, I was also upset. If my mom was different, if she'd been a normal mom and encouraged me to make friends with Will instead of shutting him out because of who his dad was, this could have always been our lives. We could have had thousands of memories together, growing up, being best friends, falling in love, and doing stuff like this all the time.

"I need to pee," Sassy announced after we'd been driving for about ninety minutes.

"Of course you do," Snake said, turning over his shoulder to look at her.

"You're the one who thought it was a good idea to get me a giant iced coffee."

"We're about halfway there," Will said. "I'll pull off at the next stop."

A few more miles down the road, Will was pulling off at an exit and into a gas station. We climbed out and Sassy ran straight into the shop while Snake followed her. I had to pee, too, but I stood next to Will while he was pumping gas.

"C'mere," he said, pulling me close with one arm while his opposite hand filled the tank. He pulled me back to his chest and wrapped his arm around the upper part of my chest. My panic must have been obvious because he whispered in my ear, "Relax." I inhaled a deep breath and let myself settle against him. "We're far away from home, nobody knows us here. That's the best part of this vacation. I'll be able to do everything I've ever wanted to do to you—hold your hand, kiss you on the street, play with you in the ocean."

"The ocean will be freezing."

"Toss you in while you yell at me not to." I turned in his embrace, looking up at him, trying to threaten him with a look. "You don't scare me anymore, Haley Winters."

"You scare me, Will Roberts," I said before I could think better of it.

The pump ticked, alerting Will the gas tank was full again. Wordlessly he leaned away, putting the cap back on and setting the pump back in its cradle. When he was done, he cupped both of my cheeks. "There's nothing to be afraid of, Hales. I love you, and I know you've never been loved before, not like this, but it's a good thing, and I'm not going anywhere." I kissed him, not having any words to say to respond.

As we were walking inside, Sassy and Snake were walking back towards the truck. "Here," Will said, tossing Snake the keys.

"We'll toss all the garbage," Snake said. Between the four of us, we'd managed to eat every scrap of breakfast food from McDonald's.

"Thanks. You guys need drinks or snacks?"

"Sassy isn't allowed to drink anymore," Snake said seriously. "If she does, we'll have to stop again in thirty minutes." She backhanded him and when he went to wrap his arms around her, she darted away from him, towards the truck, making him grin before taking off and chasing her.

Will and I held hands while we walked into the shop, and the feeling gave me butterflies harder than any time we'd ever kissed, fucked, or made love. We could never do this at home, and as sexy as a secret affair was at times—this—the normalcy of holding his hands in public was all I really wanted. Sometimes I wondered if our relationship would survive out in the open, and not just because of who our families were, who we were, but even away from home when we could. Would it be different? Would it be less?

No.

The answer was no. It wasn't different, and it wasn't less. It was more, so much more.

Will only dropped my hand when we separated by the bathrooms. And when I finished, he was waiting for me, right where we'd separated, and as soon as he saw me, his hand extended in offering. I interlocked our fingers again, and we walked through the shop. "You know what Sassy and Snake like," he said. "Pick them out some snacks." By the time we collected drinks and snacks, Will paid like fifteen bucks for everything, but looked completely unfazed.

Back at the truck, I saw Snake sitting in my seat in the back, leaving the front seat open for me. As I climbed in, I saw his arm draped around Sassy while she leaned into him, and I realized that for them, this was new, too. Their relationship was secret as well.

While Will pulled back onto the highway, I passed Sassy and Snake their drinks and snacks, and Snake immediately took the coke-a-cola zero sugar away from Sassy, making her try to fight him for it. I gave them their little moment and turned my attention back in front of me. Will's hand wrapped around my thigh, and it stayed there until we pulled up to his family's beach house.

"Wow," I said, climbing out. It was gigantic and absolutely beautiful. The blue paint perfectly matched the color of the sea it looked out on. It was modern, with floor to ceiling glass windows. "This place is beautiful."

"Come on," Will said, pulling my hand. He and Snake carried all the luggage in from the truck, refusing to let Sassy and I help, even when they had to make multiple trips to get the groceries.

"Can we stay forever?" Sassy asked while opening the sliding glass door and stepping out onto the deck. The sounds of the waves crashing against the shore, the smell of the ocean, and the sun high in the sky brought me a sense of peace I'd only ever known with Will.

"I wish."

Neither one of us had ever seen the ocean before. Her mom would have loved to take her on trips, but couldn't afford it, and my parents didn't care enough to help Chloe and me ever leave Lake City.

It was like everything and nothing I'd ever imagined it to be. Standing there, I felt small, inconsequential to the rest of the world, but when I heard the screen door open again and felt Will stand behind me, his hands on the outside of mine where I leaned against the railing, I knew that even if I was insignificant to the world, I was Will's entire world, and that was better than meaning something to the entire world. I didn't need celebrity status, or to be famous; all I needed was the man who had me wrapped in his arms.

Everything that came after that was just a bonus.

"The pool is heated," he said. It was only the beginning of April and still cold out most of the time. "Wanna swim?" He whispered in my ear.

"Sure."

I'd take any excuse to see him shirtless.

Will gave us a quick tour of the house, and showed Sassy and Snake to the room they could sleep in, which was strategically on the opposite side of where ours was.

"Get naked, Winters," he said, taking his shirt off. I rolled my eyes, but stripped. Will didn't hide the way he checked me out as I slipped into a yellow bikini. "Fuck me, doll."

"Later," I winked. That wasn't how he'd meant it, and we both knew it.

"You're so beautiful." He walked towards me as I checked him out, too. The muscles from his football career were still prominent, and I'd only recently learned that he actually worked out a lot still, lifting weights with Jordy. His swim trunks had little sailboats on them and I laughed. "What?"

"Your shorts."

"Mom bought them for me." I only laughed harder, causing him to growl low in his throat. "Careful, doll. I'll have you bent over this bed, that bikini pulled to the side, and my dick in you faster than you can blink."

"And that's a bad thing?"

"Never." Will wrapped me in a hug. "You're so beautiful. You should always be in just a bikini."

"I might get cold in the winter."

"I'll keep you warm."

Finally pulling away, he grabbed two towels from the closet and, like always, took my hand while he walked me back downstairs. Snake and Sassy were already in the pool when we got there. Snake was swimming after her while she screamed and giggled, and cursed at him not to get her hair wet.

"I'll help you wash it later," he said suggestively. And the promise of him naked in the shower with her was enough to make her cave as she let him catch her. I watched as he lifted her in his arms and tossed her into the deep end of the pool, laughed as her arms flared wildly, and she yelped just before her body hit the water. Snake swam towards her, and as soon as she came up, she wrapped her arms and legs around him, forcing him to tread water for the both of them.

The pool seemed to be designed backwards, with the deep end being where you walked towards first. I couldn't resist the opportunity, and as soon as Snake and Sassy were out of the way, standing in the shallow end, I shoved Will roughly into the pool.

"Shit!" When he came up, I was laughing like a maniac and he glared at me, those blue eyes promising payback. "Remember, doll, you started this little game." I gulped and backed away, but Will was quick, and out of the pool before I could even take two steps back. He used his arms to push himself all the way out and stood up, not even needing to turn on his butt or get on his knees. Fuck, that was sexy; he was so strong.

My thoughts made me freeze and forget I was supposed to be running from him. And I realized too late what was happening. Will had his arms around my waist and my front pinned against his, lifting me and easily walking with me to the edge of the pool. "Will! Have mercy," I begged.

"You started it," he reminded me again before stepping off the ledge with me in his arms.

When I came up, I sputtered out water and pushed my hair out of my face while Snake and Sassy laughed from the shallow end. Will reached for me and pulled me against him, pushing his wet, chlorine tasting lips to my own. I let him kiss me, trying not to drown at the same time. Making out while treading water wasn't an easy task.

I broke the kiss and swam around him quickly, climbing on his back. "Call it even?" I asked, hopefully.

"For now."

Will swam toward the shallow end with me on his back. "Want to play chicken?" He asked.

"What's chicken?"

"You and Sassy on mine and Snake's shoulders. You try to push the other off."

"Okay," Sassy said, excitedly.

Will dove under water and shocked the hell out of me when his head went between my legs and stood up with me on his shoulders. "Fuck, it's cold up here," I whined. Snake attempted to do the same to Sassy as Will had done to me, but Sassy squealed and wiggled too much, making them both topple into the water.

"Try sitting on the edge of the pool," Will told her. She did, and Snake settled himself between her legs; this time, she made it into the air and stayed there.

"So we just try to push each other into the pool?"

"Yup," Will said.

I put my arms out toward Sassy, and she did the same. We giggled and screamed, trying to push the other off. Will's hands were tight around my thighs while he weaved with me, using his strength and those sexy ab muscles to keep me centered on his shoulders, but Snake was just as strong as Will and kept Sassy easily on his shoulders too.

"Shit!" Sassy squealed when I finally shoved her hard enough to fall backwards into the water. She came up for air and Snake reached for her, pulling her back to safety in his arms.

"Nice job, doll," Will said.

"Thank you."

"Again," Sassy said.

Snake helped her back onto his shoulders, and this time it was me who went tumbling into the water. I giggled like a fool, for the first time in my life actually feeling my age. I wasn't worried about Chloe; she was safe. I wasn't worried about being caught with Will. Nobody here knew us, and we had privacy in the beach house. I wasn't worried about my future or escaping the trailer park. I was only concerned with soaking up every minute of fun I could with the man I loved and my two best friends.

CHAPTER 31

THE PIER

Haley

"Can't we just stay here forever?" Sassy asked, the words nearly a whine. "We can go get Chloe and Buck and just come back."

"I wish, but we need to finish school."

We'd been at the beach house for four days and only had two full days left before we had to make the trip back to Lake City. But my feelings were the same as Sassy's; I didn't want to leave. Being away from everyone who knew us—free to touch, laugh and kiss in public—took our relationships to an entirely new level.

Deep laughter coming from the hallway pulled our attention away from our breakfasts. Will and Snake came walking into the kitchen together, both shirtless and sweating, a basketball in Snake's hands.

"Where were you guys?" Sassy asked.

"Playing hoops in the driveway."

Will sauntered over to me and gave me a sweaty kiss. "Morning, doll."

"Hey baby."

Sassy and Snake were still lost in their own early morning moment while Will plated his own breakfast. "Snake and I were thinking we could go to the pier today. We haven't been there yet."

"Sounds good to me," I said.

"Me too," Sassy said.

Snake and Will being so close still tripped me out a little, but this trip would have been a lot worse if they didn't get alone.

"Wanna shower with me?" Will said, wiggling his eyebrows after he'd cleaned up the mess from breakfast.

"Sure," I agreed.

"We're leaving in an hour, with or without you," Snake shouted down the hall to us. "Ow!" He quickly exclaimed, and I knew Sassy had backhanded him for his suggestive remark.

Will pulled me into the master bedroom and then the bathroom. He had his basketball shorts and boxers down in a few seconds flat, leaving me still standing there in my pajamas. "Get naked, Hales."

"You know we're not having sex," I told him as I stripped.

"Fine," he pouted. "Later?" He asked hopefully.

"Later," I promised, making him grin as he finally pulled my naked body into the shower with him.

Will let me wash his hair and body while I ignored the raging erection between his legs. Little Will would have to wait. When I was done, Will washed me too, letting his firm hands rub all over my body until I was ready to beg him to fuck me against the tiled wall, but I wouldn't give in that easily. Once we finished, Will handed me a towel. Fifteen minutes later, we were down in the kitchen waiting for Snake and Sassy so we could leave for the pier.

"What's at the pier?" I asked.

"A few carnival style games and rides, shops, food. It's on the beach, you'll love it, doll."

"You gonna win me a prize?"

"As many as you want." He leaned in to kiss me, but before he got the chance to deepen it, we were interrupted by Snake and Sassy coming in.

"Ready?" She asked, gleefully. I'd never seen my best-friend as happy as she'd been the past few days; I'd never been this happy before either.

"Let's go."

Will drove us along the coastal road about thirty minutes south until we got to the pier. I saw it miles before we actually got to a parking lot. It had to be close to a half mile long extending into the ocean with lots of people walking on it.

The weather was gorgeous, sunny, warm and would be close to seventy-five degrees. My hair blew in the wind coming in from my open window, and the sun warmed my face, and Will's hand was on my thigh, sliding underneath the dress I wore warmed my leg. He'd gotten it for me on our second day at the beach—a light purple dress with cutouts along my back and thin spaghetti straps to hold it up. Dresses weren't usually my style, but he'd looked so happy when he'd told me how good I'd look in it that I'd tried it on. He loved it so much, I'd had to let him buy it for me and wore it just for him. His thumb grazed back and forth against my skin, making me tingly.

Will finally found a parking spot in the very back of the parking lot; it was still early in the day, but it seemed like we were late arrivals. Will paid the parking attendant and put a tag on the dashboard.

Even though we were far away from home, I still glanced around, slightly anxious when Will interlocked our fingers and tugged me in the direction he wanted to go. Sassy and Snake were in the same position as us, following close behind, and I felt myself relax. Nobody from Lake City would be here, especially not anyone who would care enough about us to notice or report anything.

We strolled along the wooden pier, walking in and out of shops, browsing but not buying anything.

After we'd walked the length of the pier, we turned around and walked back. "Which game are you going to play to win me my prize?" I asked Will when we approached the first set of games.

"Your choice," he said, kissing my forehead.

"That one." I pointed to a basketball hoop in the middle. "Let's see if you're any good, since I missed you playing this morning." Will looked cocky, and I found it ridiculously attractive, as he walked up to the guy manning the game. He pulled his wallet out and handed over a bill. "What's he got to do to win me that big one?" I asked, pointing to a giant owl.

"The barn owl? Good choice, especially as a gift from your man. They mate for life."

"So do we," Will said, tossing me a sultry wink that contradicted the sweetness of his words. "What's it gonna take to win it?"

"Step back behind that line," he said, pointing at what I'd thought was just a random line on the boardwalk. "Sink four out of five shots and it's yours."

"Good luck, baby," I said, kissing him before stepping away to give him space to shoot. I didn't have a lot of faith that he would win. Will didn't play basketball. If he was any good, he would have played for the school's team, right?

But the cocky smirk he gave me when he sunk the first shot had me rethinking his abilities. It was the same smirk he'd flashed me countless times before fucking me. I hadn't seen it in a while, not since we got back together, but one I'd seen often in the early days when we were enemies with benefits.

He sunk the second shot and winked at me.

"Asshole," I mouthed the word at him, and his smirk turned into a wide grin. The third shot bounced off the backboard into the net. I shook my head and watched as he sank the fourth shot.

"Winner!" The guy said. "Want to take your fifth one, anyway?"

"Come here, doll." I walked up to him. "Wanna take a shot?"

"Sure," I said, knowing I'd miss.

"C'mere," he whispered and pulled me in front of him. "Hold it like this," he said, putting my right hand under the ball and my left on the side. "This hand shoots," he said, tapping my right hand. "And this one guides." He tapped my left hand while he spoke.

"Back up," I told him, nudging him with my elbow.

"Can't focus with me so close?" He whispered teasingly in my ear.

"Stand as close as you want," I quipped defiantly.

He pushed himself against me, touching my elbows while I took the shot.

And missed.

Horribly.

It didn't even go high enough to hit the rim or net.

"Good thing you're good at other things." I elbowed him in the gut lightly, but he turned me in his arms and hugged me, right there in the middle of the boardwalk. I loved being able to be so open with him, so affectionate. He bent down further to steal a kiss, but I didn't let him get away, instead I pulled him closer and staked my claim on him right there in the middle of the crowd, showing everyone that this crazy, annoying, goofy man-boy was all mine. I wanted us to always be like this.

"Thanks, man." Will said, finally pulling away from me. He handed me a giant stuffed owl, and I hugged it tight to my chest.

"I'm sleeping with this tonight. You can find another bedroom."

"Not a chance." Will wrapped his arm around my shoulder and walked us further down the boardwalk with Sassy and Snake traveling close behind us.

"What are you going to win me?" I heard Sassy ask Snake.

"Whatever you want, baby girl. Point it out and it's yours." I slowed my pace, knowing Sassy would slow hers as she looked at the games and their offered prizes. We hadn't made it much further than the basketball game when Sassy squealed. "That one!" She shouted, pointing to a gigantic stuffed kitten, one that looked exactly like the movie *The Aristocrats*.

"Hmm… seems familiar," Will husked in my ear. That was the kitten on my pajamas the night he'd snuck into my trailer. After all this time, that had still been one of the best times. I should have known then he loved me, that this was more than just enemies with benefits.

I loved him then too.

Snake kissed Sassy before walking to the ring toss game. Will and I stood back, watching while Sassy and Snake shared the same moment we did, Snake winning a prize for her and her excitedly jumping around and throwing herself at him. He caught her with one arm and held the other out for the prize. When she finally untangled herself from him, she grabbed the stuffed animal and squeezed it to her chest.

"We should have done this at the end of the day, now we have to walk around with these prizes all day."

"Stay here," Will said. "I'll take them to the car."

"I'll walk with you," Snake offered.

Bros.

"Here," Will said, handing me a twenty-dollar bill. "Go order a pizza from that pizza place, and we'll meet you there in ten minutes."

"Okay." Will kissed me before taking the owl from my hands and walking back towards the car with Snake. They looked so ridiculous, each carrying the giant stuffed animal. It completely contradicted their size and muscles, and it made me giggle.

Sassy and I walked arm in arm into the pizza place and ordered a pepperoni and sausage for the four of us along with four drinks.

"I HAD SO MUCH FUN TODAY, BABY," I SAID TO WILL WHILE WE WALKED back to the car. He held my hand, holding me close. We'd spent the entire day at the boardwalk, eating way too much junk food, laughing, playing, and being teenagers. We'd never been able to be like that with each other anywhere but the Hillview parties.

"So did I."

We stayed late, watching the sunset over the water until it completely disappeared.

"Are you serious?" I exclaimed through my laughter. Not only had Snake and Will taken our stuffed animals to the car, but they'd decorated them. They were both strapped in, a bottle of soda between their legs and a bag of popcorn between them.

"We had to feed them if we were just going to leave them in the car all day. Look, I even cracked a window."

"Window was my idea," Snake piped in, making me laugh harder.

We were all so tired on the drive home we barely spoke, choosing to let the radio fill the silence and the quickly cooling spring air wash over us.

"Goodnight," Sassy said as soon as we walked into the beach house, pulling Snake behind her.

"Tired, baby?"

"Not too tired," I said suggestively, pushing my body against his.

"Good girl."

Will pulled me eagerly to the bedroom, and I followed with just as much enthusiasm. "So I've been thinking," I said. "Things have been amazing since we got back together, admitting that we love each other."

"Why do I sense a but?"

"Don't you miss the *'I hate you'* sex?" I asked, glancing up at him.

"Was it ever I hate you sex though?" He asked.

"The pretend hate you sex then."

"Are you telling me you want me to fuck you like I did in the janitor's closet?" I loved that smug smirk he gave me, so cocky and full of confidence. And he was absolutely right. That was how I wanted him to have me. *'I'm in love with you sex'* was amazing, but I needed a little variety.

"Yes."

Will didn't even hesitate. He grabbed me by my throat and pulled me closer, ducking his head and capturing my lips. I felt the love there, but his hand squeezing my throat and the low growl he let out reminded me so much of the times in the janitor's closet that I could pretend it was the beginning.

When he finally pulled away, leaving me panting against him, his blue eyes bore into mine. "On your knees, Winters." Maybe I should have clarified that I wanted to be the one in control, but it didn't matter because the way he spoke had me shivering for him, already dripping and needy. Using his grip on my neck, Will guided me to my knees. "Slutty Haley Winters on her knees for me," he tutted. As he spoke, he opened his pants and let them fall to the ground. "Open."

I opened my mouth, waiting eagerly for him to shove his cock in it. His shirt came off next, and then he slammed himself inside of me. He moaned when I started bobbing my head up and down on him. One hand on my head, he guided me on him while the other pulled my nipples through my shirt and bra, making me moan around him. The hand on my head dug into my hair, fisting it while he forced me up and down, making me choke and gag like we both loved. "Look at me, dollface." Fuck. That nickname. He hardly ever called me dollface anymore, it was always shortened to doll. Adding face took me back to the beginning, all those months ago. "You know I like to look at your eyes when you choke on my dick." Will used the hand in my hair to tilt my head back, so I was forced to look at him. "Whose dick is in your throat?" He asked, his voice rough and dark.

"Yurths," I tried to say.

"Say my name, dollface. Whose dick are you choking on?"

"Vill Vobertzz." I could barely get the words out, but that was exactly what he wanted. His head fell back, and I watched his throat bob while he pushed and pulled his hips back and forth.

"Fuck, doll," he grunted. I moaned around him, taking him all the way to my throat and holding him there. Both his hands went to my hair, forcing me to stay on him with my nose pressed against the base of him. When he finally pulled me off of him, I panted for breath, spit dripping out of my mouth, tears running down my face. "A perfect fucking slut."

Will pulled me to my feet and wrapped his hand around the back of my head, dragging me in for another searing kiss. I melted into him, giving him the dominance I usually wanted and needed. Hand around my throat again, he used it to push me away, backwards so that I tumbled onto the bed. Standing at the foot of the bed, he bent over me, pushing my dress above my hips and pulling my panties down. "If I hadn't bought you this dress, and I didn't love it so much,

I would rip it off of you." He'd momentarily paused our pretend to hate you sex to say something sweet. I loved this dress and I loved it even more because he bought it for me. Dress bunched at my hips and naked, bared to him from the waist down, he pulled the dress and my bra down, exposing me completely to him. Kneeling in front of the bed, he pushed my thighs open, but instead of bringing his mouth to me, he used his hand to slap four of his fingers against my pussy.

"Will!" I shouted. He repeated the action, making me writhe for him.

"Such a needy slut," he said. I watched as he smirked wickedly, tantalizingly slowly running his finger through my slit while ignoring my clit. "So wet for the man you hate."

"I hate you so much," I growled.

"Say it again."

"I fucking hate you."

He groaned before finally descending on me and wrapping his lips around my clit. My hands went to his hair, holding him there while he built me up with his tongue and slid two fingers inside me. "Fucking soaked," he grunted against me before flicking his tongue against my clit. He worked his fingers fast and hard inside me, shoving them as deep as he could, all the way to the last knuckle while his fingers curled and pushed against my g-spot. He moaned against me, adding another sensation to everything I was feeling.

"I hate you," he grunted, pulling away to look at me while he kept fucking me with his fingers. "But I fucking love this cunt."

He'd said those exact words to me before, probably more than once, but the time I remember most vividly was in the chemistry lab, after we'd gotten back together the first time.

"Are you gonna come for me, dollface?"

"Yes!"

His lips wrapped around my clit again, sucking harshly while his fingers continued to work me. "Come for me."

My back arched and my pussy clamped down around his fingers while I came, a loud cry leaving me. Will didn't give me a moment to come down before he flipped me to my stomach and pulled my hips up, slamming into me from behind, forcing my tits to sway wildly in time with his thrusting. "Oh fuck!"

"Say it again," he demanded.

"I hate you. I hate you. I hate you."

"But?" He taunted.

"I love your cock. Fuck Will, you're the biggest I've ever had, the best."

"Damn fucking right I am." His hand lifted and came down on my ass, spanking me. He was being so rough that I couldn't hold myself up anymore. I moaned and cried out as he pounded himself into me, murmuring under his breath how much he hated me.

"I'm going to come again." My hands fisted into the sheets and my body tightened right before I exploded around him again. My eyes clenched shut and I saw stars, all the while Will never stopped his thrusting, fucking me through my orgasm. Only when I was done crying out did he pull out of me and roll me to my back. As he climbed onto the bed, I scooted back, making him chase me until he finally grabbed my hips and stilled my movements just before he grabbed both my ankles and set them on his shoulders, bending me like a pretzel underneath him, and slid himself back into me. "Oh shit," I groaned. He felt so deep like this, his long, thick cock stretching me.

"You feel so damn good, dollface." I groaned at the nickname, remembering that I was supposed to hate it.

I looked up at him, watching pleasure wash over his face while he thrust himself inside me over and over again, bringing both of us closer and closer to orgasm. He rubbed my clit with every thrust. Even if I wanted to stop the coming orgasm, I wouldn't be able to.

"Will, I'm going to come again."

"Where do you want my cum?" He asked. And I knew what he wanted, what he needed. He wanted me to beg for it.

"In me," I whined.

"Beg for it, Haley. Fucking beg like the cumslut you are."

"Oh fuck. Will! Please. Come inside me. I need it. Please. Please. Please!" I whined for him desperately. My hips lifted, meeting his thrusts, trying to make him lose control and finish inside me.

"Not good enough," he said darkly. I cried out in protest, but he silenced me by wrapping a hand around my throat. "You want it? Try harder."

"Will! Please. I'm desperate for you. I'm a slut for you. Please give it to me," I cried, actually feeling desperate. "I-I. Will! Please!"

"Fuck," he grunted. "Come for me, doll. Come all over my dick."

My pussy squeezed around him as I came, no sound coming out of me as my entire body shook beneath him. He groaned on top of me, finally stilling his thrusts and spilling himself inside of me.

Will collapsed next to me, wrapping me in his arms and rolling me on top of him. "I hate you, too," he whispered, making me laugh. "Come on, we should shower."

Will pulled my body off the bed, leaving me to finish taking off my clothes while he walked to the ensuite bathroom. I heard the shower turn on, and by the time I got there, he was already under the spray. Stepping in, I wrapped my arms around him from behind. "I'm going to miss this," I said, kissing the middle of his back.

"When we get home or when you're in New Hampshire?" I froze. We hadn't talked about what happens with us when I leave.

"Both," I whispered.

"What if you didn't have to?"

"What?" I asked, confusion making my brows furrow. Will turned, wrapping me in his arms. I tilted my head up, my chin digging into his chest while I looked up at him.

"I want to go to New Hampshire with you."

"You're serious?" I asked.

"Deadly serious. You told me too late, so I missed the deadlines for fall semester, but I can apply for spring. And in the meantime, I can work for a few months. I love you, Haley, and I don't want to be without you."

"You'd do that for me? Leave your family, your friends, your home?"

"When are you gonna figure out that I'd do anything for you, Hales?"

"Soon," I whispered. Tears filled my eyes as we stood under the spray, still wrapped in each other's arms. "I'd love for you to come with me."

My tears fell against his chest as he hugged me under the warmth of the water.

CHAPTER 32

THE SHERIFF

Haley

Time moved too quickly. Graduation was only weeks away, prom even less than that. With Will, things were amazing. He'd applied for a bunch of jobs in New Hampshire, and I still couldn't believe he was willing to give up everything in his life to move across the country with me.

But Chloe's teacher didn't need her to babysit anymore. Because the end of the year was coming up, she didn't work as much outside of school. That meant we were both home more, which meant more beatings for me and two since we got back from spring break. The second one was the worst, leaving me with two black eyes. When Will saw me the next day in school, he'd nearly lost his damn mind.

But that wasn't strange.

What was strange was how my father reacted. He'd given my mom two black eyes and then told me to move in with Snake. Our wedding was planned for the day after graduation. It wouldn't be happening, but our dads had arranged everything, even a dress.

They were fucking nuts.

Chloe cried and protested about me leaving, so my dad said I could stay until the wedding.

How generous.

The last two beatings made Will angrier than I'd ever seen him. He'd threatened to get his dad's gun and shoot my mom. I talked him out of getting himself killed, but I hadn't been able to stop him from convincing Snake we needed to tell his dad about the animals, which we were finally doing today after school.

I sat in the cafeteria looking at Will, who was looking at me, but speaking to Jordy next to him, even with his focus completely on me.

I grabbed my phone to text him.

Me: our spot
Baby: race you

I grinned at my phone. "I'll be back." Sassy and Snake knew where I was going. I hurried to our spot, wanting to be there first.

"I win," I heard his voice as soon as I entered the small closet. I could hear the smile in it, and it was my favorite sound.

"Cheater."

"Sore loser."

He pinned against the wall as his lips collided with mine. He was so familiar at this point I had everything about him mesmerized—his touch, his kiss, the feeling of his shoulders under my hands.

Everything.

"I can't wait to get to New Hampshire, where we can do this all the time without hiding."

"Me either," I whispered.

"I'll pick you up after school behind the church."

"I'll be there."

"I love you," he whispered, hands cupping my face.

"I love you." With those words, I slipped out of the janitor's closet and back to the cafeteria.

"My dad will be home any minute," Will said while the four of us walked into his house.

The mood was somber, none of us ready to put it all out there, but it needed to be done.

"Hi guys!" Will's mom greeted us as we walked into the kitchen that smelled like cookies. Their house always smelled amazing since she was constantly baking.

"Hi," I greeted her, walking right up to her and wrapping my arms around her, loving her motherly embrace.

"We need to talk to Dad when he gets home."

"Is everything okay?" She asked, voice full of motherly concern.

"It will be."

Will wrapped his arm around my shoulder and pulled me against him, kissing my forehead, and his mom had hearts in his eyes while she looked at us. "Well, the cookies are fresh and so is the lemonade. I can make sandwiches too if you're hungry."

"We're okay, Mom."

"I'm hungry," Snake said at the same time Will spoke.

"Coming right up."

Mrs. Roberts was never as happy as she was when she was taking care of us.

Will grabbed the plate of cookies and set them on the table while I grabbed the lemonade and glasses. Will fidgeted with my hand on the table, clearly anxious. "It's gonna be okay," I whispered. He looked at me and nodded before kissing me. He pulled away just in time for me to see his mom setting a mountain of sandwiches on the table.

"Thanks, Mom." She came around the table and kissed his head before ruffling his hair. He let her and I smiled at how much he loved her.

"I'll be upstairs." She had a hobby room upstairs where she did all kinds of stuff: painting, sewing, reading and writing.

We each ate a sandwich and a few cookies while we waited, not saying anything. The usually relaxed atmosphere around us was tense; we all knew what we were about to do. There was no going back once we told Will's dad. When we heard his squad car pull into the driveway, we all sat a little straighter, and I glanced at Snake, who gave me one curt nod. We were the only ones who were about to confess to illegal activities.

"Hey kids, what's up?" His dad greeted.

"Hey Dad, we need to talk to you."

"Everything okay?"

"Not really."

He glanced up from the mail he was sorting in his hands to look at Will. "What's going on?" He asked, sitting with us at the table.

"Haley and Snake have some things to tell you… about Viper."

His head snapped to me like he couldn't believe I'd actually betray my father. I'd been wanting to do this since I was five years old.

"We just need to know that we'll have immunity for anything we may say that incriminates us."

Sheriff Roberts didn't even think about it before answering. "Absolutely, no questions asked. Neither of you had a choice considering who your fathers are, but this is a choice, telling me. And it's the right one."

Snake relaxed visibly, and I leaned into Will, letting him wrap his arm around me.

"Which one of you wants to start?" He asked. He pulled out a small notebook and a pen, waiting for one of us to start talking.

"I will," Snake said. Sheriff nodded, turning his attention to him and waiting expectantly. Snake took a deep breath, his shoulders lifting before he blew out harshly. "The gang has always been small fish in drugs and guns. There were too many other players for Viper to ever really break into the market, but I know where the stash houses are. It's not a lot of weapons or drugs, but it's enough to get him locked up for that alone."

"Where are they?"

"The drug stash house is in a cabin with no real address. You've got to take the access road about three miles up the mountain and then go left onto the dirt road and drive about three miles into the woods, but it's heavily guarded, but not by the men. The men have all been pulled to the club's newest stash house." The animals. "The guns are in the same spot, but the gun cabin is about a mile further into the woods."

"How do they prevent people from finding it?"

"They've got security cameras set up, and dogs. Aggressive dogs."

Sheriff wrote everything down.

"And what's the newest endeavor?"

"Exotic animals."

"What?" Sheriff asked, his brows furrowed in disbelief. "What type of animals are we talking about?"

"Everything you can imagine," I answered. "Tigers, venomous snakes, monkeys, birds, even wolves. They're shipped in from Asia somewhere, and he's moving product quickly."

"Where's he keeping them?"

"A makeshift warehouse. It's up the mountain," Snake said.

"Christ," the sheriff cursed. "If one of those escaped and got into town it could be a disaster. I need to get animal control involved and the feds. And Judge Richardson needs to be informed so I can get warrants."

"You won't be able to get a warrant from him," I said. Snake was the only other person in the room who knew that he was on the take. "He's been in my dad's pocket for years."

"Sonofabitch!" Will's dad yelled. His gigantic hand slammed on the table as he stood up, throwing the chair back and making it tumble across the floor. I flinched at his violent outburst, and Will threw him a warning glare while pulling me close. "I'm sorry," he said, running his hand down his face and picking up the chair. "I knew. I knew and I could never prove it. What does your dad have on him?"

"Judge Richardson is gay. He's got a thing for eighteen-and-nineteen-year-old boys at the club a few towns over."

"Family values my ass." I couldn't help but agree with him.

"Dad had him followed, got pictures and threatened to expose him. He's been using it against him ever since."

"You never said," Will whispered to me.

"I don't want to blow up Mackenzie's life," I said to him. "I'm sorry I didn't tell you, but I didn't want to hurt her. I already took you from her." I tried to joke and make light of the situation and it worked because Will grinned at me before leaning in and kissing me chastely.

"Her life is gonna get blown up," Will's dad said. "It's not your fault, Haley, it's his. I have to arrest him. Do you have proof?"

"Only that I've seen him at our meetings."

"Me too," Snake said.

"But my dad will do anything to stay out of jail, including turn on him."

"Your dad is going to jail," Will growled. "Richardson can walk, but your dad is getting locked up for life, and so is your birth giver." He refused to call her my mom.

"She's not innocent in all this, either, is she?" Sheriff Roberts asked with a shake of his head.

"No, she's not, but there's one more thing about my dad before we get to her."

"What?" He asked, sitting back down.

"He killed Hound."

"Your dad?" He looked at Sassy. She nodded, her lip wobbling as her emotions took over. Snake wrapped her in his arms and rocked her while whispering softly to her. I couldn't understand what he said, but it soothed her.

"How do you know?"

"My mom told me," I said. "My sister isn't my dad's kid, she's Hound's. Dad found out that mom was sleeping with him and killed him. I've got no idea if he knows Chloe isn't his."

"Can you prove it?"

"I only know what my mom said, but ever since he died, Sassy and I have always assumed he died at the hands of the club. We thought it was club business but turns out it was just an affair."

"This is a lot of information," he said. I watched as he took a deep breath and blew it out, reading back over his notes. "My deputies and I can't handle this ourselves. I need to call in someone else, but it's going to take time to corroborate all this information and get some surveillance. I can't just go arrest him."

"We know," I said. "We were actually hoping to make a request about when it would happen, our graduation."

"I can probably make that work. Any particular reason why?"

"I need to leave for school after and I need my sister safe."

"Your sister is still only fifteen. What happens to her?"

"We want to take her in," Sassy said. "We're getting jobs after graduation and can take care of her."

"If you can prove she's your family, it will probably work."

"We've got a DNA test," Sassy told him.

"Okay. I'll try to keep child services out of it. Now, tell me about your mom." I knew he knew. Will must have told him, but I didn't know what the extent was, how much detail he had. Will trusted his parents and he would have asked them for advice.

"She's abusive, but only to me, not to Chloe. She hates me because I'm Viper's daughter. I've got pictures." I opened the file on my phone of the saved pictures Chloe sent me and slid my phone across to him. The emotions on his face were easy to read as he scrolled through: anger, disgust, shock.

"How long has this been going on?"

"As long as I can remember," I said, wiping the lone tear that fell from my eye.

"This is enough. She's being arrested too."

"Thank you."

"I need to catch Viper in action. If I can't get him on surveillance with the animals, guns or drugs, I need to catch him at one of the stash houses."

"I'll call him whenever it's about to go down," Snake said. "I'll tell him there's a problem, and he needs to get there."

"That's a risky plan. You'd be putting yourself in danger."

"I'm in danger every day," he said. "Viper could kill any of us at any time for any reason. He's got no idea I don't want to be with Haley, that we're not getting married."

"What?"

"My dad and his dad have this mafia style arranged marriage planned for us the day after graduation. Snake is supposed to take over The Southside Gang and I'm supposed to be his dutiful housewife."

"This just keeps getting crazier and crazier."

"Sassy and I have had to hide, just like Haley and Will."

"You kids should not be dealing with any of this shit. I should have put him away years ago."

"You've been trying," I said.

"Not hard enough." He seemed ashamed of himself, but I didn't know what else to say to him, so I let it go. "Will you be able to keep yourselves together? Pretend everything is the same."

"We've been doing it all year." Snake scoffed at my words, but they were true. Hell, we'd been pretending our entire lives.

"I'll contact the closest FBI office and go from there. I'll need to get a federal warrant to go around Judge Richardson. If I need anything else from either of you, I'll have Will contact you. We'll only meet here."

"Thank you, Sheriff," I told him sincerely. He nodded curtly before heading up the stairs.

The four of us sat there silently for a few minutes. I was mentally and emotionally exhausted. I had a feeling, low in my gut, that something was going to go wrong with this takedown. Were we being naïve to believe we could get away with this? Trying to take down my father.

Will's dad had been trying for at least fifteen years and he'd been unsuccessful. How could a couple of kids outsmart the leader of the gang?

"You okay, doll?" Will asked. I turned to look at him and offered him a soft smile.

"Just worried."

"Come on," he said. "We all need to relax. Let's get in the hot tub."

"We don't have bathing suits," Sassy said.

"Snake can borrow one of mine, and I think you've got an extra one here, don't you, Hales?"

"I should."

The four of us made our way upstairs, and Will grabbed a swimsuit for himself and one for Snake.

"Seriously? Sailboats?"

"They're cute," Sassy grinned at him. Snake huffed, but took the offered trunks.

"Here," I said, handing Sassy a green bikini. "Your chest will spill out, but it'll at least cover your nipples."

"That's a shame," Snake said. Sassy backhanded him, but grinned while she took his hand and dragged him to the guest bedroom so they could change.

"Are you sure you're okay?" Will asked. He closed the distance between us and wrapped me in a tight hug. My face pushed into his chest, and I inhaled his familiar scent, letting it calm me.

"I don't know that I'll be okay until this is all over."

"I'm here for you," he whispered before kissing the top of my head. "Whatever you need."

"I know."

"Come on. You need to relax."

"I can't stay too long. I have to pick up Chloe from Mick's."

"Just an hour," he said.

"Okay," I agreed easily.

I pushed the nervous thoughts out of my head and changed, eager to relax with my man and our friends.

CHAPTER 33

THE PROM

Will

School was rapidly coming to a close. It was already Prom and we were going, but it took some convincing to get Haley to agree to come with me because she hadn't wanted to. She'd been so stressed since we told my dad about Viper's exotic animals. She kept her guard up constantly, a learned trait to survive living with her parents, but she was jumpy all the time now, like she was waiting for the other shoe to drop, that she couldn't believe she was so close to being free.

Haley would be shocked when her name was called as Prom Queen. It was the only way I could guarantee at least one dance with her.

Somehow she'd convinced Sassy to go who obviously convinced Snake.

A few more weeks, that was it. A few more weeks and this would be over and I could finally fucking claim her in front of the entire damn town without worrying about Viper killing one or both of us. Then we'd be together in New Hampshire.

I'd found a construction guy who was hiring summer labor, and he'd agreed to hire me after one phone call. He sent me a few references from guys on his crew who had worked for him, which I appreciated. He also had a spare room above his garage that he rented out to summer help for cheap. It was perfect, close to where Haley would be staying on campus, and it would give me time to settle in and make a plan for spring semester.

There wasn't anything close enough to Dartmouth for my liking. Keene State college was the closest, about an hour away, but they had an art program, making it perfect. And an hour away wasn't all that bad, definitely better than being clear across the country from her, and if after the summer I found a place about thirty minutes from campus, I'd be halfway to her. We'd make it work because we loved each other. I wasn't smart enough to go to Dartmouth, my girl was a genius.

"You look so handsome," Mom gushed when I walked down the stairs in my rented tux. I wanted Haley here to take pictures with and put a corsage on her, but she and Snake had duty at the animal warehouse. She would have to hurry to get ready, but she promised she'd be there.

"Thanks, Mom."

"Can you at least try to get one picture of you and Haley together?"

"I'll make sure someone takes one," I promised her. I'd ask someone to do it discreetly while we danced the King and Queen dance.

"And you're coming back here after?"

"Yes."

"Be safe," Dad said. The real meaning of his words was telling me not to knock her up. Or maybe to avoid Viper. Either one could be true. Maybe it was both.

"I will be."

Mom forced me to take pictures with both her and Dad before I was finally free to go.

The familiar drive to the school was easy, but just like Haley, I'd been anxious since we'd told my dad about hers. Things were so good, and I was terrified something would change and she'd be ripped away from me.

I can't lose her.

She's it for me.

For my entire life, Haley-fucking-Winters is the only one I want.

Who knew?

I'd been so spaced out that I completely forgot Prom wasn't at the high school like Homecoming had been. With a shake of my head, I pulled out of the parking lot and headed towards the only banquet hall in the county. Half the kids we went to high school with would end up getting married there in a few years, just like my parents had gotten married there.

Haley and I would get married, no doubt about it, but she deserved more than the life this small town could give her. And I was going to give it to her.

When I pulled into the parking lot, I saw her immediately. Her head was back as she laughed, her body shaking while Snake laughed with her and Sassy looked between the two of them like they were crazy. For a long time, even after getting to know Snake, I'd been jealous of him. He'd been her best friend for her entire life, and if that first day of pre-kindergarten had been different, I would have been too. It was mostly hard for me to believe that anyone could know her, be around her all the time and not fall in love with her. She was just that amazing, but then I saw Snake with Sassy. It was clear he loved Sassy the same way I loved Haley, making my worries vanish.

Haley's dress was made by Sassy, just like her homecoming dress had been. This one was blood red and complemented everything about her. It fell to the floor and was strapless. The material was tight, clinging to her and pushing her chest up. Her hair was up, a braid wrapping around her head and hiding into the strategically messy bun. She had more makeup on than normal and the shade of her lipstick matched the shade of her dress.

She looked like a dream, a fucking sinful dream I never wanted to wake up from.

When she stopped laughing, she spotted me. Even from so far away, I saw the way her eyes raked me up and down in the tux. I filled it out well, but knowing she was looking had me sticking my chest out a little extra. She licked her lips, and in that moment I decided as soon as the King and Queen dance was over, I was dragging her out of here. We'd be lucky to make it out of the parking lot before I had myself buried inside of her.

My dick already throbbed in my pants.

My little minx shot me a wink and sauntered into the banquet hall.

And when I got the first look at the back of her dress, I thought I would come in my pants. The tube top style front wasn't what the back was. It was completely open, save for one piece of fabric keeping the dress up. The rest was open, letting me see all the way down to the top of her ass. On the lower right side, part of her tattoo peaked out, and I wanted to run my hands all over her. While walking, she turned her head to look over her shoulder at me.

She was torturing me on purpose.

I panted after her, knowing I couldn't do what I wanted to, but I wasn't going to take my eyes off of her all night.

The banquet hall was decorated in an 'under the starry night' theme—the most basic Prom theme to ever exist. But I didn't care about the decoration. I cared about Haley, our dance, and getting her the hell out of there and into my bed.

I wandered around looking for Jordy. I found him sitting at one of the tables, Mackenzie in his lap. "Hey man," he said, offering me a fist bump. I felt so bad for Mackenzie; she had no idea that in just a few weeks she was going to have her entire life blown up. She was supposed to go away for school, so maybe she could leave early and go somewhere no one would have ever heard about what her dad did.

Her mom's life was about to be blown up too.

Maybe her mom knew?

Didn't they say that a woman always knows?

"What's up?"

"This dance sucks."

"Don't be so mean," Mackenzie whined. "Once I'm named Queen we can go."

She wasn't going to be named Queen.

I'd made sure of that.

My girl was the only Queen here.

I sat next to them and watched Haley dance with Sassy and Snake. She looked like she was having a great time, especially for someone who didn't even want to come at all. I drank punch, watched Haley dance and counted the minutes until the announcement of Prom King and Queen.

About two hours into the dance, the DJ finally shouted into the mic that it was time for the big announcement. Everyone probably expected it to be Mackenzie and me again since we'd been Homecoming King and Queen, or maybe they'd expect Jordy and Mackenzie since they were the 'it' couple of the moment.

Ms. Smalls, one of the chaperones, walked up to the DJ and took his mic. The rest of the students formed a half circle while they waited for the announcement.

"Carver High, your 2022 Prom King is..." She paused dramatically. "Will Roberts!"

My classmates cheered for me while I walked up. "Thanks, Ms. Smalls." She set a crown on my head, but I had to duck for her to be able to put it on.

"And your 2022 Prom Queen is..." Ms. Smalls gasped audibly into the mic. "Haley Winters?" Her enthusiasm was replaced by surprise. And there were only crickets from the crowd, nobody expected her name to be called. The asshole part of my brain made me sneak a glance at Mackenzie, who looked stunned.

I couldn't see my girl anywhere and everyone started looking around for her. When the crowd finally cleared I saw her stunned face staring right at me. She knew, I knew she knew. I couldn't grin at her, not like I wanted to. It would give us away.

There were indistinct murmurs, people trying to figure out who voted for her.

Me.

I voted for her and made sure I voted a lot.

Slowly, she started walking towards where I was standing. "Thanks, Ms. Smalls," she said when she finally made it to us. My girl was completely stunned. Ms. Smalls put a crown on her head as *Perfect* by Ed Sheeran started playing. "Do we have to dance?" Haley asked. I knew it was a game. We couldn't seem too eager to hold each other.

"It is tradition," Ms. Smalls said.

Haley let out a heavy sigh and rolled her eyes at me before walking towards the middle of the dance floor. I followed her, trying not to appear too eager. Everyone stared at us while I put my hands on her waist and started to sway with her. The open back of her dress let me feel her skin under my fingers.

"What did you do?" She asked.

"I saw the way you were looking at homecoming. I loved you then, doll," I whispered. "You're the only one I want to dance with."

She bit into her lip, preventing the smile that she wanted to give me.

I wanted to pull her closer, but I didn't want to push my luck. We danced to the song, and I sang the lyrics softly, caring only a little that I might be giving us away.

"We're leaving after this. Meet me at the truck." I'd parked far away so that nobody would be able to see her climbing into the passenger side.

As soon as the song ended, Haley let out a disgruntled noise and pushed me away from her. Everyone laughed, and I just shrugged my shoulders, acting as if I didn't care. I did, and I had to remind myself that it was all an act.

She loved me.

And soon she could show me in public.

Just a few weeks.

I walked away towards where Jordy was still sitting with Mackenzie in his lap. "I'm out."

"Later, man," he said, offering me a fist while Mackenzie didn't even acknowledge me.

I checked that nobody was watching as I walked out and headed straight to my truck. "Took you long enough," I heard her say, but I couldn't see her. She walked around the bed of the truck, looking fan-fucking-tastic in her dress. God, she was so damn beautiful.

"Get in, doll. I can't wait to get you home and get you out of that dress."

"What makes you think we're having sex?" She asked in her teasing tone. I glanced behind me, making sure no one was around before taking two giant steps towards her. I had my hands on her hips and our bodies pushed flushed together before she even knew what happened. Rocking my hips, I let her feel how hard my dick already was for her.

"Tell me you're not as wet as I am hard and I'll believe we won't be having sex." Her mouth opened and closed a few times, but no words would come out. I could count on one hand the amount of times I'd seen Haley Winters speechless. "That's what I thought. Get in the truck, Hales." I pulled myself away from her and walked to the passenger seat. I had the car already started when she finally climbed in.

"So, you took a play from Gossip Girl?" She asked.

"Gossip Girl?"

"It's a show. One of the characters rigs the prom vote to make the girl he loves Prom Queen."

"And here I thought I was being all original," I grumbled. She laughed at me. "I wasn't going to let another dance go by without me being able to dance with you at least once, Haley." She gave me one of her shy smiles, the ones that showed me she was feeling vulnerable. I reached across the cab and squeezed her hand, letting her know it was okay, that she could be as vulnerable as she needed to be with me—always.

Haley's little game, pretending she didn't want to fuck, lasted until we pulled into the garage and not a second longer. As soon as the garage door was shut behind us, she jumped me right in the front seat of the truck. I hadn't even unbuckled before she had her hands on my pants and unbuttoned them. She had my dick out and in her mouth before the car even turned off.

"Fuck, Haley," I groaned when she swallowed me. Her head bobbed up and down while she slurped on me, bringing me so much pleasure I thought I'd die from it. I fisted my hands in her hair, but it didn't feel like hers. It was sticky from hairspray and not the soft strands I was used to. I dug my hands in anyway, forcing her to take more of me until she gagged on me. But she wasn't deterred. "Tell me how even when we have an empty house, full of beds, I still don't fuck you on one," I groaned.

She moaned around me before pulling her mouth off and wrapping her hand around me. "Are you complaining?"

"Fuck no," I grunted, lifting my hips into her hand. "But I wanna taste your pretty cunt on my tongue, doll."

"Bed."

She left me in the truck, running towards my bedroom, making me chase her... with my dick out.

When I got to my bedroom, my girl was on my bed, legs spread in invitation. I stalked towards her and tugged on her ankles until her ass was nearly hanging off of my bed. "Will," she whispered sexily.

"Shh."

I knelt on the floor in front of the bed, pushed her dress up and slid her panties down. "Soaked," I commented. "Just from sucking my dick. My own personal slut." Her retort died on her lips when I wrapped my mouth around her pussy and licked her from opening to clit. I repeated the action until she was writhing beneath me, begging.

"Please, Will!" Finally, I wrapped my lips around her clit and pulled it into my mouth, sucking while I flicked my tongue against it, making sure to take my time building her up, loving how she squirmed for me. Her hips bucked as she tried to get closer to me, to force my face deeper into her pussy. I pushed two hands onto her lower stomach, forcing her to stay still. "Oh god. Yes! Will!"

Her body bucked as she came, covering my face in her cum.

When I pulled away, I licked up everything I could reach with my tongue.

Her body still shook with aftershocks while I stood and stripped myself out of my tux. When I was naked, I pulled her body off the bed and spun her so I could figure out how to get her dress off of her.

It was too damn sexy.

"This dress, doll. You're lucky I didn't drag you into the bathroom like I did at homecoming." She pushed her lips against mine and I lifted her in my arms, carrying her naked body to my bed and laying her down in the middle of it before rolling us so that she was on top of me. "Ride me," I said, lifting both hands to slap her ass. She moaned and slid her pussy up my length, ending when the head rubbed against her clit. Without sliding in, she rode me, letting me get lost in the sensation of her lips against me while she chased an orgasm. "You look so sexy," I watched mesmerized, as her tits bounced and her hips rolled.

She'd gained weight since spending so much time at my house, finally being able to eat her fill. Her stomach was softer, rounder, her thighs thicker, her chest fuller. She was sexy before, and she'd be sexy no matter what but looking at her like this—fuck. She was fucking perfect.

"Will, I'm going to come again."

"Come all over me, Hales. Take what you need from me."

Her fingers dug into my chest while she rocked a little quicker, changing the pressure to get it just right, until she tumbled over the edge. Her head bowed back and her entire body extended and stiffened while she cried towards the ceiling, my name falling from her lips like a litany and I was her God.

She collapsed, falling sideways, completely spent.

"Not what I had in mind when I said 'ride me', doll."

"Fuck me, Will. Please. Oh god, I need it."

"Such a greedy girl."

"For you Will. Please."

I rolled her to her stomach, letting her lay there. She wouldn't be able to hold herself up. Settling myself behind her, I pushed into her, and laid down on top of her. I pushed my head next to her, letting my lips linger on her neck. She turned her head to search for my lips and I interlocked our fingers together while I rocked into her slowly. I took my time building her up.

"It's too much," she whined. "Don't stop, Will."

"Never," I whispered, nipping at her earlobe. I felt her wet pussy tighten around me, telling me she was close. "Come for me one more time, doll. Let me feel you squeeze my dick." She whined and rolled her hips, humping the mattress. "Dirty fucking girl. Are you using the mattress to play with your clit? My little pillow humper." I teased her.

"It's too good, Will. I can't. Fuck, I'm gonna come!"

"Me too, baby. Come with me, come on!" As soon as I felt her squeeze around me, I exploded, filling her with my cum while we both moaned loudly into the mattress.

"Fuck," she cursed as her body shook still. I pulled out gently and rolled off of her, pulling her with me so I could wrap her in my arms.

"Come on," I said. "Let's shower."

"Can't. Move."

I kissed her exposed shoulder and rolled off the bed, scooping her in my arms and carried her into the shower.

Whatever the fuck I did to get so lucky to have hate turn to love, I'd never know.

CHAPTER 34

THE GRADUATION CEREMONY

Haley

The day I'd been waiting for my entire life had finally arrived.

Graduation day.

And, more importantly, the day my parents would be arrested.

Will assured me that my father would be arrested during our graduation ceremony. His dad had been keeping him in the loop, which I was sure wasn't standard protocol, but because I was his son's girlfriend, it seemed like he was okay with breaking a few rules. Obviously, neither of my parents were attending, not that I wanted them too, but somehow it still hurt. On the outside, I looked like the constant rejection didn't bother me, but the reality was that it did. I wanted to have their love.

I may always want it.

That was normal, wasn't it?

Despite what they'd done to me for my entire life.

Sassy, Snake, and I pulled into the parking lot, the two of them in his car behind me. The parking lot was already full, but I spotted Will's truck immediately. I couldn't wait to see him in his cap and gown. Since Prom, we hadn't spent as much time together as I liked because Chloe wasn't babysitting. We saw each other every day at school and snuck away whenever we could to the janitor's closet, but I'd only been able to spend one night wrapped in his arms in his bed.

I didn't sleep well without him anymore.

"Ready?" Snake asked. He was nervous, but it wasn't about graduation. The raid would start any minute. Any minute our dads would be arrested and our lives would be changed forever—for the better. Snake and Sassy held hands, done hiding their relationship. They didn't need to anymore. We were free. My dad would be arrested on a federal warrant and so would Judge Richardson. He wasn't going to walk away so easily this time. Sheriff Roberts decided to do it after graduation so he could at least see Mackenzie graduate.

I smiled at Snake and Sassy's PDA. Could Will and I stop hiding already, too? I wanted to.

We walked into the gym where we were told to line up by last name. Winters was at the very end of the alphabet, meaning I wouldn't be close to them or Will. It didn't look like anybody was lining up, so we stood around.

"Doll," I heard Will call my name from behind me. A few people were looking at us, but all I could see was him. He looked at Snake and Sassy, surprised to see them holding hands. His eyes flicked back to mine and I could read the question in his eyes. Could we do it? Could I let him kiss me right here in front of everyone?

Yes.

I could.

I wanted him to.

He took one step towards me, and I moved a step closer to him in return. "Can I?" I didn't let him finish his question, instead, I wrapped my arms around his neck, and pulled him to me, pushing my lips against his. Will groaned contentedly and wrapped his arms around my lower back. He pulled me closer, our graduation gowns pushing together and wrinkling. Neither of us cared.

"Holy shit," I heard a few people mutter while others whispered, "look."

"Fucking finally!" And that was Jordy. Will released one of his arms and even with my eyes closed, I still knew he was flipping off his best friend. The murmuring got louder, but I didn't care. I was finally kissing him, claiming this man as mine—for life.

When Will finally broke the kiss, I was breathless and dizzy and so fucking happy. I'd been happy with Will this entire year, but it wasn't like this, not with the knowledge that we would be free to let everyone know that we were a couple.

"My dad texted me," he whispered. "The raid is starting any minute." Somehow it had only just then occurred to me that his dad would be missing graduation in order to arrest my dad.

"Will, shit. When I asked, I didn't realize that it meant he'd be missing this. It's such an important day."

"It's fine, Hales. If it means you're safe, I don't care. He'll come to college graduation. This is just a single day in a long list of days we're going to get to celebrate together."

I still felt guilty, but he kissed me until I was smiling against his lips, long past caring that everyone could see us.

"I love you, Winters," he said, loud enough for the people around us to hear.

"I love you, asshole."

He grinned at me and kissed me one more time before there was a yell from Principal Potter to line up.

Me making out with Will in the middle of the gymnasium wouldn't be the most shocking revelation my classmates got today— me being valedictorian would be.

I went to stand in my place in line between Savannah Waters and Samuel Zin, second to last in the class. It was going to be a long graduation ceremony. I could hear the trudging of footsteps on the gym floor as my classmates made their way outside onto the football field. It seemed like years ago that Sassy and I went to homecoming to watch Will play, although she didn't know why we'd gone.

As hard as falling for him had been, letting him into places I'd locked up and thrown away the key to, I wouldn't change anything. It would have been nice if we had parents who hadn't hated each other, if we could have been a couple longer and open through all of high school, but Will was who he was because of his parents and I was who I was because of mine. Maybe in order to get to here—this happy place with him—I had to deal with my parents being who they were.

Was it worth it?

Yes.

To be with him, everything was worth it. I could see the back of his head, standing taller than ninety-nine percent of the other students in the class as he walked out into the sunny May afternoon.

The roars from the crowd were loud, happy parents, grandparents, and siblings cheering for their graduates while we took our seats. Chloe was out there somewhere, the only person in my family there, but she was also the only real family I had, except for Will, Sassy, and Snake. People always say blood is thicker than water, but that's not the true saying. The real quote is *"the blood of the covenant is thicker than the water of the womb"*. The real meaning implies the bonds we create, the family we choose can be stronger than the one we were bound to by blood.

In my case, that was certainly true.

My chosen family bonds were stronger than the ones I had with my parents.

Once I finally walked to my seat, we were invited to sit by Principal Potter. I listened to his speech, stating how he had never been prouder of a Carver High graduating class than he was of ours. He said that every year, and next year he would stay the same exact thing. It was laughable as I listened to him go on about our achievements, academics, sports, in the community. I listened, but only because when my name was called to give my speech, I didn't want to miss it. Sassy once told me a story about one of her cousins.

The girl had gotten a scholarship, but didn't know it was coming. She was flirting with the guy sitting next to her and her name had to be called not once, not twice, but three times before the girl on the other side of her finally told her. She was so embarrassed.

I would be too.

"Now," Principal Potter said. "To give a short introduction of our valedictorian, one of our valued math teachers, Ms. Smalls."

I had no idea she was introducing me.

"Thank you," she said, standing at the podium once the applause died down. "I'm going to keep this quick. The student you're about to hear from has worked harder this year than any student I've ever had in the past. Despite immense personal turmoil, living in a way no high school student should have to live, she made us all proud, staying at the top of her class and reaching a scholarship to the school of her dreams. She's going to do amazing things, and I, for one, can't wait to continue to root for her. Ladies and gentleman, your valedictorian for the Carver High class of 2022—Miss Haley Winters."

Stunned silence.

Once I stood up and started walking, the applause slowly started and I could hear my sister yelling in excitement. It was a surprise even to her. Proudly, I walked to the podium. Ms. Smalls hugged me before retreating and leaving me to address the audience.

"I'll give you all a moment to pick your jaws up off the floor." My opening one liner got a few chuckles from the crowd. "I'm Haley Winters, and only one other person on this field today knew about this. His name is Will Roberts." I had to wait for the murmuring of the crowd to die down before I continued to speak. "Before this year, Will and I hated each other, or thought we did and pretended to." This wasn't my planned speech at all, but I was winging it, speaking from the heart and saying my piece. "Somewhere along the way this year, we stopped hating each other and started loving each other—in secret—because of who my parents are.

"But that's all changed now. I was accepted to Dartmouth University and received an independent scholarship covering all my expenses. I'm standing in front of you today without any parental support. They don't even know I'm valedictorian. Me being here is an accomplishment all on its own, and I'm not going to be modest about that, even if it makes some of you uncomfortable. Life is too short. This year I learned about love, something I'd never wanted to know anything about before, but Will taught me everything I could possibly want to know.

"In case you haven't figured it out by now, this isn't your usual graduation speech. I don't have anything to say about the future because I don't even know what mine holds. I won't fill the speech with cliches about the opportunities or struggles we'll face in today's world; we're already all too familiar with them anyway.

"I had other plans for this speech. I was going to spill family secrets and leave this town in flames, but like all my other plans this year, those changed."

Before I could finish my speech, the sound of gunfire rang out. Terrified screams followed quickly after and people were running for cover, towards the school, towards their cars, wherever they thought they were safe.

"Haley!" I heard Will shout my name. He was moving towards me, pushing students out of the way to get to me. Snake and Sassy were hot on his heels, with Snake shielding Sassy's head and body with his own, an arm thrown over her back while he forced her to duck down. "We need to go! Now."

"What's happening?"

"My dad texted me. The raid went south. He thinks they're here for the judge."

"Oh fuck."

"Daddy!" We all turned to see Mackenzie. She was screaming bloody murder, the sounds coming out of her hysterical, and when the crowd finally broke, I saw her dad slumped over, blood covering his shirt, and I screamed too.

"We need to go!" Snake yelled. He and Will took complete charge, dragging Sassy and me towards the parking lot.

"Wait! Where's Chloe?" I said, stopping and pulling myself from Will's grip. I was already turned around and heading back to the field to get her.

"She's with Mick and Buck," Sassy said. She was out of breath and had tears streaming down her face. She was terrified. "They won't let anything happen to her."

"They're here for us," Snake said. "We've got to go."

Will tugged my arm again and ran as fast as he could while pulling me until we were in my car. "I'm scared."

"Get in the car, Haley. We need to go. And we need to go right fucking now!"

"Sassy," I whined for my best friend.

"Now!" Snake shouted. Sassy shook like a leaf, terrified but let Snake push her into the car. I was too stunned to move. The sound of gunfire didn't stop; it was getting closer.

"Right-fucking-now Haley! Get your ass in the car. We've got to go."

Finally breaking free of the spell, I climbed into the driver's side of my car. "We'll call you," Will said to Snake before climbing into the passenger side. He didn't even have his seatbelt on before we were racing out of the parking lot. My tires screeched and the smell of burning rubber filled my nostrils as I pulled away.

"Where are we going?"

"We need to get somewhere safe, out of town."

"Won't work," I said. "Dad will have the main roads manned by his guys. What did your dad say?"

"Your dad and his guys started shooting and took off on motorcycles before they could catch them."

"Nothing else?"

"He only sent one message."

"What about your mom?" I asked. I was driving, but I didn't know where. Traffic was a nightmare. People were running stop signs and red lights, driving on the wrong side of the road. I swerved and barely missed people and cars as they ran and drove for their lives. Will stripped out of his gown and tossed his cap into the back of my car. I did the same with my hat but couldn't get out of my gown while I drove.

"She texted me telling me she's fine." He had his cell phone in his hand like he was waiting for it to ring. "Dad always taught her how to assess somewhere when she got there, and to find the nearest exit in case she needed to escape. She'll text me when she gets home."

The sun was nearly blinding as it got lower and lower on the horizon.

"We need to get off the road," I said. "Where can we go?"

"We can't lead them back to my place." He thought for a moment. "Can we take one of the backroads out of town?"

"They might be blocked too."

Before I could offer any other suggestion, the roaring engine of a motorcycle could be heard behind us. I glanced in my rearview mirror to see my dad and Bull behind us. "Fuck!"

"Faster, Hales." I punched the gas, honked my horn and swerved around a car in front of me. Glass shattered, and I knew my back windshield had been blown open by a bullet. I ducked and swerved again.

"Are you okay?" I shouted at Will.

"Fine. Are you?"

"Yeah."

Will hit a few buttons on his phone and put it to his ear. "Fuck," he cursed before dialing again. "Dad!" He shouted into his phone. "Viper and Bull are behind us."

The sounds of the motorcycles got louder.

"Fuck! Now there's more."

I drove as fast as my car would allow, driving so recklessly that I could've killed us both, but if I didn't get us out, we'd both be dead anyway.

"We're heading north up fifteen."

Will cut the call and turned to look out the back of the car. More gunfire could be heard, and I knew they were aiming for the tires.

"Dad and his deputies are coming down this road. The feds are with them."

I pushed the gas pedal down harder, willing my old clunker to go faster.

"Hales," Will called. "Look at me." I turned my head just for a moment to look at him. "You've got to get out. They only want one of us. They'll take me, but you've got to get out of here. Don't stop."

"Will, what are you talking about?" I asked him hysterically.

"Don't stop, Hales. Let me go. Go live your life."

"Will!"

"Fucking promise me, Haley."

"I can't."

"You have to. This is the only way."

"I can't, Will, I can't lose you."

"Promise me, doll. Don't stop," he begged, his voice breaking as he asked me to do what we both knew I couldn't.

"Fuck! Will. I promise. I promise," I cried, the words coming out broken and intelligible. He unbuckled. "Don't!" I shouted at him. "Whatever you're about to do, don't even fucking think about it, Will Roberts!"

"I love you, Haley. For-fucking-ever."

"Will!" I watched, completely terrified, as he opened the door handle. "No!" I cried as he opened the door and rolled himself out of the car. That crazy move alone just might have killed him. I screamed, horrified, with hot, fat, salty tears streaming down my face as I watched in the rearview mirror.

He isn't dead.

He isn't dead.

He isn't dead.

The prayer in my head was answered when I saw him sit up before moving to sit on his knees. All the motorcycles behind me stopped. The sun set in the background and I watched, frozen, as they surrounded him. I heard sirens and looked out the windshield just in time to see three sheriff's cars and half a dozen unmarked cars fly past me.

They would get there in time, they had to get there in time to save him.

Glancing in the mirror again, I only saw partial flashes of my man. The cars kept coming in and out of my view, blocking him from me.

But the last thing I saw made me throw up all over myself.

Will was on his knees, my father next to him, a bat or a tire iron in his hand.

Whatever happened after that was blocked by the cars.

"Will," I breathed his name, letting the tears fall freely as I did the last thing he asked me to.

Don't stop.

CHAPTER 35

THE WAITING

Haley

My foot pulled from the pedal without me having made a conscious decision to do so. In the thirteen years I'd known Will, I'd never willingly done his bidding, not without putting up a fight, even if they'd only been fake ones this last year.

What the fuck am I doing?

Now was not the time when I would start listening to him.

I slammed the brakes and turned the car around in the worst three-point turn of my life and sped back to where the cars were parked and abandoned, holding my breath the entire time. I had no idea what I was about to see, but I needed to see it, needed to see Will.

I slammed on the brakes again just in time to not crash into one of the unmarked cars I assumed belonged to the feds.

"Will!" I yelled.

The scene was something out of a horror film. There were bodies everywhere—my father's guys and the feds. Thankfully, it didn't look like any of the town's deputies had been hit.

"Will!" I yelled again. The lights from the cars were blinding and I couldn't find him in the chaos. Someone yelled for me and I thought it was one of the deputies, like I wasn't aware that I was in the middle of the battlefield, but I had to get to him. I needed to yell at him for what he'd just done, thinking he could leave me, thinking I'd leave him behind.

Never.

"Will!" I cried. "No, no, no!"

Will's dad sat on the ground, Will's body in his arms, while he rocked him back and forth. Blood poured out of his head.

He's not dead.

He's not dead.

He cannot be dead.

I ran to where his dad was holding him. "My boy!"

"Will!" I shouted his name again. "Baby," I whined, falling to my knees next to him. More sirens sounded out, and the ambulance came into view. "The paramedics are here. They're going to help you." His eyes were closed, and he looked so pale.

"There!" Someone shouted to the paramedics when they finally stepped out of the ambulance. "The boy."

Will was eighteen, a man. My man, but laying there so pale, he looked like a little boy in his dad's arms.

I can't lose him.

Not now, not after everything we've been through.

"Sheriff, let him go so we can work on him."

They had to pull him away from Will, and I stood to give them room. They shouted a bunch of medical terms I wasn't familiar with while I watched as they cut his shirt from him.

"Please," I whispered, wiping tears from my eyes.

"You fucking bitch!" My father's voice in my ear caught me off guard. "It was you, you're the fucking rat. I thought it was your whore of a mother. I killed her for it. They'll find her in the trailer."

I wasn't sad my mother was dead.

Not even a little.

She deserved what she got, but I didn't have time to process those thoughts because my dad had his arm around my neck and a gun to my head.

"Put the gun down!" Sheriff yelled at him, his own gun trained at him, pointing right at his head. I didn't dare breathe. "There's no way out of this Viper. If you kill her, I'll put you down." This was the most physical contact my father and I had ever had, for as long as I can remember. I can't remember a single time he hugged me. This embrace was volatile. I dug my nails into his massive forearm, trying to force myself free. "Fucking stop," he hissed in my ear while cocking his gun.

One second. I was only one second away from death. I squeezed my eyes shut, not wanting to see what would happen next. If I could have closed my ears, I would have. I let images of the last year of my life fill my mind: Chloe, Sassy, Snake, and Will.

Will.

The year with him was the best of my life. He'd given me so much in such a short amount of time. He would survive; the paramedics would make sure of it, and if I didn't, if I died by my father's hand, I wanted him to remember how much I loved him and how much we'd grown and changed together this year.

"Viper!" The sheriff shouted in warning.

"What? Let her go so you can arrest me and put me in a cage for the rest of my life? I'd rather die."

I didn't expect to see or hear or even feel anything else after that. I expected the darkness of death, but I was pushed to the ground, landing directly on my face. The first and only decent thing my father had ever done for me.

Gunshots rang out, and I covered my head with my hands, crying into the mud.

"Haley!" I lifted my head to see Ian running at me. "Are you okay?"

"I think so."

He helped me to my feet, and when I looked behind me, I saw my father's lifeless body on the ground, blood pouring out of his chest.

He was dead.

My nightmare was finally over.

Except it wasn't.

"Will?"

"They took him to the hospital. Let's go." I raced as fast as my trembling body would let me to the passenger side of the sheriff's car.

"Somebody get my wife and bring her to the hospital!" He shouted.

The air smelled metallic, like gunfire and blood.

It was a smell I'd remember for the rest of my life and try to forget for as long as I lived.

"He's going to be fine," he said. "He'll be fine. My boy is strong." I couldn't speak. It felt like my tongue weighed a thousand pounds with the weight of everything that had just happened. I wasn't sure if he was trying to convince himself or me.

"Do you have your phone?" I asked. I needed to call my sister and Sassy. He grabbed a cell phone from the console and handed it to me. I dialed Chloe's number, holding my breath, praying my dad hadn't gotten to her, that she hadn't been hurt in the total chaos that had started during graduation.

"Hello?" Her soft, shy voice trembled when she picked up the phone.

"Chloe, it's me!"

"Haley, thank God, I've been so worried."

"I'm fine. Are you okay?"

"Yeah, I'm with Buck and Mick."

"Will's hurt," I said, choking on the words that didn't seem real. "Can they get you to the hospital?"

"Yes, of course. I'm on my way."

"I'll see you soon."

"I love you, Hilly."

"I love you, too, Squirt."

I cut the call and immediately dialed Sassy's number. "Hello?" She shouted into the phone. She sounded scared, like Chloe had, but her voice held more determination.

"It's me."

"Haley!" She cried. "Oh my god. Are you okay? Did you guys make it out? Where are you calling from?"

"I'm with Will's dad. Will is- oh god, Sas, he's hurt. I don't know if he's going to be okay." I hadn't wanted to say the words his dad and I were both thinking, but hearing my best friend's voice had been my undoing. "Can you meet me at the hospital?"

"We're on our way. He'll be fine, Haley. He won't give up on you. He loves you too much." Her words had another strangled, hysterical cry leaving me, and I couldn't say anything else, so I just hung up.

We pulled into the parking lot and the sheriff pulled into a handicap parking spot and flew out of his car, not even bothering to close his door. I did the same, having to run to keep up with him.

"My son!" He shouted as soon as we were through the emergency doors.

"Sheriff," a nurse greeted him. "They took him to surgery."

"Is he going to make it?" The nurse was quiet, clearly not wanting to lie or give us false hope. "Is he going to make it?" He shouted at the poor nurse.

"Sheriff, his condition is very serious. The CT showed significant brain swelling. They're opening a hole in his skull to relieve some of the pressure, and he had significant other traumatic injuries to his chest and stomach."

As soon as the urge to vomit came back, I realized I was still covered in it from when I'd puked in the car. And it stunk.

"Haley!" I turned to see my sister running to me. She didn't care that I smelled or was covered in puke, hugging me, pulling me completely against her anyway. "Thank God you're okay."

"Mom and Dad are dead," I whispered to her.

"Good." Her words caught me off guard, but I shared the sentiment. Mick and Buck stood somewhat awkwardly off to the side, watching our interaction. How did you comfort two girls who'd just lost their parents but weren't sad about it?

"Haley!" My name was called again. This time it was Sassy. Chloe didn't release me and Sassy wrapped her arms around both of us in a sister hug, the only possible hug that could calm me at this point.

I needed to see Will.

I needed him to be okay.

"Linda," Will's dad said. I turned to see his mom running towards his dad, watching as they embraced and cried against each other.

"I can take you to the waiting area," the nurse said.

I held Chloe's and Sassy's hands while we walked behind Will's parents toward the operating room waiting area, Buck, Mick, and Snake following behind us.

"Haley," Linda said, wrapping me in a hug once we were at our destination.

"I'm so sorry," I whimpered. "This is all my fault."

"My son loves you. That's nothing to be sorry about. He got his reckless streak from his father." I let out a choked laugh and she smiled at me. "Have some faith, hunny. He's not ready to give you up."

But that was where she was wrong. He had been ready to give me up, to set me free, even if it cost him his life.

That type of love was rare, and I wasn't ready to lose it, wasn't ready to lose him.

Once we were settled into the uncomfortable chairs, me between Chloe and Sassy, all that was left to do was wait. And hope. And pray.

FOUR DAYS.

Ninety-six excruciating hours, that's how long it had been, and Will still wasn't awake. When they'd rolled him into surgery, his brain had been dangerously swollen. The neurosurgeon and the general surgeon worked simultaneously, stopping the bleeding in his abdominal cavity and burrowing holes in his skull to drain the swelling in his brain. The doctors were confident he was out of the woods, that he'd live, but they couldn't even begin to guess what type of permanent damage may have been done to his brain.

I hadn't left the hospital or his bedside. My friends brought me food and clean clothes and I showered in Will's hospital room.

I wouldn't leave him.

Not now.

Not ever.

"Still not awake?" Jordy's voice didn't startle me. He'd been coming at the same exact time for the past three days.

"No," I said.

Mackenzie broke up with him. Her dad was killed in the attack on graduation, an attempt to silence him and keep him from talking to the feds. Not that it mattered. She'd told him that she needed to process everything on her own. Not that I blamed her. It was a lot of information, not only was her dad a judge on the take, but he also cheated on her mother repeatedly… and was gay. It was a lot for an eighteen-year-old to deal with.

Only three members of the gang remained, Snake's dad and two low level newbies. Bull had killed one of the federal officers, guaranteeing him a life sentence. Snake was finally free too. All the gang kids were finally free. Not all of them wanted to be, but they were. Thankfully, there hadn't been any other casualties, no innocent lives taken by the crossfire. There were a few minor injuries, but my dad and his men had only gone after the judge, Will, and me.

Jordy would sit quietly next to me for an hour before he stood and left, giving Will a gentle tap to the chest as he did. Watching his best friend so broken made my heart break further. Will's parents wouldn't be back until the morning. They came at seven am on the dot and left at five. They knew I was with him, and that I wouldn't leave him. They needed to take care of each other while their son clung to life.

Jordy and I sat silently for the hour he stayed. We'd never really spoken before this and although he was mine and Will's biggest cheerleader—a fact I'd only recently learned—I didn't know how to act with him around and Will lying lifelessly in a hospital bed.

When Will woke up, we'd figure out how to navigate a friendship. But I needed my man for that.

"I'll be back tomorrow," Jordy said. I watched, tears filling my eyes, as he tapped Will on the chest. It was his way of trying to wake him up and telling him he was there, that he'd been there every day.

When Jordy left, I climbed onto Will's bed with him. I wasn't supposed to, but I needed to be close to him and I was careful of all the wires attached to him. His skull was closed now, the holes covered with metal and the skin of his skull stitched. He was going to be so upset when he woke up and found out they'd shaved all his hair off.

It would grow back.

It was just hair.

All that mattered was that he woke up.

"Hales," his voice croaked, terrifying me and catching me completely off-guard.

"Will!" I said, happy tears finally filling my eyes. I pulled away so I could watch him blink his eyes open. He looked confused and exhausted. "I need to text your parents."

I texted his mom quickly. I was so fucking happy he was awake, but I was livid.

"I hate you so fucking much, Will Roberts."

"What?" He asked, voice shaking. "Tell me I didn't dream about everything that happened this year. We're in love."

"You are an idiot!" I whispered. I wanted to scream at him at the top of my lungs, but I didn't want to hurt him anymore. "You rolled out of a moving vehicle. That alone could have killed you, but then you decide to face my dad and his men. Alone! Alone Will. You could have died. You nearly died. What would I have done without you?"

"Gone to school, changed the world like I know you will."

"I'm not the girl who needs the boy to save her."

"You think I don't know that? You've been saving yourself for eighteen years, Hales. But I'm the boy who needs to save the girl. Dying for you would have been worth it, baby." Tears filled my eyes, and I shook my head at him. "C'mere. You're too far away. I want to hold you."

"You almost died, Will. Do you understand that? There are holes in your head where they had to drain blood from your skull. Your stomach is cut open from where they had to stop the internal bleeding. They beat you within an inch of your life. I've never been so scared."

"Haley, come here," he said, his voice harsher this time. I walked back to the bed, and he winced as he sat up to grab my hands. "I love you. I will not apologize. I would have done anything to save you, to get you out."

"You can't die for me. Promise me you won't ever do something so reckless again."

"I can't. I'd do it again if it meant you got out."

"Will," I cried, my voice breaking.

He pulled me down onto the bed with him and pushed my hair out of my face. "I love you, Haley, so fucking much. I won't apologize. Don't ask me to because I don't want to lie to you."

I lifted my eyes to look at him. He looked at me with so much love in his eyes. "I'm so mad at you still."

"Be mad, baby, be as mad as you want. But don't make me say I'm sorry when I'm not. Don't make me." I sobbed and fell against his chest. His arms wrapped around me and he rocked me. "I'm okay, Hales. I'm alive, I'm not going anywhere. We're okay."

While he held me, I felt his tears against my face as they mixed with my own. I had no idea how much time went on as we held each other, but we didn't pull away until the door was opening and his family was walking in.

"I should have been the first call when he was awake," his nurse for the night said to me.

Oops.

"Sorry," I said, pulling away and giving her space. Will's mom wrapped her arms around me while the nurse did her assessment, asking him random questions about the day and year while making him follow her finger. He had to push against her hands with his feet and squeeze her fingers. He had to lift all of his extremities and stick his tongue out and touch his nose. In any other circumstances, I would have found it hilarious.

"The doctor will come see you soon."

She left after that, but not before giving me a look, telling me she wasn't happy I hadn't called her first.

"My baby boy," Linda cried, wrapping her arms around her son. His dad hugged them both and rocked them both back and forth.

Snake, Sassy, and Chloe walked in while they were still embracing. I hugged all of them. And when Will was free of his parents, they all hugged him too, even Snake, who'd only ever hugged me and Sassy. They held each other like they were brothers and it made my heart clench.

"What happened?" He asked.

We all exchanged a look, trying to decide who would tell him what.

"My parents are dead."

"Fucking good."

"Language," his mom chastised him, but he didn't even pretend to apologize.

"My dad killed my mom. He thought she was a rat. Your dad shot my dad."

"Thank you," Will told him.

"William!" His mom yelled at him again.

"No, he's right. Thank you."

"What else?"

"Judge Richardson died at graduation. Mackenzie broke up with Jordy. He's been here every day."

"Tell him I'm awake and come by in the morning." I nodded at him. "What else?"

"I called Dartmouth and delayed my acceptance by a semester. I'm not leaving until January second."

"What about your scholarship?"

"I called the benefactor. I told them the story, and they didn't even believe me at first, but after talking to your dad and then calling the FBI field office, and they confirmed the story, they agreed to waive the job requirement. But I only get seven semesters of tuition. If I can't finish on time I have to pay for the last semester myself."

"What about the rest of you? Where are you living?" He asked Chloe.

"We actually had a few suggestions for all of you," his mom said before Chloe could say she'd moved into Sassy's with her. "We have a huge house. Chloe, we would like to invite you to live with us for the rest of your high school career, longer if you need it. Sassy and Snake, we have a guest house by the pool. It's basically a studio apartment, small kitchen, bathroom and a living space with a bed, couch and TV. We'd like to invite you to live there. You can save money while pursuing whatever careers you're interested in by living with us. It's safe and warm. I'll cook dinner and lunch for all of you." She was crying as she spoke. "Because Will is leaving with Haley."

"I am?" He asked.

"You got accepted to Keene State College for the spring semester. I'm sorry I opened your mail, but I didn't know if you were going to be able to wake up to read it."

"Congrats, baby."

"You're serious?" Sassy asked.

"We are," Will's dad said, wrapping his arms around his wife.

Sassy and Snake exchanged a look. "That would be great," Snake said, offering Will's dad a hand.

"Especially since it's not easy for broke newlyweds."

"Newlyweds?" I shouted the question.

"We got married," Sassy said to me, but she was looking at her *husband*.

"I couldn't wait anymore," Snake said.

"I didn't even get to be your best man," Will pouted, making us all laugh.

I walked to Will's bed, sitting next to him on it. He pulled me closer and forced my head to his chest.

When I started my last year of high school, I had no idea it would be anything like this. My plans for escape hadn't gone like I wanted. They'd gone decidedly worse. I nearly lost the love of my life.

But he was going to make it.

Chloe and Sassy were sisters.

Sassy and Snake were married.

I was wrapped in Will's arms.

Things turned out exactly like they were supposed to.

The boy who was supposed to be my sworn enemy turned out to be the love of my life.

EPILOGUE

THE HAPPINESS

Haley

5 Years Later

"Hales, come on, we're gonna be late."

"It's your art show," I shouted out the open bathroom door. "You can be late to your own show."

I heard him sigh.

He'd be singing a different tune when he saw me in this dress.

My man was nervous, and it was adorable.

Will had graduated with an Art Degree from Keene State College the same time I'd graduated from Dartmouth with a degree in Quantitative Social Science. Tonight we celebrated Will, but tomorrow we will celebrate me. During my junior year, I met a girl named Taylor, who was a developer. With her help, and some financial backing from a crowdfunding site, I launched an app that had changed thousands of lives.

The app was built to help people who came from homes like mine. I'd created a network of families that wanted to help shelter kids from their abusive parents. Will's parents helped me work out the legality, but we made it work. I had a team of lawyers who helped each and every kid free themselves from abusive situations. And because my network didn't give any of the families who took kids in money, it took away the system that had people in it who only took kids in for a payout and put them in worse situations than they were in to begin with.

It had started in California with Will's family being the first. Logan's dad, Sheriff Parks, who was in the town over, was the second, and it spiraled from there. By the time I graduated, I had fifty networks set up in fifteen states.

Kids just like me were getting the help they needed, the help I could never get.

I was doing exactly what I wanted, making a difference in the world, and doing it with Will by my side.

After graduation, we'd moved to New York City, where he had great opportunities as an artist. He'd had two shows before this one, but this was the first that was all his.

Chloe worked hard while living with Will's parents and earned a scholarship to NYU. Leaving her had been hard, and I'd been sad when she hadn't wanted to go to school in New Hampshire or Vermont, but she'd been right. I loved the Northeast, but I didn't want to live in New Hampshire permanently. Will and I had dreamed of living in the city since we left Lake City. It had been the right choice.

Chloe and Mick broke up in her junior year, and she'd dated a string of guys, but nothing that stuck.

Sassy had eventually told her mom and Buck about Chloe being her dad's daughter. Buck was ecstatic to have another sister, but her mom obviously took the news hard.

Snake and Sassy still lived in Lake City. Despite everything that happened, they didn't want to leave. Will didn't know, but they flew out to surprise him and see his show. They lived in Will's parents' guest-house for three years. Snake now owned his own mechanic shop, and Sassy was the most sought after salon owner in the county. She did lashes, nails, was a renowned colorist and waxing specialist. They were thriving.

And pregnant.

Sassy was five months along, and I couldn't wait to see her pregnant belly.

Will and I still weren't in a hurry to get married or have kids. We were only twenty-three. We had plenty of time for that. There was no rush when we both already knew that we would be together forever anyway.

Will's parents had also flown in for the occasion—with Will's little sister. Cora was turning three soon, and she was obsessed with her big brother. Even though they'd never lived together and only saw each other a few times a year, Will was her favorite person. She demanded that his parents FaceTime him every night when they tucked her in so she could say goodnight to him too. It made me want to rush babies a little because he was too damn cute with kids.

I gave myself one last once over in the mirror before heading out of the bathroom and towards him.

"Fuck me," he breathed. He looked damn good too in a dark gray suit with a white shirt and a blue tie. The sapphire blue of his tie matched my dress. The dress fell to just above my knees, with thick straps and a deep V cut, showing my cleavage. It was tight, hugging all the curves I had, the ones Will could never keep his hands off. "You're so beautiful."

"Thanks." I kissed him, ignoring his annoyed groan since he knew I'd leave lipstick on his lips. "You look nice too. That shade is killer on you." He gave me a glare and wiped his lips with his hand.

"Come on, you naughty thing, before you make us even later."

"Me?" I asked, fluttering my eyes.

Will rolled his eyes at me and pulled me from our apartment and to the elevator while ordering a ride on his phone.

"I'm so proud of you," I told him while we stood on the street. I was praying my makeup wouldn't melt away in the humidity. I missed the California weather, that was for sure. He grinned down at me and kissed my forehead.

We'd had our share of fights since leaving Lake City. I'd managed to convince the scholarship benefactor that it was cheaper for them to let me live thirty minutes from campus, in an apartment with Will. We'd rented an apartment between both of our schools and lived there for four years. We'd had to make a few adjustments living together, but despite the occasional fight, which was normal for couples, we were still as ridiculously in love as we were in our senior year of high school all those years ago.

The ride to the show took about twenty minutes in the heavy evening traffic.

"Are you nervous?" I asked when we stepped out of the car and walked towards the entrance.

"A little," he admitted.

"I can't believe you haven't let me see any of the pieces or even told me the name of the show."

"You'll find out soon enough, doll." Will took my hand and opened the door for me. It was already busy in the studio, people walking around looking at the artwork.

Artwork that was all drawings of... me?

"Will," I breathed his name.

"Here," he said, handing me a program.

Profound: A collection by Will Roberts.

Profound. He'd titled the show after me.

And all the artwork was of me. If you didn't know him or me, you might not be able to tell, but it was me—my eyes, my lips, even my nose and ears, drawings of the back of my head, of my head thrown back while I laughed.

They were intimate.

"Will," I breathed his name again, tearing up while I took everything in.

"It's dedicated to you. None of this would have been possible without you, doll."

"I love you."

"I love you, too."

Will pulled me deeper into the studio. "Hi!" Sassy yelled as soon as she saw us.

"No way," Will exclaimed, running up and hugging Snake while I hugged Sassy.

"Look at you," I exclaimed. "You're glowing."

"I missed you so much," she said.

"I missed you too."

"I missed you more!" Chloe shouted, hugging Sassy. While they'd both lived with Will's parents, they'd gotten as close as sisters should be. I didn't like admitting that in the beginning I was jealous, but ultimately they were sisters too and that didn't take away from my relationship with either of them.

That was something I'd had to work out in therapy. There were a lot of hours sitting with a therapist in college, undoing all the damage my parents did to me. It was hard, but it was necessary. Will even went with me a couple times. He wanted to help, and sometimes when things got dark and I got lost in the memories of my youth, he couldn't pull me out. He wanted advice on how to help.

Every time I thought I couldn't possibly love him more, he did something to prove me wrong.

I hugged Jordy, who had walked up to us too, and then my sister before Will hugged them both. We were standing around chatting, hogging all of Will's time when he should have been mingling with his other guests, and just as the coordinator was coming to tell him exactly that, his parents and sister walked in. Cora ran straight to him, launching herself in his arms. He scooped her up and twirled her, making her giggle like crazy until he settled her on his hip.

He hugged both of his parents and then I did before they hugged everyone else.

"You really need to mingle," Stefan, his coordinator, said.

"Yes. Come on, little lady," he said to Cora, setting her down and taking her hand. "Let's go show you off."

"These are all of you?" Sassy asked as I watched my man walk away.

"Yeah, I had no idea."

"They're amazing."

"But who is going to want to buy them?"

"Lots of people," Stefan said. "Half the pieces have already sold."

I caught up with Sassy and Snake, promising we'd make a trip right after their son arrived. Chloe would come with us, and probably Jordy too, since he, Snake, and Will were a bro trio.

I took the offered champagne while Sassy whined about not being able to drink. Snake laughed at her and pulled her close. "But you can eat all the snacks." That perked her up.

"Ladies and gentlemen, honored guests," Stefan said from the podium. "Thank you for coming to the first show of Will Roberts. It's certainly not going to be the last. And we're going to hear a few words from the artist himself about the collection."

"Thank you," Will said. He still had Cora on his hip as he stood in front of the podium. "This collection is titled *Profound*, and it's dedicated to my girl. When we were in high school, she wrote an essay about me, about our complicated love. It got her moved from Dartmouth's waitlist to acceptance, so you know it was good. What we have is absolute. Without her, none of this would have been possible, and there was never any other option for the subject matter or title of my first show because it's as much hers as it is mine. Thank you all for coming."

Will stepped away from the podium and walked straight to me. He passed his sister to his mom before cupping my face and kissing me. Since we finally could show our love for each other in public, it's all we'd been doing for the last five years.

"You're still an asshole," I whispered against his lips. He chuckled before pulling away.

"And you're still dollface." I grinned and pecked his lips before reluctantly releasing him.

I mingled with my friends, family, and Will's adoring fans as the show went on. At some point, I lost track of him, and when I went in search of him, I was quickly pulled into a darkened closet.

"Dollface," he husked.

"What are you doing?" I asked.

"Bringing us back to the beginning. Tell me how much you hate me."

We still liked to play sometimes. And this felt all too familiar, just like the first few times we'd been together.

"I hate you so much," I growled.

"Fuck, I hate you too."

His lips attached to mine as he plundered my mouth. I fisted my hands in his shirt and pulled him close, not letting him control the kiss. If we were going back to the beginning, I was in charge.

Will tried to pin my hands above my head, but I snapped my wrists away and wrapped a hand around his throat. "Be a good boy for me, Will." He moaned, low in his throat, the sound primal and even all these years later, it still made me drip for him.

"Dollface," he grunted. His hips thrust against mine, seeking contact.

"Think you can make me come, asshole?"

"Yes," he growled.

"I doubt it," I taunted him.

His hand reached up my skirt and pushed my panties to the side, finding my dripping pussy. "So fucking wet, dollface. I thought you hated me."

"I do. Now shut up."

He grinned and despite the dark of the janitor's closet we were in, I could see it. His fingers pushed inside me, curling expertly. He'd always been able to get me off quickly, but now, with years of experience, he could make me come embarrassingly quickly. I was determined to fight it off. I squeezed my pussy muscles around his fingers, pulling him in while his thumb brushed along my clit.

"Will," I whined. "Harder!" I demanded, remembering I was in charge.

"You better hurry, doll. You don't want to get caught, do you? How embarrassing for slutty Haley Winters to get caught with Will Roberts's hands up her dress."

"Fuck," I moaned. His hand covered my mouth. "We can't get caught, doll. I'll be a good boy if you're a good girl and keep quiet." I nodded my head against his hand and my eyes rolled back.

"Make me come," I demanded when he uncovered my mouth.

"Yes ma'am." His thumb pushed against my clit harshly, stroking it like he knew I loved while his fingers pushed in and out of me. I spread my legs further, giving him better access to me while I climbed higher and higher. Just as I was tumbling over the edge, I pushed my face into the crook of Will's neck, letting it muffle my moans. "Fuck," he grunted. "You're squeezing me so tight." When I finally finished, he pulled his fingers from me and brought them to his lips, licking them clean. "I want you on your knees for me, but we don't have time. That'll have to be for next time."

"Next time?" I asked as he spun me around and pushed my dress over my hips. "This is a one-time thing, asshole. Never again."

"We'll see if you keep saying that when I've got my dick in your cunt."

I whimpered at the words. He always switched it up on me these days. I could never keep control, and usually I didn't want to. I didn't need to. I could be vulnerable with him. Both hands on my hips, he pushed himself into me, making me moan as my head fell back. One of his hands stayed on my hip and the other went to my throat, squeezing while he thrust himself in and out of me.

"Tell me how much you hate me, doll."

"So much, Will. I hate you so much."

"And your pretty little cunt? Does she hate me, too?"

"No," I admitted breathily.

"She loves me, doesn't she? Loves my dick."

"Yes," I whispered.

"Who knew bad girl Haley Winters would be such a good girl for me?"

"Harder. Faster. Fuck, Will, please."

"So desperate you don't even know what you're begging for."

I bit my bottom lip to keep myself from saying anything else and let myself get lost in the sensation of his cock stretching me like he always did, pounding himself into me.

It wouldn't be as bad as it would have been in high school, but getting caught fucking in the closet at his art show wouldn't be great either.

"Oh god," I cried when he snuck his fingers in my panties and rubbed my clit while he pushed in and out of me. "Will," I moaned.

"Fuck, hearing you moan my name is the sexiest thing." He grunted behind me. "I'm gonna fill you," he growled. "This cunt is mine."

"No," I said.

"Fucking mine, dollface. Say it."

"Asshole," I hissed at him.

I loved playing this game with him.

The movements of his fingers against my clit stopped. "Say it, doll, or you don't get to come."

I whined in protest and shifted my hips, using his hand against me. The hand on my hip dug in harshly, making me moan at the pleasure-pain. "Fucking say it."

"Yours Will. My pussy is yours."

"Good. Fucking. Girl." Each of his words was punctuated with an impossibly deep thrust until we were both tumbling over the edge, coming together and moaning the other's name.

When Will finally pulled out, he put my panties back in place and turned me in his arms.

"Just like old times."

"Even better."

"Better?"

"I like pretending to be your enemy better than actually being your enemy."

"Me too, doll. Me too."

Will opened the closet door and peeked his head out before pulling me out.

Nobody was looking at us.

And just when I thought we hadn't been caught, I saw Sassy staring at us and moving closer.

"Some things never change," she said.

I looked up at Will. "Some things only change for the better.

ACKNOWLEDGMENTS

To my husband with the never ending patience, somehow I can write 130,000 words about love, but I can never find the right ones to give to you. Thank you for your constant encouragement, for believing in me even when I don't believe in myself, and making me laugh when writer's block makes me want to pull my hair out, and, most of all, thank you for being the calm to my chaos. The way you love me is what inspires me to write men who love their women right.

To my Patreon subscribers, who are never short on feedback and guide me on my journey, none of this would be possible without you. Your generous pledges allowed me to quit my job as a nurse and pursue my dream of writing. The amount of love you have for this book still astounds me.

To my friends, who know me better than myself and weren't surprised when I said I wrote a romance book, thank you for the endless support and consumption of my work.

ABOUT THE AUTHOR

Violet Bloom is my pen name because my actual name is ten syllables long, and even in The Netherlands, where I live and my last name originates from, people often mispronounce and misspell it.

I'm a registered nurse by trade, with a Bachelor of Science in Nursing, and I worked in health care, in two countries, for over a decade before deciding to peruse a new dream—writing.

I come up with my best plots doing hot yoga, only to forget them when the instructor reminds me to focus myself in the room. My second best ideas come right as I fall asleep, only to be forgotten in the morning. My favorite place to write is in a tropical paradise, sitting next to a pool with a cool breeze coming in off the ocean, and a drink in my hand.

I live in the Netherlands, with my Dutch husband and our dog, sipping tea in the morning and single malt scotch in the evening.

Follow Me On Social Media:
Instagram: @author.violetbloom
TikTok: @author.violetbloom

For more of her work, find her on Patreon.
Patreon: www.patreon.com/vlb1389
www.violetbloom.me

Published works:
Worth the Wreckage

Printed in Great Britain
by Amazon